Rest Now, Beloved

Blake S. Lee

ISBN: 1508754039
ISBN 13: 9781508754039

"Writers, at least those who take genuine risks,
who are willing to bite the bullet and walk the plank
have a lot in common with another breed of lonely men"
...Truman Capote

Dedicated to all who inspired, all who stood by me,
all who believed in my ambition;
those who lived this story,
and those who gave this story to me

But mostly to my husband and family
Don, Blakeslee, Sara, and
Jennifer for the time she took for a closer look

Sera Schilling

TENSION CHARGED THE large room. Before the paper went to the editor for final approval, there was scarcely time for last-minute proofreading, necessary revisions, or the rechecking of sources demanded by the managing editor, Richard Mosier. Journalists scurried through the labyrinth of desks, tables, and equipment, their faces crumpled into strained expressions. Telephones rang. News reports flashed over computer screens in furious urgency. Fax machines spat out breaking news.

But there I sat.

Alone in my drab gray little cubicle.

I was eager to join the frenzy, full of ambition and energy.

My pencil point was as sharp as I like it. My textbooks on journalistic ethics and source materials were stacked in the corner, beckoning to be opened and used.

But my inbox was empty and my phone was silent.

The top of my desk was too organized. There were neat little piles of inconsequential things.

I felt the stinging, demoralizing frustration that comes with lack of involvement.

And, I needed an assignment.

It was 1990. I had recently earned my master's. Now, as an intern just two months shy of a crucial six-month review, I had to find a story that was worthy of an article, then write and publish that article under my byline, to win a contract of employment with the newspaper.

Time was running out.

I glanced across the cluttered newsroom to the man who held my future in his hands. Isolated from the chaos in a glass-walled office sat a scowling Albion St. James. He tilted back into his chair behind his large antique oak desk. Deep in thought, he absently watched the bustling room and frequently checked his wristwatch.

Suddenly, Richard's voice called out to me across the din.

"Sera!" he yelled. "Grab line three, would'ya?" He stood next to his desk, jabbing a forefinger at his telephone receiver. I automatically reached for my phone, punched the button, and put the phone to my ear.

The voice on the other end of the line was a male, probably elderly. He mumbled and was difficult to understand.

"I'm sorry sir, but I can't understand you," I told the voice as I doodled with my pencil on the top page of a clean yellow legal pad.

He cleared his throat. When he spoke again, though wheezy and muffled, his voice was clearer.

"It's that article on the front page of the local section in this morning's paper," he said. "About a murder case back in '33. Tells how the sheriff's forensic team reexamined this old case and they are now saying that it can be closed. They say they've solved the mystery behind it. They say it was an accidental death. Miss . . ."

"Schilling. Sera Schilling."

"Miss Schilling, that's crap. It was flat-out murder."

Although I'd read the newspaper earlier and had seen the article, I had read it with dim interest.

"It's a crying shame," he continued, "that's what it is. Closing the case. Uh-uh."

"Hold on a moment," I said as I quickly brought out my copy of the morning's edition and shuffled through to Section B, Local News.

There it was: *'33 Homicide Case Finally Closed: Accidental Death.*

"I know that kid was killed," he was saying. "How do I know? Because I was in charge of investigating the damn thing back then, that's how. You might want to check. My name's Pete McGraw."

The article was about the disappearance and death of a young boy, Christopher Abkhazian, in July of 1933. It described the initial homicide investigation by the police department and then the sudden change of authority to the San Diego Sheriff's Department which dismissed it as accidental death by drowning. The case was never closed. Currently a team of forensic detectives won a federal grant to re-investigate the old case using modern scientific techniques. There was, however, no evidence on which to use these methods. Most of the article recapped old testimony and introduced hypothetical conjectures on the part of experts.

There were pictures of the child in 1933, alongside a current photograph of his matronly sibling. The caption under the sister's picture read: *Finally my family and I can put Christopher's death to rest.*

"Okay. I've read the article, Mr. McGraw."

"I tell you that kid was murdered; it was *not* an accidental death."

I scrawled the name Pete McGraw, the victim's name, and the date 1933 on the yellow pad, tore out the article from the paper, and clipped it to my notes. "Okay, okay," I said, after he'd stopped his ranting. "So you believe that the Abkhazian boy was murdered. But that was a long time ago. What's the point in rehashing it? There seems to be nothing to justify more work on this old case. And besides, the boy's sister is *thankful* that the case can be closed."

The old man's voice blasted into the phone: "An unsolved homicide is never closed. If it was accidental, it should have been closed back in '33. Obviously, the sheriff's department couldn't indisputably prove that it was accidental then, not with the autopsy, a coroner's jury, and a Grand Jury disagreeing. So, it couldn't be closed. As a reporter, Miss Schilling, you should be asking: Why now? Why after all these years. My gut says there's a cover-up. If we don't act fast, files will be purged. If there is any remaining evidence, it will be tossed. Everything will be forgotten. And someone will be freed of it.

"Consider this: When that forensics group reinvestigated this case, did they call *me*? I was lead detective on the case, but nobody called me to ask for my findings. And I had them. Believe me, I had hard evidence. I had a suspect in custody.

"Miss Schilling, I understand your reluctance. You're probably thinking: why waste my time on this? Murders happen every day. Violent crimes happen every two seconds. You're out for fresh stories, not old, moldy ones. If I guess right when you hang up the telephone, after talking to me, you'll crumple up the notes you've been taking and toss them into the can."

Guiltily, I flattened the crumpled sheet of paper I'd ripped from the virgin legal pad to take sparse notes from the old man's call. I looked at my notes: *1933. B.C. or A.D.? Pete McGraw. Retired San Diego Police. Forensic team wrong in findings/death not accident. Refer page B-1,* and the date.

"You know Mr. St. James, Miss Schilling? Albion St. James?" Not waiting for an answer, he continued: "Well, the two of us go back a long time. Tell him we spoke. You've got my name, Pete McGraw. He'll know me." I took down his telephone number and we disconnected.

Later in the day when things had settled and most of the staff had left, I took the crumpled sheet of paper and a clipping of the article to Richard, who was now relaxed and sitting back in his swivel chair. The top of his shirt was unbuttoned and his tie loosened. Sleeves were rolled to his elbows. Dark afternoon growth was sprouting around his chin. He was sipping a cup of coffee and laughing with Betty, the department secretary. They both smiled as I joined them. They shared a joke and we laughed together. Still chuckling, I handed the notes from the telephone conversation to Richard, which I'd stapled to the article regarding the forensic work.

"What's this?" he asked.

"I'm following up on the call you gave me this afternoon. The caller is a retired cop. He worked this case back in 1933." Richard glanced at the clipping and nodded. I continued, "He said the sheriff's forensics did a superficial job of reinvestigating this case and their conclusion that the child's death was accidental was wrong."

Richard took a minute to re-read the article and look over my notes.

"I thought this was nothing but a space filler. St. James pushed it through. I'm surprised someone called on it. What do you think, Sera?"

"I checked. The caller was the lead cop on this case, and he knows St. James."

"He knows St. James?"

"He said he and St. James go back a long time."

"And this Pete McGraw was the lead detective on this case?"

"Yes."

"It might be interesting stuff," Richard said, shrugging his shoulders and handing my notes back to me. "Who knows? Maybe; maybe not. Ask St. James. He'd be the one to tell you whether it's worth your time to pursue it."

The senior editor intimidated me as he did most everyone working under him. St. James could shatter a reporter's self-esteem with a dash of red ink or he could boost an ego sky high with as little as an approving glance. He was also known to fire on whim, unconcerned about union consequences. Outside lawyers loved him. They made money off his impulsiveness. My review was due. I needed that publishable article, not this moldy old case.

I knocked on St. James's door, making the glass rattle in its pane. The old man was brooding over some paperwork on his desk. Without looking up, he grumbled, "Come in."

The door clicked behind me, shutting me in his office. There I stood, alone with *the man*. I waited. Finally he glanced up over his reading glasses. "Yes, Miss Schilling? You got something for me?" A semblance of a smirk stretched his mouth. "Your six months are coming up. Got your personnel file right here." He patted a mound of files and loose papers on his desk. He was still eyeing me over his half glasses with that narrow, barely indiscernible smile. "Well, come on in! Have a seat, gal." He pointed for me to take a seat in one of the two chairs facing his desk. His own chair creaked loudly as he leaned back into it.

"Richard gave me a peculiar telephone call this afternoon," I began, and then hesitated.

He motioned with his hand, prodding me to continue.

"The caller, a man by the name of Pete McGraw, said he knows you." I explained the article, shoving it across his desk toward him, and described the conversation. Mr. St. James glanced at the article and then back at me.

"McGraw?" he asked.

"Yes. He said his name was Pete McGraw."

A vacuum of silence sucked up all sound and my voice dangled foolishly in the air.

"Pete McGraw, *Irish*." St. James ruminated. His voice was distant and his eyes glazed by memories.

Finally he laughed. "For the gods' sake! Pete McGraw! McGraw's still alive? Imagine that! I'd wondered whatever happened to him!" His eyes resumed that faraway gaze and he grew silent. I waited.

Suddenly he seemed to recall that I was in the room. He pushed the article back across the desk to me and stood up. He reached for his coat hanging on the rack behind his desk. As he pulled the coat on, he said, "Yes. Go ahead. See what you can make of that phone call, Miss Sera Schilling. Go out and talk to the man. And then get back to me."

Pete McGraw

THE OLD MAN hung up the phone. Shaking his head, he placed both hands on the small telephone table to steady himself, then caught his reflection in the wall mirror. With profound dismay, he examined the withered face staring back at him. It was deeply etched with lines and bewhiskered with white and black stubble.

"Kate!" he shouted. When he heard no response from his nurse, he thought she'd probably gone shopping, and then he remembered her telling him so.

He glanced around the cluttered living room and inhaled the smell particular to age, disease, inactivity, and old things.

Pete McGraw sighed deeply and shook his head.

"That old moth-eaten case has been driving me nuts for too many years. I've got to let it go. What the hell can I do now about the old thing, anyhow?"

He pulled a handkerchief from his robe pocket and patted his wet forehead, then swiped once or twice under his nose. He shuffled over to the ancient roll-top desk that was loaded with papers. There was mail was addressed to "occupant." The envelopes remained unopened. Under the stack of mail, there were books and magazines given to him as gifts from well-meaning neighbors.

Cheaply framed photographs of various times in his life deco-rated the wall behind the desk. In the center of this grouping was a cross-stitched Serenity Prayer. He read aloud the first line: "God grant me the serenity to accept the things I cannot change," and he chuckled ironically. "Guess I'd best apply that to little Chris's murder."

He added, "Got to let it go," and this time he said it with resolution.

There was a black-and-white photograph of a group of policemen from the 1925 police souvenir album. Five of the men were stern-faced and sat stiff as statues on a wooden bench, their arms folded officiously across their chests. Their spit-polished boots reflected the camera's flash. They wore the heavy wool uniforms with the high-necked collars of the time. Pete pointed at each in turn and one by one spoke the names of the men in the picture. The caption at the bottom read: *Special Detail: Morals and Liquor.*

The policeman in the center of the group was the only one who appeared relaxed. As with the others, his arms were folded across his chest, but his long legs were stretched out casually in front of him and his cap was pulled down rakishly onto his forehead. This man with the self-satisfied cockiness, with the handsome, chiseled features and the wide, Irish smile, was Pete's father.

"You were my hero, old man," Pete whispered.

Another picture, taken about two years after that, showed a newly inducted officer, Peter W. McGraw, Jr., standing proudly in front of his first automobile, a Model 40 Ford. This car doubled as Pete's patrol car for quite a few years.

"What a hot rod I thought that was!" He chuckled.

Pete's prize Model 40 was introduced in 1933. Pete had ordered one of the first off the assembly line from Ford's factory, back in Detroit, Michigan. He was proud as punch about that car, too. He recalled when it finally arrived in San Diego, how he had showed it off to the other fellows in the department. Sporty, a convertible top, the "deluxe" model had wood graining on the window frames and the instrument dashboard. Rounded and skirted fenders, bowed bumpers, and wire wheels made Pete's car look more elegant than the now outdated Model Ts it replaced. It was sturdier with its stretched out wheelbase. And faster with the new V-8 engine of this particular model. When he let loose the throttle he'd have himself a grand old time, frequently pushing the speed up to sixty miles an hour on the open highway. Sure, he'd gone into hock for what he considered the prize of a lifetime. It cost him nearly six-hundred dollars, plus shipping costs. That was a whole lot of *cashola*.

But it was well worth it.

That car had provided him countless moonlit rides around the hills of San Diego with his arm around pretty gals. This was something few other fellas could offer their girlfriends. He and his date, cozying into the deeply cushioned leather seats, would purr along those bumpy roads under the summer moon and sea-sweet breezes of Southern California.

Pete removed an age-yellowed framed newspaper article from the wall. A picture of his partner, Joe Deutsch, and him was featured. They were squatting on the ground, examining a set of tire tracks left behind on a dirt road. Pete recalled posing for the camera as they reenacted a scene of their investigation into the Agua Caliente money heist in 1929. The caption beneath the photograph read: *Officers Peter W. McGraw and Joseph Deutsch examine the bullet-riddled money car from the Agua Caliente Casino in Tijuana looted in a daylight murder holdup.* Another picture showed three Mexican guards standing next to the corpse of one of the robbers, who was slumped against the money car with a bullet hole the middle of his forehead and looked mighty dead.

Pete recalled how the other bandit had managed to escape in one of the police vehicles during the confusion of the shootout and how Chief Peterson placed an all-points bulletin to bring him in dead or alive. Pete told Joe: "I'm going to get the son of a bitch, buddy."

And that he did.

The newspapers wrote it up like an episode from *Superman*.

It was an open-fire, hostage situation. The bandit was holed up in an apartment in a three-story building in downtown San Diego with a female hostage. The standoff had lasted nearly three hours. He stood in front of a window on the second story, holding the woman in front of him, knife blade to her neck, and yelling demands for a getaway car through the open window. Giving in, Chief Peterson had just called for the car and ordered the police to vacate. Already automobile doors were slamming and engines coughing into operation as they began to leave.

The chief didn't know that Pete McGraw had already left the scene.

It wasn't the first time that Pete McGraw would disobey orders.

Pete had entered the building from a back-alley basement stairwell. He climbed the stairs to the second floor. Upon entering the hallway, he saw curious occupants standing outside their various doors. He cautioned them to return to their apartments. One woman warned Pete that the bandit had an "arsenal" with him. Pete knew for a fact that he had a machine gun. He'd used it on the officers from the window.

He easily found the apartment where the action was taking place. Much to his amazement, when he tried the handle, the door opened easily. He glided into the apartment noiselessly until he could see the bandit, who had replaced the knife with a handgun. The slight, fragile female hostage was being held upright by his well-muscled arm. There were drops of blood on her neck, nicked by the knife earlier. Pete saw that she was losing strength; her knees had buckled. Only the bandit's grip kept her from falling. She was becoming deadweight. Her captor had become desperate. He tightened his hold around her waist, growled for her to stand up, and shoved the gun into her neck with his right hand.

Pete realized that where he stood just inside the door was at an awkward angle to his target. He had to make the shot immediately and from where he stood, because even the slightest movement might alert the gunman to his presence. Pete saw that much of the woman's body stood in the way of a clean shot. He had to make his one shot work. And that had to be to either the top of the gunman's head or his neck. If the bullet went even slightly off, Pete ran the risk of hitting her instead. Pete took aim, held his breath, blinked stinging perspiration out of his eyes, and pulled the trigger.

He saw the flash of fire, watched the robber stiffen and then corkscrew to the ground. By the time Pete crossed the room to get to him, the man lay motionless, blood running from his mouth and his dark eyes open in death's sightless gaze. The bullet had penetrated his neck, less than an inch from the top of the woman's head.

Pete now pulled a small cardboard box from a drawer in the roll-top desk and opened it. He removed the green and gold California Medal of Valor that Governor Ralph had pinned onto his uniform. The governor flew by airplane all the way from Sacramento to do it, too.

Pete was just twenty-one years old, the youngest policeman in California's police history to be awarded such a distinguished medal.

At the awards banquet, when Pete posed for a picture standing alongside City Hall big wigs, he was fully aware that in the audience a pair of glistening blue eyes were glued on him with awe.

Now, in the emptiness of his living room, the old man signed heavily. "Connie," he said aloud and felt himself fill up with emotion.

Well now, Connie was another, very complicated story. Whenever his wife crossed his mind, Pete felt that heavy pain that comes with boundless guilt. Death in itself is incomprehensible. But there is never finality to grieving when one can't clear away dishonesty. Then it's always too late to make amends.

He had loved Connie, certainly.

He'd fallen for that five-foot-one little spitfire hook, line, and sinker. When he first saw her across the dance pavilion at Balboa Park, he'd been a young cop and she was still in her late teens. She was standing with a cluster of girlfriends when the band struck up.

"Keep your eyeballs in their sockets, Irish!" Joe chided him when he caught Pete mesmerized by the pert little blonde.

"Watch me! I'm going to dance with that one!" Pete responded without taking his eyes off her.

"Holy smoke, you rascal, you don't even know how to dance!" Joe reminded him.

"Just you watch and see," Pete said, grabbing two cups at the punch table and holding them for the chaperone to fill.

Pinching his thumb and forefinger together tightly to hold the delicate handles of the china cups, he purposefully marched over to the group of ladies. Connie was still laughing at an inside joke, her delighted laughter the tinkling of high-pitched chimes. He held out a cup and beamed. When she saw him standing there with punch spilling over the sides of the cups and splashing on the wooden floor, she stopped her laughing, smiled, and took one of the cups he offered.

"Miss—" Pete's normally resolute voice suddenly faltered.

"Connie. Connie Brewer," she replied, returning his smile.

This gave him the courage he needed to ask for her dance card.

"Sign your name here. And here," she instructed, pointing to the two available dances. As he bent to sign his name on the card, the fragrance of her White Rain Shampoo made Pete dizzy. He returned to his partner and coolly bragged about his success.

"Damn!" he whispered to Joe. "Dances number four and twelve. And I got the last dance!"

"You son of a bitch!" Joe snickered.

Suddenly Pete's thoughts were interrupted by the front door banging open. Kate Kersel stepped into the foyer, arms loaded with plastic bags of groceries.

"Bought a few things," Kate explained unnecessarily. Looking at him with the practiced eye of a caregiver, she asked suspiciously, "How are you feeling, Mr. McGraw?"

"Okay, I suppose," he responded, and once more pulled the handkerchief from his robe pocket and mopped his face.

"A rest, perhaps?" she prodded gently.

"Guess you're right. Okay, I'm headed back to bed." He gave her a smile and put the photograph back over the spot of wall it had protected for years.

Pete felt the sudden wave of nausea and light-headedness that preceded a bout of pain and headed down the hall toward his bedroom.

"A little light lunch, perhaps soup, might taste good to you. I'll bring it back to you in a shake," she called after him.

He grunted in reply that he wasn't feeling that hungry.

Damnation, how it ached even to walk sometimes! Every damn muscle, bone, tendon, ligament, and organ complained about having to do its simple God-given task. And the damnable hall grew longer every day.

It was evident that while he was blustering on the telephone with that young gal at the newspaper, Mrs. Kersel had been busy tidying up his bedroom. She'd opened the drapes and sunlight streamed through the window. Pete's eyes watered with the morning's brilliance, its vivacity seemingly mocking his decrepitude. The leaves of the eucalyptus tree outside his window fluttered happily and cumulus clouds billowed high in the cerulean sky. He heard an automobile's engine bark into operation from somewhere down the street and the screech of metal wheels on cement as a small group of boys skateboarded past his house on their way home from elementary school.

There was a time when Pete would have thrown open the window to let in the outside air, but the warm comfort of the stuffy bedroom embraced him. The sheets were folded back and the pillows fluffed up invitingly. He sat down heavily on the edge of the bed, shook off his slippers, and reached for the newspaper Kate had folded neatly on his bedside table. The local section, with the article that earlier caused him impotent rage, was on top. The boy smiled at him from a photograph accompanying the article.

McGraw shook his head and grumbled. Put the paper down. Shook out a pill from the brown bottle conveniently set on the table and washed it down with tepid water. *My lifeline*, he thought, *these damnable pain pills.*

His jaw clenched in irritation as he recalled the earlier conversation with the woman at the newspaper. Her disinterested voice resonated in his mind. She said she'd take his message to St. James. He had all the doubt in the world that it would get that far. Hell, she was bored with something as archaic as a 1933 police case.

He wondered what she looked like. Young, and probably very pretty. All young girls were pretty these days. And she was insolent. That was the way of this generation, the "X Generation." She probably laughed at him after they disconnected. Thought his enduring passion quaint.

Strange that he was sweating now. And it wasn't even warm in the house.

And St. James? He probably wouldn't remember him.

"It doesn't matter anymore." His voice sounded hollow in the empty room. He pulled his legs up onto the bed, laid the newspaper in his lap, relaxed back against the fluffed pillows, and closed his eyes to memory.

He remembered the unkind night that he had to do what many cops are eventually faced with having to do: tell the parents that the cause of their child's death was brutal murder. He and Joe had ridden out to the Abkhazians' house to share that ghastly duty. The door was opened by the dead boy's father, a thin, dark-featured man of Armenian heritage. The reverend still wore the dark clothing with the white clerical collar that he'd worn earlier at Benbough's Mortuary, where Pete had taken him to identify his son's body, and what, before that odious task, he had worn for Sunday church service. Now, facing Pete once again and this time at his front door, he avoided the policeman's eyes, turned, and led him and Joe into the living room.

They were all there, the Abkhazians. The grandparents sat motionless on the sofa, somehow fading into the shadows of the gloomy room with their black clothing and dark hair and skin. Their eyes followed Pete and Joe accusingly, severely. Two young children, their eyes wide in childish curiosity, surveyed the uniformed policemen. Their mother looked like a rag doll that had been carelessly tossed into an overstuffed wing chair. Her hair stuck to her wet face in dark ringlets. She had silently watched the two cops enter the room. Now, as they stood together awkwardly just outside the vestibule, their presence seeming to occupy the whole living room, she averted her eyes. She then buried her face in the curly hair of the infant she held in her lap and nervously kneaded its shoulders. The reverend excused the two older siblings from the room. Hand in hand they left, stopping every so often on their path down the hall to the bedrooms to look over their shoulders, to check out Pete and Joe.

Pete began to say what he had to say, but the words stuck in his throat. The reverend understood and whispered Pete's unspoken message into his wife's ear. She blanched, sucked in air, and screamed out shrilly. She struck her chest with her fist as though she wanted to rip her heart out. Then she erupted from the chair, pushed her husband away, and rushed from the room, bent over awkwardly from the weight of the infant she carried in her arms. Pete heard a door slam from somewhere in the back of the house and the gut-wrenching sobs that couldn't be muted.

The two cops took their leave. They put their caps back on their heads and pushed through the front door, outside to the balmy July evening of rising stars. The thin splinter of a new moon was beginning to peek over the treetops and a mockingbird sang its lullaby.

They stumbled away from the house, speechless and forever changed.

Mrs. Kersel now stood at Pete's door quietly, not wanting to break into his thoughts. She smiled when he opened his eyes and acknowledged her. Taking his smile as an invitation, she walked over to the bed. *She is a wise, wise woman*, Pete thought, as he objectively watched the pleasant little nurse take his pulse and his temperature, then gently adjust the covers around him without a lot of female twaddle.

"Did you ever tell me, Kate, how I was so lucky to get you?"

"No. It's my secret, Mr. McGraw." He loved it when she smiled, when the twin dimples deepened in her plump cheeks. "Let's just say an angel picked you out for me to take care of. Now you get some rest. I'll be about if you need me or change your mind about some-thing to eat."

Sera

WHEN I THINK about how technology has advanced since 1990, when I was assigned this case, I realize how hands-on it was back then—a paper trail. I spent much of my time, when I was an intern at the *Observer*, doing research for other reporters in the newspaper archives, which were located in the basement of the building.

Newspaper records, microfilm, and maps were kept there along with other San Diego historical artifacts. Temperature-monitored glass cases displaying various relics from the past gave the archives a museum-like feel. One such case had a poster depicting Rosie the Riveter. She might well have been San Diego's own, working at Consolidated Aircraft Industries during "Blitz Boom," in World War II. To women of America, driven from their homes to work in industries for the war effort, Rosie was a symbol of a feminism. In a way, I connected to her image: the determined look on the woman's face, her hair pulled back under a polka-dot bandana, and her arm held high in a salute to female workers. Its message to me? Women are unstoppable.

In my own way, I felt I was unstoppable too. I'd worked my way out of my hometown of Santa Linda and through college by juggling two jobs at a time. Now I barely made it on an intern's pay. I was determined to make my place in investigative journalism, and nothing would get in my way. This case wasn't what I thought I needed to gain recognition, but at least it was my own. Little did I know. It's the things we don't expect that make the biggest changes in our lives.

The elevator door closed behind me, and I scouted out the area. It was, as I expected, pretty empty. There were two people reading at tables in an adjacent room and the librarian, Davis Hornfield, at the front desk. As I filled out the log, I smiled a greeting at him. He nodded a response. Hornfield seemed to have morphed into another relic of the archives. A reincarnate Ichabod Crane came to mind: hooked nose, dome-shaped head, hooded eyes, gangly legs, and the overall appearance of someone who has kept out of the sun most of his life and holed up in this mausoleum for too many years.

The bank of file cabinets housed rolls of microfilm. Each drawer was labeled by year and the various newspapers that had been copied. I found and removed the box containing a roll labeled "1933."

I took the microfilm to a viewer, threaded and fast-forwarded it to July 19, where I found the first of a series of articles describing the disappearance and subsequent death of Christopher Abkhazian. I began a rough timeline of events.

Tuesday, July 18, 1933: Christopher Abkhazian disappeared.

Wednesday, July 19, 1933: First newspaper article: Child missing. Massive search by volunteers.

Thursday, July 20, 1933: Police pursue case as a missing person.

Sunday, July 23, 1933: Body of missing boy found in San Diego Bay. Autopsy report: homicide. Officer Peter McGraw promoted to lead detective in charge of investigating child's brutal murder.

I made copies of a series of articles that were published in the paper, describing the tips that had been called into the police department by self-proclaimed witnesses. Some of the journalistic accuracy concerned me, like one article telling of two different witnesses who had spotted the boy at two separate locations at the same time.

The search was described as the most massive in San Diego history. It centered on Balboa Park, its zoo, a children's playground in an area called the Pepper Grove, and the merry-go-round with thousands of volunteers.

On July 23, the boy's corpse was found floating "inconceivably mutilated" in San Diego Bay. My eyes scanned the article until they found McGraw's name: "The newly hired Chief of Police, Doyle, promoted San Diego Police Officer Peter W. McGraw, the recent Medal of Valor recipient, as lead detective of this case."

The fact that McGraw had earned a police medal, combined with St. James's apparent high opinion of him, stoked my interest—and curiosity as to why the forensic team hadn't gone to him for information when he had been so initially involved in the investigation. He seemed cognizant, was so available, and eager to discuss the case.

By the Friday after the boy's body had been found, McGraw admitted that little or no progress had been made in finding the child's murderer. "How long will killings in San Diego city and county go on?" he was quoted as asking. "There's a fiend loose in our community, and we need to find him before other children are put into harm's way." He said he was going to use "any and all men—or the entire police force if need be—to track down the killer." The paper included a photograph of Detective McGraw. Though his face was shaded, I could see that this man McGraw was at one time a very handsome and imposing man.

I was curious about other killings that he had mentioned. A related article in the same edition of the newspaper referenced six unsolved murders in two years, which seemed a very disturbing statistic for the young city of San Diego. I red-flagged the crime in which the victim was a twelve-year-old girl murdered in 1931, which was a couple of years before the death of Christopher Abkhazian. I thought I'd research her death later to see if there might be a connection.

The paper followed the jurisdictional change of command from the police department to the sheriff's department, citing as a reason the location where the body was found: in the water. At that time, apparently the sheriff's department had jurisdiction for all crimes occurring in bodies of water within the county. From the start of their investigation, they believed the boy had died an accidental death by drowning. McGraw, it seemed, was always intent on pursuing it as a homicide.

I stretched and looked around the archives. The clock on the wall read that it was after six. The ceiling fixtures had been dimmed to save energy and I was alone. I made the necessary copies and put the microfilm box back, packed up my stuff, and left to go home.

Paco

IT WAS JUST after ten o'clock in the morning in East Los Angeles. The fire-engine red Porsche Boxter swept into the parking lot of a small strip mall and spun into a space outside Sal's Taco Shop. The driver's bulk made his exit from the low vehicle a lumpish, laborious effort. He ran his hands through his thick jet hair, adjusted his leather belt, and tucked his shirt into his pants, noting the dampness around his waist and under his arms from sweating during the long drive. Checked his watch. Sal set the meeting up for ten. Paco was on time, as was his predilection. Paco jangled his keys until his fingers found the silver key that would unlock the front door to the restaurant. Before pulling the door open, his dark eyes scanned the parking lot to see if he was being followed. Finding the few cars parked there empty of occupants, he felt relieved, slid through the door, and then quickly shut it, listening for the comforting click of the dead bolt.

Paco walked through the now-empty restaurant to the door marked "office" in the rear of the building. He used his knuckles to rap sharply on the door. Salvador answered immediately.

"Paco, my boy!" The older man pulled the door wide open and stood to the side to allow Paco to enter the small, cluttered room. He gave Paco a genial slap on his back. "Welcome back to the barrio! Where you been hanging, *Ese*? Heard you went up north." The smiling man pointed to a faded, upholstered chair placed in front of his desk. "Sit! Rest your bones, *amigo*. I got a little business deal I gotta talk over with you."

Paco plopped into the chair, looking relaxed but keeping his eyes on Salvador. "Had a little business of my own to clean up in San Luis Obispo," he said in a low voice.

The old man grunted. "No glad to see ya? What? No what's up?" Salvador's face hardened. "Remember who I am—*El Papa*. What I've done for you! Life's been pretty damn good since I took you off the streets, eh? Don't you forget it." As quickly as the old man's mask had disappeared, it reappeared again with a smile. He reached down and slapped Paco on the arm good naturedly as he passed the reclining young man in the chair. He rounded his desk and sat down behind it.

Salvador kept his eyes fixed on the younger man as he spoke. "There's this lady down there in San Diego. She wants a little, ah, business done. Lady's husband is very important. That means this job's gotta be handled with *muy discreción*. Everything is to be between you and her. Got it? Her husband is not to know anything about it. Or you." When Paco didn't respond, Salvador continued: "This lady got the word from a guy she knows down at the San Diego newspaper that a young reporter by the name of Schilling is going to be doing some work on an old case that she wanted buried. Now, look here. She is to call the shots. She wants this gal off the case. Scaring the reporter might be all you have to do."

Salvador grunted as he twisted in his chair and finagled a roll of bills from his pants pocket. He fanned a few off the top. Looked up, cleared his throat, and then removed a few more. As he handed them to Paco, he said: "This will set you up."

Salvador then reached into his desk and withdrew a folded sheet of note paper. He gave it to Paco. "This is what I got on Schilling," he explained. Remember, Paco," he said, holding his finger aloft, *"con muy discreción."*

Paco counted the bills and pocketed Salvador's note. "I got to be in San Diego how long? He asked.

"As long as it takes, my friend," Salvador answered.

After a few minutes Paco walked out of the dark and empty restaurant into the parking lot. He stretched and+ yawned, rotated his neck. He unlocked the door to his red Porsche, feeling the adrenaline begin to surge through his veins, as it always did at the beginning of a job. He smiled greedily. It had only taken seven minutes to make nine-hundred dollars. Listening to the sweet, churning motor of his car, he glanced at the dashboard clock. Now he had an hour's drive to make—depending on the traffic on highway five south.

Sera

I UNLOCKED THE door and stepped inside my cave, relishing the warmth the wall heater gave off. It was nearly seven o'clock. I felt achy-tired from sitting in front of the viewer for most of that Friday after McGraw's telephone call and my subsequent assignment from St. James. Sighing, I picked up my mail, which lay scattered on the floor near the front door mail slot. It was the usual stuff: mostly coupon books, circulars, and catalogues advertising merchandise for Christmas shopping. But, tucked in with the merchandising was a letter from my mother. I poured myself a glass of wine, shoved the thermostat up a notch, and collapsed on my *damn-ugly* futon to read what she had written.

Mom's news about Santa Linda was pretty much the same provincial chitchat as always, but she had a witty way of filling me in on local gossip. Before she closed, she'd invariably add a few lines of advice. This letter repeated her concern about my decision to live in South Mission Beach. She wrote that she thought it wasn't the safest place for a young woman to live by herself. Perhaps a roommate? Then the caveat: a *female* roommate. Also, it might be best to find a quieter part of San Diego. After all, did I remember how she was kept awake nearly every night during her short visit by the loud and raucous music and laughter that swelled by the nearby Surf Rider Bar? And since she was unfamiliar with the surfing life, she associated surfers with drugs, and the fact that this was a surfing community always worried her.

The turn of my mother's letter somewhat depressed me. I carefully refolded the letter and put it down. I considered my "cave," as mother had called my apartment, and had to admit that it was sort of gloomy, since it had only one window that emitted direct sunlight for a short time in the late afternoon.

But it struck me how I had been able to brighten up the place with only a couple of gallons of sunshine-yellow paint. I had covered the window with wide-slatted blinds that I picked up at a garage sale and painted glossy white. They didn't quite fit the window, but they worked. The white of the blinds set off the yellow walls in a crisp and chipper way. Above where I lay on the futon, a plant hung from the ceiling. It was near the window, where it could take advantage of whatever rays pushed their way into the room. I furnished the studio apartment with cheap, used furniture that was purchased from Goodwill stores and garage sales, including this *damn-ugly* green and gold paisley futon that had a deep rut in the middle that conformed neatly to me.

No, Mom, I thought, *I love where I live.* I was only a half block from the Pacific Ocean. Every night as I left downtown San Diego and drove over the Mission Bay Drive bridge, I felt freedom. I tossed off workaday constraints. I had never once felt unsafe living here. There were so many neighbors about my age coming and going at all hours of the day and night. Most of the other women also lived solo in small apartments. As far as a social life, I seldom felt lonely.

The "sonata" wind chimes, a rare splurge that I bought in Hillcrest, clanged furiously outside the window. On nearby Mission Boulevard, automobile tires swished through puddles left behind by the earlier storm. Lively fragments of music and occasional hearty laughter, the noise my mother detested, always sounded welcoming to me. On the sidewalk below my cave, I could hear the sodden footsteps of an occasional walker.

Fighting lassitude, I pushed myself out of my futon, grabbed my running shoes, and pulled on sweats for a quick jog along the beach. I did this most every night. The run would reenergize me and it might clear my mind.

The weather had pushed folks indoors, so the boardwalk was deserted. The low cloud cover made the sky particularly dark. The lights along the boardwalk looked hazy in the misty air, but they lit the pavement and reflected warmly in the puddles.

I returned to my apartment after about forty-five minutes. During the last part of the run, the idea of a pizza had crossed my mind—pizza always tasted good on cold, rainy nights. I wondered if one of my friends might be available to share one.

Coincidentally, as I opened the door the first thing I saw was that the message light on the telephone was blinking. Before listening to the message, I grabbed a kitchen towel and wiped my face, which was wet with moisture from the damp air. As I tossed the towel on the counter, I noticed a subtle but unfamiliar fragrance in the air that I didn't recognize. It wasn't the scent of the perfume I wore. It was harsher, like a man's aftershave. My first thought was that someone either had been in my apartment while I was out—or someone was still there. Hairs on my arms bristled with the thought. I had to consciously calm myself down before I checked out the small apartment. Nothing seemed out of order. I then began to wonder if I had imagined the odor. I went back to the spot where I'd originally noticed it, and sniffed. No, a scent was definitely there. I glanced up at the heating vent in the wall, then shook my head and smiled. *Dummy*, I thought, the odor had probably wafted through the wall between my apartment and the one next door that was shared by three single young men. I admonished myself to stop acting childish. There was nothing there. It was nothing.

I punched the message button and smiled. My friend Michelle had left a message for me to meet her for a pizza at Tony's New York Style Pizza on the Boulevard. After a quick shower, I dressed warmly in jeans and an oversized wool sweater, and then hurried to meet my friend.

I couldn't sleep that night. Couldn't relax. Lay in my futon frozen stiff, keeping my eyes on the front door. I couldn't shake the feeling that someone had been in my apartment. When I got up Saturday morning, the fragrance lingered faintly in the air, pushing me to act.

At ten o'clock, I was one of a few early shoppers waiting for the manager to unlock the front door at Macy's, to let us in. I wondered if I could remember the fragrance of what I thought was a men's after-shave well enough to identify it.

So, at the men's department, I began aftershave sniffing. When finally I could identify it, I was exultant. It was Yves Saint Laurent's L'Homme aftershave. I asked the clerk for a sample. It didn't give me much encouragement to hear him say that I'd made a good choice; it was their most popular aftershave.

When I returned home, I took my sample of L'Homme to my next-door neighbors. Did any of them or their visitors use this after-shave? Their response to my inquiry was negative. When I mentioned that I'd smelled it in my apartment after I returned from my jog the day before, they shared my concern and suggested I get the locks changed. A simple solution, but I couldn't help but recall my mother's foreboding as I dialed the manager's number. I hate it when she's right. In this instance, was she? And if so, who could have broken into my apartment—and why?

Pete and Sera

First Interview, October 23, 1990

TUESDAY MORNING AT exactly ten o'clock, I pushed the doorbell a third time and paced back and forth impatiently on the brick porch. The numbers above the door were the same as I'd written down: 421. I knew I was at the right house. Why wasn't anybody answering the door?

Pete McGraw's house was in a neighborhood of post–World War II stucco bungalows. His neighborhood, South Park, overlooks pristine blue-white San Diego cityscape and the Pacific Ocean in the distance. I was impressed by the hushed feel of Lomas Street. It was tree rimmed with sunlight dappling onto the pavement through the leaves. Not only were the homes older, I got the impression that most of them were inhabited by older people. Mature hedges encased well-kept but modest homes, which had a closed-off look. Drapes were drawn tight over front-facing picture windows and garage doors were shut. An orange neighborhood watch sign posted on a utility pole warned intruders of community vigilance. There was nobody on the sidewalks. There was no traffic. Only a smattering of cars were parked on the street.

Over the years, the strong Southern California sun had faded the homes to light pastel shades. Brilliant bougainvillea spilled over fences. Most Lomas Street homes displayed well-tended and colorful front-yard flower gardens. At 421, however, only a few defiant weeds poked up through dry, caked clay soil.

With a final jab at the doorbell, I turned to leave, more annoyed than disappointed, but I was stopped by the sound of metal scraping metal as a rust-bound window was being forced open.

"Someone there?" a male voice called out.

"Yes. I'm looking for Pete McGraw."

"Are you Sera?"

"Yes. Sera Schilling of the *San Diego Observer*. Your housekeeper set up this appointment last week. Did she forget to tell you?"

"Sorry. Wait a minute. I'll be right there."

The window shut with a bang.

Moments later, I heard the metallic click of the bolt being released. The heavy oak front door was pulled open.

"Yes, she told me about setting up this meeting. I've looked forward to it. But I must've drifted off. The medication, you know. They load you with the stuff." He held out his hand to shake mine. His broad smile swallowed up his face, immediately melting my frosty introduction.

Following behind him, I noticed how he shuffled to keep his balance, hunched over a wooden cane, and with apparent pain. He wore a sports coat, slacks, and an immaculately pressed white shirt. "She's still out food shopping, I guess," he mumbled.

"We don't keep a whole lot of food in the house," he apologized. "But, can I get you some coffee, water, something?" I declined, remembering how difficult it was for him to get around.

"Let's go in there, then." He pointed to seating in front of the fireplace in the living room and began his arduous walk in that direction.

Windows covered by heavy drapes might have made the room oppressive, but actually it was comfortably warm and hospitable on that moody fall day. The pleasant, somewhat pungent wood smell of many fires burned in the stone fireplace over the years filled the air. In heavily trafficked areas, hard use had worn the wooden floor finish to a dull, bleached appearance. On the wall behind a roll-top desk loaded with piles of mail, local newspapers, and magazines hung a grouping of framed pictures. In the center of the grouping was an Alcoholics Anonymous serenity prayer that had been neatly embroidered by an unknown feminine hand.

McGraw led me to the room and sat down heavily on the sofa, leaving me the choice of one of the twin ornate, antique chairs that looked very uncomfortable. As I sat down, its horsehair stuffing crackled under my weight. I set up my equipment, a yellow lined legal notepad, pens, and a tape recorder. McGraw watched me closely as I did this and smiled. I returned his pleasant smile and pressed the "on" button.

"I'm at the home of Peter McGraw, retired San Diego Police Officer. It is now 10:17 A.M. on Monday, October 22, 1990. The purpose of this interview is to discuss the article that was published in the *San Diego Observer* on October 19, 1990. Mr. McGraw, who was chief detective in charge of the investigation of the Abkhazian boy's death, believes he has information to add to this article. Do you have anything to add?"

I saw him bristle. His words were measured and emphatic: "To answer your question, do me a favor and reread the article your paper printed very closely. There's nothing there. I am sure that you'll agree with me that the work done by that forensic team was slipshod at best. Miss Schilling, I was the chief detective in charge of investigating this case as a murder, as you know. I can honestly say that I did as good a job as I could. I had answers. I had concrete evidence. I had witnesses. Had a solid, confessing suspect. But jurisdictional politics got involved that took the case away from me. The San Diego Sheriff's

Department pursued this case as an accidental death from the time they took it over. And now after all these years they've done it again. I am very sure that after you've researched all the facts, you will share the position of the police department."

"Please continue."

"Let's begin at the beginning. First, a little foundation. The early thirties were the waning days of Prohibition in San Diego. Our city was a small border town of just under one hundred and fifty thousand residents who were still reeling from the aftershocks of the Great Depression. We didn't have it as bad here as most of the rest of the country because there was agriculture in fertile Mission Valley, cattle ranching, and of course, the ocean. Fishing boats lined the harbor; tuna nets with cork buoys covered the piers to dry. Canneries meant work. We pinched pennies—had to, because of high taxes from the failed growth of some land speculation by our city fathers.

"You've heard of the 'Roaring Twenties'? Those things were going on when my dad was captain of the San Diego Police Department's Purity League. Vice, it's called now. There was bootlegging, speakeasies, back-room poker games, and cat houses in the Stingaree.

"As the thirties moved on, however, the social pendulum began to swing to the right. Purgative committees sprouted up to rid the city of criminals, bootleggers, and others. There were women's committees like the Women's Convention Center and the Committee of Six Hundred. We had a strong-fisted P.T.A. There was vigilantism. San Diego men deputized themselves, and wearing stars and guns succeeded only in pushing thugs just over the border into Mexico. They made the problem worse.

"It was a joke. When these vigilantes pushed the crooks into Mexico, they had wide-open opportunity south of the border, safely outside legal regulation, where they could sell what was illegal in the U.S. to U.S. citizens. Tourists were attracted to Mexico, where illicit goods and services came easy. Almost overnight, Tijuana changed from a dusty border town. Tijuana was known as 'Satan's playground' back then.

"Soon big-time machers, like Wirt Bowman, James Crofton, and Baron Long, came to Tijuana. They were called the 'Border Barons.' By pooling resources, they hired an architect and built Agua Caliente, a fancy resort rivaling Monte Carlo. Agua Caliente had a casino, spa, golf course, tennis courts, and later on, its famous racetrack. Since booze, racing, and gaming were illegal in California, Agua Caliente's guest list became studded with blue bloods, Hollywood stars, diplomats, politicians, aristocrats, foreign kings, and even wealthy Indian maharajas. All the tourist money was bypassing San Diego to be spent in Mexico. All this was going on before the 1930s. We wanted that money for ourselves.

"One of Agua Caliente's notable visitors was Bugsy Siegel. He took the Border Barons' idea north to Vegas and built that up. City fathers saw what Siegel did and wondered why the same idea of an open town like Vegas wouldn't work here in San Diego. If gambling and racing were legalized and if prostitution were regulated like in Las Vegas, San Diego might bring back the crowds that otherwise would be headed to Tijuana.

"This idea ignited hostile disagreement. City fathers argued that San Diego become an open city, legally allowing gambling and regulated prostitution like Vegas. They had their supporters, as you can guess.

Others argued for what they called a "closed town," the good, old American values, those that followed the settlers from America's puritanical east, to its heartland, and finally to the coast. Family, home, school, and church would be protected with what they thought would be positive community growth coming from real estate expansion, good urban planning, education, and culture. There was some speculation that Christopher Abkhazian's death might even have been a hostile reaction to the boy's father, a minister with an extensive following. He spoke out against opening up the city. He created quite a stir, and pissed off not a few of the city's big wigs."

"This was before Prohibition ended?"

"Yes. You're right. Prohibition ended in December of 1933. Before that there was rum-running, bootlegging, smuggling. As kids, my sister and I would listen to my dad's stories that were as exciting as any radio mystery.

"Before the 1930s, rum-runners used a network of border tunnels and the ocean to smuggle in booze. My dad told of shootouts from the cliffs in what is now Torrey Pines State Park. When cops got wind of a delivery, they'd lay in wait at the top of the cliffs, armed and ready. The ocean ran red with spilt blood, my dad said."

"They'd just shoot them?" I asked, incredulously.

"Back then, cops weren't something to be reckoned with. And another thing, only a fool would drink that rotgut. Reminds me of one time that my dad was involved in a big bust. They were bringing in some dangerous smugglers.

"Dad told us that they jailed the smugglers, but they didn't find the stash. A few days later, he took my sister and me out to Dutch Flats. Said he had some looking around to do. Mom didn't know he had a gun in the car. She wouldn't have allowed us to go if she'd known. We turned off the main road and bumped along for a while on a dirt road before stopping the car a little way down from an old green-shingled farmhouse. He took his Thompson sub out of the car. He told my sister to wait in the car, and for me to come along with him. You can imagine how jealous my sister was of me then!" The old man chuckled at the memory.

"Dad told me to wait outdoors while he checked out the house. He said to holler if I saw anything or anybody on the grounds. He made a show of the gun to dramatize the danger of it all. At first, I was very excited to be told to stand guard, but after a while I got bored and decided to take a gander around for myself.

"There was a rotted-out chicken coop in the side yard. No chickens; only dried-up chicken crap on the ground. I went in and scuffed around in the dirt and crap with the toe of my shoe. I wasn't looking for anything, so I was surprised when my foot hit metal. It was a steel plate. I knew immediately that I'd found what my dad was looking for.

"I ran to the house and yelled to my father to come quick. Together we went back to the chicken yard. We found four other round steel, quarter-inch-thick covers of fifty-five-gallon drums. Inside the barrel was whiskey—if that's what you'd call it. Oh my God, Sera! There were maggots, flies, and filth floating on the surface of the putrid liquid. My dad took a stick and stirred the rotgut. 'Pete,' he said, 'this is the so-called American whiskey. It's distilled from potatoes, rotten cactus, or whatever else is to be had down in Mexico, and it's being sold to people to drink. It can make them blind; it can even kill them. With good liquor available, because you know people will always want to drink it, and under heavy national and local management, we can save lives.'"

"I guess he wanted San Diego to be an open town?" I asked.

"Yeah, he always thought that San Diego being a border town and a navy town, things should be available but heavily regulated. My folks had many heated arguments about just that."

McGraw took a sip from his water glass, put the glass back on the table, and smiled. "But, I've digressed. You asked me to tell you about myself. I was born in Chicago—in 1908. There were two of us, my younger sister Cathy and me. My ma was from Ireland, and my dad was Irish-American. We were poor as church mice. A lot of folks were hanging it up to move out west to California. 'The land of milk and honey,' but I'm sure you've heard that cliché. So, the McGraw family went west, too. I remember that train ride very clearly because it wasn't the most comfortable trip a person could take, unless that person had money and could afford a sleeping car at night. I was about twelve when we came out. It was a good move for us because my dad found employment, we could afford a house, and the schools were pretty good. I followed my dad's steps when

I became a cop when I was around nineteen. Straight out of high school."

"Thank you." I prodded, interested but growing impatient. "Now, to the point of this interview."

"To clear the air, and I meant to ask you straight on, why aren't I talking to the reporter who wrote the story?"

I shrugged. "I guess because she's leaving the paper, is moving out of the area, and is taking a job at another newspaper. Actually, I don't know why St. James assigned it to me."

"Then, you know little or nothing about this case?"

"I spent several hours in the newspaper archives yesterday, Mr. McGraw. I put a timeline of events together, surrounding the child's disappearance, a little about the investigation—*your* investigation— through to the time that the sheriff's department took it over." I showed him my timeline.

He looked it over and nodded. "Good start. Now about the article in the paper, it is B.S. Honey, I know what I know, and I know flimflam when I read it." He paused, frowned, and then began to poke himself in the chest with his finger. "*I* was there when they pulled the child's body in from the San Diego Bay. *I* was at the mortuary where they ran the autopsy immediately after we left the waterfront. *I* was one of the first to read the doctors' autopsy report. *I* sat in on the coroner's jury and listened to their verdict of homicide. *I* hunted down a suspect who confessed and showed me physical evidence. *I* pieced this damnable puzzle together and was ready to take it to the D.A.'s when the sheriff's department took it over. *I* watched them mishandle evidence. And now, recently. If the forensic team wanted good, sound information, they should have come to me. Nobody did."

McGraw wiped perspiration from his forehead. He took a few sips of water and put the glass down.

As kindly I could, I asked, "Why not put the case to rest?"

"Why not? I just told you why not. Because I know when we're being screwed over. Like I told you, someone wants this case closed and forgotten real bad, and will go to any length to see that it happens."

"Mr. McGraw, as a reporter I deal with facts. What you just said sounds a little wild."

"Okay, you've got a point. Facts. You need facts. Let's take another close look at what the sheriff's forensic team said in the article."

I brought out the article from my attaché case, and read it out loud.

"Let's start at the beginning. Why did they choose this particular case to reinvestigate? It is very old, as you said. It happened more than a half century ago. Another thing is: Is there any new information offered? They requested federal grant money to pay for the costs for using modern technology. Then they admit that evidence was either missing or too old to use DNA testing anyhow. Do they offer any new opinions or bring in any witness statements offering a new or different perspective? No. They restate published testimony from 1933."

"What types of equipment or tests were used by medical examiners in the thirties?"

"Good question. Back in '33, they were beginning to compile somewhat of a fingerprint database. Very rudimentary, you understand. They used blood type analysis. They had hand-typed lists of criminals. That's just about all."

"Very fundamental, wasn't it? And prone to error?"

"Yes, I agree. But back then, San Diego was a very small city. People knew each other. As a cop, I knew who was taking a look at the evidence. I knew the professionals. I knew those that had no agenda other than to figure out who *done* it. And remember, our city being fairly small at the time, most people knew what made other people tick. I personally knew the pathologists who did the autopsy on the little boy, and I knew they were honest, credible, and trustworthy. And they were medical doctors."

I attempted to sit back in the chair, but the horsehair crackled, and the straight back didn't allow for much comfort. I couldn't help but smile at the old man who was watching me intently, waiting for validation.

"Okay, Mr. McGraw," I said. "I'm biting. I will start researching in depth. How 'bout you tell me what you know and I'll go out on my own and see what I can find to support what you tell me?"

McGraw replied, "Thank you. Your time and interest are appreciated more than you know. I'll begin at the beginning. On a summer day in July of 1933, a little boy disappeared . . ."

McGraw's Story

THE DAY AFTER Christopher Abkhazian went missing, Chief of Police Alton Doyle called a meeting. Most of the department had yet to set eyes on him. Doyle was newly hired by the city council under the recommendation of the city manager, Fred Winters. Doyle had been recruited from San Diego's big-sister city, Los Angeles.

Cops grumbled. Sure, it was true that the department had its share of problems, but was it necessary to bring in an outside man? Surely, San Diego had men capable of the leadership the force needed. Most of the guys wanted the cliques broken up and the low morale boosted, and they wanted to support their chief. But did they trust Doyle? He was rumored to maintain questionable alliances in L.A., in spite of his handle, "Chief Cleanup." His management style was questionable, too. He was said to turn cop against cop, encouraging them to rat on each other in spiteful competition.

Pete took a wooden chair in the sweltering staff room. His partner, Joe, handed him his coffee mug, which he'd filled with hot coffee. Glancing at his wristwatch, Joe smirked. "You look like you can use this, Irish! Late night in the Stingaree?"

"Nope." Pete took the coffee. "Thanks. Why don't you buy me a new mug while you're at it? This looks a little messed up."

"Ah, it ain't so bad. It's got character." Joe pointed at the chips and stains. "Has your name on it."

Pete answered by taking a noisy slurp of the coffee.

Joe tipped back in his chair, balancing against the wall and crossing his arms across his chest. His cap was pulled down over his forehead, barely covering the playful glint in his hazel eyes. "You set to meet our chief? Chief Cleanup?" he asked.

"Alton H. Doyle."

"What does he make in the lineup of top cops? A baker's dozen?"

"What's this meeting about?" interrupted Officer Sparling.

"The missing kid, most likely. Was in the paper yesterday and today."

The door opened suddenly and the chief made his entrance, creating a curious hush in the crowded room. Barely five and a half feet tall, round-faced, and portly, Pete's first opinion of him was one of profound scorn. Doyle wore full regalia: a uniform stiffly starched and too blue, medals pinned and proudly pinned on his chest. (*How'd he earn those?* Pete wondered.) With his manicured nails and polished skin, Pete thought Doyle looked as his nickname implied: too clean to be trusted.

The men stood noisily and saluted their new chief. He returned their salute and took his place behind the podium. There was no introduction, no opening joke, and no smile. Doyle took a wooden pointer and firmly tapped it on the intersecting lines on the wall map indicating Ash Street and Fifth Avenue in downtown San Diego.

"Okay." *Tap. Tap.* "Now, most of you have read in the paper that a seven-year-old boy went missing Tuesday morning. The last time his parents saw him was at their cleaning store around 0830. He left the establishment with a friend. We got the report of a missing person at 1800 that night. Men, we are still in the twenty-four-hour regulatory period for missing persons and we will allow the newspaper to continue to write of it as such, but my sense is that we should begin immediately investigating it as an abduction. To that end, I am mobilizing this-here force to get the culprit and get that child back to his parents safe and sound. We will be working this as a crime, and men, as you know in any criminal case, time is the enemy."

"Sir." The chief was interrupted by Gus Hildebrant's hand. Gus had a reputation for his outspokenness. Doyle nodded at the officer to stand.

"Begging your pardon, but this is San Diego, sir. Not Los Angeles. Kids in San Diego are free to roam around the city. Everybody knows everybody, and it ain't unusual for kids to roam around unattended. This causes a problem because when little Johnny doesn't come home for lunch, parents overreact. They panic and call the cops. You see, sir, kids go missing all the time down here because of that freedom they have. But most of the time we find out they were with relatives or friends. We may be jumping the gun by going after this as a crime right away." He looked around for support, and there was a guttural murmur of confirmation by other men in the room.

Officer Stevens pushed his chair back, stood, and saluted. "That's correct, sir. We don't get riled up, because every time kids show up."

"Yes, sir," Hildebrant continued. "The blat shouldn't have run that article so soon. When the paper does that, it only gets people all lathered up. It didn't give enough time for things to settle out. The boy will probably show up at a friend's."

Another guttural murmur of agreement was heard among the men.

The chief nodded slowly, cleared his throat, thanked the two officers, and motioned for them to sit down. He paused to make eye contact with every individual in the room, cleared his throat again, and said, "As you all are aware, this department has been in pretty much of a mess these past few years. The paper has called us a revolving door of chiefs, and truthfully that is not far from the truth of things.

I want to stop that door from revolving. I plan to keep this job. First, I need to instill some trust in our police department by the citizens of this fine city."

He banged the podium with his fist. "You're right in the fact that the city is already 'lathered up,' as you put it." He held up a hand-drawn poster. "See here? I took this off a telegraph pole just outside headquarters. A three-thousand-dollar reward has already been raised for information leading to the arrest of guilty persons. I'm stressing the word *guilty*. Um, I wonder if any of you noticed the line of so-called witnesses stretching nearly half a block up the street. Lathered up?" He shook his head and worked his bottom lip with his teeth. His voice grew loud, and the jowls on his pudgy face shook. "This afternoon a massive search of Balboa Park has been organized by the Women's Civic Center, and already an inordinate number of San Diego's citizens have signed up to participate. Men, we are looking at a thousand folks, perhaps more. Good stuff, but not so for us, because they'll be stepping on evidence or stomping over footprints if they exist. And if I follow your plan of non-action, by sitting back on our haunches and waiting for things to take care of themselves, as you believe they indubitably shall, any crime scene, if the crime did happen as it very well might have, and if it happened in Balboa Park, then all important evidence, if it exists, will be all tore up. Now, if it pleases you, gentlemen, let's get on to the business of being policemen." He turned and tapped the intersection of Fifth and Ash once more.

"I personally questioned the parents of the missing boy yesterday. Our department psychologist sat in on the interview. We observed them closely, and then compared our opinions. The doctor and I agreed that they were genuinely frightened about the welfare of their son, Christopher. We are convinced that they are uninvolved in his disappearance and that our department needs to look outside the family for answers.

"This is what happened as we understand it. While the boy was eating his breakfast in the back of his parents' store here (*tap, tap*), another youngster barged in to tell him about a robbery that took place the night before, on Monday night at Hulsizer's Jewelry Store down the street." He tapped the pointer at a location just south of Ash on Fourth Avenue. "Jackie Cohn—that's the name of the boy's chum—is the son of the people who own the fur shop, here" (*tap, tap*.) "I have already met with this Jackie Cohn and his parents. The boy gave me a good rundown of their whereabouts the day the boy went missing. This is what he told me: They left the cleaning shop together at about 0800 Tuesday morning and headed to the jewelry store. After that they visited Kress's Department Store. They split up after that; Jackie had to return to the store to be driven home for violin practice. He left Christopher here" (*tap, tap, tap*), "at this trolley stop. Christopher said he was going to take it to the zoo at Balboa Park.

"What I got from the Abkhazians was somewhat the same story, but from a different point of view: that the last they saw of their son was when he ran out of their cleaning shop with Jackie Cohn. They said he didn't come back to the store for lunch, as was his habit. They didn't grow too concerned until around closing time, at 1800, when he still hadn't returned. They called the Cohns, who told them their son, Jackie, returned alone at noon to be driven home for his violin practice.

"As to identifying characteristics, the Abkhazian boy had a small mole on the right side in the back of his neck, just below the hair-line. He is short for his age, three feet, two inches, and thin, weighing approximately fifty-three pounds. This we got from school records—Mountain View Elementary. His mother told us he just lost his front left central upper incisor. And was wearing brown corduroys, a white shirt, brown jacket, tie shoes, and socks."

The chief paused and gazed once again around the room. "It is our job, men, to answer the unasked questions and fill in the blanks, and to *find that little boy,* dead or alive." He issued a plan of action with assignments. A second all-staff meeting was calendared for the next morning. Partners McGraw and Deutsch were assigned to Balboa Park to participate in the search that afternoon.

McGraw's narrative was interrupted by the front door of 421 Lomas Street banging open. A short, rotund woman with a pleasant middle-aged face stepped into the foyer. She dragged a shopping cart behind her.

"Oh!" she said when she realized her intrusion. "I'm so sorry to interrupt you." She unbuttoned her coat as Pete introduced her to Sera as his nurse, Mrs. Kersel. Sera noted that other than her ruddy complexion, the woman's entire color scheme was gray: she had gray hair and eyes, and was dressed in gray tweed trousers and a gray sweater set. She felt an immediate liking for the nurse, who appeared very attentive to the old man. She saw how Mrs. Kersel searched his face professionally while asking him, "Are you not too tired, Mr. McGraw? May I refresh your water?" Then she responded to his body language as he shook his head impatiently (obviously annoyed with her interruption and eager to resume his story) by smiling sweetly and taking a step back. As she turned to leave the room, she quietly reminded him not to forget a doctor's appointment in—she checked her watch—about an hour. "You'll need to get ready, so we'll need to leave here by . . ." Pete's frown stopped her. "I'll go out to the kitchen and put the food away, "she said instead, and left the room.

McGraw wiped his forehead with a Kleenex and tossed it on the table next to the other. He sighed, apologized needlessly, and continued with his narrative:

"Everyone struggled to make ends meet during those penurious times. Most of the folks went about their own business, keeping personal matters to themselves. When the newspaper published the headlines that the boy was missing, something happened in this city that I had never seen happen. Christopher Abkhazian became San Diego's poster child. To find him, everyone banded together. A new drive, a new purpose drove the entire town, and there was unprecedented solidarity."

Officers McGraw and Deutsch had been assigned to oversee searchers of what we used to call the pepper tree playground area of Balboa Park. It was already swarming with people, dogs, and horses by the time they arrived. Under various banners, volunteers had gathered into search groups: the Boy Scouts of America, the San Diego Women's Civic Center, the San Diego Parent-Teachers Association, Allied Veterans of Foreign Wars, the Crime Prevention Committee, and others. Equestrians from the Balboa Park Riding Club sat on high-strung horses that pawed at the ground impatiently with their hooves. The German Shepherd Tracking Team was there. Dogs barked eagerly and lunged impatiently on their handlers' leashes. Students from San Diego High School, La Jolla High School, and Coronado Academy were let out of school early in order to join the search.

Under the San Diego High School banner, Pete saw Dr. Hugh De Witt, his old high school principal. De Witt's formidable leadership was respected, unquestioned, and impeccable. But at the time that Pete was a student, Pete wholeheartedly despised the man. While admonishing him one day for some misconduct or another, Witt had made the observation that he didn't hold much hope for the youth's continued academic achievement. He predicted Pete wouldn't amount to much; that he'd be *just* a cop like his father. Now that Pete was the proud recipient of the distinguished Medal of Valor, he wished he could flaunt it at the principal who had been so pessimistic about his future.

The Santa Ana winds raked the leaves in the lofty eucalyptus trees, adding commotion to the scene below. Mrs. Rudolph Kennard, Jr., president of the Women's Civic Center, was commandeering the control booth with the W.C.C. flag snapping cheerfully in the dry wind. Portly Mrs. Mable A. Sterling was applying red sashes with the emblem of a cross and a flame to individuals in her massive collection of concerned mothers united under the banner of the San Diego's Women's Vigilante Group. Joe and Pete split up to oversee searchers in separate areas of Balboa Park. Joe accompanied the veterans, while Pete went to the playground area.

Later, when they were driving back to headquarters, Joe hooted, "You should have seen those guys from Fighting Bob Squadron, Irish! Most of them could hardly walk. They were deaf and almost blind. Damned if Kennard didn't give those old geezers the canyons to search. What a circus! There they were, clambering up the steep canyon walls on all fours. That crone has as much common sense as God gave a goose. Wouldn't you think she'd have the good sense to put those high school kiddies out there in the canyons, not those old joes?"

"Seems as if," Pete agreed thoughtfully, "since most of them kids have used those caves in the canyons for playing hooky from school for a smoke or some pussy, they'd know where to look."

"Experience talking, Irish?"

"Nah, not me. I was a fucking saint in high school. Just you ask old De Witt. He loved me. He'd tell you what an angel I was."

As he tossed his cap into the back, Joe noticed the brown bag on the seat. "What's in the bag?"

"Found a pair of men's skivvies in the brush off the playground. There was blood on them."

Joe's double take nearly broke his neck. "Yeah? You don't say?"

"Taking them to the lab."

"Right," Joe said, nodding his head coolly as though finding a pair of bloodied men's underwear near a children's playground was normal. They continued their ride in silence.

On Friday morning, promptly at 0800, the second staff meeting regarding the Abkhazian boy's disappearance took place at police headquarters. The chief gave an update. He had spoken to each leader of the various groups who searched the park the day before. "*Nada,*" he said dismally. At headquarters, officers had sifted out over fifty viable witnesses of the over three hundred. *"Nada,"* Doyle said again, shaking his head. No vital information had been learned.

"And after questioning these witnesses, you would think the boy grew wings," the chief chuckled sarcastically. "He would have had to have been in several places at the same time. Two women said they drove the kid out to La Jolla at eleven thirty, Tuesday morning. A cabbie said he saw a boy he swore was Christopher on the corner of Broadway and Second at noon. Another person said he saw the kid on Fairmount and Home avenues at the same time. And another fellow said the kid was thumbing a ride near Wonderland Park in Mission Beach around midnight."

He continued: "Christopher collected glass marbles. The kind that are popular with kids his age. His father said that Chris took great pride in his collection. One in particular: the orange cat's-eye marble. That marble was missing from his collection, according to his father. This may or may not be important. One last thing: this summer Christopher was allowed to ride streetcars without supervision and frequently rode streetcars numbers one, nine, and seven."

Pete stood and asked to be acknowledged. "Sir, were the streetcar drivers questioned? Did any of them see the missing boy on Tuesday?"

"Good question, Officer McGraw." Pete felt his face fill with blood from the chief's personal recognition. He wondered how he'd known his name. They'd never been introduced. "I pulled all drivers on those routes into headquarters for questioning. None had seen the boy that day.

"To continue, I forgot to mention Christopher's interest in the zoo and the children's area at the pepper tree playground. Those places were, of course, covered in the search"—he paused and referred to his notes—" by Officer McGraw. Nothing came up at either place, other than a pair of men's underwear with bloodstains on them. They have been sent to the lab.

"Some of you might have heard of Christopher's father, Adam Abkhazian. He carries a large following as lead minister at South Bay Baptist Church. He also runs the summer revivals out in Dehesa. Apparently these revivals are very popular and are actually going on now. Reverend Abkhazian is of Muslim roots, having been born somewhere in the Middle East. He converted to Christianity as a young man, and later went on to pursue his Ph.d. at Fuller Theological Seminary in Pasadena. Abkhazian is an outspoken proponent of maintaining San Diego as a closed town. Talk is, his mouth has ruffled not a few feathers in downtown San Diego. He also has been fervently pushing the drawing up of a city code prolonging Prohibition indefinitely in San Diego.

"The Reverend Abkhazian is married to a woman named Catherine, who is a pianist. She performs under her maiden name of Lindow. Some of you more cultured fellows may have actually attended one of her concerts at Spreckels." (The men guffawed at the chief's tongue-in-cheek sarcasm.) "She also is the organist at her husband's church.

"Finally, the rest of the Abkhazian family includes the grandparents, who take up residence with the family, and three siblings: Doris, five years old; Mary, two-and-a-half years old; and Albert, who is eighteen months old."

Again the meeting was adjourned after discussion. The chief still maintained that Christopher Abkhazian was probably the victim of a crime.

● ● ●

"Mr. McGraw," Mrs. Kersel inquired.

Sera looked up from her yellow legal pad.

The housekeeper was standing just inside the living room wearing a patient smile along with her overcoat.

The old man began to bluster at her interruption. "Okay, okay!" he finally responded – grimly, but with a wry smile. He held his palms up in hopelessness. "Worse than a wife!" he said with a glint in his eyes. "Guess we've got to cut it short for the day. Can you come back tomorrow?"

Sera returned his smile and gathered up her things. There was no way she could be but understanding about the situation, the old man, and the sweet, caring nurse.

Sera

CONTINUING WITH MY investigation, I called the sheriff's department and got the name of one of the investigators who had worked on the Abkhazian case with the forensic team. I was given the name of Bob Tindall and a telephone number where he could be reached.

When I called Mr. Tindall he was initially resistant to letting me question him about the article, saying it was a done deal. He questioned why the newspaper was investigating the story it was responsible for publishing. But he eventually agreed to give me an hour of his time. He suggested we meet at Denny's Restaurant in Santee if I hosted. Denny's had a cowboy breakfast that he enjoyed, and it only cost $5.99.

It was picturesque driving east along I-8 in the early morning. The highway dipped into the El Cajon Valley. The unusually heavy rains of the past few days had enlivened the underbrush on the surrounding environs to a lush California sage-green color. The distant peaks of the Cuyamaca Mountains were topped with a sprinkling of snow, the first of the winter season. The white of the snow drew a sharp silhouette in the rich cerulean sky.

After a while, I exited the freeway and eased through hilly terrain on a narrower paved road. Here, the scene changed to a rural, somewhat ramshackle community. Bordering the highway were small ranch-style homes and fenced pastures with various livestock: cows, goats, and horses. Porches held sleeping dogs. Side yards frequently had sagging, disused clotheslines. In the front of many of the houses, pickups and old Chevy sedans with broken windshields or missing doors and wheels were rusting in high weeds.

The town center of Santee had a smattering of small mom-and-pop businesses, repair shops, beauty shops, small appliance stores, and finally the strip mall where the sign advertised Denny's Restaurant.

In the reception area, a number of people waited for open tables, mostly senior citizens. I looked around the restaurant and immediately spotted an individual sitting solo at a booth in the back. He waved. I crisscrossed through the tables to join him.

Tindall's bulk filled the bench, his paunch leaving little room between him and the table. He had a neatly groomed white goatee and his dome was completely bald. I suspected he was only a few years younger than McGraw, but in much better health in spite of his obesity. Tindall's gray eyes reflected intelligence and, thank goodness, warmth, despite his initial resistance to our meeting. He stood as I took the seat on the opposite bench and offered me his hand to shake. He had a great and very contagious smile.

"I've already ordered, Miss Schilling. I got the cowboy special. You may want to try it. It looks like you could put a little meat on your bones, if I can be so candid."

I declined the cowboy special, ordering coffee and toast instead, not at all bemused by his familiarity. *Next he'll be calling me "girlie,"* I thought, as I set up my equipment and pushed the "on" button on my tape recorder.

"I'm Bob Tindall," he said, leaning across the table and speaking into the machine. "Retired from the San Diego Sheriff's Department as a sergeant after nearly forty years' service, currently volunteer on the sheriff's forensic team . . ."

"When did you retire, Mr. Tindall?" I asked.

"Let's see, that was back in '83. You're here about the article that reported the reinvestigation and formal closure of the Abkhazian case in 1933. I can accept partial responsibility for the information that was published in the *San Diego Observer.*"

"Why did your team choose that particular case to reinvestigate?" I asked.

"I can speak of my own interest in the case, but that takes a bit of an answer. I began my career in law enforcement in 1939. This was six years after that boy's death. I was about twelve years old when the boy was found floating in San Diego Bay. The case and all that went on around it made a bit of an impression on me. During the time that the police department was investigating it as a homicide, our city acted as though it were under quarantine for the plague or polio or something. We kids were not allowed the freedom that we were used to. Our folks were terrified that a maniac was stalking our streets, on the lookout for children to brutalize. The papers fed their fears.

"A sense of normalcy returned to the city when the sheriff's department took over the investigation. And when Doyle was right-fully fired, people relaxed. Then, once again, we kids were allowed to play sports once more, go to the zoo, take the streetcars, and go to the movies.

"A group of us retired investigators occasionally take on cold cases to reevaluate. I remembered this case from my childhood and found out that it hadn't been formally closed, although the sheriff's department concluded that it was an accidental death. Since I had a personal interest in the case, I suggested that we look into it. And what we found was what your paper published."

"Can you describe how you came to your conclusion?"

"We used the information and materials we had available to us."

"You could test evidence? You had reliable witnesses to question? You could apply modern techniques to this material?"

"Not actually." He looked down at his eggs and poked them around on the plate with his fork a bit. "Like I told you, we had very little to work with. Unfortunately, when the San Diego Sheriff's Department took over the case in 1933, most of the things were sent out of town to Los Angeles. This was under the order of the sheriff. He probably thought it wise to change the venue because of the public hysteria in San Diego. It was a good move on his part in most ways. They had better lab facilities up there than we did in San Diego. But the downside was that records and evidence were lost or destroyed by the time we got around to reinvestigating. They told us that case information had been purged long ago. So we were left with just a few things that we had kept on our own cold case shelves."

"But you accepted federal money to reinvestigate the case?"

"I think that's where we got the money. Look, we weren't lying or mishandling the money. As I understand it, the feds give us blanket funding for cold case investigations. I suppose that this was one we chose to spend some of the resources on."

"Interesting."

"Say, about those cold case shelves, you might be able to take a look at what we used yourself. That is, if the box hasn't been shredded since we did our work."

"Shredded?"

"It's closed formally now. Once a case is closed, records can be tossed. Anyhow, if it still exists, you might find it in the sheriff's headquarters downtown. I know that a transcript of a key witness is in the box, the boy's, the Cohn boy. You will find that interesting if you read it."

"Good idea. Other than DNA and technical equipment now available in forensics, what were some other techniques you used?"

"Answering that question causes me a little embarrassment, Miss Schilling, because as I just told you, we had very little to work with. Jackie Cohn's statement was one of the few things we had. That's the transcript I was talking about. You've heard of Jackie?"

"Yes."

"Poor kid. To have a friend die like that."

"What the nine-year-old child said back then is what you based your investigation on?"

"Yes. And there were experts' opinions we got about the injuries done by marine life to the boy while he was in the bay. What the police department thought were mutilations back in '33 were merely marine life damages."

"You didn't mention any of the experts by name."

"We didn't? Their names weren't any secret."

"May I have the names of these experts?"

"Yes, of course you can. Just call me. I'll give their names to you if you wish."

"Thank you. To move on, I get the impression that you didn't have much respect for the police department of the time, Mr. Tindall."

"You couldn't be more right. That's why I made it a future goal when I was twelve to become a sheriff when I grew up. No, Doyle was a joke. He was our chief of police. He had no management skills, tried to exploit the poor boy's death to win a following, and was about as corrupt as a person could be. He was fired by the city manager for doing a poor job. He went back to Los Angeles. He had a bad end, too. Word was he mixed with racketeers and the like. At any rate, someone put a bomb in his automobile, which was parked in his home garage, and when he started the car up one morning it exploded. He lived, but it broke just about every bone in his body."

I asked him about Pete McGraw.

"Shoot! You mean the old son of a bitch, Irish?"

"Yes. Irish." I laughed, misreading his body language as he said Pete's nickname.

"Yes. That's what they called him. And he *was* a son of a bitch."

"You knew him, then." I smiled, gratified that someone besides St. James was personally acquainted with my primary source, but as I

watched Bob Tindall's expression constrict into a scowl, I began feeling tentative about his affirmation.

"Yeah, I knew McGraw," he responded, less than enthusiastically.

"He was quite the hero," I ventured, watching his face fall.

"The *hero* you say?" He shook his head slowly and screwed up his
mouth in disgust. "Nah."

"We're talking about Pete McGraw?"

"The one and the only," he replied caustically.

I raised an eyebrow. "From what I've read, learned, or personally
felt about Pete McGraw, he seems a good man and was well respected
as a police officer."

"I can't argue with your opinion, Sera; I suppose there were a few
who might have thought well of the man."

"For one, my senior editor, Albion St. James," I asserted, wondering at my desire to protect the old man. Tindall's words stung. And
they also made me wonder about McGraw's character...the Serenity
Prayer on his ego wall—.

"I know St. James," he said, swishing his hand through the air dis-
missively. "But Pete McGraw. He was a low-down and dirty son-of-
a-bitch cop. The guy I knew of diddled with the prosties on his beat.
Took bribes. Was a sloppy lush and got thrown off the police department because of booze. And that's not all. If my memory serves me
right, he had a fling with the little mother of the dead boy. Now that I
think about it, McGraw's impropriety just might have been the reason
why the Abkhazians left San Diego."

I noted Tindall's opinion in my notes. Then I asked, "Am I right to
assume that those are the reasons you didn't ask for his notes on his
investigation into the boy's death when he was involved in the case
in 1933?"

"You're damn tootin'. He'd lie anyhow. Never trust a drunk."

"Wasn't it a bit one-sided for you to only use the sheriff's old
material?"

"You could think that, but we felt it was the only *reliable* material."

"Carver? Sheriff Carver?" I queried of the sheriff who was in charge of the investigation in 1933. "You served under Sheriff Carver, is that right?"

"No, never got to do it. He was before my time with the department."

"Did you know him personally?"

"No, I am afraid not. I knew him by reputation."

"What was his reputation, then?"

"He had an excellent reputation."

"And this you gathered this from—?"

"Mostly from my father's opinion. Dad served under Carver and knew him as well as anybody could."

"Your father was a deputy sheriff?"

"That's right."

"And your father thought highly of Carver?"

"Yes, he did, and for good reason. Hank Carver was a hell of a nice guy. He was of the old stock: American, down to his core. Honest. He was a charitable man. When he was sheriff, he raised the funds by himself to set up a camp for juvenile offenders in the South Bay. Worked at that until he died. He died young, as I recall, of cancer. He was Christian man, and he was also a member of the Masons. A big fellow, but gimpy. War left him with a bum leg. That's the First World War, mind you. Before he went into politics, he was a businessman, involved in real estate and insurance. He was elected sheriff in the late twenties, and held that position for two terms, for eight years. When he inherited the Abkhazian case from the police, he stood up before the Board of Supervisors and demanded only the best in the way of investigators. They used Virgil Green. Has the name Virgil Green come up in your research yet?"

"No."

"He was a top-notch investigator that Sheriff Carver brought in on the case; and take it from me, if you're looking for heroes in this story of yours, *they* were heroes in the real sense of the word. Not the other, McGraw. Green was a hard-boiled detective of the Philip Marlowe vintage. He was brought down from L.A. to head up the sheriff department's investigation of this case. Have you read about the torso murder up in L.A.?" Not waiting for my response, he continued, "Well, Green was the private investigator who solved that notorious case. And it was ingenious detective work, that's what it was. What happened was that a female torso had been dumped in a culvert up there off Mulholland Drive. The killer tried to destroy her identity. He cut off her hands, legs, and beheaded her. Slightly over-kill if you'll excuse my macabre attempt at humor. Green was hired by L.A. to handle the investigation of the case. In the end, he not only identified the woman, but went on to solve the case by matching a single strand of hair that he found on her body to her doctor's hair. Then he got the good doc to confess to killing her, too. The doctor eventually hanged for it."

"Was that the Black Dahlia Murder? I thought it was never solved."

"No. Not that one, but another case very much like it."

Little more was said that would help me in my investigation aside from the location of the material for the cold case, if it hadn't been shredded. I thanked Mr. Tindall for his candidness, paid the bill, and took my leave.

As I drove back to the city, my mind was a muddle, wondering whose memory to believe. It became clear to me that so far all that I had been hearing was just that, memories. I needed to get my hands dirty, as my mother would say, and get down to work. Dig for the answers. Actually, in the end, Tindall didn't offer anything other than what had been published in the article. But he sure painted another picture of Pete McGraw.

Pete and Sera

Second Interview, October 24, 1990

WHEN I MET with McGraw for the second time, he seemed eager to begin. His "spot" had been set up for his comfort during our interview, probably by his caregiver, Mrs. Kersel. There was a glass of water and a box of Kleenex next to the sofa on the side table. As I organized my things, plugged my tape recorder into a nearby wall socket, and pulled out my yellow legal pad on which to continue my notes on this case, he told me he wanted to talk about the initial days of the investigation under the new chief, Doyle.

I flipped through the yellow pad for a clean page to take notes. My eyes fell on the starred, circled notation I'd made during Tindall's interview regarding Pete's alcoholism and his possible involvement with the mother of the deceased boy. I looked up at him. His rheumy eyes, shining with eagerness, searched mine—so hopeful, so anxious. As much as I wanted Pete's elucidation on these matters, I wasn't comfortable broaching the topic so early in our relationship. He might become defensive and clam up. Instead, I decided to bring it up later, at a more opportune time.

We reviewed what we had discussed the day before, and McGraw outlined what he planned to cover. When I saw that he was ready—after he had taken a sip of water, removed a Kleenex and wiped his forehead, and finally relaxed back into the sofa—I told him I was ready for his story. His eyes took on a faraway look as he seemed to recall the long-dormant memories.

Pete's Story

AS THE WEEK progressed, Christopher Abkhazian's name was on everybody's lips, headlining the newspaper, and whispered in the undercurrent of speculation that it was another homicide.

By Friday, when there had been no news about the child's whereabouts, a frightened restlessness stirred up the city. The police understood the people of the city they served, and knew it wouldn't be long before this state of vexed alarm turned into all-out panic. There were signs of it already: People had begun to bolt their doors (a practice that was unheard of in San Diego before the recent rash of crimes), and children traveled with chaperones (seldom was a child seen unattended). At playgrounds throughout the city, bands of mothers protectively enclosed their innocents. There was also a shift to extreme conservativism in the political mood. The newly formed Women's Vigilante Group published demands in the newspaper that the city be cleansed of immoral dance halls, offensive burlesque theaters, Chinese opium dens, and gambling. They denounced the lax enforcement by police of speakeasies and their open advertisement over the radio in public announcement slots. A letter to the editor appeared in the newspaper from Mrs. Rudolph Kennard of the Women's Civic Center, suggesting, "All known degenerates, feeble-minded persons, the congenitally perverted, prostitutes, and homosexuals should henceforth be kept in humane but permanent confinement." And the newspaper moved editorials to the front page, feeding growing wholesale paranoia with unsubstantiated speculation as reasons for the upswing in crime.

Threatened, folks turned to religion, raising church attendance by nearly 12 percent. Previously meek-mannered citizens dusted off the cobwebs (and their shotguns). Many went door to door, ringing doorbells, carrying petitions for signatures. Keep San Diego a closed city, they argued. Strengthen law enforcement and tighten laws and regulations.

And the Reverend Abkhazian kept on preaching. His fold continued to increase.

Six Murders; None Solved. Two-Year Spree Ends with Missing Child! Screamed the newspaper. *Boy Now thought Dead*, blazed the front-page headline. The ensuing article reminded its readers of the recent rash of homicides where the victims were children or young adults. It went on to utter a warning: "Parents, do you know who to trust? Take care because the perpetrator of these dastardly crimes could be anybody: the friendly milkman, the generous clerk at the corner grocery store who, sympathetic to a family's needs, allows bills to pile up and 'borrows' ration cards from the register to pay for necessary staples, the neighbor next door who is kind to children but keeps mostly to himself, or a parasitic bogey man, who is invisible to adults' eyes but shows himself to children, and then preys on their innocence."

After succeeding to rile up San Diego's citizens, the newspaper began a blame game by pointing fingers at the San Diego Police Department. Articles connected the Abkhazian boy's disappearance to the other murders. The press implied that the ineffectiveness of the police department was related in part to a lapse of morality by heretofore solid policemen as the end of Prohibition drew near. It charged the police force with disorganization and with both real and imagined problems, ranging from organized crime to political corruption.

Pete admitted that it was sadly true that the police department was in an appalling state of affairs. The turnover of seven new chiefs within a three-year period had been justifiably compared to a revolving door by the newspaper. And now, another new police chief! And who was this new chief but an outsider brought to San Diego from Los Angeles by the city manager, who touted Chief Doyle's unblemished reputation of unwavering probity. But whispers among the police force based on rumors from L.A. put holes in the manager's belief, making the chief a much doubted new leader.

On Friday morning, a very somber chief of police ordered a follow-up briefing to the police department's Thursday's meeting regarding the missing boy. Most of the men came into the hall with cups of coffee in hand, and they took their seats more quietly than they had when they met before.

Chief Doyle, with his customary soldier's stance, took his place behind the podium. As before, medals and ribbons were placed on his uniform with dazzling symmetry. Patiently waiting for all the seats to be filled and the room to become orderly, he perused a stack of loose papers in his hands. Every once in a while, his eyes would glance up from a sheet of paper he was holding to meet the eyes of one of the policemen in the room, then back to the paper. After a while this caused group consternation, and the rumbling of conversation quieted into a curious hush. Eyes in the audience shifted warily to each other after meeting the eyes of their chief. He'd frown, then look down and write a notation, and then shuffle the paper into the back of the stack. Finally he cleared his throat and gave a general salute, which was immediately returned by the policemen.

In a deep, chesty voice that belied his diminutive size, the chief reviewed the work that had been done on the case. Pete flipped open the new notebook with the genuine cowhide cover that he'd bought the day before at Hayward's Stationery and Paper Store for on-the-job note taking. He called it his "police journal." He wrote rapidly, trying to keep up with the chief. His intrigue had spiked. He felt the verve in his gut that that he got when a new case started becoming personal to him.

The chief again briefly outlined the route the youngsters took "scouting about downtown," then splitting up at noon, at which time they went their separate ways. Jackie returned to his parents' shop, as planned, to be driven home for lunch and his violin practice. He had no idea about where his friend had ventured other than Chris saying that he was taking the streetcar to the zoo. When he left him, Christopher was headed to the stop on Second Street and Broadway.

In addition to Jackie, detectives questioned any persons who came to the station with information. As before, the so-called witnesses didn't pan out.

Under pressure by certain community groups, a new list had been compiled naming criminal offenders living in San Diego, and one by one these "despicables," as Doyle called them, were being brought down to headquarters for thorough questioning.

The chief said he had wired an inquiry to personal acquaintances "of the higher order" in the Los Angeles Police Department, requesting any information they might have about criminals and known perverts who might have moved from their jurisdiction into San Diego's, or vice versa. A reply was expected soon.

To conclude, Chief Doyle thanked the men for their contribution at the search of Balboa Park and commented on the frustration the several thousand searchers must have shared with the department after such an exhausting, discouraging, and hot day.

The chief then outlined the next steps in the ongoing investigation. That day World War I veterans from the Fighting Bob Squadron were organizing a search of Coronado Shores. Over five hundred Boy Scouts of America were going to walk the mud flats at the San Diego Bay waterfront. The three-hundred-something members of the San Diego's Women's Civic Center were canvassing the neighborhood where the Abkhazian family lived, going house to house. And finally, the chief announced that he had assigned specific sites to designated police teams of two. Having said this, Doyle called out names and handed out assignments.

Pete unfolded his sheet of paper, took a look at their assignment, raised an eyebrow to Joe, and then handed him the paper. Joe read the assignment and returned the dubious expression of his partner, who simply shrugged his response. Pete folded and pocketed their assignment.

Chief Doyle was adamant that this case was extremely time sensitive. Although it hadn't officially changed its status from that of a missing-persons' case, the passing of time would be disastrous if the case turned out to be more sinister—it was already well outside the twenty-four-hour window so crucial to a criminal investigation. What the chief didn't admit, and all the guys in the room knew, was that Doyle had to make headway if he wanted to keep his job. The new chief of police, a scapegoat for a bloodthirsty newspaper, stood tallest in the line of execution.

Saluting the men once more, Doyle left the room.

For a while there was an uncommon silence in the room that would be normally filled with the guffaws and hoarse laughter of a bunch of raunchy males. This was followed by the low hum of conversation as the officers made plans and offered speculation.

Pete and Joe listened to snippets of conversation: How could a child simply vanish into thin air? This was a town where everybody knew everybody and gossip traveled faster than radio waves. If someone was acting strangely, or if something seemed out of kilter, almost everybody within the city limits would know about it before the end of the day. They were moving too slowly. The kid had to be dead. The culprit had to be found; that's all there was to it. Expand the search outward into county lands, across the border into Mexico, and up into Los Angeles.

What about kidnapping? The chief hadn't mentioned the possibility of a kidnapping. And nobody brought it up to ask him. Had the parents heard anything that would indicate that the boy had been kidnapped, such as a ransom note? Was something taken from the child and sent to his parents?

Pete thought common sense pointed to an act of murder, not a kidnapping. Yes, there had recently been a rash of kidnappings going on back east, but not here in San Diego. And if the boy had been kidnapped, wouldn't the kidnapper have chosen a family that could afford to pay a substantial ransom? Recent kidnap victims in Chicago and New York were connected to people of notoriety, wealthy industrialists, or entrepreneurs. Pete's thoughts turned to Charles Lindbergh, the famous aviator. Lindbergh was the victim of a horrendous, gone-wrong kidnapping. But then, he'd been rich and famous. Pete considered how San Diegans felt keen possessiveness of Lindbergh and his family during the trial and later execution of the man convicted of the deed. They were endeared to "their own Lindy" because hadn't his 1926 monoplane, the *Spirit of St. Louis*, that took him on his famous international flight, been made by San Diego's Ryan Flying Company?

Thinking about the Abkhazian case, Pete wondered about the motive. Was it sensationalism? Recognition? Sexual depravity? Certainly not easy money. The Abkhazians weren't wealthy; they were common working folk. The boy's father had to work two jobs just to make ends meet for his large extended family that lived in a small bungalow in North Park.

Pete watched the room begin to empty. He and Joe remained in their seats. Pete gazed into the distance deep in thought, folding and unfolding the assignment the chief had handed to him earlier.

"I was just thinking . . ." Joe said.

"Let's have it."

"The chief said that he'd checked out the family, didn't he?"

"Yeah."

"Wasn't the boy's father pretty outspoken about San Diego remaining a closed town?"

Pete nodded. "I think that's true."

"It could be that, or the interracial marriage thing."

McGraw nodded somberly. "They're Armenian, huh? The reverend's family. She's Caucasian. That would make the kids mixed."

"The Klan. It's another angle to keep in mind. Both of them are good angles."

Pete agreed. "I can see why Doyle wants this handled in a quiet way, but I think we need to get moving or time will get away from us." He once again unfolded and studied the paper the chief had given him.

"How come we got downtown? That's prime."

They were two of the youngest rookies in the department, so they expected to be placed somewhere out in the boondocks, with the experienced guys strategically placed downtown. Their assignment was to retrace the boy's last journey on the day he disappeared. They would re-interrogate the boy's parents, neighboring shop owners, merchants, the parents of the friend who had last been with Christopher, and anybody at all who might remember something when his or her brain was picked.

Pete's Story

IT WAS NEARLY ten o'clock by the time Pete and Joe drove up Fifth Street. Pete pulled into a space in front of Abkhazian's Laundry and set the brake on his car. This was a quiet part of the downtown area. They saw but a few pedestrians, whereas a few blocks south, sidewalks were busy with early shoppers. Every now and then an automobile would putter down the street past the two cops. In contrast, at this time of the morning on Broadway, streetcar bells would be dinging, automobile horns hooting, and horses' hooves clomping rhythmically as the farmers brought produce in wooden wagons to the open market.

The Abkhazians' shop had a "closed" sign on the door. It was dark inside. Pete knocked anyway. Only silence and the echo of emptiness answered.

"Got their home address, Pete?" Joe asked.

"Yes." Pete consulted his notebook. This new mystery had already ignited a spark in him. He'd taken it on his own to drive by the home of the missing boy, and the address was among the first notes he'd written in his police journal.

"Out on 47th Street. We'll take a ride out there later. First, let's get a sense of the boys' day as they spent it down here." He consulted the notes he'd taken at the earlier meeting.

The first place the two youngsters probably went together was to the Model Boat and Airplane Co., a hobby shop located across the street from the Abkhazians' laundry.

When they opened the door to the hobby shop, a small bell on the door frame announced their presence. *What a kids' treasure trove this store is*, Pete thought, looking around the crammed shop. Piled high from floor to ceiling were all sorts of hobby and craft items. There were woodworking kits, model automobile and airplane kits, electric train sets, dolls of all sizes and styles, magic kits, and science kits. It kind of made a man want kids, or to once again be a kid himself. Either way, he'd secretly like to try some of the stuff out.

Pete's thoughts wandered to Connie and their childless marriage. He decided to speak to her when he got home that night. He needed to impress on her the importance of having a son. Or daughter, for that matter. He considered the trouble he had bringing up the subject of children. She'd turn it around and remark about the many times that he'd returned home in the early hours of the morning smelling like beer and sex. He hated himself for his compulsions. But it was all so easily attainable—the girls, pretty as they were, and the booze. Around the girls, and with the booze in him, he felt desired and virile. Sex in his marriage? Well, it had become purely functional. No doubt about it, he was to blame for Connie's iciness. And children? It was no wonder that Connie always veered away from the discussion of parenthood. She simply didn't trust him. And why should she? He'd change; he resolved it then and there. And that was that. And he'd make a promise to her that he would keep his promise for once and for all.

When he got home tonight he'd greet her with a big smack-o-la. He'd nuzzle the side of her neck just under the jaw line where she used to like it, and then, locking their bodies together in a tight embrace, he'd walk her back to the bedroom, and then—he'd romance her, pleasure her, and gratify her so that she'd want him as badly as he wanted her. A son would surely follow. Or a daughter. His imagination started a dull burn in his groin and sudden body warmth that wasn't entirely caused by the summer's heat.

McGraw's cheeks flushed bright red when he realized others were carrying on a conversation around him. He occupied himself by filling in some inconsequential notes, vaguely listening to them.

Mildred, the clerk, had been standing on the top rung of a step-ladder. As she climbed down, she flashed Joe a wide, flirtatious smile and batted her eyelashes. "I haven't seen you for a while, Officer Deutsch," she said, taking the time to lift her skirt and reveal her legs as she climbed down the ladder. Pete did a double take on Joe's expression.

"Oh, I guess we were here about the first of the month, as normal." The young officer tipped his cap, then removed it and placed it on the countertop. *Damn*, Pete thought, was Joe blushing? "I don't think you was in when we came by."

"You know? That might be." She placed the merchandise that she had hoisted down from above onto the counter next to Joe's cap. She twisted a spit curl on her cheek around her finger as she flirted with him. "I was out sick with that grippe that's been going around. It kept me in bed for nearly a week."

Pete glanced from Mildred to Joe and back to Mildred again, astonished at the fireworks taking place between them. For the first time Pete noticed that Mildred was kind of cute, if a fellow liked a gal with a little meat on her bones, dimples in her cheeks, and brains in her hind quarter.

"Martin in?" Pete asked, his voice a little too gruff.

"Yes, but he's in the back of the store." Giving Joe a lingering smile, she turned and sashayed to the back of the store calling out, "Mar-*tin*!"

"What the hell, Joe?" Pete chuckled under his breath.

"Jealous, eh Pete?"

"Nah, man. I'm a married man. You and Millie?" he whispered. "What's that about?"

"I'm *not* a married man, my friend, as though that put a damper on your little nocturnal escapades. Ho! When did wearing that gold ring ever stop you? I've seen how your peepers follow a babe with great gams. And what about that little butterfly up there in the Hotel Stockton?"

"Jesus! Clam it, would you, Joe?"

"Testy, partner, testy!" Joe laughed.

Their joking was cut short when the owner, Martin Hubble, pushed his corpulent body up the aisle and behind the counter. Millie followed him. The owner smiled when he saw Pete and Joe. He had one of those ageless faces.

"To what do I owe the pleasure, gentlemen? My calendar says it's barely the middle of the month." His expression darkened when he read the policemen's grim faces. His eyes shot from the cops to the little darkened laundry store across the street. His once beaming face suddenly grew taut and distressed. Mildred's eyes had followed his. Suddenly her expression grew serious. "Oh," they said in unison.

"We're here to ask you a few questions about Christopher Abkhazian," Pete began, removing his cap and setting it on the counter next to Joe's.

"Cops was in here a couple days ago asking questions, Pete," Martin said.

"We know that. We just have to go through it again, so if you don't mind, anything you can remember, even the smallest detail that you might not think important, might be helpful in our investigation."

"Of course. Anything I can do," he said. "You know, I was shocked when I read the paper on Wednesday about little Christopher going missing. It's a crying shame, that's what it is: a poor little innocent fella like Christopher being caught up in something."

"Why do you say, 'caught up in something'?" Joe asked.

"I don't know what I meant, but just speculating, I guess. See, I've been hearing how his dad's quite a rabble-rouser about keeping San Diego a closed town." Pete and Joe exchanged glances.

"You know Reverend Abkhazian well?"

"No, I do not. Just by reputation."

"Ministers do that," Joe observed.

"What?"

"Get up on their soapboxes."

"I'm not talking about in church. I wouldn't know anything about that. But he sure has a big following down in some church in the South Bay, that's true. What I'm talking about ain't all about Jesus. He's becoming pretty political and has said some things to offend some of our city's anointed ones. That's what I've heard, anyhow. Now then, the boy was different. Oh damn. Why do I say 'was'? We don't know he's dead. He ain't dead, is he, officers?"

"We don't know that he is dead. We are still treating him as a missing person," Joe offered unconvincingly.

"You know Christopher well?"

"Yes, I guess you could say I knew him as well as anybody," Martin said, massaging the jowls under his chin. The big man's concern was obvious.

"Tell us what you know, Martin," Pete said.

"Well, after the other policemen left, I got to thinking. It seemed to me that he came to our shop that very same day that he disappeared."

"Time?" asked Pete, who was now busily writing in his notebook.

"Oh, I don't know." He paused. "It was early, because we hadn't officially opened up for business. Millie was still setting some of them sale racks outside. The door wasn't locked, so he just came in. He was in a hurry. His buddy was waiting outside. Chris just wanted to know if his mail order had come in. He'd ordered a kit of the de Havilland Albatross."

"Albatross? That's a bird, isn't it?" Joe said.

"Plane, you dummy!" Pete chuckled, elbowing him.

Martin continued. "I told him it hadn't come in yet, so they was gone almost as quick as they came."

"Christopher and Jackie Cohn?"

"Yes."

"You know Jackie well?"

"Uh-uh." The proprietor shook his head, his jowls responded like Jell-O. "He's been here only once, I think."

"I take it that Chris came to your shop quite frequently?"

"You're right. He likes to come in here to get supplies for his model airplane hobby. This being summer, he was in the shop most every day that he came downtown with his folks. Pays for supplies himself. He earns the money doing some odd jobs around his parents' shop, and I give him a nickel here and a dime there for sweeping up and tagging some of the merchandise. He saves it up and spends it on kits. Whenever we get a delivery, he's bound to come over to see what new things we got."

"Lindy was Chris's hero," Millie put in.

"Lindy?" asked Joe, smiling at her with the stupidest grin Pete had ever seen him wear.

"Charles Lindbergh," Pete answered with irritation. He watched Joe look away from Millie as his cheeks turned crimson.

"Lindbergh, of course," Joe said under his breath.

Millie giggled.

Pete cleared his throat and turned his attention back to the shop owner. "Would you call Christopher a happy kid?"

"Not happy, more thoughtful than cheery."

"Okay," Pete said, noting that. "Other than what you know about Mr. and Mrs. Abkhazian from your customers, what do you know about them personally?"

"I only know them to wave at, or tip my hat to the missus. Now, she's a pretty woman. The reverend's a foreigner. Turk? Armenian? Don't get me wrong, officers. It wasn't that they weren't friendly. They were busy with those children and the shop. Besides the cleaning shop, there's the church." He clicked his tongue thoughtfully. "These are pretty strange times. A Turk who's a Christian minister. A handful of kids. Has to work two jobs. It's tough. Anyhow, Chris came over to our store alone quite a lot, so I got to know him well, but not his folks."

"Tell us all you remember about him," Pete requested, notebook open and pencil in hand.

"How he looked?" Pete nodded. "Let me see." Martin's hand took to rubbing little circles under his chin again. "He was small for his age."

"Small, like his mother's tiny," Millie offered.

"He is extremely shy, wouldn't you say, Mil?"

"Yeah, sure. Very shy, the poor little guy. Remember his nervous habit of fluttering his hands when we asked him a question? And when you tried to teach him something new, Martin, remember how quickly he'd lose his interest, start looking around at other things, go wandering off?"

"But he made model airplanes," Pete observed. "That calls for concentration, don't it?"

"You make a point, officer. He put beautiful models together, and I think he did these on his own. I suspect that he had a hard time learning from someone else."

"And he stutters slightly, huh, Martin?" Millie added.

"Yes."

"And, dark eyes. Jet black."

"So dark you could almost see your reflection in them."

"Eyes like his father's, I'd guess. And freckles," she added, smiling sadly and wringing her hands. "Don't forget about his freckles, Martin. Remember how we'd tease him? We'd say we'd make him rich. We'd give him a penny for each freckle that he counted. Remember that, Martin?"

The big man nodded. "That's right. We sure kidded him about those freckles."

"And he got up to nearly a buck one time, remember?"

"Yes. That's right. Seventy-eight cents, if I recall right."

"Paid him, too, we did."

"That was a million bucks to the boy, wasn't it, Martin!"

"A million bucks. That's what it was. Then we started kidding him when he said he found new freckles. We told him that he already counted this one or that one and that he couldn't count freckles more than once."

"And he was left-handed."

"That's true. He was left-handed."

"We kidded him about that, too. Marty, remember how you'd ask him which hand he was using, and he'd say his left hand, and you'd say nope, that he was using his right hand, he'd get all balled up, and say no it was his left hand, and you would say it's your right one, isn't it, it's the one you're using so it's your *right* hand, but he'd say it was his left hand, not his right hand—"

Pete stopped writing and looked up at them. Joe's face contorted in confusion. "Hold on," he said. "His right hand was his left hand or his left hand—"

Pete held his hand up and said, "Never mind, Joe."

Finally, Martin cleared the air by saying simply, "I guess what Millie is trying to describe is how it took him a while to feel comfortable around us." He went on to explain. "Chris was a very quiet boy," he said.

"At first, when he first started coming over, we had to work to get him going. Talking, I mean. Later we couldn't shut him up. He stayed and stayed. Acted like he didn't want to leave the store."

"What was he, seven? Yes, seven. Turning eight soon. Remember how he told us about the party?"

"Yes. How he was going to have this one and that. How he was going to have ice cream and cake. How they was all going to go to the zoo because that was his most favorite place."

"We wondered if it were all true, officers. The party and all that, you know," Martin confided to us. "His folks didn't look the type to throw kids' birthday parties. Pretty serious folk."

"Well, his father, Martin. Perhaps his mother was less stern."

Martin nodded in agreement.

"Are there any other merchants or shop owners here that we should talk to who might have been friendly with the Abkhazians?"

"No, can't say that I ever saw them mixing with others down here. They came, worked, and left. That was their routine. That's all."

"What about Christopher? Did he ever mention any particular friends other than Jackie Cohn?"

"No."

"Christopher never mentioned any friends from school, nor did we see any of his friends coming downtown with him, huh, Marty?"

"Not except that Cohn boy. But, you've got to realize I only knew Christopher when he was in downtown. I know nothing about his school chums."

"What did you think about Jackie?"

"Well, he acted a little bossy, but maybe because he was a little bigger and older. You know how boys pack," Mildred observed.

"But he seemed to be a nice boy. Anyhow, he was always polite," Martin added.

"Do the cops have any suspects or ideas about where he might be?"

The two policemen shook their heads.

"It's a terrible, terrible thing."

Millie scowled. "It's just like that little girl."

"Yes," Martin agreed. "It was in the newspaper this morning. The Brooks girl they found up there on Kearny Mesa a few years ago?"

"She was killed." Millie shivered visibly. "It was vicious. Horrible, is what it was. You don't think something like that might have happened to Chris, officers?"

Ignoring her question, Pete continued, "To get back on track, let's go to the day Christopher disappeared. Do you remember what he was wearing?"

"His brown jacket," Millie answered quickly. "That's all I can remember about what he was wearing. At the time, I thought it would be too hot a day for a jacket, what with the heat spell we've been having."

"Yes. Tuesday was another scorcher."

"Do you recall anything about what he was wearing, Mr. Hubble?"

"No. It's as Millie says."

"Did the boys talk about their plans?"

"Plans?"

"Did they say anything about where they were going after they left your shop?"

"I don't recall. I'm sorry . . ."

"Did they talk about going to the zoo?"

"No, can't think that they did."

"What about Hulsizer's?"

"Wait a minute. Yes, come to think of it, they did say something about the robbery at Hulsizer's the night before. I guess that's where they might have headed after they left the shop. They left the shop like greased lightning. That's what they did."

Pete and Joe thanked them, told them to call if they remembered anything else, and left the shop.

The day was already heating up with the glaring Santa Ana sun beaming down on the city sidewalks.

"Going to be hot," Joe grumbled. Pete agreed.

"Why the hell did they give us wool uniforms to wear?" Pete asked.

"Heard someone in apparel had a love affair with a ewe."

And they both laughed, walking together with matched steps in the easy way of companions accustomed to each other's gait. They stopped at a café and bought two cups of coffee. Pete read through the notes that he'd taken at Hubble's. They cross-checked their observations and reflected on Chris's personality, his parents, the father's position on open or closed city, and the child's seeming fear of authority. They agreed that another close look at the parents was critical. Joe reminded Pete that Chief Doyle already questioned the Abkhazians. Pete countered that a second questioning wouldn't be a bad idea. They were interested in Jackie Cohn, too, of course. Although he'd already been questioned by the police, his tongue might have loosened up since a few days had gone by. Pete nudged his buddy and ribbed him again about Millie. Pete slapped down the change and they left the café.

Outside, Joe took out a package of clove gum from his pocket, shook out a stick, popped it into his mouth, and began a loud snapping—a New Jersey art form, he once bragged. Joe's family was from Newark.

• • •

The plaque over the door of Hulsizer's Jewelry Store read "Established 1870." A family-run business, it was now managed by the grandson of the original owner, who had set up the jewelry store down near the original San Diego wharf in the city's first commercial center. As the city spread north over the years, the store moved to its present location. It was a regular stop on the policemen's beat, and it was apparent that the elderly proprietor was very glad to see the two cops he'd grown to know and trust over the past years.

Both of the policemen saw at first glance how the old man had been aged by the robbery. Naturally thin, he now looked fragile. He was sweeping up broken glass from the wooden floor. He reached over and offered a bony hand for Pete to shake. Pete didn't want to squeeze it too tightly for fear of breaking it. Jeez, but it was hard to see old people victimized. Old people and young children, too. Bad stuff.

"First time I could get to this." He held the broom up. "Detectives just left." Elias said, still grasping Pete's hand.

"Burglars made a mess of your shop, Elias," Pete said, noting the broken glass on the floor from the display cases and the front window, which had been broken as a method of entry. It was now boarded up, making the interior of the shop dark. "Looks like they cleared you out of most of your things."

"Oh, I kept some of my better stuff in the safe. Thank God. They didn't get to that."

Pete wrote his impressions in his notebook. Either the robbers had been interrupted before having the opportunity to attempt to break into the safe or they lacked the expertise of professional thieves. And he noted that he was naturally referring to the *burglars*, not *burglar*. His gut reaction was that the burglars were youths.

"Sixty-two years, then this. Some might call me lucky for only having this one robbery in all that time." He looked up. The elderly proprietor's filmy gray eyes scrutinized Pete's questioningly. "But then with all the police protection I've paid for, it never should have happened at all, eh, Pete?"

"Didn't happen on our shift, Elias."

"I'm aware of that. But what the heck am I paying for, then?"

"We do the best we can," Joe put in, kicking a shard of glass with the tip of his shoe into a pile the proprietor had swept.

"The police will find the culprits, Elias. Don't you worry about that." Pete tried to sound convincing.

"You *are* the police, Pete," Elias snapped.

"Yes, but actually we're here on another case. We're retracing Christopher Abkhazian's movements on the day he disappeared."

Elias shook his head, took a deep breath, and clicked his tongue. "Yes. I know about that."

"Do you know Christopher?"

"Just by appearance."

"Did you know his parents, the Abkhazians?"

"Knew them only by sight, as well."

"We understand that Christopher came up here with a friend early Tuesday morning."

"The day I found all this," the old man said, sweeping his arm at the devastated little shop.

"That's right."

"He came in with a buddy of his. Jackie Cohn. You asked if I know Christopher. I know Jackie Cohn better."

"Oh yeah? How's that?"

"My family attends the same synagogue as the Cohns."

"Describe Jackie."

"You mean what did he look like?"

"Yes, and anything you can think of about his personality."

"Well, Jackie's a nice kid, a little on the heavy side and somewhat big for his age, nothing outstanding about the way he looks, just a normal-looking kid. He's a little bit older than Christopher. I think he's nine. And what was Chris? Seven, I think. Jackie told me that he and Chris became friends this summer. They both came downtown with their parents, and of course you know their shop is just down the street. Let me see. You want to know about Jackie." He set the broom against the counter. "One thing I know is that Jackie is very musical. His mother says he's been playing the violin since he was five years old. Could play Mozart by the time he turned eight. A child prodigy. I heard him perform before our congregation one holiday back, and he took the house down. That kid could play Israeli folk tunes as good as he could play classical music."

"What is your opinion of the Cohns?"

"Oh, I don't know. They seem very nice. They live up there in Mission Hills, near Presidio Park. Charitable people, they do a lot of fundraising, mostly for young artists and musicians. My wife and I attended one of their affairs at their fine home. It was a fundraiser for our city orchestra. My wife got me to pledge my life away, culture nut that she is. Anybody who was anybody was there."

"Are you familiar with Jackie's older brother, David?"

"Not very well. I do know he's quite a bit older. From what I've heard, he's given his parents a run for their money. You know, kid stuff. He seems to be of a different lot than Jackie. Jackie got the talent, while David acted out."

"Can you tell us about Tuesday, when Jackie Cohn came here with Christopher Abkhazian?"

"What do you want to know?"

"Do you remember anything about their visit—what was said— any plans they happened to be making?"

"Let me see . . . I want to be as precise as I can about this to help you in your investigation. It's very, very frightening to have a child just up and disappear like this. It was early in the morning . . ."

"Tuesday?"

"Yes, of course. I was alone inside at the time, sitting in the back at my desk, looking over some insurance papers the agent left behind. The glazier had already come and gone. He'd gotten the measurements for the replacement glass and left. Police detectives had already been here to take my report, the insurance agent had come with his paperwork, and then he left, too. The carpenter was cutting that piece of wood to cover up the window. The two little guys barged into the shop. Christopher Abkhazian and Jackie Cohn. Voices high and loud, outrageous and irritating, they were full of questions. What was taken? Was it mostly jewelry or money that the crooks got? I'll tell you, officers, I was in no mood for their nonsense. Excitement to them; tragedy for me. Questions. Questions. Questions. Was it taken by the mob? Ho!" The little man chortled cynically. "A syndicate in little San Diego? I told the kids that they watched too many of those gangster movies they make up there in Hollywood and ushered them out of the store. Told them to be on their way; that Jackie's parents wouldn't like to know he was pestering me like that."

"How long did they stay here?" Joe asked.

"I don't remember how long. Five minutes might be a long shot. Like I told you, I had no patience for them and moved them out of the shop as quickly as I could."

"Did they say where they were going?"

"I heard Jackie say something about buying some candy at Kress's. Chris had a dime and Jackie wanted him to buy some licorice for them to eat."

• • •

Joe and Pete walked the several blocks farther south to Kress's Department Store. The manager took them to talk to the sales clerk in the toy department where the boys had been. She vaguely remembered the two boys because she'd had to yell at them for sliding down the stair banisters. No, she didn't know for a fact that she yelled at Chris or Jackie in specific, because boys were always doing that. It was bothersome, and it was dangerous, too. They could've fallen from the banisters, for crying out loud.

Buster, the store's doorman, recalled two boys with their bags of licorice sticks. It had been around ten A.M. He told them they'd get the worms from eating sugar so early in the day. They'd run off down the street, laughing and stuffing their faces.

"To the east?" Joe asked the man.

"No. West," the doorman responded. Thanking him, Pete wrote down this new information that they had headed in the same direction in his notebook. The cops left the store and headed back up Fifth to where their car had been parked in front of the Abkhazians' laundry shop. On the way, they discussed the conversations they'd had with the three merchants. All of them were helpful in framing a timeline for the morning Christopher disappeared. They had learned a bit about the boy, his friend Jackie, and some of their summer habits. The two cops agreed on one thing: the sequence of time they spent at each of the places didn't work out. They would have left Kress's long before noon. Where had they spent the missing window of time between Buster's suggestion of ten o'clock and the twelve o'clock time Jackie had returned to his parents' shop?

The sign was still on the door of the dark shop.

"Guess we'll have to go to the Abkhazians' home," Joe suggested.

Pete didn't answer. He backed his car out of the parking place, shoved the gear into first, and headed north on Fifth Street. Three blocks down, he turned right.

"When they left the store, the kids went west," Joe observed. "So why are we headed east?"

"We're going to the zoo."

"Okay." Joe tossed his cap into the backseat. "Maybe it's just my German stubbornness that isn't grasping your Irish impulsiveness, but good old-fashioned common sense whispers to me in my hairy ear that since Buster just finished telling us that the boys went west, wouldn't we be clever fellows to follow up on his idea and go west to check out the waterfront?"

Pete chuckled. "That's what I like about you, Joe. You take detours to get to your point."

"Well, why then?"

"You can call it an itch I gotta scratch. I want to personally check the zoo out to eliminate it as a possibility. All kids love the zoo. Jackie might have been wrong about the time they separated. He's just a kid, anyhow. What do kids know about time?"

"But, wasn't the zoo searched on Thursday? And isn't it some other team's assignment?"

"Yeah. It is. But I want to do it myself. Doyle didn't mention talking to Dudley, and I know Dudley fairly well. He'd be the one to ask if Christopher made it there. He knows about every kid in the city by name."

"Dudley?"

"The zookeeper."

"I agree that the zoo is a good place to check, but someone else is doing it. Pete, my hunch is that the arrows are pointing to the bay as where they would've gone if they went somewhere together. That'd be the place to check, with all the sleazy water rats living down there."

"After the zoo, we'll go down to the waterfront. Remember the report Doyle read at this morning's meeting? Jackie told the investigators he had to go home to practice his violin, and based on that, that's where they might have split up. Like I said, they may have left Kress's together and headed west; and, then Chris could have caught the streetcar on Broadway and headed up to the zoo alone while his buddy went back to his parents' store. Might've mixed up the time."

"Either that or the kid's lying."

"Or the parents are by saying he was back at the store at noon. If Dudley has nothing new to add to what he told the detectives before, we will go on over to the bay. Fact is, I'm beginning to get hungry. By the time we get there after going over to the zoo, I'll be ready to eat an elephant."

"Or a whale."

Pete laughed. "Or whale. You're right. More whales to be found at the ocean than elephants! I'll even foot the bill for a cup of that good chowder at Yankee Bill's."

"Now, that's an offer that I can't turn down. Not even on a steamy day like today! Free grub is free grub."

• • •

By the time the two policemen arrived at the zoo, the gates had just opened. There was a mere smattering of visitors filing past Dudley, the zookeeper. The officers watched him take tickets from each visitor, answer questions, and point this way and that around the grounds. Finally he saw Pete and Joe. He nodded as though he wasn't a bit surprised.

"Not here to see the animals, I'd wager." He smiled, but his eyes displayed sadness.

"Nope. We're here on an investigation. We would like to ask you a few questions."

Dudley called for backup from one of the attendants, and the three men headed for a bench where they could talk quietly. Pete and Dudley made initial small talk and introductions were made.

"This is about Chris, isn't it?" Dudley asked.

"Yes."

"You know this is the first time cops have questioned me, personally. I've seen them here. Some of our employees were questioned. I was sure they'd question me because I know all the kids who come here pretty well. But they never did."

"That's what I figured, Mr. Dudley."

"What?"

"If anyone would know Christopher, it would be you, being that you've been zookeeper for almost as long as I remember."

The man nodded. "When Chris didn't show up on Tuesday as I expected, I told Emma—that's my wife—something was off. Then I saw the paper, that he was missing and all. I was hoping that he'd just run off, you know like kids do sometimes, but that was a few days ago. Now I'm not so sure."

"So, Christopher was a regular visitor here."

"Regular as San Diego sunshine. One or two times a week this summer. But like I said, when he didn't show on Tuesday, I knew something was off." The elderly zookeeper shook his head sadly.

"Christopher usually came alone?" Pete asked.

"Yes. Sure did. Took the streetcar all by himself, too. I told him I didn't think that was a good idea, him being so small and all, but he told me he always took the same cars and knew the drivers. And his parents were all right with it."

"How long did he stay when he came?"

"Stayed most all afternoon. Followed me around like a shadow. He loved the animals."

"And you were planning to see him Tuesday?"

"Yes. Kept an eye out for him all day."

"Why on Tuesday?"

"It was like this: when he came on Monday afternoon, he was expecting to see the Siamang gibbons. It's our new exhibit. You should visit it."

"I'll make a point of it."

"People get a kick out of watching them. Hearing them. They're pouch gibbons and make a lot of noise when they get riled up. They blow their under-skin pouch up to about the size of an indoor baseball, and then they whistle it through their mouths. What a sound it is! Christopher couldn't stop laughing."

"So, why did you expect him to come again on Tuesday?"

"Well, on Monday the exhibit was closed for some unscheduled maintenance. The kid was all smiles when he came, but when I told him it was closed, he was disappointed to the point of tears. You know kids. No, maybe you don't yet. You'll see. They got no patience for nothing. The little guy acted so sore that I got to feeling kind of rotten myself. I told him if he came back the next day— which would have been Tuesday, of course, the day you want to know about—I would see to it that we'd get one of the attendants to show him some of the equipment—the storage rooms, the hospital, some of the inner workings. I told him that Bets—that's the female polar bear—just gave birth to a cub. He got so excited about seeing it. He wondered where the animals were put when they cleaned their cages and I told him when he came, I'd show him. He was real happy when he left on Monday, and was planning to return on Tuesday.

"I asked Frank—Frank works with the anthropoids, you see—to set it up for the next day. He told me he'd be glad to do the little guy a favor. The kid was one of my favorites. Quiet little boy, but a real little sweetheart of a kid." He paused a moment, apparently reflecting. His eyes teared up. "Anyhow, all day Tuesday I kept a lookout for him; but as I told you, he never showed up. When I read in the paper that he'd gone missing—oh, gosh! It's too bad! Like I said, I thought he just forgot. Kids forget things; they get on to new interests as the whim strikes 'em. But then, Chris seemed different than most kids."

"Oh? In what way?"

"Other than having a sincere interest in the animals here?"

"Anything you saw in the boy is important. Even if you might not think so."

"Different . . . well, let me see. Well for instance, you know how little boys tend to get rowdy. When we get classes on field trips from schools here at the zoo, it ain't the girls who give us much of a problem. The boys throw things at the gorillas, or try to feed gravel to Queenie—"

"Queenie?"

"One of our two female elephants. Queenie and Empress. Of the two, she swallows anything coming close to her trunk and then gets constipated because of what some kid fed her. But Chris never caused any problems. He loved doing little jobs we'd give him."

"How'd he act around other boys?"

"I can't say that I saw him with other kids. I got the hunch that Chris was sort of a loner. Maybe it's because he's small for his age and a sweet kid—I'm not calling him a prissy kid, but then I'm not saying he wasn't a bit of one—the sort of kid that would be bullied by bigger fellows."

Pete noted this, recalling what had been said about his friend Jackie being large for his age and somewhat bossy.

"So Chris usually came alone to the zoo."

"That's right. I got the hunch that he felt safe with me. It took a while to gain his trust, but after he got to know me, I enjoyed having him around, as I told you. One time I tried to talk him into joining one of those summer classes they have for schoolchildren, but he liked just to hang around me. I didn't push it much after that." Dudley took a handkerchief from his pants pocket and swiped his nose fervently, as if ashamed of his emotions. "You think he's all right? I mean, you don't think a pervert got to him, or—?"

"At this point we're still looking for a missing child," Joe repeated.

On the way to the car, Pete suggested that Joe follow up by questioning the driver for the number seven trolley. They discussed plans for the rest of the day, ending with a visit to the Cohns. Pete said he'd stop by the Abkhazians' house by himself.

•   •   •

By the time they left the zoo and drove over to San Diego Bay, it was nearly noon. Hungry for his promised bowl of chowder, Joe pushed the pace to Yankee Bill's Eatery, which was situated at the end of a short service pier. Below them, water rats skulked in and out of the pilings. Rubbish bobbled on the surface of the water, and small waves slapped incessantly at the wooden pier. They passed a tuna boat, the *Maria Rosa*, which was moored there. She pulled at her cleats. The chains groaned and clanged and grated against the wooden pier. Pete observed that it looked like the boat had just returned from a fishing trip. Hemp fishing nets were spread out to dry in the sun. Under a small tornado of squawking seagulls, the smell of fish and brine combined with the guttural Portuguese voices of males as they worked cleaning the hold. Fish guts and rejected carcasses were randomly heaved overboard into the bay. Gulls dove and shrieked and tore fiercely at the scraps. A black naval ship lumbered across the harbor on its way to open water. The dismal groan of its horn bade a sad farewell to happy furloughs on land. A trail of black coal smoke from the stacks spiraled into the pristine blue sky. There wasn't a breeze in the air. The sun glared down relentlessly on the cops. Streams of perspiration trickled down their backs and necks, and behind their ears under their caps.

There was little relief from the heat inside Yankee Bill's. There was a fishy, suffocating stench to the air: thick cigarette and cannabis smoke. Salty sweat. They took a table. Joe sat with his feet planted under it and Pete sprawled back in his chair. He tossed his cap on the table. The man who called himself Yankee Bill attended their table to take their orders. Pete had told Joe that Bill boasted the best chowder on the West Coast. Yankee Bill was another transplant to San Diego, coming from Boston, the chowder capital of the East Coast. Bill was a ruddy-faced, bandy-legged old salt of the sea. A short, grimy apron was tied around his waist and his shirt was opened at the chest, revealing curly gray hair and part of a tattoo inked over his heart. Joe thought it was enough to take away a weak man's appetite: the smell, the grubby customers, and the unappealing proprietor. But he was hungry.

They ordered, ate, then settled back satisfied into their wooden chairs, lit up their Lucky Strikes, and studied their chipped and stained coffee mugs. Joe had to admit that his chowder was the best he'd eaten, well worth the dime it cost his partner.

Pete began indiscriminately discussing the Abkhazian case. Joe understood his strategy. Pete called it "fishing." He cast information about and, if they were lucky, the bait would be taken. They might get a lead or two. Pete thought if someone saw the boy down here at the bay on Monday, the cops' conversation might stimulate that person's memory. Someone overhearing them might want to talk about it. And he was right. They got a strike.

A crusty seaman seated at the counter appeared to Joe to be tuning in to Pete's voice. He watched the old man take a final drag on his cigarette and then resolutely stub it out. Joe saw that the man's hand was shriveled up from paralysis, which required him to hold his cigarette between his thumb and forefinger—typical of what Pete understood was called Jake's paralysis from alcoholism. As the man slid off the bar stool and headed clumsily across the wooden floor with the symptomatic *tap-click, tap-click* of a toe-heel gait, Joe's diagnosis was confirmed. Toxins in the wood alcohol had started the old man on a swift course to his coffin.

"Heard you guys talking," he said to Pete. "You're working the case of that little guy they can't find."

"Yeah, that's right."

"Got a tip for ya."

"Yeah?"

"How much is it worth to ya?"

"Depends on what you've got to say. What'd you say your name is?"

"Deuces. When you hear what I've got to tell you fellows, it will be worth at least a bill."

Pete took a dollar from his pocket and put it on the table. When the man with the name of Deuces reached for it, Pete put his hand out, covering the money. "Uh-uh," he said. "You have to earn it." Then he plopped a salt shaker on top of it. There was a suspenseful hush in the restaurant while others looked on expectantly and boldly listened.

"You guys hear of a fellow who calls himself Stoogies?"

Snickering was heard in the restaurant. Pete tried to pinpoint its origin, but as his eyes darted around the room, gazes were lowered.

"Nope. Can't say that we have," Pete answered, moving his schnozzle away from the man's breath. A dead rat smelled better.

"Stoogies has these, um, visions."

Pete once again heard the muffled snickering. "What do you mean, visions?"

"He sees things in these visions he has."

"Oh yeah?" Pete was not impressed.

"He told everybody he knows all about what happened to the kid that's missing."

"Where is this fellow, Stoogies?"

"I'll take you to him."

Pete picked up the dollar bill and pocketed it.

"Hey!" Deuces protested. "That would be mine."

"Take us there and then maybe I'll give it to you."

Leaving two dimes and a nickel on the table to cover their meal and tip, the two cops followed the ex-boatman down the waterfront, stopping just short of the Broadway Pier. The old man held out a greasy forefinger and pointed.

"See Shantytown, down there? Stoogies lives there. Anyone can tell you what hut is his."

"So, that's where we're headed, you and us."

"Nah. I don't want Stoogies to know I narked on him. He's easy to find. Just ask anyone. They'll tell where to find him."

"No going."

"That's the way it is. You can pay me now."

"Ah, nah." Pete shook his head and frowned. "You're not getting a dollar for this. Not until after you take us there and we shake hands with this guy, Stoogies."

Grumbling, Deuces lead them farther south along the shoreline. Farther away from the piers, away from fishing, away from activity. Their shoes were swallowed by the mucky earth and made a sucking sound as they walked. Pete groaned, remembering the spit shine he'd had Jimmy, his shoeshine man, give him before the meeting with Chief Doyle the day before. The withdrawing water of the San Diego Bay at low tide left behind translucent jellyfish, broken seashells, crustacean shells, tin cans, bottles, and bits of various other refuse in its retreat. In the heat, rivulets of perspiration trickled down the valley of their backs. Pete cussed to himself as the wool of his uniform began to scratch against his skin. He wiped his forehead and under his eyes with his hand and saw that Joe was doing the same.

Shantytown was a settlement of shore dwellers, society's bottom feeders of the most despicable kinds: bums, alcoholics, and addicts. There were also migrants who came to California with hopes of finding employment and dreams of respite from economic and natural calamities in the farm belt of the Midwest and the industrial East. Makeshift dwellings built from various bits and pieces of tin, cardboard, wood boards, and shingles provided shelter. The city council had wanted to close down Shantytown for several years now, but the number of transients was constantly on the rise. The thought crossed Pete's mind that this was one helluva place to send the Boy Scouts to search.

Their guide led them to one tiny dwelling, rough boards pounded together with a makeshift tin roof.

"This is his place," he said as he banged heavily on the tin roof. "Stoogies, it's me, Deuces. Got some people that wanna talk at ya."

"Go 'way," grumbled a raspy voice from within.

"No. They gotta talk at ya. It's important."

"Take a fucking hike."

"Goddamn it!" Deuces' fist struck the metal roof. A deep moan was heard inside.

"Cut it out, for crissake, Deuces. Give a man a rest."

As the banging continued, the moaning from inside turned to cussing, then to swearing and yelling. Finally, Pete saw a dark head poking out of the opening. The rancid smell of stale alcohol fumes mixed with cannabis was released into the sea air.

Liver disease was apparent in his yellowed eyes. He glanced from Deuces to Joe to Pete and back to Deuces. As he swore under his breath, he spat an arched spray of sputum that landed with a splat on the coarse, mucky sand. "What the hell, Deuces? What'cha doing, bringing two fucking bluecoats down here?" He glared at the guide.

"Move your sorry ass out of there," Pete ordered.

"Shit," he cussed as he crawled out through the opening. "Can't a body sleep off a bout with John Barleycorn in peace?"

Stretching, yawning, and scratching, he asked, "Now that you got me up, butt me." Pete nudged Joe and he reluctantly shook a cigarette from his pack.

"Grease my palm," their guide demanded, holding out a rigid hand toward Pete.

"You Stoogies?" Pete asked, fishing out the promised greenback from his pocket.

"Could be."

"Go buy yourself a quart of moonshine," Pete told Deuces, holding the dollar in his fingers.

"Two. Price has gone up since I had'a bring you here."

"You're getting one smacker." The old man looked at the crumpled dollar bill in his hand, grumbled, and slunk off, leaving crescents in the muck where his boots sunk in.

Stoogies crumpled up his face into a look of disgust, coughed up phlegm, and spat a wad of it into the grimy sand. "Jeezus, ya can't trust anybody no more. Cops don't keep their word. Pals rat on ya. Gimme a light, wouldya?"

"Give the man a light, wouldya Joe?"

Joe lit the cigarette.

Stoogies inhaled deeply. "Whatever you say I did, I didn't."

"Nobody's here to accuse you of anything. Not yet, at least. If you can help us, we'll leave you alone. If you know something and don't help us, that's aiding and abetting, and that's a crime. You'd go to the slammer for that. So you'd best come clean."

"Like I said, I didn't do nothing."

"We need some questions answered, that's all."

"And answers cost moola." He held out his palm and motioned with his fingers.

"You get paid what you're worth."

"Two bucks?"

"Depends on what you have to tell us."

"Go ahead." He hawked up another mouthful and spat it onto the sand next to the other jelly-like wad. "Go ahead and ask."

"You were on the waterfront this past Tuesday?"

"Yeah." He inhaled deeply, smoke spewing slowly from his nostrils and mouth.

"We're looking for any information about the little boy that went missing on Tuesday."

"Naaaaah!" He held up his hands defensively, his eyes frozen with fear. "Oh, no you don't! I didn't do nothing to hurt any kid."

"We're not saying you did. We have information to believe you might have seen him here."

"From Deuces? That fucker!"

"Information is all we need, at least at this point in our investigation."

"Oh, well." Stoogies was visibly relieved. He scratched behind his ears, looked at the money Pete held in his hand, scratched his crotch, and took a final drag on the cigarette. "As I told Deuces . . ." He flicked the butt into the sand. "See, I get these visions, see."

Pete told him to just tell them what he thought he saw.

"I had this vision that I saw the kid up there on the pier."

"Shit. This is a fucking waste of our time. And *your* money, I might add." Joe counted on his fingers. "Let's see—two Lincolns for the soup, an Indian head, a bill to Deuces, and one or two to this lumber head. Let's split."

Pete protested with his hand. "Let's see if you're weaving a good yarn. Describe the kid for us, then. What'd he look like, what was he wearing, and anything you can remember about him."

"Yeah, all right. He was just a little pecker, a white boy. Had brown hair. Big eyes. He was running. Skeered shitless. My vision, he was running to beat the devil down the middle of the old Navy Pier."

Joe was stubbing the toe of his shoe in and out of the sand, creating a puddle, while shaking his head dubiously.

"*Okay*—go on," Pete said.

"You wanna know how he looked." Stoogies scratched behind his ear again. "Got another smoke?"

"Got another cigarette, Joe?" Joe frowned as he shook another cigarette from his pack of Lucky Strikes and handed it to the man.

"How he looked in my vision. Let's see. The kid was dressed in dark colors. Black, black, brown—" He snapped his fingers and lit up. "That's it! He was wearing all brown. That's what it was. Brown jacket, brown pants, tan shirt under the jacket." He saw the stunned look on the cops' faces. "I'm right, ain't I?"

"Could be. Or you could have read it in the paper."

"Could've, that is if I could read, Officer."

"Well, go on with your vision."

"So, this little pecker in my vision is hauling ass down the pier towards the water."

"Which pier was that?"

"Navy Pier. That's what I just told ya. Anyhow, in my vision, I think: Kid, you'd better stop before you fucking run off the end of the pier. But still he keeps on running. You know how it is in dreams? You can run and run and run like the devil's chasing you. Your brain tells you, man, the place ain't that long and the kid should have already gone off the end, but he keeps running and running, forever. Huh?"

"I didn't say nothing. Just go on. Was he alone? In your vision, your dream?"

"Nah. He was being chased. Behind the little guy is another fellow, and this guy is shadowing him. Chasing him. There ain't no other people there in my dream, so he's got to be going after the little pecker. He was running to beat the band, too. Bigger than the kid, he could run faster, and he was gaining on the kid, too. The boy keeps looking over his shoulder at the other fellow."

"Bigger? Older?

"Both. He was bigger and older. A youth."

"Not another boy about the missing kid's age? But a bigger kid?" Pete asked, thinking of Jackie Cohn.

"No. A youth, like I told ya."

"A youth could be thirteen, fourteen, nineteen . . ."

"I guess about nineteen. Twenty. Shit, I dunno."

"White? Negro? Tall? Fat? Blond? Dark haired? Details?"

"A cracker. White, to you." Stoogies glanced at Joe. "About your height. Not as heavy around the breadbasket. Brown hair. So in my dream, I want to be Superman and fly to the boy to save him from going over the end of the pier and from the guy after him, because I know he's evil. So I shadow the youth. Running to beat the band. I gain on him, and he hears me behind him, he turns around and looks at me, and he's a mean son of a bitch, too; his face can freeze the titties off a witch. Stopped me in my tracks. In my vision, that is."

"Now that's plain nasty. Titties on a witch," Joe echoed sarcastically.

"Nope. Was the face of the Grim Reaper. That's what it was I stared into."

"That's a pretty good yarn if I have to say it myself, Stoogies," Joe quipped. "It's always a good thing to know what the Grim Reaper looks like so's in case you really do run into him."

"Hold on there, partner," Pete said. "Let the man continue. So, what'd he look like?"

Joe frowned at Pete incredulously. Pete pulled his partner aside, opened his notebook, and pointed. "Remember that window of time? And I'm still a bit rubbed by his description of what he said Christopher was wearing. I don't remember reading about how the kid was dressed in the blat. Do you? And don't you remember Millie saying he was wearing that brown jacket?"

"Not me either. Could have been on the radio?" Joe suggested.

"Here? A radio down here?" Pete waved his arms at the squalor. "Let's go out on a limb and say that in a muddled, inebriated state, he might have actually seen something going on, but he's having problems describing it. Let's hear him out."

"Okay. It's your cash," Joe said, and they turned back toward Stoogies. "Go on with your story."

"Where was I? Oh, the youth. When he turned around, he gave me this very creepy smile."

"Words! We want words! Describe him."

"Okay. Let's see. He was a white guy, probably around twenty or nineteen. Medium build. Wore a white shirt with tails out over black trousers. Dark hair. A little bit on the long side. Curly. Or wavy. Deep-set eyes. Couldn't see the color. Long face. It was his smile that I remember best. There was something about it—something . . . I know! It was a bit off."

"What do you mean by that?"

"Listen." Stoogies took one last long drag on the second ciga-rette, and then dropped it to his feet next to the first. Grinding it into the sand with the toe of his shoe, he said with clear resolution: "This is who you're looking for. This is the guy who done the little boy . . ."

"Done? What do you mean when you say 'done'?"

"Killed, done him in."

"Oh hell, we don't know that he's dead. It's still just a missing per-son's case."

"Killed. I mean killed," the man repeated resolutely. "You will find that little fellow is dead. And the guy you're looking for has a crooked front tooth that sticks out and catches his top lip when he smiles. It makes his smile sort of lopsided. And he has, like I was telling you, the look of Satan. You'll know him when you see him. That's the guy who killed the little boy."

"You think I wasted my money?" Pete later asked as they returned to the pier.

"Shit, man! He's just a fucking low-down booze head. But what you said about Millie's statement about the jacket is interesting. As far as you wasting your money, I do know that you just pissed away a couple days' wages."

"He kept saying the kid was murdered."

"Give it up, Irish! We will find out when we find out. Right now your real problem is how you're going to explain the shortage in your wages this week to your wife. We pissed away time, too," Joe grum-bled, glancing at his watch. "It's now nearly two o'clock."

"You've got that right."

"What's next on the agenda, Partner?" Joe asked, making a delib-erate effort to change his tone.

"The Cohns. Jackie Cohn's home."

Checking his wristwatch, Joe said, "That should be it for the day, I figure."

"Yeah, we'll meet the kid and see what's up. Then later, if we need to, we can set up another interrogation downtown. After that we can call it a day."

• • •

The Cohns lived in Mission Hills near the old Presidio, the Spanish fort overlooking Old Town. As they drove up the winding hill, Pete observed that the higher they went, the bigger the homes were.

"I'm always befuddled by what kind of business tends to get along when the rest of the nation is going to pot."

"Uh-huh." Joe nodded.

"Can't figure that out. Hell, Connie would like a mink coat as much as the next lady. She doesn't need furs, but holy smoke! She stands in breadlines and counts her rations just like everyone else. I'll bet the rich get someone else to do that for them."

"You're damn tootin'," agreed Joe.

"Look at these places! I think I could fit at least six houses the size of my bungalow in one of these."

The little Ford took a right onto Fort Stockton Drive. The Cohns' home was easy to find. Its address was on a brick wall enclosing a large residence set in a landscaped yard.

"Not too shabby. Somebody's not hurting for money."

"Well, it's not us cops, and that's the damn truth of it."

The late afternoon breezes wafting up the hill from the ocean below felt refreshing to the two officers as they stood in the portico of the stately home.

A maid in uniform—black dress, starched white apron, and perky cap—pulled open the massive oak door after they rang the bell. When she saw the two policemen standing outside the door, her eyes grew wide. She began to shut the door, telling them that the mistress wasn't seeing any visitors. Pete stuck his foot in the door.

"Oh, we don't need to bother the missus, not just yet anyhow. We came to see Jackie. Is he in?"

"He's in the middle of his violin lesson."

"We can wait."

She hesitated, and then she pulled the door open for them enter. "Wait here," the maid instructed before she climbed the stairs leading to the second story. Indeed, from somewhere up the stairs they could hear the faint sound of a violin.

"Damn!" muttered Pete. "This vestibule is as big as our living room."

"Reminds me of the Lincoln Memorial in Washington, D.C. We visited there when I was a kid." Joe was referring to the liberal use of marble in the room.

A white marble fountain with a life-sized statue of a cherub riding on the back of a fawn bubbled in the center of the room. The marble staircase wound its way up the second story. The leaded glass on and above the front door refracted the afternoon sunlight, scattering prisms over the white marble floor. A towering Queen Palm stretched nearly all the way to a dome over the second story.

In a matter of minutes, the maid returned and primly told them that Mrs. Cohn had asked that they wait in the living room. She would be down shortly with her son. She guided them into the plush-carpeted living room.

The room was loaded with antiques, oriental rugs, tapestries hanging on the walls, Egyptian or Grecian statues (they didn't know which), and original artwork whose artists' names were lost to the policemen. The heavy, maroon drapes were half drawn over the picture windows, which overlooked a landscaped backyard with mature verdant bushes and assortment of roses that were startling in their superabundance.

They went to stand at the window and admired the view.

"It's a fucking park, that's what it is," Joe observed in a whisper.

And a park it seemed. Roses of every conceivable shade of red, orange, pink, and yellow nodded and waved amiably in the cheerful summer breeze. Manicured privet hedges, brick pathways, and wide garden steps led to a gazebo. There was a furnished summerhouse surrounded by flowery trees and another fountain.

"I'm sorry to have kept you waiting," a woman's voice interrupted. They turned to see two silhouettes backlit by the sunny vestibule.

It was the first time Pete had laid eyes on the boy he'd heard so much about. Now faced with him, he felt a little shaky questioning Jackie for two reasons: What did he know about nine-year-old boys? He could only compare the youngster to himself when he was nine, and the two were as different as day and night. For one thing, this boy hid behind his momma. Pete would never have done that, even at nine years old. He also felt that this young fellow might hold a key to the mystery of the disappearance of the Abkhazian boy, and he didn't want to upset the apple cart by being too aggressive or be ineffective by not being pushy enough.

"Jackie just finished his violin lesson."

As she spoke, the maid was showing a gentleman out the front door.

Pete's eyes questioned her regarding the visitor's identity.

"Jackie's violin teacher, Officer." Pete nodded. They silently watched the teacher's departure until the front door closed.

The maid gave a small curtsey as she passed by the living room entrance, but her mistress's voice stopped her. "Marta! Did you offer the gentlemen iced tea? Lemonade? Cookies?"

"Nah! That's all right. We just ate," Joe protested, patting his stomach.

"Nonsense. It's a hot day. I'm sure it would taste good to you. I believe Jack will have a glass of lemonade, Marta. Would you desire iced tea or lemonade, gentlemen?" she repeated.

"Lemonade is good," they said in unison, to which the maid dipped briefly into a second curtsey, then disappeared.

"Please sit down, officers." Mrs. Cohn waved her hand toward the sofa.

Pete took a second to take in what he was observing in the small, demure Jewish woman so that he could phrase his questioning inoffensively and productively. She wore her wealth as easily as a Chanel wrap on a fashion model, but he had the sense that there would be no fooling around her. After all, she was a business woman and ran a successful fur shop in the center of the city.

The two cops sank heavily into the densely stuffed couch, which was in keeping with the formally furnished parlor in this fifty-year-old house. Connie would say it wasn't trendy like the more popular minimalist furniture, which she adored. *But those roses*, Pete thought, remembering the park-like backyard. *She'd love her rose garden to be as splendid as that.*

They introduced themselves, then politely placed their hats on their knees. Mrs. Cohn took one of the chairs in the grouping. Jackie went behind his mother's chair and stood with his hands on her shoulders. He was a pretty serious-looking kid, and considerably overweight. Pete wondered what kind of a friend he could be to the younger boy. Was he the bully that Martin Hubble suggested he might be?

Pete began his interrogation by asking Jackie how well he knew Christopher. Jackie replied that he'd known Chris at school. They had met on the school playground during recess. Jackie admitted to playing with the younger boy only because he was bored when he had to come downtown with his parents. Chris, he explained, was the only fellow near his age to play with.

"We understand that you were the last one to see Christopher before he disappeared on Tuesday."

"Tell them, Jackie," the mother urged after a tense silence followed Pete's question.

"I already did, Mother," he whined. "Why must I go through it all over again?"

"Yes, I know you have, dear. Then, what we'll do is: I'll tell the officers what you told that nice Mr. Doyle the other day—"

"He's our chief of police, Mrs. Cohn," Joe said, smiling amiably.

"Well then, *Chief* Doyle. So I'll tell them what you told me, and you interrupt me if I get anything wrong, all right, Jackie?"

"Yes, Mother."

"Come. Have a sit-down here next to me." She patted the twin chair next to hers and smiled at her son. Then, she responded to Pete's question:

"Christopher was a very shy, quiet child. He would stand for an indefinite time without saying a word if he was not spoken to. But he was a cute little guy. He was very small for his age."

Pete noted this in his notebook and nodded at Jackie to have him continue the story. As the boy remained taciturn, the mother took over, continued speaking for him, saying that she was repeating what Jackie had told the chief. Noting this, Pete understood that he needed to speak privately with Jackie, without his controlling mother present.

And the story she told was the story as Pete had heard it, read it, and thought about its holes ever since the police were first briefed on the boy's disappearance. Jackie seldom interrupted or corrected his mother, but sat listening attentively. Her story ended as Pete had heard it each time before: the two boys separated after visiting Kress's, for Chris to catch the streetcar on Broadway and Second and Jackie to return to the shop to be taken home for lunch and violin practice. Pete noted the window of time that still hadn't accounted for, but knew that this would not be the time to pursue this with the mother so ready to take over. Again the idea occurred to Pete that he needed to get Jackie alone, without his mother around.

Pete asked Jackie, "Wasn't Christopher supposed to return to his parents' shop for his own lunch?"

"If my son said they split up, Officer, that's exactly what they did," Mrs. Cohn responded. Her tone was icy.

"You two fellows hung around together quite a bit this summer, didn't you?"

"Yes, Officer. They did," his mother said, looking narrowly at Pete.

Keeping his focus on Jackie, he continued: "Did you and Christopher usually go back to your parents' shops for lunch at lunchtime?"

"Officer—"

"Mrs. Cohn, if you please, I'd like Jackie to answer this question. Jackie?" he prodded.

The boy kept his eyes lowered as he responded, "I had to. Always. To practice. But Christopher didn't always go back to the shop for lunch. Not like me. Sometimes he went home."

"To his own home, you mean?"

"Yes. Sometimes he went to the shop, and sometimes he would go to his own home."

"By streetcar?"

"Yes."

"The Number Seven?"

"I think so, yes."

"So occasionally he took the streetcar back to his home on Forty-Seventh Street? For lunch, instead of going to the store for lunch?"

"Sometimes he did that."

"You didn't think it strange that this day, Christopher decided to go and catch the streetcar before lunchtime to go to the zoo?"

"No."

"And he didn't tell you why?"

"He said something about the zoo. But I thought he might have gone home for lunch after."

"Okay. So he might've gone somewhere else instead? I mean, you didn't really know where he ended up. He only said he was going to the zoo. He might have gone someplace else."

"Maybe. He liked to go to the park. He liked the zoo. He played sometimes at the pepper tree playground."

"You said 'liked.' Is there a reason you might believe he's not alive?"

"Officer. Keep asking questions like that, that would upset my son, and you will have to leave this house, immediately," Mrs. Cohn blustered.

Pete apologized for the harsh way he'd asked the question, then continued: "But he didn't say on Tuesday."

"He already said he didn't, Officer. Is there anything you forgot to mention to the other policeman—I mean Chief, Jack?" Mrs. Cohn turned toward her son. He responded by a slight shake of his head, still looking down. Pete could see tears coursing their way down his plump cheeks. The boy's mother reached over and patted him on the shoulder.

"Officers, I can't tell you how much all this has affected my boy. Here's Marta now. Thank you, Marta. Set down the tray on the coffee table; would you, please? I'll serve. Would you bring Jackie a handkerchief, please?"

Mrs. Cohn offered the cookies to the officers. Ice clinked refreshingly against the crystal pitcher as she poured the pale yellow liquid into two glasses. "Since the day his friend Chris disappeared—" she glanced at her son affectionately and said, "Take a cookie, Jackie"— our boy Jack hasn't been able to sleep. Isn't that true, baby? Some mornings we've awakened to find him sleeping on the floor at the foot of our bed. Other times he has needed to come into our room during the night because he has such terrible nightmares. Other problems, too. Of a personal nature." The boy's face turned pink. Pete immediately assumed the problems were of a nocturnal urinary type that children sometimes suffer from when insecure. He made note of it in his notebook.

The maid returned with a small, embroidered hanky and handed it to the boy.

"And up till today he hasn't been able to keep up with his violin practice. That's why you were kept waiting. Jackie wanted to show me that he'd taken up the instrument once again. He played a little recital for me. And I might add that it was very beautifully done, Jack." Her tender smile was lost to her son, whose tears had increased.

"All this started, as I said, the day Christopher Abkhazian disappeared. It has been a nightmare for our whole family, but mostly for Jackie. I'm sorry—Jack, you want to be called now. You know how boys are, don't you, officers. He doesn't want to be called Jackie any longer. How much longer must my son remain in this room?"

"Just a few more questions, Mrs. Cohn." To Jackie, Pete asked, "So, once again, at twelve o'clock or thereabout, you went back up Fifth Avenue, that's north, and your friend went—in which direction?"

"To the streetcar stop," the boy mumbled.

"And that was where?"

"I guess it was up the street from Kress's."

"That's west. Did you watch him cross the street to get to the streetcar stop?"

"I don't remember."

"Did you actually see him at the streetcar stop?

"I don't remember."

The boy's face flushed, and tears balanced on his eyelids.

"Jack, think about it for a minute. Did you actually see him at the streetcar stop?"

"No. Yes. No. I just don't remember." The tears fell.

"That's it, Officer. He has already answered that question. I think you're badgering him now." The boy sobbed. "That's all right, Jackie. They're just leaving," she said comfortingly.

The boy nearly shouted. "When I left him, he went in that direction. That was the last time I ever saw Chris."

"Officers, please—Jack, you may leave us now." The boy bolted from the room, sobbing. They heard him scramble up the staircase and slam a door upstairs. "You see how distraught my child is, officers? I couldn't let you go on like that."

"We understand. We just need some confusion cleared up. Then we'll be leaving."

"Thank you. I actually have a commitment I need to ready myself for."

"We understand. Just a couple questions, please."

"Only if it's just a couple, Officer McGraw."

"Please describe when you first heard that the boy was missing."

"It was about six o'clock, closing time, when Catherine Abkhazian rang to see if Christopher might be still with Jackie. I was stunned. I told her that Jackie came back to our store alone at noon, and that he and my husband, Marvin, left soon after that to go home for lunch and his violin practice. She told me not to worry, so I didn't. I didn't mention it to Jackie or even tell Marvin that she'd called. Actually, I forgot all about it until the morning paper on Wednesday. I was shocked when I read that he was missing. Right away I asked Jackie if he knew anything about Christopher. Jackie broke down immediately. He was crying so hard that it took me quite a while to get the story out."

Joe asked, "Why was Jackie so broke up about it? I mean, little boys know that other little boys might disobey their parents' rules to go to other places. After all, he is just missing as far as we know and as far as the newspaper has said."

The woman's face colored. "Imagine if a close friend of yours up and disappeared, Officer, and you had been the last one to spend time with him. My son is extremely sensitive. He takes all his responsibilities very seriously. He was a good friend of Christopher's. Considering all those things, it would be difficult for a child not to cry, unless he had a heart of lead."

Pete asked, "When Jackie finally talked to you, what did he tell you?"

"It was the same story that he told your chief when he was taken downtown for questioning." Again the mother's cheeks reddened. "What is happening in our city? It used to be so safe. Everybody knew everybody. But now? Now all this riffraff is pouring into San Diego like garbage floating on the Tijuana River after a hard rain. I'm not sure any more about where San Diego is headed. I would have never let my children go to any playground alone. But kids are always there unsupervised. You're cops. You know what kind of predator children attract."

Pete nodded his head, sharing her worry. Then he looked up and asked, "What can you tell me about David?"

"I'm sorry, Officer. David? What do you want to know about our son David?"

He prodded her to respond, motioning with his hand.

"David's nineteen. But you're not here about David. I wanted to tell you about those places like the pepper tree playground that Christopher was allowed to go to on his own. They attract the wrong type, that's what they do. And mothers are just too lenient with their children. Mark my words: *"Rien, amabilité non égale, la bonté ou innocence n'est épargné dans l'oeil de l'aigle!"*

Pete and Joe's eyes met as they shrugged at their ignorance of French. Before Pete got a chance to ask her what she'd said and how it related to her elder son, the front door banged open.

"That's him. That's David, now."

The youth stood just inside the door when he saw the two cops. He scowled and began to jog up the stairs.

"Come in here, David," his mother demanded. "These officers are investigating the little Abkhazian boy's disappearance."

The youth stopped midway on the stairs and turned. "Don't know nothing about him," he replied. Then he hoofed up the rest of the stairs.

"David!" she called from the bottom of the stairs. There was no response from upstairs. She turned crimson and apologized.

Pete found the youth's behavior very curious, but kept it to himself. As he stood up from the sofa, thanking Mrs. Cohn for her time and the refreshments, he made a mental note to find out more about David. When he mentioned that he might need to talk to Jackie again, he noticed that her pleasant demeanor suddenly faded. Her mouth stiffened as she asked: "Why again? That would be three times. Oh no, Officer. I can't let that happen. He's been through too much—"

"I'm not saying I'm going to, I'm saying I might have to, and it might also be necessary for us to talk to your husband and your son David."

"I don't see why; what can they add? Neither my husband nor our older son knew Christopher at all well. You heard him yourself. Why do you need to question them—" Her voice faded away as she perceived the iron look on the Irish cop's face. She closed the door behind them tentatively.

As the two men approached the car, Pete pulled on Joe's arm, holding him back.

"Stop me if I'm wrong. I don't remember Doyle saying anything about questioning the father, do you?"

"No. Didn't Mrs. Cohn say he is up in Los Angeles for a fur show?"

Pete agreed. "And, he didn't mention questioning that kid David, either." The image of the older boy flashed in Pete's mind. So did the jeweler's inference to David being problematic for the Cohns.

"Pete. There's more going on than we know about."

"I want to question Jackie again, without his mother around."

"I agree."

"I was just thinking: You remember what Elias said about David this morning? Something like the kid gave his parents a run for their money?"

"Right."

"What do you think he meant by that?"

"My mom always said that when my brother and I caused her problems. It meant we were a handful. We were."

"I sort of figured that. Listen, I've got an idea. It would mean that we split up our jobs. I'll go out to the Abkhazians and poke around a little bit and you go downtown and stop by the courthouse. See about getting a judge to sign a subpoena to bring David down for questioning. And his father, too, while you're at it."

"Good idea. What about Jackie? You wanted to get at him alone, you said. A subpoena for him, too?"

"Let's hold off on him for now. We'll get to him later when he's a little more relaxed about us."

"And you want me to follow up on the streetcar driver of the Number Seven?"

"Yes. That's a good idea."

"Hey, what the hell was Mrs. Cohn saying in French?"

Pete shrugged. "I figured it was something about the park attracting creeps because there were children there."

"Yup." Joe bobbed his head, agreeing emphatically. "Where now, boss?"

"I'm taking you to your car and I'm going home to Connie. She and I have a little business matter to work out."

"Say, Irish, you got an itch that needs scratchin'? About David, I mean."

"You've got that right. I don't know what's tickling my brain about that fellow. The case is giving me the heebie-jeebies. I've got a bad sense about it."

"Yeah, it's looking that way."

Pete stopped walking, turned around, and stared at the house. For a while he said nothing; then he suddenly hit his thigh with his fist.

"Dammit, Joe! I am fucking afraid for that little boy, Christopher. My gut tells me we're getting into something damn ugly."

• • •

"Sera," McGraw said, suddenly interrupting his story, "I'm getting a little worn out. Could we set up a time for us to continue?"

The intern looked up and saw that indeed the old man looked wan. She agreed, and they set up another appointment for the next morning. As she put her things away, she remembered a question she had wanted to ask McGraw.

"The article mentioned another Abkhazian sibling by the name of Rose. I haven't checked yet, but I got the impression that she lives locally. Have you met her?"

"I was also surprised that Christopher had a younger sister living here. I never thought any of them would have come back to San Diego. Last I knew, they were somewhere in Missouri or someplace east. I thought the same thing when I read the article that she lived locally, so I looked up her name in the telephone directory. From the area code, I figure she lives somewhere up in the North County. I called and told her who I was and why I was calling. She was polite on the phone, but she said she was satisfied with what the sheriff wrote in that article."

"Isn't it strange that she would be so indifferent about meeting a policeman who had led the investigation into the death of her sibling—even though she apparently hadn't even been born at the time he died? I know I'd be."

Pete shrugged. "I thought so, too. So I kept her on the phone a while and told her some things about Christopher. She seemed to soften. She finally agreed to talk with me. She couldn't then, but she said she would call me back at another time. So far she hasn't, and I'm not putting any money on her doing it, either."

"I'll contact Rose," Sera promised.

Pete and Sera

Third Interview, October 24, 1990

SOME DETRACTORS SAY Southern California has no seasons. That's not true. Take autumn. When the sun is low on the horizon, shadows are stretched, and colors are richer. The hills that were bleached by the summer sun to shades of tan have become verdant as the rainy season begins. Pristine true-blue summer skies turn moody in October, laden with lofty cumulus clouds. These aren't the white puffballs that dotted summer skies; these are heavy and darker, outlined with striking whiteness. Sometimes sun rays slant from heaven through the openings in these banks of clouds and reach to the earth to touch it with spots of light. Sera recalled some of the farmers back home calling this phenomenon the "fingers of God," and smiled at the thought of her small town. Now, in this season, she loved San Diego especially, when clouds are painted in hues of rose, gold, and peach pastels with the lesser light of the season's weaker sun.

She playfully scuffed through the fallen liquid-amber leaves that had spilled onto the sidewalk on Lomas Street. Her thoughts grew distant once again, to her mother's home in Northern California. Winter would be coming on with a vengeance at this time of the year.

She would be wearing boots and woolen clothing. Downpours, heavy winds, and sometimes sleet would bore through the fabric, chilling her. She kicked a small pile of leaves into the air so that they grace-fully fell—red, yellow, ochre, and green jewels.

As Sera turned onto the walkway leading to 421, she saw the drapes fall back into place on the picture window. She thought warmly of the old man who'd held them aside, looking for her.

Just as she reached the door, it was yanked open enthusiastically by Pete's sinewy hand. There he stood, with that wonderful smile that deepened the dimple on his cheek and crinkled up his blue eyes. As before, McGraw was immaculately dressed. He wore a crisply ironed white shirt and pressed slacks.

"You're on top of it, today," the young intern said lightly, passing by him into the house.

"Yes. I've got a list of things to talk about," he replied with a new, pleased lilt to his voice. They took the same seats as they had before and Sera remembered the promise she'd made to herself to sit in another, more comfortable, chair. But where? There were two chairs and the small sofa in the seating group. Pete always sat on the sofa. What was she to do? Sit right next to him?

"I don't recall an autumn as rainy as this one has been," Pete mused as Sera organized her things.

"It's an El Niño year," she responded, distantly.

"That has something to do with the ocean," Pete said.

"Yes," she affirmed, looking up at the elderly man, and then she smiled. "Warmer water temperatures, more rain on land. I just recently needed to use my wet suit for ocean swimming. I fre-quently do the deep-water swim out of La Jolla Cove. Swim the buoys."

"That's impressive. I can see doing that in the summer, but in the winter?"

"The wet suit keeps me warm. Rough-water swimming has become so much a part of me that I couldn't imagine going several months without swimming there. And they over chlorinate public swimming pools." She paused. "I have a ton of things to do today after I leave here, Mr. McGraw. Shall we get moving on your agenda?"

He nodded; then his face tightened. He sighed and took his glass of water from the table and sipped thoughtfully. "Today we tackle hard memories for me," he warned, and then began.

Pete McGraw's Story

"ON THE SUNDAY morning following the boy's disappearance, I was dead tired from working a double shift, and finally on my way home. What happened was that the cop who normally relieved me had called in sick with the grippe or something. I took his shift for the extra money. So with two shifts behind me, I had worked all night.

"It was about nine in the morning. I wanted nothing better than to get home, to sleep. Heading in that direction, I received a call from dispatch.

"Back in those days, some of us had a transmitter installed in our cars. It wasn't a perfect system, not like the two-way car radios that came about five years later. In fact, we called the old one-way radio system 'flying on one wing,' because there was no way for Dispatch to know if we'd received the signal or not. When the light on our dash went on, we had to find a call box to call back to Dispatch for further information. It was pretty crude, as you can well guess. I could've simply turned off the transmitter under my dashboard and said I never received the call, and then continued on my way home. Nobody would have known the difference. But to me, there was honor in being a policeman.

"When I found a call box, I wasn't much surprised by Dispatch telling me that they'd found a child's body. I *was* surprised that it had surfaced in the San Diego Bay. My heart told me it was the Abkhazian boy they'd found. Chief Doyle gave the directive that all available officers on duty were to go down to the waterfront to maintain order.

"I parked my car on the street near the entrance to Navy Pier. Four or five policemen were standing guard there, keeping the people already gathering from going farther onto the pier and getting in the way. I told one of the senior officers about my double shift and asked if I was needed, saying that I wanted to go home to catch up on my sleep. He told me he thought they had things under control there at the crime scene and filled me in on what was going on. Mostly out of curiosity, I walked a little way down the pier to have myself a gander. It was a dismal sight I took in: a couple of policemen were holding grappling irons. Chief Doyle, the police surgeon, and the county coroner with the ambulance were there. They were lined up at the edge of the pier, grimly looking out over the water, watching the slow, cumbersome progress of a sheriff's patrol boat as it lugged the pathetic bundle to the pier.

"The morning's low clouds still hung heavy on the water. The sun hadn't broken through yet. There was a chilly and piercing sadness in the air. There was the drone of the engine on the sheriff's boat. There was the foghorn out in the bay, moaning its ominous warnings at regular intervals. There were the cries of the gulls as they circled, squawking and cawing over the incoming boat. The size of the crowd was growing as onlookers meshed together on the shore, watching the dreary scene play out.

"The policemen on the pier scurried to tie up the rowboat to a stanchion. The muted sound of commands could be heard as the strong-handed policemen, using their combined brawn, maneuvered the deadweight up onto the deck with grappling irons. Finally the corpse of the child came into view. Bit by bit, it was lifted until it reached several feet over the pier, and then it fell with a terrible thud. A mound it was—of sodden cloth, ghost-white, seawater-eaten skin, a tangle of seaweed, and a puddle of seawater.

"I heard the combined groan of the onlookers. They knew or sensed whose little body it was that they were looking at out there. The groan was followed by anguished silence. Women fell into the arms of their husbands, sobbing. I heard occasional male voices explode. Here and there, fists were raised in impotent protests. The police blocking the pier tightened their barricade, linking arm in arm to keep the crowd from coming on the pier.

"From what I could see, the crime scene was well attended, with all the appropriate parties there. Thinking I had already endeavored to make myself available and had been told that everything was under control, I wasn't needed, I made up my mind to simply leave. Even now as I tell it, Sera, the weight of that moment hangs heavy on my heart. At the time, the absolute tragedy of the scene was compounded by my own exhaustion. What I was watching cast a spell of utter despair. Now Sera, I'd seen dead bodies before, but that was beyond anything any human with a heart can tolerate. I turned around and began walking slowly in an easterly direction, toward the street and to my car.

"I'd almost gotten to the end of the pier when I felt a strong hand grab my shoulder, pulling me around.

"It was Doyle. I was shocked speechless. Automatically I saluted him and said, 'Sir!' He returned my salute and formally addressed me by name: 'Officer McGraw,' he said, waving his arm in the direction of the small group now clustered around the little boy's body. 'It's a sad thing, this.'

"Together we watched the men at the end of the pier. The surgeon and coroner were kneeling side by side, blocking the view of the tiny corpse. The surgeon was apparently dictating his observations to a cop who was taking notes in a small notebook. The doctor was on his knees across the body from the other two.

"The chief turned toward me, harrumphed, and said, 'Heard tell of your dad, son. Heard that there never was a more upright vice cop than Bill McGraw. He's been gone, uh, how long?'

"'Died in '30, sir.'

"'That so? Well, son, I hope to God that he didn't take all the respectability and diligence required of a good cop with him when he went.'

"I thanked him and returned the compliment by mentioning Doyle's reputation in Los Angeles that preceded him. A little bull, if you know what I mean. He nodded, thanked me. 'Already some enemies down here, *guldarnit*,' he muttered under his breath. Then, once again, he fixed his disarming myopic eyes on me. 'Officer McGraw, there's another thing . . .'

"'Sir?'

"'Your reputation is that your feet fit in his shoes,' he said.

"'Thank you, sir.' I was wondering where this was going, impatient, dehydrated, and exhausted as I was. I smiled and said something like, 'I'm afraid that's not completely true, but I'm working on it.'

"'No siree. That's what I hear. And that you received the Medal of Valor for that Agua Caliente heist.' I nodded again, growing more impatient. I was personally pleased by this conversation, but I thought it was inappropriate considering the time, the place, and the occasion. At that point, it was wearing me down.

"'Congratulations!' He slapped me on the arm. Out of the corner of my eye I noticed other policemen glancing at the two of us curiously. He continued: 'I knew of only one other fellow who got that medal, and son, he was at least twice your age.' The chief took off his cap, scratched the back of his head, and then put it back on. Looked past me. I joined him in silently watching the activities at the end of the pier, wanting to walk away to my car but not daring to do it. His face tensed up. He worked his jaw as though he were ruminating on a thought. His eyes darted between the activities and me. The investigators were searching through the boy's clothing now.

"Finally he focused on me. His eyes, distorted and magnified behind his thick lenses, held my own for a lengthy period of time; then he ran them up and down my body, scrutinizing me from head to toe, sizing me up.

"'Officer McGraw, I want you to take charge of this case.'

"I protested. 'Sir, there are others much more experienced than I.'

"'Perhaps, but based on what I know of you and the urgency to get things moving, I'm promoting you to lead detective here and now. We're under the gun, so to speak.' He glanced around at the crowd of onlookers. 'It's a matter of time before reporters get here with their cameras and yellow press attitude. And when they do, I'm sure they'll blast us again. McGraw, I mean to get this crime solved, and put the son of a bitch who did it on the hot seat or behind bars until he rots. And damn it, do it yesterday. I'm aware of what the papers are saying: that it's been nearly a whole damn week since the boy went missing. But you can read. You've read what the blat is saying. Bad thing for our department. Bad thing for our investigation. As you know, it's true that too much time has gone by. We've got to hustle our sorry asses.

"'Go join them down there. Read over the notes from the good doctor and add your own observations.' He motioned toward the end of the pier. 'After they cart the little guy to Benbough Mortuary, you get the father to ID the body. Then you go back to the mortuary. They'll be running an autopsy. Wait for it to finish. If what the doctors say is what I'm certain they are going to say, there's no more *dicking* around; we've got ourselves a murder case. After that, come down to headquarters. I'll have the paperwork ready for you to sign for your promotion to chief detective so you can begin your investigation immediately.'

"The chief and I joined the others who were finishing up with their examination of the body. The ambulance attendants were ready to take it away. The chief told them to wait and let me take a look at the body before they did it; then he told them I was to be in charge of the investigation as chief detective and from that minute on, they were to follow my orders. He stayed for a while, watching me as I discussed the notes the doctor had taken to what I saw. Then Doyle left to speak to the crowd.

"The first thing I did on my new assignment was to question the two sailors who found the little fellow's body floating in the water. They said they had been returning to their ship after a twenty-four-hour shore furlough, at about 0645. On their way, around the area of the turning basin, about fifteen hundred feet offshore, they saw something half floating in the water. It was difficult to identify that it was a body because it was covered with sea grass and other floating litter. As they drew closer, they realized what it was and attached it with rope to the rowboat. They went out to their ship and alerted their commander about their discovery. He put out the call to the sheriff's department, who responded with the two escort boats. They towed the corpse from there to Navy Pier."

"What's a turning basin?" Sera asked, interrupting the old man.

"Good question. A little history. The Bureau of Engineers had dredged a portion of the bottom of the San Diego Bay to make it deeper for the larger ships. They used the silt as a foundation for what is now the San Diego Int   Airport. I'll bet you didn't know that piece of trivia."

"No, I didn't know that. An   why did the sheriff's department bring the body in an   ake over the investigation after the body was delivered to the pier?"

"Another good question. The two law enforcement agencies had different jurisdictions, Sera. The San Diego Sheriff's Department had control over all the county water; the police controlled the land. Note: jurisdiction was always an issue in this case. And I mean down-and-out contentiousness over who should lead the investigation. We started the investigation; they took over. I felt they bollixed everything up from the get-go. And Sera, think about it—they still can't let go of this case," he blustered. Then he began to hack. He took out a handkerchief and wiped his brow. "But, we'll get into that later. I'm getting off track. Where were we? Yes, the little boy's body."

Sera waited for the old man to regain his composure.

He continued, finally.

"Then I examined the body. I recall commenting to the doctor that I thought the boy overdressed for a hot July morning, as it had been that Tuesday when he went missing. He agreed, and pointed out how carefully and completely dressed he was. His shoelaces were double knotted; his jacket was buttoned right up to the collar button, making it tight against his neck; his shirt under the jacket was also buttoned up to the top. His pants were buttoned up and the belt was tightly clasped.

"Wasn't it Milly at the craft shop who mentioned how overdressed the child was for such a hot day?"

"That's right.

"Maybe she was smarter than she looked," Sera kidded, recalling Pete's remark about her having her brain in her hindquarters.

He chuckled. Then he continued.

"We found some things in the boy's pockets: there was a fountain pen that had a broken point, a small nail with a short piece of twine attached. Neither he nor I noted any bloodstains on his clothing.

"At the pier, we only were doing the preliminary examination. Removing all the underclothing was going to be done later at the autopsy because the skin was in such poor shape and removing the soggy, clinging clothing could have torn it away. But we did notice some obvious injuries: the tip of one of his fingers was cut off at the knuckle, there was a deep wound on the inside of the right wrist, and his neck was bruised on either side by what looked like human hands.

"The ambulance took the body away.

"I picked up the Reverend Abkhazian and drove him to the mortuary to identify the body. I'll never forget how very cool he was as he looked down on the horrendously mutilated face of the boy who had been taken from being in water for a period of time. Water destroys tissue and bloats features. But, he was able to identify him as his son.

"For several hours after that, I waited for the doctors to finish the autopsy. This, by the way, is very important in a water case like that one. A medical examination needs to be done immediately after a body is taken from water. It was about three hours later that they had completed the procedure and had their preliminary report. Their verdict? The cause of death was homicide, with evidence of sexual abuse.

"I finally got to go home. Connie held dinner for me. I didn't tell her at first about my promotion. But I kept teasing her that I had some news. She was dying of curiosity. Instead, we waited until the chief's announcement over the radio that night."

"Mr. McGraw," Mrs. Kersel's voice called out. She stood in the doorway to the kitchen, an apron on and a dish towel in her hands. "I don't want to interrupt, but I don't think you remember that we have a doctor's appointment."

"I completely forgot about it," he replied to the nurse. Then to me, he grumbled, "Darn it, Sera. I had other things I wanted to cover today."

"It's all right. I have my own list of things to do, Mr. McGraw." Sera closed her notebook. "I'll make note of where we stopped today and we can begin there when we meet the next time." She reached over to the coffee table for the tape recorder. As she was about to turn it off, Pete reached over to stop her.

"Just a couple more points, Sera. Then we'll call it a day. I wanted to tell you about the coroner's inquest that took place after that, and the funeral.

"Joe and I sat in on the inquest along with Doyle, pathologists, the district attorney, and a few others. I don't recollect who they were at this time. The doctors repeated their findings of the autopsy. The jury wasn't out long. They returned with their verdict, which concurred with the autopsy surgeon's. Their verdict was that the boy died from a heinous and brutal attack.

"The murder investigation began in earnest, but a week had already gone by, losing us precious ground. The newspaper succeeded in terrifying our citizens by comparing the Abkhazian boy's murder to others like it, like the Chicken Coop killings up in L.A. in the small town of Wineville, and a rash of kidnappings in the east. And then it went on to criticize the police department. Not that criticism wasn't needed. During the past three years our department had gone through a rash of turnovers of chiefs of police, which left it in a disorganized state of affairs.

"I remember the newspaper running a psychological profile of the killer. Now Sera, this was sixty years ago, when psychology was in its infancy. But all in all, it was close to what we found in our suspect. If I recall right, the profile said the killer would be a young man, under thirty years old, who could fit into most society, appearing normal. It went on to suggest that this person had character flaws, like anger issues or gender confusion. The killer would have come from a stormy childhood, and this experience would cause churning inside of him until he exploded, like a bomb. His actions were sadistic: he gained pleasure from seeing pain inflicted on his victim. The profile also suggested that the killer would be a megalomaniac, thinking he could get away with anything at all without being caught or would boast about his crimes.

"Sera, another thing: in those days the newspaper was anything but politically correct, bordering on complete disrespect or irresponsibility for what went into print. The articles turned ugly and presented vivid descriptions of the brutality the child might have endured during the time before his death. The paper used the term 'bloodlust.' All this only succeeded in traumatizing San Diegans and turning them against the police department for not being more assertive in the investigation, earlier on.

"One of the things I did in the early days of my new job as chief detective in charge of this homicide was to go out to Glen Abbey Cemetery to attend the boy's burial and look the crowd over for any suspicious people.

"I stood about halfway up the slope. Looking down the hill, I could see the slow procession of the funeral cortege. This was led by a black hearse and a black Plymouth, which I knew carried the Abkhazian family. A few automobiles followed, and behind them a trail of darkly dressed people walked. This procession snaked its way slowly up the winding asphalt drive.

"Every human being is required at one time or another to perform the act of burying his or her dead. This was sadder than usual because the grave was so small. And the savage brutality of the manner of death was at odds with the peaceful beauty of the burial site.

"I heard car doors open and shut, the sound of the coffin scraping the metal on the floor of the hearse as it was pulled out, and the quiet commands of the captain as he directed Christopher's school chums who acted as pallbearers. The pine box was a heavy burden for such little boys to carry. It was joggled up the steep hill to the grave by their unsteady legs and thin arms. The flood of people seemed to multiply in number as they climbed the hill. I had anticipated a crowd, not the whole city. The paper estimated there were over two thousand mourners there. I thought there were many more than that.

"My attention had been focused on the sedan that followed the hearse. The reverend was the first to step out. He mopped his brow with his handkerchief and straightened his black clerical suit. What a pompous little guy he was, I thought—I had always thought, since I first met him. He held the car door open for his parents. They were Armenians—I guess I mentioned that to you earlier. Soon two young children stepped out and took hold of their grandparents' hands.

"Then their mother stepped out of the sedan."

Pete suddenly stopped talking as he recollected that there was nothing graceful about the way Catherine got out of the car. She was small, lean, and fragile. He recalled her dark-eyed beauty, her curly hair that couldn't be controlled by the small, round black hat framing her lovely face. Her veil had been cast aside, so Pete could see how she kept her eyes focused on the ground. As if sensing Pete's fixation, the reverend suddenly stopped, glanced in Pete's direction, and turned toward his wife. He reached up and took the veil in his hand and pulled it down over her face. Pete quickly averted his eyes.

After a few minutes of silence, Pete continued: "It seemed to take quite a long time for everyone to get up the hill as near to the grave as they could crowd. I kept distant by remaining on the outside, so I could move around and keep my eyes out for someone who looked like he was out of place.

"I heard fragments of a song being sung by the reverend. The paper later stated that he had written it for the occasion. After he had finished singing, the casket was lowered into the grave and some of the members of the family poured a shovelful of dirt onto it. The boy's mother refused to do it.

"Then I heard a bloodcurdling scream from somewhere in the crowd. I pulled out my gun and elbowed my way to where the sound came from.

"It was about twenty yards away from the grave. I saw a woman pointing at a crudely built, small wooden cross stuck into the ground there. I pushed my way up to where she was and saw immediately what had so frightened her. On the cross, printed in black paint, was the name 'Virginia Brooks,' the name of the young victim whose body had been found up on Kearny Mesa. There was not a person in the city of San Diego who didn't know her name and shudder in terror at it. She was a young girl who was killed, terribly mutilated, and whose body was left on Kearny Mesa just a few years before. Her murderer was never found.

"There was a sealed envelope attached to the cross. The Abkhazian name was written on the envelope. I opened it carefully, to keep from destroying any fingerprints that might have been left behind. It held a single, folded piece of white paper. Written on it was simply the words 'We understand. The Brooks Family.' To the Abkhazians, that note meant someone personally knew the anguish they felt and genuinely shared their sorrow. For me, it made a connection. To me it cemented the suggestion of the similarity of those two crimes and the fact that I might well be on the trail of a serial killer."

• • •

Sera had let herself out. Pete hadn't realized how tired he'd become. His throat was suddenly sandpaper dry. He called out to his caregiver and asked her to refill his water. As she was about to remind him to get ready for his doctor's appointment he held up his hand, stopping her. He said he knew; there was time for him to rest a while, then he would get ready.

What Pete wanted to do was to finish out the memory of that first day as chief of detectives. The memory was bittersweet, and oh, so clear.

Pete wanted to think for a moment about his wife, Connie, on that Sunday, so long ago, after his promotion. Of a slew of memories, this one figured for one of the sweetest. On the day of his promotion, by the time he reached the driveway of the little bungalow at 421 Lomas Street, he was punchy from exhaustion and emotionally spent. It was almost six o'clock, and he wanted to listen to Doyle's radio announcement that was scheduled for seven o'clock.

Pete tossed his cap onto the rack and called out to his wife that he was home. He heard her reply from the kitchen for him to take a seat at the dining room table.

How Connie managed to pay for the pork roast, she kept a secret. Unknown to her husband, she'd saved money out of their budget to splurge at the end of the month for a pound of pork, which ran fifteen cents a pound. Friday, she'd walked to University Avenue and taken the Number Seven all the way to the butcher shop on Broadway to pick it up. She was adamant that for once they'd have real meat instead of that disgusting canned deviled stuff. She'd kept the pork on ice for Sunday's dinner. Today, after it had been cooking slowly for a couple of hours, the rosemary she'd picked from her kitchen garden and used in the gravy had filled the air with a pungent spicy fragrance.

There was something about Pete's demeanor, outside of his apparent tiredness, that sparked her curiosity the moment she walked through the door carrying the platter of pork, potatoes, and applesauce. When she mentioned this, he responded by saying with a smirk, "Later." He shoved the meal down his throat without much comment about the dinner she had prepared with so much care.

She tried to fill in the silence with small talk, but his mind was somewhere else. And to her disappointment, he didn't seem to notice the small bouquet of roses she'd picked from their garden, nor the stiffly starched and sun-bleached table linen that dressed up their Sunday table. She watched him eat ravenously and quickly.

At precisely seven o'clock, he turned on the radio. Connie, having finished washing the dishes, came to join him on the sofa to listen to the news. He worked the dial. Static crackled, and there was an irritating whistle until the dial landed on station KGB. Molly Freeman, First Presbyterian's soprano soloist, was singing a sizzling rendition of the "Star Spangled Banner," then Pete and Connie, hand over hearts in the privacy of their small living room, solemnly echoed the Pledge of Allegiance. They sat while Mattie and Elvie sang a jingle: "It never rains but it pours," advocating the benefits of iron in Morton's Salt. Connie picked up her knitting, and to Pete's disgruntlement, began her incessant chattering.

"San Diego Sunday Evening News!" the announcer said. Pete nudged her and asked her to listen. She smiled and nodded and promised to be quiet.

"Ladies and gentlemen, we have a special and important announcement from our Chief of Police, Alton H. Doyle." There was a pause, a crackle of static, and the sound of the microphone being tapped.

"Oh Petey, I do hope this is good news."

Pete shushed her when he heard the familiar "harrumph" of his chief, followed by his deep, clear, and bold baritone voice.

Connie squeezed Pete's hand and smiled at her handsome Irish husband, then lay down her knitting and reclined into the couch with her tiny feet crossed on the coffee table next his size-twelve mahogany calves'-leather lace-up shoes that he'd spent almost five dollars on. Pete gazed down onto the top of her blond hair and inhaled the fragrance of the White Rain shampoo she customarily used. He placed his arm around her shoulders and gave a squeeze, suddenly overcome by the warmth of his emotions. He kept his eyes on her face and watched her expression grow hardened into solemnity with the sound of the chief's voice.

"My fellow San Diegans," Doyle boomed. "Many of you don't know me, as I'm new to this beautiful city. I am proud and honored to have accepted the appointment by your city manager, Fred Winters, as your new chief of police. After tonight, I will have this space in time right here on your dial to fill you in on police news.

"After a professional career in your sister city of Los Angeles, I can truly tell you that San Diego is a city on the upswing. As Chief, I pledged to Mr. Winters and now I pledge to you to help guide San Diego through its somewhat rocky adolescence.

"San Diego promised opportunity to you as well as me. Some of you came here for personal reasons. Some sought a better life than you had in the agriculturally depressed Midwest, the overpopulated urban centers, the smokestack-poisoned industrial cities, or closer at hand, across the border in Mexico. This city of eternal sunshine beckoned to those of you who were spent—both in money and drive, used up from financial failures with the onslaught of the Great Depression, or from unemployment in the industrial East, from the dustbowl calamities I mentioned, from the corruption of political power mongers, or from fears of gangland activities. You brought your families; you wanted to raise your children in an environment of peace. You came here because San Diego seemed to you the proverbial land of milk and honey. In all physical aspects, it ostensibly promises a sweet life.

"We have one of, if not the best, natural climates in this grand old U.S.A. I can tell you that firsthand. I'm a product of the East Coast. I am proud to have been educated at an Ivy League university. I threw my snowshoes away, tossed my wool suits and top coat, gave my shovel to my neighbor next door, and then I boarded the train with my wife to move to the West Coast.

"And these natural elements have been our insurance against complete devastation from the calamities elsewhere. Sadly, many Americans are still struggling. But here we've a natural harbor that offers port to navy vessels, ocean liners, the tuna industry, and merchant shipping. In other cities east, starving people stand long hours in breadlines. Here we have food to eat: we've got fish to catch in the inexhaustible Pacific Ocean; we've got farming in Mission Valley, with fertile soil from the flooding of the San Diego River, where we raise fruits and vegetables. We've grazing land for dairy cows, and we've rangeland for beef cattle.

"While other cities back east stagnate in production shutdowns, job layoffs, and such, we draw profits from tourism as cruise lines, railroads, and now our airport with scheduled passenger flights bring in money. Basic economics: When money is exchanged, the economy is kept healthy.

"You as San Diegans, I am told and firmly believe, are upright and solid people. You wish to raise your children with good, wholesome family values, and to pursue your own individual lifestyle. Our Constitutional Bill of Rights insists that this—the pursuit of happiness—is your natural and indelible human right.

"But beyond unfortunate turns of the economy, beyond draughts and windstorms, beyond calamities beyond our control, there are people amongst us with corrupt intents.

"When Mr. Winters was given the responsibility of selecting a new chief of police, he said to me—and I'll use his very words—'I have had repeated revelations of laxity in enforcement laws, in vice, gambling, cases of corruption in city and county governments, and the board

freeholders who were elected back in '29.' San Diego couldn't continue to depend on a ragtag-run police department to safeguard our
children. So your city manager went outside your city to select somebody who would boost police morale and reform its tattered ranks,
and mop up the soiled litter of corruption on the floor of City Hall.
When he offered me the job, I was a private detective in Los Angeles.
My reputation is widely known there. *Cleanup* Doyle is what they
called me, because I've made public the names of private and well-
known citizens who were enmeshed in corruption and criminal activities. Their names were published in the L.A. papers. For my entire
life, in fact, I have had but one objective, and this, my friends, I carry
with me to San Diego—and that is to stamp out crime, shed light on
dirty deviants no matter what handles they might have for surnames,
and bag criminals so they won't further harm our society. And more
urgently, so that they won't harm our children.

"San Diego sits on the edge of transition, my friends. There are
some who ask: should San Diego be an open or closed town? Well
now, it is already very obvious to me that most of you family men
came here for a haven from the devastation suffered in the economi-
cally distraught and broken cities and farms you left behind, a new
and clean slate offering rejuvenation and renewal, a perfect place to
raise a family with values of the Christian type. These are the reasons an open city will simply not work for San Diegans. Why not? Over
two hundred transients invade our city every single day. They are the
wretchedly poor that need to be fed, clothed, and housed. These
unfortunate people may be alcoholics, drug addicts, or mentally ill.
They live down on Squatters' Row on the waterfront; they inhabit the
alleyways behind our homes, and beware! They raid our iceboxes at
night while we sleep. In the light of day, they stop us on the streets
begging for a nickel or a dime—as though we have money to share.

"'Why not?' you may ask. 'Why shouldn't we legalize gambling
and prostitution, and promote bars once Prohibition is ended in
December? Look at Las Vegas!' you may say. It has drawn in money to

build beautiful, successful casinos; there, money is exchanged, and didn't I say that when money is exchanged, everybody profits?

"But take a reality check, my friends. Who is it that benefits, indeed?

"Take a closer look at home. You have noticed that there's been a crime wave in San Diego over the past few years. Vice is rampant! Our homes are not safe; our innocent children are victimized. The San Diego newspaper reminds you daily of the crimes that go unsolved, and the predators are still wandering our streets.

"Are you sitting down, my friends? Do you ladies have your hankies within reach? Now to get to the point of this message, and it's a very sad message that I have the unfortunate duty to relate to you. It's about our city's own beloved son, Christopher Abkhazian.

"Is there among you a single soul who doesn't know the name Christopher Abkhazian? He was the seven-year-old child who disappeared just this last Tuesday, and whose disappearance inspired many thousands of you to personally volunteer in the widespread search for him. My hat goes off to you for taking the time and showing the concern. We all cared deeply. We all have prayed to have Christopher Abkhazian home safe and sound. We've prayed in our churches, our cathedrals, and our synagogues.

"But just today the beaten, brutalized, and broken body of that seven-year-old child we came to love was discovered in the waters of San Diego Bay.

"Now as a result of this dastardly discovery, the number-one priority of your police department is to unearth and bring to trial the party or parties responsible for the contemptible and outrageous attack on this young child. I promise you that we will lift every rock, turn and expose all dung, to expose this culprit and every other deviant pervert who tries to burrow and hide. And we will try them in our courts; and we will fry them in the electric chair. Justice will prevail, my friends. On that I pledge my solemn oath. But to have that happen, we have a lot of work to do.

"Don't deceive yourselves. This is war! The oldest conflict known to mankind is the fight for good over evil. We all have to fight to keep San Diego pristine. We have to identify the demons first in order to remove them from our society. We need to utilize all manpower—that's you, my friends. And we have to professionalize the campaign by organizing under sound leadership—that's your police department. When I took on the responsibility as your chief of police, I was given a job to do, and I pledged to do it. And I will appoint the best police officers that our city has to offer to support me in this pledge.

"Some of you knew Bill McGraw, who died a few years back. If you didn't have the occasion to meet him personally, you might have known of him. He was quite a fellow, I am told. He was captain of the vice squad in your police department for a time and did a pretty good job of starting the cleanup campaign in the Stingaree and other areas of ill repute in our fair city. But this man left a legacy to our city, beyond his own splendid accomplishments in freeing San Diego from criminal elements that festered and infected our community's health: he bequeathed to us his son, Pete McGraw . . ."

"Oh, Pete!" Connie gushed. "It's coming, isn't it? The part you wanted me to hear." Pete smiled, held a finger to his lips, and winked. Her blue eyes sparkled as she wrinkled her nose and put her fingers to her mouth to comply.

Chief Doyle continued. "Officer Peter McGraw joined the San Diego Police Department in 1927, a year short of his twentieth birthday. As some of you have read in our paper, he received the distinguished Medal of Valor in 1929, for bringing the culprits to justice in the renowned Agua Caliente Money Heist. Hear my words! This young man fills his father's shoes. As was his dad, Peter is a family man, a man who follows the dictates of morality, conventionalism, and American traditionalism; he's a square shooter, a decent human being, and a police hero.

"Today I promoted Officer Pete McGraw to lead detective in charge of the investigation of this child's homicide. And ladies and gentlemen, make no mistake—it was homicide. Murder. This sad revelation was brought to light after a thorough medical examination today by a team of qualified medical doctors and then confirmed by Coroner Gunther Chester's jury. Officer McGraw has already begun his investigation and promises to give it his tireless attention. Your responsibility, my friends, is to work with this man, to help us seek closure of this case. All of your calls, all of your leads—no matter how insignificant they may seem to you—should be forthwith directed to Detective Peter McGraw through police headquarters. My friends, I am confident that his leadership combined with the professionalism of our brave police department, and your awareness, will bring the culprit to face the consequences of his evil act."

When the chief finished his speech, Pete had turned to Connie and saw that tears were coursing their way down her cheeks. "I'm so proud of you," she said, looking into his eyes and molding her body to his.

Pete did't thoughts were elsewhere. He wondered how Diego remaining a conservative, closed tow ose at City Hall who were touting it as an open, fair-ga ity. He also needed to explain to Connie, that there was still a job for him to do before he could call it a day. He made a telephone call to Joe and told him he would be picking him up for the sad but important duty confirming to the Abkhazian family the results from the examination earlier that afternoon. This, he had never had to do before; this, he dreaded more than anything else he could possibly imagine.

• • •

Now, in the quiet of his living room, Pete withdrew a tissue from the Kleenex box and wiped his eyes. It surprised him that along with the memory came tears. Mrs. Kersel watched him and gently said, "You see, Mr. McGraw, you've exhausted yourself. Miss Schilling stayed too long."

"I'm okay, Kate. I'm ready to leave now for the doctor's. I'll be all right."

He looked at her pretty, round face and saw that her look of concern had melted into a lovely smile. Pete felt gratified at that. She was someone very special to have beside him in these waning days of his life. With her by his side at the doctor's, he felt he could accept whatever the doc had to say.

Better than a wife, he thought, somewhat cynically.

Sera

AFTER MY INTERVIEW with McGraw, I spent the rest of the day checking the facts regarding the Abkhazian boy's death. The first stop was at the County Administration Center on Pacific Highway.

I needed a copy of the death certificate for Christopher Abkhazian. Getting it would be a simple process. I'd pay a small fee, fill out a simple form, and after a short wait I'd have it.

What I read shocked me! What a disparity between what it said and what I knew! The boy's body was found on July 23, 1933. *August 12th* was recorded as the date of death on the death certificate. Three weeks' difference!

Then, what they reported as cause of death! "Accidental Death" was checked on the death certificate. Everything I'd heard from McGraw was "homicide." An unsolved homicide case is never closed; if the boy's death had been accidental, it would have been formally closed sixty years ago, instead of remaining unsolved on cold case shelves for the sheriff's forensic team to close now.

I walked over to police headquarters to see if anything might have been stored regarding the case. The archival department was located in the basement of the building.

A female officer checked the records on her computer. "There is a homicide listed in 1933, of a Christopher Abkhazian." She read on and reported, "But the records indicate that we have nothing in storage because of jurisdictional change of control of the case. All pertinent information and materials would have been given to the sheriff's department for their investigation."

My third stop of the day was the sheriff's department headquarters in Kearny Mesa. When I found the officer in charge of cold case storage, I mentioned Tindall's name by way of an introduction.

The officer checked cold case records and told me that the Abkhazian material was marked to be shredded since it was redesignated as a closed case, but added, "The shredders are supposed to be here tomorrow, so it hasn't been picked up yet."

When he returned, he carried a small cardboard box. "You're in luck, Miss Schilling." He pointed to the "closed" stamp and the date. "You can go through the stuff inside the box. Don't take anything from the building, though," he cautioned, and then added, "You might want to keep it under wraps that I let you go through it."

There were only a few things in the box: some telephone messages, a bound, court-certified transcript of the interrogation of Jack Cohn by Virgil Green, Private Investigator, and crime scene photographs. Tindall had mentioned the transcript.

One photograph illustrated what Pete described to me about the day Christopher Abkhazian's body was found in the bay. There was a small cluster of policemen huddled around a small mound lying on a wooden pier. In the photograph there was a grappling hook, the police ambulance, two attendants wheeling a gurney toward the body, a sheriff's skiff anchored just off the pier with a sheriff deputy and two sailors monitoring the unfolding drama, and a naval ship in the far distance.

I pulled out the second photograph. It was so shocking that my first impulse was to bury it. It was a candid, morbid police photograph that revealed in detail the mutilated face of the boy.

This image terribly affected me. Somehow by seeing the photographic evidence, the horror of his death became very real to me.

I thought about the picture I'd copied along with the article in the newspaper and dug it out of my attaché case.

Here showed a healthy, boyish face. Totally typical. Ageless in an innocent, juvenile way. He looked like any seven-year-old boy. He could be living down the block now in 1990, dressed in a Little League uniform with his baseball bat propped on his shoulder or skateboarding on the Mission Bay boardwalk. It was his cute little thirties haircut with the straight, smoothed-down hair, its no-nonsense middle part, and the *Little Rascals* style of a layered ridge around his head that hinted at the time in which he'd lived.

Twenty-two years old and single in 1990, I hadn't thought a whole lot about kids in general. Those photographs, however, kept me brooding for a while. That the boy was beautiful was plainly clear. His eyes were soft and dark, his smile sweet. His focus was slightly at an angle, as though the picture caught him while quickly turning away from the camera, avoiding it and yet wholly aware of it. I became fixated on the boy's face. Eventually I realized an emotional connection was growing inside of me. This picture right from the start—all right, irrational as it might sound—triggered an emotional *bond* with me and this child whose death took place sixty years ago. The deeper I looked into the eyes of the child in the photograph, the more I felt an uncanny sensation that Christopher Abkhazian was looking directly into my heart.

I went back to inspecting the contents of the box, including the dozen or so telephone messages. I took note of the callers' names and the dates of the calls. Chief Doyle had telephoned Sheriff Carver on several occasions toward the end of July. This was when the change of jurisdiction would have taken place. An article dated August 1st described this. Others described exhuming the body; having a second autopsy run in Los Angeles at the municipal crime lab up there; and the department hiring outside, objective experts, namely Virgil Green, an investigator from Los Angeles, and his background. Sheriff Carver was quoted in one article as saying that Doyle was "a publicity hound" and McGraw was a "hound dog with a cold, barking up the wrong tree."

There was a certified statement dated August 7, by a Los Angeles County autopsy surgeon, Dr. A. F. Williams, following the exhumation of the Abkhazian boy's body on August 5, 1933. This second autopsy was performed by Williams and attended by Dr. R.E. Terry; Dr.W. Field; Dr. J.J. O'Shea; Sheriff Carver; Gunther Chester, the San Diego County coroner; Rice Packard, Ph.D., and a few others. Dr. Williams's statement read: *The opinion of doctors in attendance is that no wounds on body were caused by a knife or knives. All mutilations were the result of crustaceans in the San Diego Bay. In the absence of incontrovertible proof that the boy was criminally attacked, all mutilations are considered the work of marine animals. The condition of the lungs indicates that the boy drowned.*

I found published accounts of conflicting opinions also in the box. On August 8, Coroner Chester made a statement to the newspaper, shooting back at Williams's statement. Chester said: *The sheriff's office's announcement that Christopher Abkhazian was the victim of accidental drowning does not solve the mystery of the cause of the boy's death. The coroner's office will continue its investigation as originally decided, as a homicide. I am a layman, but I have seen many bodies taken from the bay. It's true that crabs and other crustaceans feed on exposed parts of the body, but never have I seen a body on which crabs have attacked parts underneath the protection of clothing.*

In a related article in the same newspaper edition on August 8, Dr. Terry, who presided over the initial autopsy, was quoted: *I performed the initial autopsy on Christopher Abkhazian. This was done immediately after the body was taken from the San Diego Bay. There is absolutely no reason at all to change my opinion that the boy was murdered.* Dr. O'Shea concurred with Terry's opinion: *The boy was killed. Mutilated, killed, and then put into the water.* Chief of Police Alton Doyle scorned Dr. Williams's theory, calling it an *insult to the intelligence of the people of San Diego County.*

The remaining item in the cold case box was a bound, court-stamped transcript of an interrogation of Jackie Cohn by Investigator Green. Reading it became tedious because of Green's habit of asking repetitious questions, but using different wording to catch the boy up in contradictions. It was a very puzzling to me that this was altogether a completely different version about what happened on the day Christopher Abkhazian disappeared.

What Jackie told Green was that the two boys went to the waterfront to fish from the piers. (What the police department understood was that the two boys had split up after Kress's, not seeing each other again.) According to this transcript, he and Christopher went along with a group of older boys to the waterfront. Christopher followed these youths to the lower level of Broadway Pier, to fish from there. Jackie, who couldn't swim, stayed safely on the top level. Jackie told Green that he heard a splash and saw his friend in the water, struggling and crying for help. Jackie saw him go under.

This new story's obvious flaws struck me. I wondered about Jackie saying that there were older boys on the pier. If there were, what happened to them? Why hadn't they been questioned? Why hadn't they tried to help a drowning boy if they had been there when he was appealing for help? I also wondered how deep the water was at the point at which the boy fell in. How high was the pier? What was the distance of the fall?

I noted my questions and made a mental point to ask McGraw more about Jackie.

Just a short walk from the sheriff's department was the San Diego Medical Examiner's. It was located within an industrial park, a cluster of office buildings and small businesses set in a landscaped area. As I walked up the sycamore-lined sidewalk, it occurred to me that this architecturally uninteresting building of tan stucco with square aluminum windows didn't seem like it should house all the sinister, gripping things associated with autopsies, violence, mysteries, and dead bodies.

I opened the glass door into a lobby of elevators, more glass doors, a floor of black and white linoleum squares, and beige walls. It didn't have the appeal of the coroner's office in my hometown of Santa Linda. I'd been fortunate to tour the facility when I took a criminology class in community college. The coroner's office there was housed in an old stone building with bricks turned dingy with nearly a century's worth of grime. Its leaded glazed windows seemed from another era. The glass was distorted by age and etched by years of grit and dust. Iron casings kept the windows intact. It had a foreboding and sinister presence. Inside, it reeked of formaldehyde. The coroner's office in my hometown seemed more like a coroner's office should be.

My three-inch heels tapped annoyingly on the linoleum floor as I crossed the lobby to view the wall directory. The morgue, the directory read, was situated in the basement; the laboratory on the second floor; and the records department was on the first floor, room 108. Albert C. Caswell, M.D. was listed as the San Diego Medical Examiner. His office was on the first floor, room 120. I signed into the registry in the records department, explaining to the clerk that I was researching an autopsy for a death in 1933.

She led me into a large, square room with its walls lined with sand-colored file cabinets. She opened a cabinet with drawers beginning in 1931 and stretching into the early 1940s. She slammed the drawer shut and yanked open the drawer below it. Muttering under her breath, she fanned through the boxes, then slammed that drawer shut and returned to the first one. "I don't get it," she complained, running her pencil eraser over the tops of the microfilm boxes that had dates stamped on the top. Down one row, down the second row, down the third, the fourth, until she looked up and worked her lips in frustration. "Damn it, I hate it when this happens. The box for 1933 is not where it should be. It's been misfiled. . . . Oh! Here it is. It's filed under July through October, 1939. That's strange. I'll have to ask Barbara about it."

The clerk explained, "I haven't worked in any of these drawers with the old tapes for a long time and I don't remember anyone else getting into them either. So there's no reason this one box should have been misplaced. Unless, of course, someone else was looking at a case of around the same date as you're interested in finding. Perhaps it's just a coincidence. Nineteen thirty-three wasn't what one would call an eventful year, I shouldn't think."

I reminded her of the recent investigation done by the forensic team of the sheriff's department and suggested that they might have taken out the microfilm for their research and then misfiled it when they returned it.

After a moment's consideration, she shook her head. "Nah. Those guys are in and out of here all the time. I've trained them better than that. Tell you what. I'll check the log."

I scanned the microfilm on the microfiche viewer until I reached the date of July 23, 1933. This confirmed that the death was in July. Not August as the death certificate stated.

There were three parts to the autopsy report: the first was the initial police report; the second, the attending physician's autopsy report; and the last, a page with an outline of a human body with sketches depicting the injuries. Following the autopsy material was the coroner jury's verdict.

The police report was signed by Detective Peter W. McGraw, Jr. In it, he outlined the facts of the discovery: time of sighting, action taken by the sailors who found the body, recovery of the body in San Diego Bay, the boy's apparel, and what was taken from the clothing. McGraw listed these items that he found in the pants pockets: A green fountain pen with a broken point, a small nail with a short piece of cotton thread on it, three red glass beads, and a chicken feather. The report described what he thought was white paint spots on the seat of the boy's trousers.

The autopsy report was signed by R.E. Terry, M.D., Autopsy Surgeon, and Elbert Cooley, M.D., Assistant Autopsy Surgeon. Terry described the wounds just as Pete McGraw had and as I'd just seen in the crime photo. The box next to *homicide* was checked and *Probable Cause of Death: Asphyxiation; multiple mutilations* and *attack* were typed into the adjacent space.

I took note of the following:

- Coroner was at site and put immediately in charge of the case.
- Removal of body to mortuary was at 0805; autopsy began at 0930.
- I quoted Dr. Terry's observations that, "Laceration on wrist is deep and sharp. Noted: Severing the radial and ulna arterial systems. The approximate amount of blood in body found is approximately 10 to 12 percent of normal. Blood type: presently undetermined. A small blood spot on the collar of the jacket."
- I quoted Dr. Terry further: "Evidence of ante mortem sexual abuse including enlarged and thinned-out rectum, so that only the peritoneum remains as covering. Anus is enlarged. Patulous is open, torn, and inflamed. Upon microscopic examination, spermatozoa found in the anal region."
- Deep serrations on top exterior of tongue match upper teeth.
- The lungs were excised and weighed. Findings: ". . . There is no water in lungs."
- Bruises found on neck. Bruise on head.

Following the autopsy report was a legal form titled: Coroner's Jury's Verdict. Most of the information in the document was redundant to what had been stated in the report. The verdict was that: *". . . the cause of death was asphyxiation compounded by multiple mutilating operations and hemorrhage. The victim was killed by one or several criminal sexual degenerates."*

I made copies of the reports and then sat for a while, absorbing what I'd read. After a while I began to think that McGraw's perspective was beginning to become clearer and more credible. *These were doctors,* I thought. *They held no misgivings that the boy had been murdered.*

On the way out, the clerk stopped me to take a look at the registry. She had book-marked it a couple pages before my own entry. She turned the registry towards me so I could read it, and pointed to a signature. It was difficult to make out the handwriting, but it looked like "Abkhazian." Recalling the boy's aunt who lived in San Diego, this seemed like a logical explanation. The clerk re-ascribed the earlier misfiling to that person. I thanked her for her help, and turned to leave. She stopped me, asking: "And why all this interest in that old case?"

I gave her some of the background, and the clerk mused, "Interesting that the sheriff's department forensic team reopened the cold case after almost sixty years. That's an awfully long time, and I'd think any evidence they had would be too old to test now, wouldn't it?" She thoughtfully tapped her fingers on the counter. "You know, it *would have* been interesting to have been able to have this autopsy performed using modern techniques, like DNA analysis."

That had been the purpose of the grant money the forensic team used for their investigation, I explained, but techniques were limited because of old or missing evidence. As once again I turned to leave, she gently restrained me.

"You know what? Dr. Caswell might be interested in speaking with you."

After a quick call, she announced that Dr. Caswell would speak with me, but his time was extremely limited.

Dr. Albert Caswell stood and smiled as his secretary ushered me into his office. He reached out across his desk with a firm handshake. The chief medical examiner was a big, imposing man with heavy limbs, a barrel chest, broad shoulders, and an enormous head crowned with bushy brown hair. He reminded me of a brown bear. His desk was heaped with files and paperwork. The red lights on his telephone blinked impatiently. But his welcome was gracious. If he felt the clerk's request an imposition, he took pains not to show it. Caswell's smile was contagious. His clear brown eyes sparkled with intelligence and revealed both intuition and compassion. They were half hidden under heavy eyebrows going to grey.

"Two cups of coffee, Bridget. How do you take your coffee, Miss Schilling?"

"Cream and sugar, please."

He glanced at his watch. "Nearly three thirty. Midday letdown. Need a caffeine jolt?"

I smiled in agreement and took the offered chair.

"So, you're investigating an old case for the newspaper? Did you happen to make a copy of the autopsy report from our records department?"

"Yes."

"May I take a look at it?"

I handed him everything I had copied. He sat down heavily and immediately became immersed in the documents. As he read aloud and mumbled comments to himself, I took the opportunity to gaze around the office at dangling skeletons and bookshelves full of periodicals and books on homicides, forensic psychology, anatomy, and the like. His assistant, Bridget, returned with two cups of coffee, smiled sweetly as she placed them on her boss's desk, and then left the office, discreetly closing the door behind her.

For quite a long while, I watched silently as he continued to examine the information. When he was finished reviewing the documents, he said, "Well now." Just that. Then he paused. He nodded his head as though agreeing with himself. Still nodding, the doctor picked up his cup of the now tepid coffee and drank most of its contents before he put it down.

"I did indeed read this article in the paper. Last week, wasn't it? It interested me at the time. It's coincidental that you brought it to me now because it got me curious. I wanted to take a look at the autopsy myself, but hadn't yet had a chance to do it." As a way of explaining his busy schedule, he gestured toward the still-blinking telephone message lights. "You have done my work for me. Now, let's take a look together at what we've got and go through it step by step. Some of what I tell you might seem repetitive to what you already know, but if I stumble on something that's new to you or something you don't understand, stop me and ask.

"Note the time of the autopsy procedure. It took place within an hour and a half after the boy was taken out of the water. That's very important, because if there is a delay in the autopsy it may become nearly impossible to judge the cause of death because the petechia break down. They dissipate. Disappear."

"I see," I remarked, but not understanding, noting *petechia* on my notepad and underlining the term.

"First question a medical examiner asks about a victim found in the water is: Is there obvious injury? A 'yes' answer, signifying that there is injury, might indicate traumatic death—depending of course on what and how serious the injury is. A 'no' answer would more than likely indicate death by natural causes. The examiner uses common sense at this point of the examination, taking into consideration the types of injuries, if they exist. And here"—he tapped the top document—"we've got injuries." He turned his attention to the autopsy illustration, "to the mouth, neck, eyes, ears, wrist, finger, genitalia, and hair. You're with me so far?"

I paused and looked up from my note-taking, nodded.

"Which of these injuries were inflicted ante mortem—before death—and which were after death?

"Ante mortem injuries were the laceration of tongue, cutting away of his mouth and cheek, the deep cut on his wrist, wounds on skull, abrasions about neck, and sexual injuries. Ante mortem sexual attacks were brutal and multiple.'

"'The following mutilations would be postmortem: gouging of victim's eyes, severing of ears, severing of genitalia, severing of fingertip.'

"He had lost about fifteen percent of his blood when he was found, according to the doctor's notes. This happened while his heart beat. Ante mortem. A major artery was severed here on the wrist. This appears a reasonable explanation as to the loss of blood. But interestingly, there weren't bloodstains on the clothing other than that small drop of blood on the collar. It's the boy's blood type: type O positive," he added.

"Then there was that bruise on his skull. It was an ante mortem injury. Dr. Terry didn't think it was what killed the boy. See? He wrote here: 'Wounds are evident on the surface of scalp, with extensive hemorrhage with some free, dark-colored blood beneath the scalp; there is extensive hemorrhage within skull and covering left lobe of brain, but no skull fracture.'

"He concluded the cause of death was asphyxiation. I agree, and for three good reasons. They are these: the two bruises on the neck, the flattened trachea, and the laceration of the tongue. Let's look at these more closely. The petechia—"

"Petechia?"

"Black-and-blue marks. Petechia can appear purplish or brownish red, and is visible through the epidermis, caused by hemorrhage to tissues under the skin. See here?" He turned the photocopy of the sketch toward me so I could see the picture as he pointed to the neck. "There are two bruises marked on this sketch. These would suggest two hands, of course." I nodded, surprised at what I'd missed when I examined the picture earlier. He took back the drawing and pulled out the report. "Here it is: 'There is extensive hemorrhage in the tissue in the front of the neck, about the trachea. The trachea itself appears flattened.

"Now to the laceration on the tongue—these two injuries are connected: the teeth marks on the tongue and the neck bruises. In most cases of strangulation you'll find an injury like this because the victim invariably bites down on his tongue during the attack. See here what he wrote? *Deep serrations on top exterior of tongue match upper teeth.*'"

He paused, then continued: "Let's consider the length of time the body was in the water in order to rule out mutilations said to have resulted from marine life."

Riffling through the police report and then consulting the autopsy report, he scratched some figures on a scrap of paper. Finally he looked up and announced, "I figure it was in the water no longer than forty-eight hours, based on the size and age of the victim and the temperature of the water in San Diego Bay, which is consistently over seventy degrees Fahrenheit in July.

"Now let's move on to the matter of damage marine life might have inflicted in such a relatively short period of time. Before and after it surfaces, one can expect a body to be attacked by marine life. The favorite areas are soft tissue areas like lips, cheeks, the cartilage in noses and ears, eyelids, and genitals.

"Fish choose to attack injured areas preferentially, just as insects do. So injuries in untraditional areas, like the entire tip of the finger and under his clothing, cause concern. I doubt marine life got to fleshy parts under two layers of clothing."

I mentioned Jackie Cohn's account of watching Christopher drown.

"Death by drowning? Not at all. Let's look again at the autopsy report about testing the lungs of the boy." He shuffled through the papers and read, *'Findings: There was no water in the lungs.'*

The portly doctor leaned back into his chair, signaling the end of his commentary. "So tell me, Miss Schilling. Why is your paper taking interest in this old case after it just published that article about it so recently?"

"My senior editor received a telephone call from the detective who worked the case in 1933. He complained about the article. My editor remembered him and respected him from the old days. He assigned me to look into what the man had to say."

Dr. Caswell nodded. "The article describing the forensic team's investigation seemed superficial, I thought. It didn't mention any new evidence, new information, or new testimony. Gets one to wondering: Why this case?"

I shrugged.

"Could somebody still be threatened by the truth behind the little boy's death? If so, who is it? Why should they want to keep the truth buried?"

"A cover-up? Are you suggesting a cover-up?"

"No, Miss Schilling." The amicable doctor's smile turned chilling. "Not *a* cover-up. *Two* cover-ups. One in 1933. And now in 1990."

We parted with a handshake. As I opened the double glass doors to the outside, the fresh, clean, crisp air never felt so good.

The day was spent, so I went home via McDonald's for take-out for my dinner. As soon as I opened the door to my cave, I noticed that the red button on the telephone answering machine was blinking. The recording put the call at 6:17 P.M., and it was from Betty, the department secretary at the *Observer*. The minute I heard the serious tone of her normally upbeat voice, I knew something was terribly wrong. She spoke in a near whisper.

"Sera, I just received a weird phone call," she said. "Some guy asked for you. I told him you weren't in. He said he didn't want to leave a message on your machine, just to tell you that there are some folks who are pissed off that you are probing into the Abkhazian case. There was something really scary about this, Sera. If you keep on, he said, something very unpleasant will happen to you. Neither Richard nor St. James is here now. I called security. Left a message on St. James's line. Be careful, Sera. Call me at home if you want to." She recited her home telephone number and disconnected.

I didn't call Betty back. But I did call Richard and left a message on his answering machine at the office requesting a meeting first thing in the morning.

Sera

I STOPPED BY Betty's desk when I got to work the next day, and asked her about her message the night before. She didn't have anything else to offer other than what she'd said in her message. As I turned to leave, she mentioned that a delivery had been made to my desk from UPS. Now that was strange. I hadn't expected any delivery.

Sure enough, an envelope had been left in the center of my desk with my name and address on a proper UPS label. I opened the envelope. Found a folded piece of paper. Written on it in masculine scrawl was the message: "Get my message?" Short, but it made its point.

I skirted the wall separating my cubicle from my neighbor's. She turned and smiled. My words spun together: Did she see the UPS man who had left this? She hadn't. I made the rounds, asking everyone with a desk near mine if they had seen a delivery man. None had noticed him, either.

I called UPS and asked for records of this delivery. It didn't surprise me when they told me that they had no record of a delivery being made to the newspaper or specifically to me.

Richard was waiting for me in the conference room. He nodded. He knew. St. James had alerted him about the reason for my harried call demanding a meeting. He pulled out a chair for me to sit down and closed the door. I handed him the envelope and the note.

"Now, what's this?" He pulled out the folded note and read it. "Now, a threatening note. Obviously about the telephone call last night."

"You know this is about the Abkhazian case."

Richard nodded slightly. "Update me."

I filled him in on what I had found.

"This is all very interesting, to say the least. But it's your safety. Do you intend to keep on delving into it, especially in light of these threats?"

"Yes. I've found too much to stop now."

"As your manager, I have to think about your future here at the paper and push you toward getting your contract, so I have to consider the value of this. You need a good, newsworthy story to work on. It's my job to help you out there. I know that you have been doing a lot of work for other reporters, mostly in the way of research. From all reports, you've done a sound job of that. I've been getting good reviews. And you know that St. James is going to be retiring. When he's gone, I can't see much of a push—if any at all—for you to keep working on this story."

"I'm not ready to give it up just yet, Richard. I could continue working on it and do something else. You know I want to get into investigative reporting—my own, not footwork for other reporters as I've been doing."

"I'm concerned about your safety as well as your career."

"I will be more alert. I know what to look out for," I said, thinking of his aftershave.

"You're a tough gal." He said that smiling.

"I've had to fight to get here and I will fight to make a place for myself at this newspaper."

Richard pushed his chair away from the table and stood up. He leaned forward, keeping his eyes on mine, his face stone serious. He put both his hands on the conference table and leaned toward me. "If you receive any more threats, let me know immediately."

"I will."

"Meantime, let's find you a good story."

Pete and Sera

Fourth Interview, October 28, 1990

"DO YOU KNOW what a *narker* is, Sera?" McGraw asked.

"No."

"A *stoolie*?"

She laughed. "Yes. A stoolie's a police informant."

"Yes. And a narker is the same thing as a stoolie—a stool pigeon."

"*Nark* is contemporary slang—an undercover policeman."

"Yeah, but back then a nark usually didn't mean a cop. Usually it was a fellow who was a real seedy character and would rat on his own momma to save his skivvies. Cops used these narks as snitches to get information. The nark giving us our first lead in this case worked as a rummy at one of those gin joints on my old beat."

"Rummy? Gin joints?" Sera couldn't suppress a smile.

"A *rummy* is slang for bartender." He returned her smile.

"Oh."

"You know the term *speakeasy* or *speako*? The Studio Club was the swankiest underground place in San Diego during Prohibition. It was down on Sixth and Juniper, and holy cow! What a place it was! Outside it looked like any old run-down building with boarded-over windows, no lights, no signs—nothing to grab ya—but inside, man alive! Tiffany lamps, stained-glass windows, hand-carved wooden ceiling beams, and gold bathroom fixtures. And the entertainment! Floor shows were brought down from Hollywood with some big names. There were jazz greats, ragtime bands, and scat singers; there were weird and fantastic attractions, like circus trainers with wild animals, magicians, belly dancers. You name it. At the Studio, all types of people mixed—the rich and the not-so-rich, and Negros could shimmy with the best of the *hoi polloi*, doing the wild dances of the time: ragtime, swing, and bunny hug.

"But all these goings-ons at the Club were nothing but fronts for backdoor hanky-panky where serious money was passed in high-end gambling. Also at the club, a fellow could drop a couple sawbucks, drop a name, and get himself some hoochy in the back. And those gals were some sweet patooties."

The young intern kept her face down, intent on note-taking, and to hide her grin as she listened to the old slang. The old man's mood was—well, very upbeat. It was a kick to listen to him pull out old banter.

"No siree-Bob! It took a lot of wheelin' and dealin', but I *made* the Studio Club part of my beat. And it paid pretty well—you'd better believe it did—to keep it running clean and quiet and smooth. And, ahem, I gotta be honest, there were some pretty nice perks in working the club.

"The owner, a fellow by the name of Wrottenberg as I recall, who had originally hailed from Los Angeles, had a lot of money and connections to powerful people up there.

"You didn't want to mess with Wrottenberg, but he and I established more or less of a collaborative relationship based on protection on my part and information on his. I could take advantage of any of the recreational activities the Club had to offer, not that I'm proud to admit it. But hell, I was young then. Some said Wrottenberg was a thug of the worst sort, mixed with heavy-duty gangsters, but I liked the man. But, like I said, I was young then.

"At the Studio Club, anything could be had, legal or otherwise; you just needed to know the right man to ask. In my case, what I needed was information. When Wrottenberg found out that I was in charge of investigating the Abkhazian boy's mysterious death, he said he wanted to help me out in any way that he could. I told him I needed some leads, so he set me up with a stoolie who also worked the bar at the Club. You bet all sorts of information is freely passed over the bar, and Wrottenberg paid him to use his eyes and ears. We did the same. This began a longtime relationship between me and my stoolie. I used him throughout my career, long after this case. We had a system that if he had something to tell me, he'd leave a dead soldier at the foot of a certain telegraph pole on F Street."

"Dead soldier?"

"An empty booze bottle. A couple of days after Wrottenberg set us up, Joe and I saw that an empty bottle on the sidewalk next to the pole. You've been on F Street?"

"Yes, of course.

"F Street is part of the old Stingaree District. Now, of course, it's called the Gaslamp Quarter. Saturday nights it attracts young adults out to have a fine evening at fancy restaurants and fine-wine bars. But back then it got to be dark and sinister when the sun went down. Come to think of it, it always has been a wild spot in San Diego. A portion of it was San Diego's Chinese district. Chinese banks, a Chinese mayor, Chinese laundries, Chinese schools, and even Chinese policing. They'd police their own gambling halls, fan-tan parlors, opium dens, and red-lamp district and kept them running quietly so we city cops wouldn't interfere. Look the other way, so to speak. That part of the Stingaree was where I met my stoolie to exchange information.

"That day, it was midday. Downright raunchy there at Noon. You can imagine that syrup   ᵗᵗing smell of the weekend's garbage behind the eateries, ro   July's heat. There were ugly, mangy stray cats fighting ov   s and fish bones. Ribbons of sewage trickled black in the gutter. And the stench from the crappers in the back alley lay like a thick, fetid fog.

"He tells us that one of the prosties who works at the club told him something that might connect with our investigation. She said that some schmuck, who'd been one of her guests, showed her some pictures. She drew a line, she said. What that fella showed to her and his demands on her were way beyond her line of acceptability. So she had him thrown out."

"Were they porn?"

"Yes, they were of kids. And this happed the weekend before the boy went missing. Joe and I felt it was too coincidental—the porn, an outsider with predilections like those, and the timing. She was something to check out."

"You mean she was *someone* to question." Sera said, half smiling and gazing at the old man.

"Yes. Shoot! Caught me there. *Question* her. But check her out is what we did, too." He chuckled and took a sip of water.

"I knew the place the girl roomed at. It was a boardinghouse run by Myrna Josie, down on Ninth and Broadway. It was early afternoon when we got there, but our lady-of-the-night was still wearing her robe. A white swishy thing." (He drew an hourglass with his hands.) "It clung nicely to her chassis. Had a white fluffy fox collar. Her hair was set in bobby pins, but she wore a silk scarf around her head. She had cold cream on her face, but even so, holy cow was she a sweet patootie.

"She invited the three of us into her room when she heard why we were there, and started right in.

"That Saturday night before Chris went missing she saw this fella at the Studio. She didn't recognize him as a local, but he looked like a big spender because he was dropping rubes at the bar like it was going out of style. She sidled up to him and asked him to buy her a drink. He ordered a panther sweat for himself and a gin and tonic for her.

"'Call me a gold digger if you wanna, but he looked like he was a catch. He was dressed in some pretty swanky duds, a silk suit, and spent money like he had it. He wasn't a bad looker, either. He was tall and thin, sharp featured, with dark hair and dark eyes. He had heavy brows and broad shoulders.'

"After *punching the bag* for a while at the bar, she takes him to the back still thinking he was a buster with a roll. But when they get to her room, he gets down and out whacky on her.

"She said gals in her profession get all types of joes, but she sets limits on what she'll handle and what she won't. She said she wouldn't service a fellow if he was abusive, if he packed heat, or if he was a degenerate.

"'That joker was a pervert of the worst sort. I told him to get out. He became threatening so's I yell for the bouncer. Before the bouncer got to my room, he skedaddled like the rat he was.'

"She went on to say that she thought that was the end of it. But on Sunday morning she was at the boardinghouse, and on her way to use the privy, when she nearly collided with him in the hallway.

"'Is he here still renting a room here?' I asked Myrna.

"'No!' the proprietor nearly shouted. 'I'm looking for the jerk myself. He split last week, on Wednesday, without paying the room rent.'

"We checked the guest book. Got to Saturday, July fifteenth. She ran her finger down the page and stopped at the name of Purdy. The date he registered was three days before the boy disappeared. E. Basset Purdy.

"She stopped me from writing down the address. 'It's a phony address. I already checked with the telephone operator up there. He is from somewhere upstate around the Oakland area, because we jawed about Frisco, how it was both of our favorite towns, how his business—accounting—took him over there a lot. He took the Creek Route ferry, he did. From Jack London Square. Told me all about it. Oh! Was I gulled! Believe me, officers, I am no flibbertigibbet! You know I've run this place for over thirty years, and I could count the bad ones on one hand. He completely took me in. He seemed so clean-cut and dapper. And well educated. He spoke the Queen's English. Was well dressed. Seemed cultured. Said he loved opera and occasionally attended performances at the San Francisco Opera. It's not usual that we get the likes of him. After our first meeting, I looked towards talking more with him. Didn't see him until Sunday night, though. He stuck to his room all day and went out until late most every night. But then Sunday night—er, rather early Monday morning— he came in swacked, singing like a canary with a cold. Woke me up out of a deep sleep. I told him to hush up. He looked like what the cat dragged in. Stumbling and farting and singing and laughing, he was. Saw me up there on the stair landing, staring down at him and looking mad as a hornet. The louse, he roared at *me* like *I* was the sight to behold. I should'ov thrown him out right then and there. But, like I told you, he gulled me. After he laughed at me, he apologized. I let him stumble off to his room and I went back to bed. He must'ov drove off after that because I never saw him again. Stiffed me, he did.'

Pete continued: "After leaving there, I drove back to the station and sent out some wires to Bay Area cities, inquiring about this fellow based on the name he put into the boardinghouse register. I didn't hold out any hope, but damn it if I didn't get a hit. There was a Basil Purdy who had a police record in Oakland, California. Interestingly, he had been arrested on several occasions for indecent exposure and solicitation. With Doyle's authority, I wired back to them to have Purdy brought into their custody so I could bring him down here for questioning.

"Chief Doyle had a habit of jumping the gun. That night he made another radio announcement about this new development in the Abkhazian case—just as he'd been giving nightly updates since the day the boy disappeared and I got my promotion. That was the chief's biggest problem. Some called him a blowhard. At the time I just thought he got ahead of himself. He told the radio audience that the San Diego Police Department would soon have a suspect in their custody for the murder of Christopher Abkhazian.

"This was the first time I flew in an airplane. A Boeing 247, as I recall. It had just come out that year, the first modern-type passenger airliner. Big thing for our little airport, having a run down here to ⬛⬛⬛⬛, and Los Angeles. It was small, though. It ⬛⬛ ats and a closed cockpit." Pete smiled. "And ⬛⬛ stewardess who provided us with blankets. They were needed. At ten thousand feet in the air, it got to be very cold.

"There were four fellas from the Oakland P.D. waiting for me at the San Francisco Municipal Airport with two squad cars. Very impressive. They were real police cars with the police logo on the side. Not like mine with a sign that I'd put up in the windshield when I used it for police work. They took me to the jail in Oakland where they held Purdy. Then I, with Oakland detectives, searched his house for anything to connect him to Christopher Abkhazian's disappearance. We found a hoard of pictures, ones like the prosti described, and some kids' clothing, mostly undergarments, that had been tucked away underneath Purdy's bed.

"I shuffled through the photographs, looking for—I was half afraid of what I might find— most of the children in the photographs were about the same age as—their faces were unclear, but there were one or two that might have . . ." He sighed and didn't go on.

"I brought Purdy back to San Diego. We kept him for a few days, but we couldn't hang anything on him to directly implicate him to the boy's murder. The underwear we'd held in evidence turned out not to be Purdy's blood type, nor was it Chris's. The only slight connection was the pornography angle. Purdy said he got the photographs from a youth he'd met at one of the clubs in the Stingaree. It was all very vague. I had such high hopes—that's how it goes. I began to thinking again about Jackie Cohn. Couldn't get it out of my mind that in him we'd find some good answers. I thought I'd take Jackie Cohn out to my fishing camp in Ocean Beach, to spend a day with him 'fishing' for information. I mean, hell, what boy doesn't like to fish? I also knew that his mother wouldn't give me permission, so I borrowed the boy for a day."

"You did *what*?" Sera asked in disbelief, looking up from writing and giving Pete a crooked smile. Pete took in her expression and laughed. Then his eyes glazed over, as they did when he began searching for a beginning point of one of his recollections.

"I drove up Presidio Hill to the Cohns' residence," he began.

Pete McGraw's Story

PETE'S CAR CHUGGED up the steep and twisting road. Ahead, the Serra Museum, a splendid building in the Spanish Revival style, a white stucco edifice topped by a red-tiled roof and bell tower and wrapped by a broad, columned portico, stretched majestically across the summit of Presidio Hill. Pete recalled the ceremony just five years before—before Connie, before the Agua Caliente money heist—that he'd participated in as one of the police department's honor guards. A ceremonial gun salute was given when Mayor Hank Clark cut the ribbon. In full uniform, the young rookie cop watched as the mayor then took the first shovelful of dirt, commencing the building's construction.

It was high summer. A hot, July afternoon just like this. Everybody was celebratory. The Hoover High School marching band played Sousa; there were balloons, clowns, kiddie rides on a fire engine that wailed its woeful siren, lemonade and brownies served by members of the Ladies' League.

It was built a few years before the Great Depression, before San Diego was cast into a belabored state of economic despair. It was when the city was in adolescence, still hanging on to innocence.

He drove past where the old Presidio cemetery used to be. The hill next to it had been bulldozed and landscaped. The century-plus-old human remains were relocated. He considered the disrupted peace of the skeletons. What stories they could tell! Presidio Hill *was* San Diego during the days of the Spanish explorers and zealous padres. Here, large numbers of captured indigenous people were brought to build the fortress with the strength of their backs and artistry in their hands. They molded natural clay soil into adobe bricks; they taught the Spanish the art of irrigation as they drew water from the nearby San Diego River to little vegetable gardens.

Along the side of the road, trees that were merely three or four feet high only a few years before when they were planted now waved their sturdy branches with the afternoon breezes and shimmered in the sun. The Presidio boundaries had been expanded. They now included Presidio Park, with stone statues honoring the early Spanish settlers, the museum, a playground, an area for picnicking, a gazebo that was popular for weddings, and landscaping including some not-so-indigenous plants, eucalyptus trees among them. Presidio Park was a well-used, *happy* place to be. Now, Pete watched children roll down the steep hill from the museum, stopping steps short of the road, and getting up dizzily and cheerfully. A couple of boys saw him in his uniform and saluted with wide smiles. His rearview mirror caught the grin on his own face as he returned their salutes.

He recalled quail hunting up here on Presidio Hill with his dad when he was a kid, when there was only a cemetery and stone ruins, and the land was barren and hard with creosote and prickly pear cactus.

Back in his youth, his dad was full of great stories of the old Southwest. Although the senior McGraw was an Irish import and had worked in Chicago's meat-packing plants, he came west and took to San Diego as though he'd written its history. Being a policeman, he loved the people on his beat and brought personal stories home to the dinner table each night. But what Pete remembered were his old-time stories. His dad, being somewhat a history buff, shared his enthusiasm with his son about the Spanish history that seeped through San Diego's pores.

His tales sparked Pete's imagination so that he could envision Spanish soldiers strutting about in their armor, beautiful Mexican maidens running away with English sea captains, and cannons booming from ships at sea.

Those hunting days were long awaited by the anxious youngster. At the time, the boy thought them much more than hunting trips; they were grand adventures. What he considered trips were actually jaunts across town. What he remembered as a vast wilderness open to hunting, was actually a city park-sized open parcel of land. He recalled long days, starting early in the morning before sunrise and ending well after the sun had set. The twosome they created, father and son, was special and complete. Framed by gunpowder and what he thought at the time man-to-man talk, they'd creep stealthily through the brush. A covey of startled partridges would take to the sky in furious flight as the hunters aimed their shotguns and fired. Feathers fluttered from the sky like snowflakes. For the day, they'd forget that there was a real world out there. Then, much too suddenly, shadows lengthened, there was a blush to the earth, and the air grew chilly. It was time to head home. His mother would greet them with her arms folded across her chest and an icy expression on her face as they stomped into the kitchen still wearing their leather boots, leaving clumps of clay around the door. But they were weary and dusty and satisfied, with their strings of flaccid birds, and she soon forgave them with a hot meal.

Now Pete suddenly remembered that he hadn't called home to tell Connie he'd be late that night, as was becoming more and more a habit the deeper he became involved in this investigation. The guilt he felt rattled his guts for not calling her earlier. There was no excuse: he'd had the chance when he was at the police station, but he simply didn't do it.

But then he might not be late after all, because his idea might not work.

If his plan worked out the way he hoped it would, nobody would be the worse for wear in not knowing, and everyone would benefit by what he found out.

In other words, they'd thank him in the end.

But if it didn't work out the way he hoped it would, he might end up in a mess.

That was something to think about—but that was if it didn't work out and he was caught. Then, he'd have to think about another career . . .

The splendid homes of the wealthy lined the pleasantly wide street that crossed the top of Presidio Hill, with the Cohns' looking as regal as the rest. Pete was greeted by the maid who stood just inside the massive front doors, whose eyes grew like saucers when she saw him. She hesitated about calling for Jackie after Pete asked for him, but Pete insisted that he'd spoken with Jackie's mother beforehand.

Jackie wasn't particularly pleased to see Pete, but when Pete suggested he grab a jacket and come with him, the boy's face lit up with the idea of riding in a car with a policeman.

"Will I see some criminals? Will we catch a robber?"

The maid was conflicted as to whether she should let the boy out of the house or not, without the parents' direct permission. "They're downtown. At the shop. I should telephone them," she protested.

But after a few awkward moments followed by a little solicitous flattery, Pete finally shut the door behind the boy and backed out of the driveway.

"Where are we going, Officer McGraw?"

"Oh, I don't know, kid. Why don't we make it a surprise?"

"We're not going to the jailhouse, are we?"

"Nope."

"That's good. I didn't like it when they took me there and asked me all those questions. Those guys burned me blue."

"Never mind them; they think they're just trying to get to the truth of it all. That's what they think, kid."

"They weren't like you, Officer McGraw. They were gee wiz nasty buzzers."

"Thank you."

"So, if we're not going there, where are we going?"

"I thought it would be fun for me to have a boy's companionship for a day. You see, I don't have any boys of my own."

"Looks like we're headed toward Ocean Beach, Officer McGraw. Are we?"

"I was thinking I'd like to take you out to the beach where you can try your hand at some ocean fishing."

"Swell! It's nearly halfway through the summer and I haven't been to the beach yet." The boy put his head out the car window and shouted out, "Hurray!" into the wind.

Jackie's chatter continued at a rapid pace until Pete pulled over at a small roadside shack with a sign advertising *Fresh Bait.*

Pete pulled the hand brake. "First we have to stop here and buy us a few sardines to use as bait for catching the fish." He began to open the car door, but stopped. He turned to face the boy squarely. "But then, you know all about that, because you love to fish, don't'cha, kid?"

"Never done it," he answered innocently; his excitement pulling his smile from ear-to-ear.

"Well, I'll be. I thought you were an old hand at it. Come along with me."

Jackie followed McGraw, mimicking his lazy stride and keeping his eyes peeled on the tall drums of bait. He half-listened to the easy conversations of fishermen sitting around inside the shack. His eyes took in the framed sepia photographs of trophy catches and the stuffed specimens hanging on the walls. His heart thumped.

Inside the bait shack, the air was thick with cigarette smoke, dust, and fishy smells. The fishermen's low and continuous burbling came to a silence as they watched the boy and the man who'd just come in. One or two nodded at Pete. Jackie's chatter never ceased as he watched Pete dip the sieve into the drum.

"Didn't you say you fished on the piers downtown?" Pete asked as he withdrew a jangle of small, shiny silver fish. The rest of the fish still in the drum that had scattered now regrouped and swam in a swirl.

"Nope. Never done it yet," Jackie confided, face peering over the edge of the drum. He was completely mesmerized by the tiny fish. They formed in a counterclockwise vortex, then suddenly and mysteriously changed direction to swim the other way.

They left the shack to drive down Newport Avenue into Ocean Beach, and then turned down Brighton Avenue. Making a sudden turn into the driveway of a small bungalow there, Pete pulled the brake, turned the key, and sat back, took a look at the boy, and frowned thoughtfully. "Looks to me that I'm going to have to get you some gear, kid. I never thought to tell you to wear shorts."

"I can roll these pant legs up. My mom won't mind." The boy leaned over and began rolling them up to his knees.

"Well then, come inside and let me get you a bottle of Coca-Cola. I keep a few out here for when I come out to fish." He pulled a chair from the kitchen table for Jackie.

"This your place?" Jackie couldn't hide the look of distaste.

Pete's eyes followed the boy's gaze, taking in the dust, the broken linoleum floor, and the dirty windows and lackluster curtains that covered them, grimy with layers of accumulated dirt and grease from cooking off the oil stove.

"Yeah, it's all mine. I come here when I can. Here's your cola." He ripped off the bottle cap on the corner of the counter and smacked the green bottle down on the table in front of Jackie. The drink fizzed over the top. He grabbed another for himself, opened it, and pulled thirstily at the bottle.

"Thanks. It's even kind of cold."

"Stays cool in that little old box, even without ice."

"Is this where you live?" The boy took a sip from the bottle, still taking in the environment, now with an indeterminable look on his face.

"No. I live with my wife at another place, if that's what you mean. In fact, Connie—that's my wife—well, she don't really like coming out here too much. I guess you can see why. To tell you the truth, I don't think it's been graced by a lady's touch in maybe a dozen years, since my mom passed away. Now, she liked it here—my mom, that is—but then she liked to ocean fish. No kidding! You look surprised."

"It's just the idea of a mother fishing. It seems weird."

"She did. And she was pretty good at it, too. But like I said, no female has been here since she died, so I suppose you could say that it's kind of a man's getaway place, you know?

"Sure."

Pete winked at the boy. "Chicks ain't allowed; that's for sure."

"They'd spoil it," responded Jackie with all the seriousness of his age.

Pete reached his bottle across the small metal table. They clinked bottles in a toast.

"Say kid, I don't bring many folks to my beach house here, so let's keep this fishing adventure our own little secret. What do you say?"

"Yeah. That's patsy. I'll keep my mouth zipped." He smiled and drew his finger across his lips.

"I'll bet you're pretty good at keeping secrets."

"Yeah! I can keep secrets."

"What kind of secrets do you keep?"

"If I tell you, they won't be secrets, will they?" the boy answered with a glint of amusement in his brown eyes.

"I guess that's true enough. But I'm good at keeping secrets, too. See here, kid?" And Pete mimicked Jackie's zippered mouth.

The boy chuckled. After a while he said, "Well, suppose I can tell you that I am the president of a very secret club."

"Oh, yeah? That's a real good secret. What do you call your club?"

"We don't have a name yet."

"How many members are in your club?"

"Only two."

"That's a pretty small club, Jackie," Pete chuckled.

"We just started it this summer," Jackie replied.

"Who did?"

"Me and Chris."

"You and Chris?" Pete echoed.

"Yeah." A shadow passed over his face. "I guess . . ." His voice faltered and he fell into silence.

Then the boy lit up suddenly. "Now that you know my secret, you've got to cross your heart and hope to die that you won't tell."

"Word of honor. Don't a lot of boys have clubs?"

"Most of them do."

"What kind of things did you do in your club?"

"Oh, adventures of a sort."

"I suppose I shouldn't ask what kind of adventures."

"It's okay. We took turns making up adventures. You know—one time it's my turn and another time it's Chris's."

"Gotcha. What kind of adventures?"

"Like the time I put castor oil in some kid's cocoa?"

"Whew! Now that's not exactly an adventure; it's mischievous." Pete chuckled. "I'll bet that happened during the school year, not this summer, didn't it."

"Yeah. It was before I started my club. It was funny anyhow."

"I'll bet. So tell me about your and Chris's adventures this summer."

The boy shrugged. "I can't think of one right now."

Pete slapped his thigh and swilled down the last of the Coke. "Now kid, time's a-wasting. We gotta see about that equipment I've gotta get for you to use."

In no time flat they were barefoot and in rolled-up trousers, walking across the sand to the beach with their pails of sardines, a net, scissors, fish line, two stools, and fishing poles. Pete baited the hook and cast for Jackie and set the pole into the sand. Then Pete told the boy that their job was to wait until they saw the pole bend with a fish fighting at the other end. He explained that the pole would naturally bend and twist along with the currents of the ocean, and that it took practice to be able to tell when there was a fish strike, or when it was caught up on some old seaweed or kelp, or when it was just riding with the currents and tidal action. He placed their stools side by side and they took their seats and quietly watched as the waves crashed on the sand, then ebbed with a gurgle, and the seagulls glided overhead on the winds, squawking noisily.

"So when you fish down on the piers, Jack, what kind of equipment do you use?"

Jackie, forgetting what he'd said earlier, responded distantly, "Oh, we make our own fishing contraption out of things we find in a junk pile."

Pete pulled back from the subject of fishing the piers and said, instead, "Tell me about Chris."

"What about Chris?"

"I guess he was your friend, so you should know pretty much about him."

"Chris? He wasn't my friend."

"Oh?"

"Chris was a bother. Always hung around me like a bad dream. My ma said I had to play with him in the summertime on account of our folks having their shops near each other."

"Whoa! I thought you liked to pal around together."

"Nah. I don't usually put up with twits like Christopher. You see, there was nobody else to play with downtown."

"Okay. Gotcha."

"So I made up the club thing."

"What? You didn't have a club?"

"No, not really."

"Kid, remember I don't have kids of my own and it's been a while since I was a kid myself, so I don't know what kids do anymore in their spare time."

"I understand."

"What kinds of things do you like to do in the summer? Downtown?"

"Me? Things I like to do?"

"Either you alone, or the both of you together."

"Chris liked to go up to the park. I like going to Kress's. Oh, he liked Hubble's. He made model airplanes and things like that. Those things bore me. I like action! But I usually ended up doing what he wanted. He'd get all whiney on me if I didn't go along with what he wanted to do. So we'd end up going to the park or the zoo. After a while it gets pretty boring downtown, to tell you the truth. It gets hard to think of new adventures."

"The days that you went to the piers to fish, whose adventure idea was it?"

"That was my idea."

"And Chris had to do what you said he should, being that it was your adventure idea?"

"Yes. That's right."

"I suppose going to see where a robbery took place, like Hulsizer's, started out to be an adventurous day for you. Didn't it?"

"Seeing where the robbery happened was a riot. There were coppers. Broken glass all over the floor. There were detectives dusting the counters for fingerprints. Old man Hulsizer booted us out. He said we were getting in the way of things. We weren't there for very long."

"And then you went to Kress's Department Store?"

"Yes."

"What did you do there?"

"Chris had a dime so we bought some candy. And we went upstairs and played with the toys until the lady told us we had to leave."

"Did you split up after that?"

"Umm, can I tell you a secret?"

"Of course you can, Jackie. You can trust me."

"Cross your heart and hope to die you won't tell anyone?" He drew the imaginary zipper over his lips, which Pete mimicked.

"Cross my heart and hope to die," Pete said, crossing his heart with his right hand.

"We went to the waterfront."

"Did you know that Chris wasn't allowed to go down there?" Jackie squirmed uncomfortably.

Again, Pete pulled back from this line of questioning. "Did you and Chris play together at school, Jackie?"

"Nah. Nobody liked him, because everyone thought he was a bit of a crybaby. He got a little bit better in the summer, though. And shoot, he was only a second grader, anyhow."

"You did know him during the school year?"

"That's right. Sometimes I would see him at recess. Like I told you, I got to know him better this summer."

"Did he tell you that he liked to fish?"

"I don't remember." Jackie shrugged.

"Wait up there now, Jackie! I think we have something at the end of the line! Now take the pole and reel it in there now, Jackie. Slow. Slow will do you. Slow. See the bobber? It's nearly inside the breaking waves there. We'll see what we got in just a minute. Slow! There now! I see it, and don't it look like a little striped bass? Here, bring her in and we'll put this net under her and cut the hook out of the mouth. There ya go! Not bad for fifteen minutes, huh?"

"Holy cow there, mister! I just damned caught a fish!"

Pete sized it and tossed it into the bucket of salt water. "It's within keeping range. Guess about eighteen inches. Not bad there, pal."

"Holy cow! I can't believe it! Geez, that's swell! Can we try it again? Yes, I'll load the hook with one of those sardines."

"You'll have to tell your father to take you fishing now that you're a champ, Jackie."

"My dad? Nah. He wouldn't like fishing."

"What about your brother? What's his name?"

"David? No. See? That how you do it?" The fish was wriggling on the hook. Jackie smiled proudly.

"That's fine, Jackie." They settled down on to their stools once again. After a brief silence, Pete asked, "Do you do any adventures with your older brother David?"

"Nah. He does things with his chums. Not with me. He thinks he's too high and mighty for me anyhow."

"So you're not close with your brother?"

"Nope."

"But he has a gang of boys he's close with?"

"Yeah. He don't talk about them. It's a secret club."

"He doesn't tell you who's in his gang of boys?"

"Nope."

"Help me out, kid."

"Huh?"

"Names?"

"I'm not sure, but I think there's one named Phillip and some of the others are from his school."

"Is it an athletic club?"

"Huh?"

"Are they into sports, like baseball?"

"They row, if that's what you mean."

"Out of the San Diego Rowing Club downtown?"

"I guess so."

"Did you ever get any idea what kinds of other stuff they did?"

"David wouldn't tell me on a bet. But, I got another secret, Officer McGraw. Promise you'll never tell?"

"Cross my heart—"

"Sometimes David sneaks out at night and goes places with his club members. He was the one who told me to go to Hulsizer's and ask about the robbery."

Interesting, Pete thought. "Does your brother David ever bring his buddies by your house?"

"Nope. Like I told you, it's a secret club that he's in. He can't give out the names of the members."

"Then how do you know about the boy called Phillip?"

"David spilled the beans one day and mentioned Phillip's name by mistake, I heard, and he got real angry—made me swear to God and hope to die that I'd not tell anyone about Phillip being a member of his secret club. You've gotta promise now, Officer McGraw."

Pete drew a zipper across his lips once again.

"Are you a little bit scared of your older brother?"

"No I ain't. He don't scare me."

Pete cast a third time. It came out short. While reeling in the line, he asked, askance, "Well then, how does he treat you?" He cast it a little farther north to follow the tidal pull.

"Huh? What do you mean, how does David treat me?"

"You see, kid, I never had an older brother. I just had an older sister. She bossed me around when I was a kid. You know, she even dressed me up as a girl when I was young."

"Nah!" They laughed together.

"Your brother—is he good to you as an older brother, teaching you things, taking you places and stuff like that?

"Uh-uh. Most of the time he doesn't pay much attention to me at all."

"Oh, I see. He ignores you?"

"Yeah. You could say that."

The two silently watched the diamonds sparkle on the waves as the sun came closer to dipping into the horizon.

"You know?" Jackie asked softly.

"What, kid?"

"My brother likes to razz me in front of the tannery men. They laugh at me. Call me names like 'Pretty Boy' because I play the violin. My dad would murder them if he heard, but my folks are never there when they get to messing me around." He added in a softer voice, "Sometimes, well, sometimes David punches me out."

"He beats you up?"

"Well, when we're wrestling it starts out one way and ends up another. It's like David gets mad and starts throwing punches, you know? Hitting at me and stuff. I probably shouldn't be telling you this because Mom says it's a family matter, but you asked, and . . ."

Pete glanced sideways at Jackie and studied the boy's taut expression. The boy's eyes were narrowed and focused on the little red bobber that floated cheerfully on the effervescent blue water.

"Have you told your father about this?"

"He'd say for me to stand up for myself. To punch him back."

"How old is David?"

"He's going to be nineteen."

"And you're what? Eight, nine years old? How old?

"Nine. Well, nine and a half. I'll be ten next year on January seventeenth."

"And I'd guess you're not quite five feet tall, or just over."

"Actually I'm nearly five feet and one and a half inches."

"Your brother is how tall?"

"Six feet."

"So you see it's not a fair fight, is it, kid?"

Jackie turned suddenly and looked evenly at Pete. His features softened. "Yeah. I guess you're right."

"So, say your brother were to tell you to take Chris down to San Diego Bay—say on a con of going fishing—would you do it so that he wouldn't beat you up?"

Jackie's face turned red and tears sprang to his eyes. He shook his head violently. "I did *not* come to the bay with Chris," he said.

Pete's put his hands up in front of his chest defensively, smiled and stepped back. Okay. Okay, you went different ways. I get it." Then, smiling at Jackie, he said, "You know, kid, I heard you play a pretty keen fiddle."

"Yeah, I guess I do." He looked at the older man and nodded slowly, his face shining with pride. "How'd you hear that?"

"Oh, somebody mentioned it. Maybe it was Mr. Hulsizer. Whoever it was said that you get paid some *moolah* for playing at the church."

"Moolah? What's that?"

"Cash-ola."

"Oh. Sure. And it's not a church."

"Of course, it's a synagogue."

"Do you like music, Officer McGraw?"

"Gee, kid, I hate to tell you that I don't know much about it. I can play a little on the mouth organ."

"Harmonica"

"Harmonica. You're right. But I would suppose that's not near as hard to play as a fiddle."

"Violin."

"I wish I knew more about music. How long you been playing violin?"

"Since I was three."

"Whew!"

"Yeah. My mom says I'm a prodigy. She wants me to go back east to study at Juilliard or someplace like that."

"And your brother?"

"What about my brother?"

"Is he musical like you?"

"David? No. Told you, he ribs me for playing the violin. Tells me I'm a pansy for doing it."

"Not if you love it like you do. Seems to me that there ain't enough people around who love what they do."

"Thank you."

"Is he going to college?"

"Who? David? Uh-uh."

"Not college?"

"David didn't get the grades."

"Did you know your brother graduated from my alma mater?"

"Alma—?"

"Fancy for my old school, where I went."

"San Diego High?"

"That's where I went. San Diego High!" Graduated in '27."

"That's crazy!"

"Did your brother know your pal Christopher?"

"Not really. David might have seen Chris around at my school when he came by to take me home."

Pete caught the hesitation and prodded him to continue.

"I shouldn't flap on him, but to come clean, Officer McGraw, David didn't care much for Chris. He said he was a pansy."

"How come?"

"Well, Chris *was* somewhat of a crybaby, like I told you."

"Bully fodder," Pete mumbled under his breath.

"Huh? What'd you say?"

"Nothing. Well, some kids get picked on for not doing anything but being who they are. And the guys who pick on them are bullies. Sounds like your brother liked to pick on little kids. That right?" Jackie nodded. "Well, then go ahead with your story. How did your brother pick on Chris?"

"Well, David, he liked to tease him and make him cry. It was pretty easy to do it."

"Bullied the kid, that's what."

"Yeah. Guess you'd say that. Wasn't right."

"Darn tootin' it ain't. You didn't like it when David bullied you, did you now? Did you tell your mother about David picking on the little kid?"

"My ma didn't care one iota about it. She just said that it's a guy thing. I thought Dave was kind of a punk for picking on a little kid like that. And me too."

Pete took a long look at the boy. Jackie was a child who should be firmly protected. He was a gifted boy. How bullying by his brother might affect his unusual talent, Pete wondered.

He said: "Let's pull in that line and recast. See how the current has brought it close into shore? I think it needs to be recast farther out."

"Officer McGraw, did you really bring me out here to fish? Or did you want to ask me questions about Chris or my brother?"

"Well now, kid, you sure ain't a twit for a nine-year-old. You're right. I did bring you to ask you questions about Chris. And your brother, too." Jackie's face squeezed into a pout. "But I did want to fish, so I thought it might be a good thing to combine 'em. Here now, take this here pole and set it into the sand there where I dug it out before. That's good. Now that you asked, what can you tell me about Christopher that you think might help me in investigating how he died?"

"I told the coppers everything the last time."

"You mean at the station house."

"Yeah. And I don't want to talk about it now, either."

Pete looked at the youngster's alarmed but determined expression. "Okay," Pete said.

Together the man and the boy watched the ocean waves glisten as the sun moved west. They kept silent, standing with their shadows growing longer behind them and their feet sinking deeper into the sand. Anxious as he was to pursue his questioning of the boy, he'd steal glances at the boy's resolute face and know any more would push him further away from any possible openness. He thought about what he'd learned from Jackie so far. He knew that his brother was in with a ring of boys who attended San Diego High School, and he knew that Jackie was afraid of his older brother for bullying him. This older brother bullied Jackie's friend, too. Why? What kind of youth was David, anyhow? And Pete wanted to revisit the story about the two boys separating on the day Christopher disappeared. His gut told him there was much more to the story. And how did David factor in? No, Pete needed to be patient. Gain the nine-year-old's confidence. Pressing him any further that day would only turn the child against him.

"Okay, Jackie. We'll save this for another time. Why spoil a good fishing day, huh?"

"That's right."

The two fishermen rode back to Presidio Hill in silence. Every so often Pete would glance at Jackie, but the boy stared sullenly out the window. Pete tried to gain the boy's attention by whistling, but his mouth was dry and the tune wouldn't come.

When he drove up the drive to Jackie's house, Pete's car was besieged by Jackie's angry parents. They threatened a lawsuit for abducting their child, and claimed that taking him without their permission was kidnapping. They'd see to it that the law would strike him down for abuse of his power—

Pete just shrugged and put his auto into reverse and backed away. "It's my job," he said, half out of the window and half to himself.

Pete and Sera

MCGRAW'S STORY DWINDLED into a thoughtful silence. Sera took the hint that he was done for the day and began packing up her things. Just as she was about to close up her legal pad, her eyes fell on the name *David*, by which she had placed an asterisk.

"Did you ever get to question Jackie's brother, David?"

"Yes. We took David Cohn down to headquarters to interrogate him. He was a slippery one, that David. Joe and I badgered him for over seven hours, but we couldn't get anything out of him."

"What were your own personal impressions about David, then?"

"David was a manipulating son of a bitch. Everything Hulsizer hinted about him I believed. During the time we had him in for questioning, he had flares of anger that would have scared the gully-by-Jesus out of me if I were a nine-year-old like Jackie. David didn't come out and say it, but he showed such contempt for Christopher that it was obvious to me that he very well might have acted on it. He slipped through our fingers. We had him, and then we lost him. He may well have been the one who killed little Christopher. We'll never know."

"Did he have that 'off-center smile' that Stoogies saw in his vision?" Sera asked, half facetiously.

Pete didn't return her smile. "As I recall, he had a front tooth that caught his lip when he spoke. I never saw him smile, but it probably would have been off-center as Stoogies said."

"What happened to David?"

"We hadn't gotten very far in our questioning about his possible connections with Purdy and his involvement in the Abkhazian case when his attorney came into the picture and got us to release him. It wasn't long after that that David disappeared from San Diego altogether. Word was that he'd gone back to live with relatives in New Jersey or somewhere."

Sera

ONCE AGAIN IN Ichabod's den, I spun through reels of microfilm, made photocopies, and wrote notes of the events following the boy's death. As I read on, I was again struck by the sensationalism of news coverage. The story surrounding Christopher Abkhazian's death made front-page headlines with shockingly graphic articles and photographs.

Over the short period of two weeks, photographs alone captured the rise and fall of McGraw. At first his picture was a common sight on the front page of the newspaper, and no wonder he was a media favorite with his good looks and cocky smile. Officer McGraw was shown directing searchers at Balboa Park the day after the boy disappeared. In uniform, he towered over other men in the crowd, carrying a billy club, wearing an armed shoulder holster, and frowning imperiously. The next picture, taken July 23, was included in an "Extra" issue published on the day the boy's body was discovered floating in San Diego Bay. It showed McGraw shaking hands with Chief Doyle outside police headquarters. Its caption stated: *McGraw Takes Command of Abkhazian Homicide.* On July 31st, McGraw stood before a microphone with the call letters "KGB." The article described the contentious debate regarding jurisdictional policies of the police and the sheriff's departments. Then, as if a changed authority would bring faster results, finger pointing ensued and articles grew vicious. The "sluggardly investigation of Doyle's department" and McGraw's experience and competency were questioned. In response, Doyle published a chain of news releases describing wholesale detainment of "gangland thugs, sexual degenerates, vagrants, and hoboes," and boasting of "broad sweeps of human garbage, and wholesale arrests of *skin-ticklers*, bootleggers, gamblers, and prostitutes." Conservatism grew, and with it came vigilantism. Women's groups armed with pens publically broadcasted and blacklisted citizens by name as "known perverts living in our fair city."

On August 8, an article stating "Competency, Finally!" accompanied photographs of McGraw and Sheriff Carver. The article told about the transfer of the investigation from the San Diego Police Department to the San Diego Sheriff's Department. Sheriff Carver, immaculately uniformed, faced the camera with the same confident smile McGraw had shown earlier. Next to his picture, McGraw was photographed as he turned away from the camera with a dismissing wave. He was out of uniform, wearing a suit that looked baggy and wrinkled. Under McGraw's picture, the caption said simply: *Irish says: "I'm through!"*

One last photograph of Pete McGraw appeared. It was next to a regularly appearing gossip column, "Undercurrents." In it, Pete was caught with a "lady of the night" on his arm down in the Stingaree. *Is this San Diego's Valorous McGraw?* Its caption asked.

By three o'clock in the afternoon, my stamina was depleted. I sighed, stretched, put my things away, and turned off the viewer.

Once in the elevator, my finger paused over the second-floor button as I considered returning to the newsroom to check my messages. But when the elevator doors opened to sunshine flooding the lobby, there was no decision for me to make. We'd had so much rain and miserable weather that I wanted to enjoy what there was left of a beautiful day.

On impulse, I decided to drive to my "cave," pick up swim gear and my wet suit, then head over to the La Jolla Cove for a late-afternoon ocean swim. The sun set early, at about five o'clock. With the short-ened hours of daylight, getting into the water, doing a half-mile swim, and returning before the sun sank would become a race against time.

Walkers enjoying the break in the wet weather had amassed at the La Jolla promenade. I parked my car near the Children's Pool, about a quarter of a mile from the Cove, and jogged north on the sidewalk. Waves crashed into the rocks on the shore below, rising in Coke-bottle green translucency. Offshore Santa Ana winds tossed lacy veils of spray into the air from the peaks of the breaking waves.

The bulletin board on the lifeguard station at the Cove reported that visibility was thirty feet and swells were mounting at three to four feet. To me this report meant that swells would be gentle, and that using goggles, I might well be able to see as far as thirty feet down into the water.

I tucked my long hair into a bathing cap and put on my goggles. I reached down and slapped the cold water onto my face. Then I stepped into the water, slowly immersing myself to get used to the temperature, and shuffled my feet in the sand to avoid startling a bat ray. Pausing briefly before diving under the waves to begin the swim, I took note of my goal, the half-mile buoy; any obvious rip cur-rents; and the timing of the waves, which seemed to come in surges of seven. My wet suit kept my upper body warm, but my feet, legs, hands, and arms tingled from the cold water. Taking a deep breath, I tucked in my chin, stretched out, and dove into the surf.

Beyond the waves breaking into the cove, underwater was gen-tle, almost serene. Sea grasses tossed. Golden garibaldi, the gem-like California state marine fish, darted through the kelp, their fins flut-tering, their mouths gaping, and their black button eyes surveyed my monstrous body above. Silvery yellowtail swam in pairs. Schools of bullet-speedy sardines raced through the water, spewing billions of tiny bubbles. An occasional crab, its bulging eyes round with fear, scurried away from my shadow into protecting rocks and grass.

Farther out, the bottom fell away. Sea grass was replaced entirely by kelp beds. There, larger and darker shapes slid in and out of the kelp jungle. And there I swam with seals, with sea lions, and next to seagulls bobbing on the surface of the water.

The pace of my stroking took over, a sweet, hypnotic rhythm: left arm, elbow up, breathe, reach, pull; right arm, elbow up, breathe, reach, pull . . . Hearing nothing but the sound of my own breathing, the cawing of gulls, and the distant sound of waves breaking on the shore, fragments of conscious thoughts commonly stream through my mind. They come, these thoughts, uncensored and unfettered.

The perfect syncretism in all muscles, organs, and parts of the body as they were challenged to the task took me through the ocean's currents, between the imposing swells, and away from the safety of the land and toward my goal. With each stroke, the quarter-mile buoy grew in size as it got closer. Beyond it lay my goal, the half-mile buoy. I charted my progress by noting my relationship to the cliffs, the caves, and the mansions built into the rock high above the ocean. And the buoys.

The sun, now hovering on the horizon, had dulled the color of the water to a murky green. One by one, incandescent lights were turned on inside the homes. I decided to shorten my swim to the quarter-mile buoy as darkness was approaching rapidly.

Before I began my swim back to shore, having reached the buoy, I took a moment to float on my back and to absorb the exquisite beauty around me, to let the gentle swells rock me, and to admire a "V" formation of brown pelicans as they flew in perfect synchrony in the sky above me.

Floating on the water, my thoughts mish-mashed until they jumped to Pete McGraw, and I found myself smiling. It occurred to me then, that I'd begun to care for the old fellow. Ironically, the research I'd uncovered somewhat excited me. It seemed to support his claim of mismanaged justice and cover-up. I enjoyed McGraw's stories about San Diego during the Prohibition, hearing his tale of the Agua Caliente money heist, descriptions of bootleg whiskey, the Stingaree, Tijuana, and the rest. And the people involved in the investigation that McGraw had described to me were becoming real: the Abkhazian family, little Christopher, his minister father, and his beautiful mother, Catherine; the merchants in downtown San Diego that Pete and his partner, Joe, investigated; Yankee Bill at his water-front eatery and Stoogies with his vision; Dudley at the San Diego Zoo; and the Cohn family in their extravagant home on Presidio Hill. And there were the people I'd met in this short time while working the case—most of all Dr. Caswell, who had generously spent nearly an hour of his time sharing his medical knowledge with me, further supporting what Pete had to say. As I thought about Dr. Caswell, I felt a sudden nudge of insight. He'd said that he believed a cover-up had taken place in the murder investigation in 1933. Then he amended this belief to "No, *two* cover-ups." And with that thought, I flashed on the note, the telephone call, and my conversation with Richard, then turned over abruptly onto my stomach and began to swim back to shore with a sort of reserved urgency.

When I am swimming alone in the ocean, the thought of vulnerability crosses my mind. I realize that my strength and skills are absolutely worthless compared to the power of the ocean. Nature takes its course.

The bank of clouds was moving in and so was high tide. The moon was mounting over the La Jolla cityscape. Finally the ocean bottom rose, the darkness below became sand, the kelp disappeared, and the sportive schools of fish flashed in and out of willowy sea grass. At last, with a final spurt of energy, I stepped out of the water onto the sandy beach, ripped off my goggles, and pulled off my cap. I shook my long hair free and emptied the water from my ears and nose. I jogged up the cement steps to the park above, feeling as light as a feather from the elation of having completed my swim.

By the time I took off my wet suit and gathered my belongings, it had grown dusky. The yellow streetlights of Coast Boulevard had been turned on. The park was almost empty, with only a few scattered walkers. There were no voices, only the cawing of the gulls, the bleating of the seals, and the breaking of the surf.

After a warming shower at home, I considered taking in a couple of beers at the nearby Surf Rider, but then reconsidered, opting to stay at home where it was warm. My new plan was to watch a little television and read in bed. But that plan dissolved as I snuggled under the comforter on my *damn-ugly* futon. I fell asleep immediately.

Sera

IT WAS HALLOWEEN. San Diego goes absolutely stark-raving mad on Halloween!

I was goaded into renting a costume by my friends. When I finally got to Buffalo Breath which advertised an assortment of Halloween get-ups, the pickings were dismal, all that were left were mostly ghetto monster masks and witch costumes. Finally, under, duress, I chose a Snow White costume—the Disney version.

So I wore that *fugly* Snow White costume to work, and after work kept it on to meet my friends at the Surf Rider for a pizza-'n'-suds party. The place was hopping by the time I got there, packed with customers in all sorts of costumes. Thinking that it would be next to impossible to get to the bar to order a beer, I took a chair at a table where some of my friends were already seated. I laughed off their comments about Snow White and purity issues, ordered a beer from a waitress, and grabbed a slice of pizza from the pan already sitting on the table. I stayed there most of the night with people coming and going, and magically, my beer glass remained filled. I kept up a steady stream of conversation without paying attention to the amount I was drinking, until I felt the beginning of a pleasant alcoholic buzz.

Well into the evening, I hadn't noticed that around me the crowd had thinned. Only then did I realize that my table, which had been earlier filled with lively chatter, was now just two of us, and my companion was putting her jacket on to leave. It was time for me to leave, too. I didn't want to mess up my review which Richard had scheduled for the next day. I finished my beer, set it down resolutely on the table, stood up just as resolutely, and started to leave. But stopped. Missing my earlier alcoholic giddiness I gave in to impulse: "Just one more beer." And that would be all.

When Jake the bartender heard me order "Jus'n," he suggested in a light tone that I'd had enough to drink.

I laughed, and pointed at my chest. "*Moi?*"

Rolling his eyes at my inebriated flippancy, he asked if I'd eaten anything. I recalled all the pizzas around me, and having eaten only the single slice nearly nine hours earlier. "Order a burger or something to put in your stomach," he suggested, and even capped off his suggestion by offering to "put it on the house." I chuckled at his worry, which I called "brotherly," and declined.

"It's my job," he said with a shrug, shook his head doubtfully, and handed me a glass of water.

"Here's to Halloween!" A shrill female voice floated over the rest of the din in the place.

I turned to see a woman about my age seated next to me at the bar. She was smiling and holding her own beer glass up for a toast. We began a conversation of sorts and discovered we had a lot in common, as drunks usually do. Before long, we were discussing everything from men to the Persian Gulf and the war on drugs. Our voices pitched and fell as subjects changed. We disagreed and then agreed. We laughed, whispered, shouted, gestured, picked facts out of the air, hugged, and laughed some more. Drank some more, too.

Our mood of spontaneous congeniality was suddenly extinguished when a male voice unexpectedly intruded: "Have you two ladies solved all the problems of the world yet?"

As most of the patrons in the bar, he wore a Halloween mask. It obscured part of his face, but he had a remarkable smile and the whitest teeth I'd ever seen. Behind the mask, his jet eyes flashed playfully. Feeling "hidden" behind my black eye-mask and disguised as a chaste Snow White, I ran my eyes shamelessly over his tight jeans, firm upper body, and broad shoulders.

"And who might you be?" I asked, pushing my mask up and asking in a voice not Snow White-ish at all.

"Does this give my identity away?" He hissed, "*Spooooooooooo ooooon!*"

"The Tick!" I said and laughed outrageously.

As he moved closer so that one arm was on the bar and the other around my back I swallowed my objection.

"I've never seen you here before," I said into a fog of fragrance, beer breath, and sweat.

"That's because I've never been here before." His face was in mine and his arm was heavy on my shoulders.

"I'm sure I would remember you," I added, leaning away.

He laughed.

"Well, have you?" He asked both of us.

"Have we what?" My companion asked with a new edginess in her voice.

He leaned over me toward her. "Have you two solved the world's problems?"

"Not yet," I said.

His naughty-boy charm appealed to my alcohol-induced recklessness.

"Let me introduce myself," the stranger said. "I know who you are, of course."

"How do you know me?" ("How do" slipped from my mouth as "*Howju*").

He chuckled at my slurring and patted me on the shoulder. Flipping his hand and flashing that marvelous smile, he said, "Got my ways."

"I'll bet you do."

"May I buy you ladies a couple of beers?" he asked.

My companion declined, saying she had to leave. "Workday tomorrow, you know."

I cheerfully accepted his offer. "One last beer," I said, the second word sounding more like "latht."

I excused myself to go to the restroom. On the way, I felt a tug on my arm. My earlier companion stopped me. "Sera," she warned me, "something about that guy, just. . ."

I ignored her, and pulled my arm away. "I'm all right," I said laughing, and continued toward the restroom.

It wasn't long after I returned that Jake announced the last call.

"Well, that's my call, too," the stranger said.

I felt a rush of irrational disappointment.

He stood, fished in his pocket for change, and dropped it on the bar as a tip. "Good luck, Sera Schilling," he said, and swaggered to the exit.

Then he was gone.

I sat for a few minutes longer at the bar, feeling depersonalized and uninvolved. Voices and music in the bar mingled into incomprehensible babble. Earlier alcoholic effervescence had deadened. My gut was bloated. My head felt heavy. The minute I stood up, the room spun. I needed to take hold of the bar for balance.

Focusing on the red letters on the exit sign, I began to pick my way toward it, one step after the other, concentrating on a path through the tables and chairs. I steadied myself on furniture as I stumbled across the room.

The Surf Rider door slammed behind me and I staggered toward the street. Normally busy Mission Boulevard had little traffic at that late hour. Sick and dizzy, I collapsed on the curb. The earlier rain had left the roads wet and puddled. Mist fell, forming halos around the streetlights. A muddled confusion set in. The street I knew so well was unfamiliar. I pulled myself up and stood on the corner watching the traffic light change from red to green to yellow to red.

Once safely across Mission Boulevard, headed west towards what I hoped was the direction of my apartment, I slumped against the brick corner of a building, zapped of energy. How could I be lost in my own neighborhood? As I pushed away from the building, my stomach lurched and sour beer bubbled up. I gagged, rushed to the curb, and vomited into the gutter.

I looked like a wretched homeless person, stumbling along the dark street after two in the morning. Standing—falling—writhing—kneeling—wet, stringy hair, bruised and muddy. Sides of buildings held me up. The gutter was my toilet to blast vomit. Humped over the gutter, an ungainly heap of knees, legs, elbows, and shoulders. Fumbling around—for shoes and the contents of a spilt purse.

At long last, I finally—and miraculously—pulled myself up the steps to my apartment. At the door I stood wobbly, fumbling through my purse for a key.

Emptied the contents on the deck.

It wasn't there, my house key. I stood up and let out a loud yowl. I must have leaned against the door. It opened against my weight. I fell onto the floor. And there, I lost consciousness.

When I came to, I was shocked to find that I was in bed.

On my *damn-ugly* futon.

The morning sunlight rudely pouring through my one and only window awakened me.

I lay motionless. My head throbbed. My mouth tasted dry, and my stomach was acid raw. I gazed at the urine-yellow of the walls and the water-stained popcorn ceiling. I shivered from a sudden chill and ran my hands down my body.

My *nude* body.

Sickened, I screamed: "Stupid, *fucking* girl! You never even got his name."

I then forced memory through as much as I could recall about the night before. I concentrated on trying to put together the stranger's features—his face, his build, his voice. It struck me then, the scent of his aftershave.

I also recalled not being able to find my house key.

I sat up suddenly. How vulnerable I was without my key. I swung my legs over the side of the futon. My feet landed on fabric. I looked down between my knees and saw a pile of the clothes I had worn, including the now-ruined Snow White costume and my bra and panties. On top of the pile lay the key to the front door. Trembling and appalled, I reached down and picked up the key.

He was *fucking* playing with me.

Stumbling and tripping, I shot to the bathroom and dry heaved into the toilet.

After I'd regained some composure, I called 911. I was picked up by a policewoman connected with the rape clinic. I spent most of the rest of the day there. The good news was there wasn't any physical evidence that I had been raped. But the frightening awareness that my attack was connected with my work on the old case was driven home. How far would this person go to scare me off the case?

For once, the cool darkness of my apartment welcomed me. Stepping through the door, the scent hit me. It was faint, but it was there: L'Homme Men's Aftershave. I locked, relocked, and bolted the front door behind me. Then I sat on my futon, staring at the door.

Pete McGraw

THE BEAUTY OF the day pushed Pete outside. He opened the French doors and stood in the doorway admiring the rose garden that at one time Connie and he had lovingly cared for. After he'd been left alone, he made it his mission to keep it up, and he'd done this pretty well until he got cancer. Now, he seldom got out into the backyard, and the roses looked neglected in spite of their abundant flowers.

Pete knew his favorite rosebush was hidden by the others and planted in back, near the fence. Among her wealth of talents, Catherine was an enthusiastic amateur horticulturist. Before she and her family moved back east to Missouri, she gave Pete a slip from her own bush. She had grafted it before her son's death and fatefully named it "Blood Red Rose."

Funny that after all this time, at the end of his life, his thoughts kept returning to Catherine. Little things would send him down memory lane.

Pete now recalled a hot July day in the early days of his investigation.

He was standing on the porch outside the front door of the Abkhazian home. He hesitated before ringing the doorbell because somewhere in that dreary little bungalow somebody was playing the piano, and it would be a shame to interrupt that pretty music.

However, after a few minutes he pushed the button. The chimes responded. He waited, but still the door remained closed and the piano played on. Pete stood there wondering what he should do. Should he ring it again? Or should he leave and come back later? He had just turned to leave when he heard the bolt on the front door snap back. The door was opened a cautious crack, emitting the homey scent of seasonal strawberries being cooked into jam. He smiled genially at the partially exposed lined face of the elderly grandmother. He introduced himself, awkwardly remembering that neither grandparent spoke English. Seeing his uniform, she opened the door a little wider. Her dark eyes scrutinized him, conveying obvious contempt—not for the man, but his purpose. At long last she gestured him in. A small girl, whom McGraw knew was named Mary, hugged her grandmother's black wool skirt and looked up at the tall officer with large hazel eyes from beneath a halo of golden curls. The elderly woman pointed toward the living room and motioned at a chair for Pete to sit in.

Pete had decided earlier to take on the interrogation of Mrs. Abkhazian without his partner, Joe. Before coming to her home, he called the South Bay Baptist Church and inquired about Reverend Abkhazian. The reverend's secretary told Pete that Abkhazian would be in his study there for most of the day. Pete said he'd call back later, and timed this visit for when he was certain the husband wouldn't be at home. McGraw thought it would be far more productive to question Mrs. Abkhazian alone. He figured that mother's candid and uncensored answers might reveal a lot, because a mother knows her children inside and out.

And there was the other reason, the one that he wasn't sure he understood, the one that made him act almost bashful.

Now he was concerned that he wouldn't have courage enough to face her alone.

Before going to the door, Pete had walked the Abkhazians' property looking for evidence of a chicken coop. Most people kept chickens these days on their property for fresh meat and eggs. The Abkhazians were no different. They had a small coop at the far end of their backyard: a crudely built wooden structure with chicken wire over the windows and on the door. There were a few hens, a rooster, and several chicks. They were Bantams, not Rhode Island Reds like the feather that he'd found in the boy's shoe.

Leaving the coop he inspected the walls of the house, looking for evidence of a freshly painted surface. He examined the concrete patio and the grass for white paint spatters, but found nothing.

He also checked out the trees growing in the backyard. Were there any Monterey pines, like the pine needle swept from the boy's mouth? The landscaping contained mostly bushes neatly pruned along the property line for privacy, and then some shrubbery. But no, no Monterey pines.

A small kitchen garden was in a far corner of the backyard, its rows well-tended, soil dark with compost and vegetables lush with summer growth. There was a small rose garden in the opposite corner of the yard. Its flowers were abundant and colorful.

All that he saw indicated a woman's touch. Nothing showed neglect or abuse. This was a household, Pete figured, run with maternal supervision. It wasn't a scene that a police officer would connect to such a horrific crime.

Pete took the designated chair in the living room. He winked at the little girl as she continued to stare at him while sucking her thumb and hiding behind her grandmother's skirt. Eventually they returned to the kitchen, leaving Pete to sit quietly.

Alone he watched Mrs. Abkhazian at the piano. Her back was to him; she was oblivious to his presence in the room.

Pete listened to the deep running chords and racing melody. Her fingers moved lightly across the keys, yet they produced a voluminous sound. Occasionally she'd stop and would repeat a phrase over and over until she seemed satisfied. She'd then continue. When she reached the end, she'd sigh and flip the pages of the music back to the beginning. Once more she'd start. She did this a number of times, and each time, to Pete's ears, it sounded as beautiful as before.

Finally she sat back onto the piano bench and relaxed into a slump. She lifted her hands and played the last chord once again. Its full sound faded into silence. Then she shut the music. Pete watched her stand and gaze sadly out the window. The morning sun fell upon her face, lighting her profile and illumining her sharp features.

Then she sobbed deeply into her hands. Her body, racked by this emotional outburst, shook violently. She collapsed back onto the piano bench.

Pete awkwardly picked at the band of his cap that lay in his lap. He didn't want to breathe; he didn't want to make a sound. He wished he hadn't come. He felt intrusive and terribly awkward. And unseasoned for this sort of thing. He had the impulse to rush out of the house before she realized that he was there. But Pete was a cop. This was his job. So he sat, conflicted and frozen by indecision.

She sighed again, cried again, groaned again, and slammed the keyboard cover shut, making the piano wires respond with a cacophonous chord.

He cleared his throat to announce his presence.

Catherine Abkhazian turned in astonishment. Her hand went to her throat. She let it fall into her lap.

"How long have you been here?"

"Not long. A few minutes, that's all," he hedged.

"I didn't hear you come in." She reached into her apron pocket and withdrew a hanky, blew her nose, and mumbled an apology.

"I can come back—" he began, but stopped as she held up her hand and shook her head.

Pete re-introduced himself.

"Of course I remember you, but you probably should just ask Adam all the questions you need to ask. I don't think I can be of much help. I'm—I'm not myself, I'm afraid."

"I actually needed to ask you some questions without your husband here, but if this isn't a good time—"

"No. It's all right, Officer. Please sit down. I'm practicing for a recital that's coming up. I'm playing this piece with the symphony. I've been having difficulty with a particular section. I think I got it, though." A small smile.

"I'm afraid I don't know much about music, but I enjoyed listening to you." His words sounded dumb.

"Thank you."

"Do you mind me asking what—what were you playing just now?"

"'Moonlight Sonata.'" She smiled. This time it was a little wider. "It is beautiful. It's very healing. It's by Beethoven, you know." Her face was mottled, her cheeks were flushed, and her eyes were rimmed with red.

"I've heard of Beethoven, of course. But that—I think I never heard anything so pretty, Mrs. Abkhazian."

She didn't answer. She lowered her gaze and thoughtfully ran her fingers through her hair.

He cleared his throat, pulled his notebook from his pocket, and brought out a pencil. "Mrs. Abkhazian, a few questions?"

"Please don't be so formal. Call me by my Christian name. It's Catherine. You want to know about Chris," she stated evenly. She pressed her handkerchief to her eyes, her nose, and was silent for what seemed a long time. "I am so sorry, Officer McGraw. Let me continue. This is the first time I've been able to sit down at the piano since . . . I thought it would—I don't know, I thought it might ease some of the pain. For me, beautiful music usually does, but . . . Oh, God! This has been the longest week." Her voice became husky. "Officer McGraw, I simply can't bear the emptiness. Everybody talks *around* my son, Chris. They avoid mentioning his name. *Phush!* Into the ground." She spat out the words. "And he's gone forever." She wrapped her arms around herself and rocked back and forth on the piano bench. "Oh dear. Please forgive me.

I just can't stop crying. It's unbearable to be so, so *alone.* With nobody to talk to."

She saw him begin to rise from the chair once again. "No, Officer McGraw. Please don't leave. It might feel good to talk about Christopher. My in-laws don't speak much English and I speak only a little Armenian. My husband, Adam—well, he has his faith, his church, his convictions. He's a very self-contained man. My parents are dead, and my only sister lives up in Pasadena. She has problems of her own. It's just so frightfully *lonesome.* With nobody talking about him, it's as if he never existed. Like he was never born." Her eyes filled up again. She sobbed into her handkerchief while holding up the other hand motioning for him to wait. Again she seemed to command self-discipline. Her voice was clouded. "Tell me, has anything new developed in the investigation?"

"In spite of what the newspaper is saying, Mrs. Abkhazian, we are making progress. I'm checking on some leads later today. They seem pretty solid. We'll get the culprit. Don't you worry."

She nodded and dabbed her eyes once more, folded the handkerchief, and put it back into her apron pocket. "Now then, how may I help you, Officer?"

She had nothing to add to her husband's previous statement about the day Christopher disappeared. "This was the first summer that Chris actually wanted to come downtown with us instead of staying home with his grandparents. He discovered Hubble's hobby shop, across the street from our shop.

"And with his love of airplanes, Martin Hubble introduced him to model airplane kits. Chris spent every free minute over there." She smiled slightly with the memory. "How he'd nag us about wanting to buy this or that kit! Come, I'll show you his room. You'll see how he loved making those model airplanes. He finished quite a few of them. He earned his own money to buy the kits. When my husband saw how much Christopher enjoyed this hobby, he began paying him a small allowance for helping us out at the store—a little bit here and there, a few cents to sweep the floors, a nickel to run a downtown delivery, some change to help at the front counter, and so on. Mr. Hubble also had him working around his shop to earn some change.

"Another thing that drew him to downtown this summer was his playmate. Quite by accident, he ran into Jackie Cohn, who was a student with Chris at Mountain View Elementary.

"Like Chris, Jackie also came downtown frequently during the summer holidays with his parents. Have you spoken with Jackie? Have you had a chance to ask him what happened that day, Officer?"

Pete looked up from his notebook into her anxious face. He assured her that he had spoken with Jackie and that he wasn't finished questioning him.

She nodded. "He's a good one to question." She sighed and continued. "Summer days when he had free time, Christopher enjoyed exploring downtown with Jackie.

"That day was unusual in that we needed Christopher to look after Albert and Mary. Chris never minded keeping an eye on them. He actually enjoyed being with his younger siblings, and they loved Chris." She shook her head sadly. "But Tuesday was different. I should have put the brakes on those boys, because from the very beginning it was an odd day. When Jackie came bursting into the shop, Christopher was just eating his breakfast in the back with the little ones. He came running out with Jackie, yelling about going to see where the robbery had taken place. I should have told him right then and there to stay. But Adam and I were preoccupied and let them leave without hearing their plans. Adam grumbled all morning about Chris's irresponsibility in leaving his younger siblings. He told me he was going to give Chris the strap when he returned for lunch. But he never came back . . . Oh!"

She trembled.

"Was he flighty?"

"No. Dependable."

"A discipline problem?"

"Not usually."

"Who disciplined him, you or your husband?"

"Discipline was my husband's responsibility. Adam strictly adheres to the Watson method."

With Pete's blank look, Catherine added: "Watson—strict discipline and rewards for good behavior."

"Okay."

"He says that I'm overly protective, that I do too much mothering in an overbearing way. Adam blames me for Chris's sensitive nature. Says I'm turning him into a softie."

"How did your husband discipline Christopher when he needed to?"

"How?"

"You said he was going to get the 'strap.'"

"Oh, that. Only on occasion. And only this year. It was an especially difficult one for Chris. Now, let me take you to Chris's room. I think it might help you understand our boy." She bent, turned, and moved the piano bench back under the piano keyboard.

How tiny she is, Pete thought, following her down the hallway wards the bedrooms. She left a fragrant wake, not perfume. Her h scent. This gave Pete a heady feeling. He was perplexed by confusion of feelings—something in between admiration and usal.

Christopher shared his bedroom with his infant brother, Albert. It a very small room, with a crib and twin bed nearly filling it. The s were painted blue. Window curtains were closed, but the morn- un pushed through the blue cotton fabric, giving an icy, opaque d to the room and a blue cast to Catherine's face, making Pete think of Balboa Park's marble statues.

She directed Pete's attention to how Chris had decorated his side of the bedroom with several model airplanes hanging by strings from the ceiling over his bed. The soft breeze, blowing through the open window, made them swing and gently knock into each other. There were other carefully assembled model airplanes on display on top of his small bookcase.

She then drew Pete's attention to the drawings Christopher had taped to the walls. Pete had to agree that the drawings were fairly good for a seven-year-old, especially the attention to detail he had taken to make the airplanes appear quite realistic.

Pete sensed that she grew more relaxed just by being in her son's room. Just picking up objects and holding them to her breast as she commented seemed to calm her. She would hold them under her nose and inhale, sniffing them intimately, and then she put them back with such tenderness that Pete had to suck in his own breath. She sat on the edge of the boy's small bed.

"One of Chris's favorite heroes was Charles Lindbergh. Most boys want to be firemen. Chris wanted to be a pilot when he grew up." She laughed, and then stopped. Her face turned rigid. "Oh my God!" she blurted, putting her hand to her chest.

"What?"

"Lindbergh's son was kidnapped. You don't think that our son was—" Her voice fell.

"We haven't seen any evidence to support it as a motive in your son's death. No ransom. No telephone calls. No notes. But, we're looking at all angles," the young officer soothed. He picked up one of Chris's models, commented on its fine workmanship, and put it back into its proper space.

"Mrs. Abkhazian?"

She looked up at him through eyes glistening with unspent tears.

"Please go on about Christopher's normal activities during summer holidays." He consulted his notebook. "You were saying how he loved going to the airfield. I understand that he went alone to the zoo and the playground at the park. He would take the streetcars by himself?"

"Yes. The city was his playground during the summer holidays this year. It was the first year we allowed him to take the streetcar on his own up to Balboa Park, to the zoo and the Pepper Grove. Since he earned the nickel for the ride and the quarter he needed for admission to the zoo, Adam felt he deserved some freedom. We always knew where he was going and when he was going to return. We knew which streetcar to expect him to return on.

"The zookeeper took him under his wing, so to speak. He seemed to take a special interest in our son."

"Mr. Dudley? I know him very well and spoke to him earlier."

"Christopher said he would let him in for a penny so he could use the rest of his money to buy an ice-cream cone or candy apple. Or, ride the merry-go-round for the gold ring. This was the first summer he could reach the gold ring."

Pete smiled, remembering his own childhood. What a prize the three-inch gold ring was to a boy Chris's age! Really gilded lead, it awarded a free merry-go-round ride to the customer who pulled it from the dispenser, changing its value from worthless to priceless.

"Did Chris fish?"

She nodded. "Jackie and he went fishing once or twice down on the piers of the bay. But oh boy! Did Adam put a stop to that when he heard! Sat Chris down and told him in no uncertain terms that the waterfront was off limits. You know why, of course."

Pete nodded. "There are some ruffians down there. Could Chris have gone to San Diego Bay that day to fish with Jackie?"

"No. absolutely not."

"And your husband agrees with you?"

"Yes. Chris knew his boundaries. He wouldn't have disobeyed his father on this."

"Could Christopher have visited one of his school chums on the day he disappeared?"

She shook her head. "Chris didn't see a lot of his school friends this summer. We couldn't take Chris to play at their homes. We were too busy with the shop, kids, church activities, and home responsibilities to have them at ours."

"And he couldn't go to their homes by streetcar? Or they to meet up with him?"

"Streetcars aren't always convenient to where these boys live. No. He had little to do this summer with his school mates."

"What do you know about Jackie Cohn?"

"I don't know very much about Jackie, to be perfectly frank, except that he was just someone for Chris to spend time with while he was downtown. Oh, one thing: Jackie's a prodigy on the violin. When Jackie heard that I am a musician, we had some of the most interesting, very mature conversations. Those times, Jackie made me feel like I was talking to an adult, not a nine-year-old boy."

"Mr. Hulsizer told me something to that effect. He also said the Cohns were very influential people in their community. Have you met Jackie's parents?"

"No. I did speak to Jackie's mother once or twice on the telephone. The first time I saw them was at the funeral. We didn't have an opportunity to speak; someone pointed them out to me.

"Both Adam and I thought Jackie seemed like a nice boy, judging from the times he'd been at the shop to call on Christopher. He was very polite. Called Adam 'Sir' and shook his hand. A good, square handshake for a little boy, Adam said. He dressed neatly. He was a little bit older than Chris. As much as I hate to admit it, because of Adam's and my absorption in the shop and all our other responsibilities, we unintentionally pushed some of our responsibility of Chris onto Jackie since he was a little older and bigger. If that isn't ironic that my son was in Jackie's company when he disappeared, and all along we thought Jackie would keep Chris out of trouble."

"I told you that I've a mind to bring Jackie downtown for re-questioning. I have a hunch that he might know just a little bit more than he has let on."

"Now, Officer McGraw, what does a nine-year-old child know about such things? How can the police do something as outrageous as hold a mere child for questioning, as though he were a hardened criminal?"

"He might be a kid, Catherine, but he also might be a witness or worse. We can leave no stones unturned."

She shook her head violently, shaking off the thought. "All of this is so horrible. It's so loathsome, despicable! The thought of bringing a youngster into it is appalling." She looked at Pete, then lowered her gaze.

"But we have to do it, as difficult as it is and sounds." Pete cleared his throat and asked, "While we're on the subject of Jackie Cohn, did you ever meet his older brother, David?"

She looked up suddenly, startled. "No. I didn't know he had a brother," she replied.

"He just graduated from high school, I understand."

"San Diego High School?" She spat.

"Yes, what of it?"

"School was difficult for Christopher," the mother replied evasively.

"He attended Mountain View Elementary School, didn't he?"

"Yes."

"He was in the first grade, for the gods' sake. How could school be difficult for such a little boy?" Pete let the question ride. In the silence that followed, he tried to connect Catherine's reaction to San Diego High School and her dead son. He asked gently: "Was there trouble with someone from San Diego High?"

"Yes. There was trouble. What I believe was the cause of Christopher's decline was that there was someone that I believe was a student at the high school who picked on my son without mercy.

"Even though I was his mother, I saw Chris for what he was. He was a quiet child, an artist, and a different sort of a boy than the rest. He wasn't a boy's boy, if you know what I mean. Not into sports. Nor Scouts. Seldom soiled his clothing with rough play. I'm afraid Adam might have been right when he accused me of making my son into a momma's boy. Chris was sweeter and gentler than most boys his age. That's the reason, I should believe, that he'd be picked on by others." She paused and then added, "And of course the other."

"The other? Another reason?"

She nodded dimly.

"What reason?"

"The fact that my husband is Armenian. That we've a mixed marriage. Chris told me one time that he was called a mulatto and wanted to know what it meant.

"Then there were the pictures Chris found in his school desk. They were crude, stick figures drawn to represent . . . I supposed they were representations of our family. You can imagine them. Kid stuff. I told Chris to not mind them. They revealed someone's ignorance."

"Did you keep these pictures?"

"Of course not! I tore them up in front of Chris's eyes and threw them away. Chris was just too young to understand racism in its complexity."

"I see." Pete looked up from his note-taking and searched her face. "So you think he might have been picked on for his softer personality and also being a child of a mixed marriage."

"Yes, unfortunately, but I don't think it came from school chums his age. I believe it was an older youth."

"What about Jackie Cohn? He was a couple of years older than Chris. Could he have been the artist?"

"Jackie is Jewish. If anyone would understand the pain of racism, I should think it would have been Jackie."

"Back to Christopher's bullying. What did this ruffian do to Christopher?"

"Teased him brutally. Beat him up. He came home from school one day with his shirt ripped, a split lip, and a bruise on his cheek. Other days he came home holding back the tears. He didn't want me to know, but he couldn't keep it from me. I went to the school and talked with his teacher . . ."

"His teacher's name?"

"Mrs. Evans. She was no help at all. So I went to talk with the principals of Christopher's school and San Diego High."

"Did they give you the name of the boy who picked on him?"

"No, Officer, they did not. McMurty was closed mouthed and sent me to Dr. De Witt at the high school. He told me that he had taken care of the issue. He knew the boy's family. It was a good family, he said. He said he personally telephoned and spoke to the father and was confident the problem was solved." She seemed unaware that as she spoke, she was pounding the bed next to where she sat with a tightly clenched fist. "It was his condescending, ingratiating, and smug manner—like he was looking down his nose at me. He's a tall man, as you know—"

In spite of himself, Pete chuckled. "I used to believe that, but not anymore."

Catherine smiled. "Yes. He wouldn't dare talk down his nose at you now. But when he said to me, 'Mrs. Abkhazian, you know all stories have two sides,'" she mimicked his voice, "I was fit to be tied. I demanded to know the name of the boy, but he didn't budge. He just shook his head and said he was in a bind. It was his responsibility to protect the rights of minor children." She paused and took a deep breath. "He ushered me out of his office as though *I* were a misbehaving student. As I got to the door, I screamed at him: 'And what about protecting *my seven-year-old child?*'

"When I told Adam about my meeting with the principals, he said he was both surprised and concerned about their indifference to our concerns, but he stopped there." She saw disbelief on Pete's face, and added: "You've got to understand my husband, Officer McGraw. He is a quiet man, a peaceful man. He tends to hold things inside. Frankly, he has the stoicism that I've tried to adopt. I have ached— Oh! I've ached— my broken heart—enough about that."

Pete found he was staring into Catherine's eyes. He fought an impulse to take her into his arms, to hold and comfort her. He turned his eyes away from her face, toward the window. Watched the breezes riffle the curtain. Then he focused on his notebook, the notes he was taking, added a caption: "Christopher's Bully," and asked, "When did these bullying incidents occur?"

"This past school year."

"Yes, I understand that, but I mean, was it happening all year, or during the spring, winter, fall? Beginning, middle, or end of the year?"

"It was toward the end of the school year. Late spring is when I became aware of it."

"One time? Several times? Ongoing? How many times would you say that Christopher was targeted by this older boy?"

"It was more than a few times. More than once did he come home after school with bruises. It seemed to occur when he walked to and from school in the morning and after school when there was nobody was with him."

"Did the bullying stop as the principal told you it would because the problem was taken care of?"

She sighed heavily. "It stopped because the school year ended."

Pete made a note to question Christopher's teacher, who might be more open than De Witt.

Pete and Catherine fell into an uncomfortable silence. Still sitting on the edge of Christopher's bed, she gazed up at the tall, burly cop with such open vulnerability that he had to look away.

He took a minute to examine his notebook and pencil stub, then said: "I need to question everyone, whether immediately or distantly involved in your family's life. Can you think of someone—an adult—who might have established a closer-than-normal relationship with Christopher? Think about it, please. As difficult as the thought might be, is there someone you might have thought acted a little off-kilter? Someone who might have ignited in you that spark of instinct that things were not quite right—some male who might have acted overly friendly?"

She shook her head. "No. Nobody like that."

"You might think of someone after I leave. If you do, would you please call me? And certainly, that older student—I will find out who he is. Chase him down and see for myself if there's any connection. Trust me."

"Oh, I do." She shivered and ran her hands up and down her bare arms. "Is it cold in here?"

"No. It's actually quite pleasant, with the breeze and all."

"I just felt a draft."

Pete reached over and shut the window. She smiled and thanked him.

"Has your husband shown any new or different behaviors that concern you since your boy died?"

"If anything, my husband has become more fervent about religion."

When he shook Catherine's hand at the door, he noticed that he held on longer than necessary and she didn't seem to object. He looked down and saw her unlined and perfect hand in his muscled, square, blunt, masculine hand.

Her dark eyes searched his face hopefully. He smiled and made a silent commitment. For Catherine and nothing else, not for prestige, not for notoriety, not for a salary increase, not even for Connie, he would pursue this case until he couldn't go any further, to get all questions answered, to ultimately put the woman's beloved son to rest.

He disengaged, replaced his cap, and took his leave as smoothly as he could.

Pete left the woman standing alone on the front stoop of her little house. Her daughter, Mary, had come to stand next to her. Together they watched Pete drive away. When he turned the corner and headed down University Avenue, he saw that they were still standing there.

• • •

He checked the address he'd written down in his police journal after the Abkhazian visit and turned north on Hamilton. He parked his car in front of a small home surrounded by a white-gone-to-black picket fence. A small boundary garden was tucked just inside the fence. Weeds thrived in the clay soil, while plantings were scrubby and brittle. A woman was on her hands and knees, using her trowel energetically, trying without much success to break up the hardpan. He called out her name, and she raised her head, smiled, and stood, affirming that yes, she was indeed Mrs. Evans. She pulled off her gardening gloves and tossed them and the trowel into the little wooden box that held her supplies. It was painted green, with stenciled yellow and white flowers on it.

"Whew! It's hot. And that's impossible work! You're here about Christopher, I presume. I've been expecting someone from the police to come."

For a second time that day, he introduced himself and his purpose. She nodded and led him up onto the front porch, where she motioned for him to take a seat. He sat back into the wooden Adirondack chair, removed his hat, and placed it on the nearby beverage table. Mrs. Evans took the other chair and smiled earnestly at him.

Her candid and sincere countenance gave Pete no reason to use small talk by way of an introduction. "To get right to the point, Mrs. Evans," he said, quite brashly, "did you know that Chris had been assaulted by an older and bigger student from the high school on his way to or from school throughout the fourth quarter of last year, when he was your student? I'm looking for his name."

He immediately regretted the harshness of the tone of his voice when he saw the effect it had on her. She shuddered visibly, then pushed herself out of the chair and smiled a bit too cheerily at him.

"I was just about ready to take a break and get myself a glass of iced tea, Officer McGraw." She fanned her face with her hand. "Would you like one, too? It's a hot day. I suspect it would taste good. It's already steeped. I only need to pour it." And she was gone, leaving Pete wondering how to make a fresh start.

He wiped his forehead and neck with his handkerchief. Sweat coursed down his back.

From inside the house were the familiar sounds of chipping at the block of ice, the clink of glassware, and the opening and closing of the icebox door. These comforting, homey sounds inside were joined by a combination of familial noises and voices coming from the small homes up and down the street. This was the music of summer: kids' high-pitched voices shouting in play, dogs yapping, screen doors banging, and neighborly greetings called through opened windows. His eyes followed the sounds from house to house.

In his police uniform, Pete felt a stranger to neighborhoods like this, filled with innocence and joviality. Until his promotion, Pete spent late hours, night after night, pounding the pavement down in the decadent Stingaree. Abhorrent as he found some things in San Diego's Stingaree, it enticed him. There, shadows slithered, music was raucous, smiles offered schemes and promises, and alluring and tender arms were easily procured.

Behind him, the screen door whined open and slapped shut. Mrs. Evans held out a glass for him and sat down again.

He started over. This time, he began by circumventing the subject he'd introduced earlier that had caused such jolting negativity. Rather, he directed questions to her experience as Christopher's teacher, to get her opinion of the boy. And so, methodically and professionally, he let the teacher describe Christopher as a nice boy to have in class, always very polite and respectful, always tidy and immaculately dressed. "This is most unusual for boys that age, don't you know?" The boy was punctual, responsible, and thorough in his homework. He was a quiet boy, and apt to be shy when he was among his peers.

As she continued to describe her former student, the words spilled faster and more emphatically. She noticeably relaxed, her eyes grew misty and took on a faraway look.

She'd never had such an industrious, compliant student. And she never thought she would have occasion to worry about him. But worry about him she did.

As the year progressed, she noticed a change taking place in Christopher. This change affected his work, his attitude, and his interaction with other students. His confidence seemed to erode. His smile became a scowl. His homework was sloppy or left unfinished. He became reticent in class. He stumbled on words when he read. She, anguished at the boy's new insecurity stopped calling on him.

His personal appearance started declining as well. Before, he'd had starched and ironed clothing; his parents had a cleaning store, didn't Pete know? Later in the year he'd show up at school with wrinkled and half-untucked shirts. "Yes," the teacher concluded. "You're entirely correct. The boy changed a lot during the year."

"Was he bruised?"

"Yes. I'm afraid I saw bruises. I'm ashamed I did so little about them, too."

"Did you think there was a problem at home?"

"No. Not in that family."

"Bullying student?"

"Yes."

"Did you try to find out who it was?"

"I think I knew."

"Name, Mrs. Evans. I need a name."

"No."

"No?"

"No? There are two reasons, officer. The first is that they were not students at my school and I only know of them by reputation."

"They? Them?"

"Yes, there's a ring of troublemakers we've been aware of."

"Who is in this gang?" Pete asked, his heart jumping.

She shook her head slowly. "Dr. De Witt, the high school principal, probably would give you their names for your investigation. I can't."

"Who happens to be camping somewhere in the mountains."

She shrugged. "I'm sorry. But you would have to speak with him to get the names. I live alone here, you have to understand, and—"

"I understand, Mrs. Evans, and the police department can pro-tect you from them. But it's one of your student's whose murder I am investigating. You may hold the key I need. Your information would be invaluable. If necessary I can subpoena you and bring you down to police headquarters to question you under oath. Knowing the way the blat has handled this case so far, they'd get wind of this and your name would be plastered on the front page of the paper. This way we could do it quietly, secretly, and nobody would have to know."

The woman's face turned scarlet. Her eyes filled with tears. "Then, by force it will have to be," she said through braced lips.

"Madam, let me warn you: the law can be pretty heavy-handed."

The teacher studied her hands as she shook her head slowly. With a deep sigh, she said, "I am so sorry."

Pete tore a page from his notebook and wrote his name and the department phone number on it.

"I need for you to call me," he said as he watched her fold it up and put it in the pocket of her housedress. "I need for you to give me the names of the bullies who picked on Christopher."

Suddenly the cacophony of friendly neighborhood noises that he'd earlier enjoyed struck a nerve. He saw the teacher's determined expression and knew he couldn't get anywhere by continuing this tea party. Not today. He handed her his empty glass and stood up to tower over her. When she looked up at him, she needed to shield her eyes against the sun. He wanted her to be aware of his height. He wanted her intimidated by him. He wanted her to fear him if she didn't respond to his questions. And he knew she was unnerved by him because she averted her eyes suddenly, crossed her arms against her chest, and looked at the floor. She'd built a wall; she'd drawn into herself.

"Mrs. Evans, school ethics is one thing, but a court of law is another. You've got to trust me on this. When I became a cop, I took an oath of office to defend and protect. I'm not here to ambush you, but damn, lady! If you've got information, we need to have it to get to the bottom of this crime. You can say I am the muscle of the court of law. Anything you tell me may help us bring in the culprit who took the life of a seven-year-old child.

"Think about it! Christopher Abkhazian, Miss Evans, your student, the boy you loved and cared for, who was cruelly attacked and coldly murdered and tossed into the waters of the San Diego Bay like a bag of garbage. This is no kidding, lady. If you know anything, I am asking you one more time to tell me so that we can get the culprit or culprits who brutalized that child."

She faltered. "I'm so confused; I don't know what to do."

"There is only one thing for you to do, and that is to talk to me. A homicide investigation works against the clock, Miss Evans. Already too much time has passed. We have few if any real leads, so we need to depend on word of mouth. You can see how important it is for us to question anybody who you think might have victimized Chris. Though they might be innocent, they might have something to say that would shed some light on my investigation."

She stood and nodded. "I'll think it over. That's what I'll do." And then she retreated into her house. The whining screen door slammed with a bang.

Pete McGraw's Story

THE DAY HAD started pretty normally. Early on, full of ambition, on that sunshiny bright morning of the day of surprises, Pete had pulled his car into his parking spot, the one with the sign marked "Chief Detective, Peter McGraw," in front of the station house. He yanked the brake and shut off the engine. Full of ideas to work on the Abkhazian case that day, Pete nearly leapt from the car in a hurry to share these with his boss.

But inside, when he caught Myrtle's sour expression, Pete knew that things weren't quite as bright as they felt outside. Myrtle, who never was without a yarn to tell, frowned at Pete, made a puzzling sound, and spun around to face the switchboard, turning her back on him. He shrugged and filed through the messages left in his pigeonhole. Glancing at the telephone operator's back, he shrugged once more and began to walk down the hall to the chief's office. Her voice stopped him. "You in a hurry or something?"

"Yup. I've got to see the chief."

"He is in, but you better hold your horses. Sheriff Carver's in there now talking with him."

Pete's heart fell. It was happening. "It's about my case. I'm going back there to join their little meeting."

"Oh, I don't think—" Myrtle cautioned as she turned around, but he was already trotting down the hall.

Pete pushed the door open and stood in the doorway, waiting to be acknowledged. Sheriff Carver, a brawny man who stood well over six feet, and one of his senior officers were standing in front of the chief's desk and were addressing Doyle, voices rough and assertive. Pete felt a wave of embarrassment about his chief, who, dwarfed by their sizes, was looking up over his thick glasses to meet their eyes. They wore their uniforms, held their caps at their waists, and stood at relaxed attention: feet splayed, and bodies straight as rods. Chief Doyle, in contrast, was dressed in street clothes. He wore a pinstriped suit, a white shirt, and a bow tie. His ruddy face, mottled by frustration and anger, poked out from between his rounded shoulders as he leaned onto his desk, looking up at the two with obvious dismay.

"They've lost patience!" Sheriff Carver drawled, his words coming slowly and deliberately.

"We're making progress, by damn!" the chief shot back. "Come, in Pete," he said, not taking his eyes from the sheriff and motioning Pete into the office with his hand. "See here? This man is the best in our department, and he's the best man for the job, Carver." The chief nodded toward Pete. "Pete McGraw, Chief Detective of the Christopher Abkhazian homicide—Sheriff Carver." They shook hands. Head to head in height, Pete regarded the older man evenly.

Carver smiled. "We've already met, haven't we, Irish?"

The chief ambled around his desk to Pete and punched him jovially in the arm. "Can your department boast of a Medal of Valor recipient? Can you provide the city with a legacy of police work the likes of which this young cop sprang from? Did you know Pete's dad?"

"Yes, of course I knew him. Not personally, though. His reputation preceded him. Our town lost a good man when your old man passed, son. What was that? A year or so ago?"

"1930, sir," Pete answered somberly.

"No joke. Three years already." He snapped his fingers. "And gone like that. He was a darn good cop, son. The best of the best. Unflappable and aggressive."

"That's right," the chief responded. "And don't you forget it, either! And including this officer here, we've got many damn good coppers in our department. We are committed to getting to the bottom of the case."

"Nah." The sheriff shook his head slowly. "Already there's too much water spilt over the dam, Al. Everybody knows that. Didn't you read the editorial in the newspaper today?"

"Yes, but we've been keeping something under wraps, haven't we, Pete."

"We have, sir," Pete responded eagerly, though he was unsure about what *something* Doyle meant.

"Oh, and what's that?" the sheriff asked cagily.

Doyle and McGraw exchanged glances. Pete spoke: "We are keeping our eyes on a key suspect."

"I thought he already went back to Oakland."

"This is another suspect." Pete mumbled, weakly.

The sheriff hooted loudly and turned his attention to the chief. "You've got *nada. Zilch!*" Watching Doyle's face color in embarrassment made Carver laugh long and hard. "Anyhow," he said finally, regaining professional composure, you've read the paper. You saw that there is a tidal wave of people thinking like we do, that it likely isn't a homicide."

"Who gives a flying rat's ass what the public sentiment might be?" Doyle flared. "Public moods wax and wane. Remember, our investigation is based on the medical examination of doctors and the verdict of a coroner's jury."

"We intend to exhume the body and run another examination."

Pete blurted: "That is unnecessary, Sheriff. Hell, you can't get more professional than the team of docs who did the first one.

Flat-out homicide. That's what they judged. Any further examination of the boy is morbid. That family has been through enough as it is."

Carver simply shrugged in response. "San Diegans have been frightened by gossip and scuttlebutt long enough. Now it's time to take new control and bring a little truth and reason back to our city."

But McGraw wouldn't have it. "And you think that publishing the transcript of your detective's interrogation of the boy, Jackie Cohn, is a way of calming people down? This should never have been published in the paper, Carver. Jackie is just a nine-year-old boy. Nothing he said has been verified. Remember, we questioned the boy ourselves. The story he told us was entirely different."

Doyle nodded. "It was rash for the paper to print it."

Carver responded, speaking evenly and slowly. "Since it was taken from a certified court reporter's transcript, word-for-word, it was about as accurate as it could be." The sheriff hesitated then went on: "Listen, Al, you've read those letters to the editor. Right or wrong, there's been speculation about your real motives in blowing this case up. You're too new in the town for anyone to have a good take on you. I know you came here with a good reputation. You've worked too hard to be discredited by mob mentality. But they might hang you out to dry if they think you might be making more of this boy's death by calling it homicide in order to get everybody all riled up. And them thinking that you're pursuing it as a homicide, when it probably wasn't, for your own political aspirations—"

The chief reddened, pulled back his shoulders, and shouted: "Now there! That's not true and you know it. And we're pursuing it as a homicide, Hank because that's where all the evidence is pointing."

Carver shrugged. "You've got to know our town, Al. It is fed up! That's what it is: fed up! Fed up with politics. Fed up with a long line of mediocre police chiefs. And mind you, I'm not including you in that. They are fed up with the notion of cops pushing the panic button—and doing it for recognition and political gain. And again, I'm not saying that's my opinion. You know that, Al. I appreciate the fact that you inherited a pretty slippery slope when you took on this here job as chief. God love you for taking on the challenge. Little thanks to it, you bet. But it's just what it is.

"We didn't come here to argue with your opinion. We came to inform you of the fact that this case is no longer yours. Got our court order. It's official. If you want to pursue an appeal through a court of law, so be it. But it would waste time and the taxpayers' hard-earned money doing it. The fact remains, this case is under our jurisdiction and we have every intention of taking over the investigation—now—so more time isn't wasted.

"I'm giving it to you straight-up and personal. And first hand. I'm set up to make this announcement on the radio tonight."

"We've spent a number of man-hours on the investigation of this case. Why—"

"I know what you're going to suggest," the sheriff interrupted, "that we combine our manpower and work together on it. In some ways I agree, and hell, I'd be the first one to agree—if it was doable. But you and me, we don't see eye to eye in this matter. Never have. Never will. It would only end up causing more lost time and confusion."

That being said, Carver nodded to his deputy and they left McGraw and Doyle standing in silence, glowering after them.

On that morning when Carver took over investigation, McGraw remembered saying to Doyle, "Guess that's that." Doyle pulled out his chair, looked up at Pete, and sat down heavily. He muttered: I suppose we'll have to hold a meeting later today to tell the department we're off the case."

"Sir? What's that mean to me?" Pete asked, hopefully.

"I can use you back, patrolling the Stingaree."

"Why can't I keep my position as a detective?" Pete asked, baffled.

"If another high-profile case comes up, you'll be the one I'll get to investigate it. Count on that, Officer." Pete was stunned. He turned to leave the office, trying to hold down his anger and frustration. He had his hand on the doorknob but was stopped by his boss sharply calling out.

"Sir?" he asked, turning around.

"I have a little issue that can use your skills."

"What's that, sir?" Pete asked, feeling hopeful.

"Well, it has come to my attention that some of my men are becoming involved with a little bit of palm greasing down there in the Stingaree. Underground clubs and such."

"I know nothing about that, Chief." Pete said, coloring.

"Word has it that prosties are shuttled out of town after raids and then cops shut their eyes when the gals come back on the next train to go back to work, almost without interruption."

"I wouldn't know anything about it," Pete insisted, feeling his cheeks burn.

Chief Doyle ignored his comment. "What I need to know is who's dirty."

Pete felt like he'd been sucker punched. "I don't know anything about what's going on down there, boss. Remember, you pulled me off that beat. Don't Hildebrant and Spauling work it now? They're good guys, clean; why don't you ask them?"

"What I've heard about your family ethics, McGraw, makes me downright shocked that you aren't jumping at the chance to protect the integrity of our department."

Pete had to avert his eyes. "I'm not saying we're all saints, but we have done a good job of keeping things running pretty safe."

"We leave graft to gangland warlords, not police departments."

"Ah hell, Chief, ain't Prohibition going to end soon? We've less than four months now. Everyone is sensing a breakdown of alcohol regulations. All they are trying to do is keep things safe during this transitional period. And the prosties, well, they're another subject. Damnation, they've been down there just as long as I can recall. Even in my dad's time they were there. There's talk anyhow of legalized prostitution. Agreed that that's not the law right now, but hell, chief, turn on my buddies? Talk about integrity! Our department is built on trusting each other."

"Pete, you're the last person from whom I would expect this baloney. I know the ilk you come from. Your dad wouldn't have shirked duty when it came to lawlessness inside the department. Like I said, I wouldn't expect you to, either. As for the end of Prohibition, we don't make the laws and we don't live by ones that are based on what's coming down the pike. Our system has laws in order to keep peace and keep our society safe. It's not like you're ratting on your cronies. Like you said, most of the fellows are straight-up. It's the ones who aren't that give cops a bad name. What you'd be doing is like separating out the chaff from the wheat. It's keeping the department honest and straight. Pete, I'm giving you this assignment for a reason, because I think you will do a fine job of it and because I trust you. We'll keep it between only the two of us."

• • •

Life sure can deal you a kicker, Pete thought to himself. Just when it looked like the police department was losing control of the case, when he felt he was finally getting nowhere in his investigation, he got a break.

One morning a few days after his visits to Catherine's and Mrs. Evan's houses, Myrtle, the switchboard operator, greeted him at police headquarters, telling him of a telephone call they had received from Catherine Abkhazian requesting Pete to return her call. While he waited for the connection, he'd whispered to Myrtle the question that kept him tossing and turning all night: Had Chief Doyle set up a meeting in regards to Carver's announcement on last night's "Talk Radio" show? She shook her head as she pulled a wire from one hole in the switchboard—a muddle of wires and perforations—plugged it into another, spoke to the central operator, gave her the Abkhazians' telephone number, and adjusted her headset. She glanced at Pete, covered her microphone with her hand, and repeated, "No."

"We've been bamboozled, Pete," she said, holding her hand over her mouthpiece and shaking her head grimly, "by that no-account Carver."

The mother's voice came across the phone in a strong, clear tone. Without beating around the bush, she asked him to meet her at Pepper Grove in Balboa Park at nine thirty that morning.

Now Pete looked around at the playground in Balboa Park for Catherine. It was already as busy as ant colony, with young mothers and their infants scurrying about in various activities. Mothers pushed their children on the swings, guided them up the ladder on the slide, held them on teeter-totters, and talked with one another with the familiarity of women who met regularly. He parked his car and put the card labeled "Police" on the windshield. He grabbed his notebook and cap, then turned to stride across the grass to the children's playground.

"Mr. McGraw. Here!" a single voice carried over the shrieks, laughter, and mother's pitched voices, the cawing of the crows high in the pepper trees, and the automobile sounds on busy Park Boulevard behind him. "Over here!" He looked in the direction of her voice.

Catherine was pushing her infant son on the bucket swings. She glanced over her shoulder at the approaching policeman. Coils of dark curls were tossed around her face by the morning wind, her cotton dress billowed, and she smiled.

It was pleasant to see a smile nowadays. They were precious and far between. Most people walked with haggard faces, heads bent to the earth, and wearing scowls. They were wearying of the long recovery after the Depression. If anyone had the right to scowl, it was this mother whose son had died. But her smile was genuine, warm, and gracious. It was dazzling. She waved and he made his way to join her. His leather shoes caught awkwardly in the sand of the kids' playground.

"Let's find a quieter place. I brought a thermos-full of coffee. Well, chicory. We couldn't afford coffee this month." He looked askance at her, wondering at her light manner. "So we will pretend we have the real stuff. Coffee is a policeman's silent partner, isn't it?" She laughed.

He took the small picnic basket from her hands and she carried her tot. Sunlight danced red in her dark brunette curls. The child peeked over his mother's shoulder and Pete smiled and winked. The child lit up with a dimpled smile and then buried his face in his mother's neck. The small boy stole another look at Pete and giggled with childish delight.

They chose a park bench just past the playground.

"There are a couple of reasons I asked you to join me today, Officer McGraw. First of all, I want to apologize for putting my emotions on display the other day when you came by my home."

"Mrs. Abkhazian . . ."

"Catherine."

"Catherine, don't apologize."

"I come from a family of stoics, I am married to a stoic, and frankly I am an aberration. I am an artist; I am musical; I am emotive, and I am prone to dramatics."

"Catherine . . ." he blustered, then faltered.

She responded by holding her hand up, stopping him. "I'm a minister's wife. I wish I had my husband's faith. But apparently I do not. But, I must learn to carry the pain," she tapped her chest, "in here. Not put it on display for everyone to see. That being said, the other thing I wanted to talk to you about was last night's radio talk."

"Oh. You listened to that."

"Yes. What Carver said made me very, very angry," she bristled and paused. She took out a couple of biscuits that she'd wrapped in wax paper for her son, removed them, and snapped them into small pieces for the child to eat. Then she removed a thermos and two cups from her small wicker basket.

"Here, Albert," she said, "look now, we're having a picnic." The child dimpled up at her, put the biscuit in his mouth, took a small bite, and laughed at Pete, the crumbs tumbling from his mouth.

"This is one time that consistency is what is needed to get to the bottom of Christopher's death." She poured the beverage. "I'm afraid this isn't fancy. I hope you can drink it black . . . You know that old adage about not switching horses in the middle of the stream? Well, it's true in my son's death as well. And it seems that's exactly what Sheriff Carver is doing by claiming jurisdiction in the case now after all that has been done on it by the police."

"I suppose it does seem like things are becoming confused between two agencies. I agree that it shouldn't be that way, because whatever momentum we've gained might be lost in the shuffle."

"That's exactly what I think. Have the two departments considered working together on this?"

He cleared his throat. "Oh, I don't think that would work."

"Why not? They would be able to combine the very best of equipment and experts if they were to combine their efforts."

"It'd seem that way."

"But the sheriff's department and the police department cannot coordinate?"

"I don't suppose so. Politics, I guess, would get in the way."

"Do not get me started on that. It makes me rabid. But I do not understand. What if they do their own investigation and come up with a different opinion than yours—? Officer McGraw, you just can't walk away."

Pete didn't respond immediately. What could he say? He listened to the continuous mishmash of melodies being sung by a mockingbird from somewhere overhead. Children scuttled here and there on the playground. He glanced at that the little boy Catherine was holding in her lap and saw the child was becoming drowsy; his eyes were getting heavy, the eyelids so transparent they were blue.

Finally he cleared his throat and said: "I'm not walking away. We're not. It's like I said: It's politics. Departmental jurisdiction. Simply put, Christopher was found in San Diego Bay and as Carver said, that's the sheriff's jurisdiction."

"I don't give a hang about jurisdiction. All I want is to have the guilty person found and brought to justice."

Pete glanced at Catherine. Her mouth was fixed. Her dark eyes, full of innocence and pain, were glued to his. He looked away. He couldn't let his powerlessness show. He watched a mockingbird chase a crow, three or four times its size, from the branches high up in a nearby eucalyptus tree. The little bird fearlessly attacked the crow over and over. The crow tried to escape the mockingbird's furor, a terrible terror. The two spiraled into the sky and out of sight.

Pete finally cleared his throat to suggest, "I could keep up my investigation, on my own, of course."

A slight smile stretched her lips.

"I still want to follow up on some leads of my own."

The child's head had dropped onto her breast. His breathing was deep and steady. A ladybug landed on his shoulder. It moved a few inches and then took off, fluttering away.

The breezes tossed Catherine's hair. Her face was flushed. "I was hoping you'd say that. I can help you."

Pete, surprised, noted a new light in her eyes. She returned his smile.

"What I need are the names of the high school boys who were bullying your son. I got no place with Mrs. Evans, and I probably won't be able to drag her downtown if we're off the case. You could help by talking to her—you know? Woman to woman—letting her know the importance of this information."

Catherine hesitated before responding. "I can do that. She called me a few days after Chris was buried. She offered her condolences. She mentioned that she had some of Chris's work she thought I would want to have. Mostly his artwork. At the time I didn't have the strength to follow up . . . It was too soon. Now perhaps I could do that, go see her. If I were to speak to her personally, she might tell me who these boys were."

He inadvertently glanced at his wristwatch. She caught this motion and began to pack up the cups and thermos. She reached over and took Pete's hand. She squeezed it.

• • •

A few days later, while Connie was finishing up dinner dishes in the kitchen, the telephone rang. Pete listened in. Connie's voice trilled with excitement. When she hung up the phone, she turned and beamed delightedly at her husband. Catherine Abkhazian, she said, was performing at Spreckels Theatre with the visiting Los Angeles Symphony. She said that because of all the work that Pete had done investigating her son's death, she wanted to thank him by giving him two tickets in the orchestra section for this concert.

At the theater will-call window, he claimed the small, sealed envelope with his name scrawled across the front. Inside the envelope were the two tickets, along with a folded piece of paper.

"What's that, Pete?" Connie asked about the note, bursting with curiosity. Pete smiled at her excitement. "It has something to do with the case," Pete explained, taking her arm and ushering her into the theater to their seats.

As they sat in their theater seats, Pete reread the note. *Good for you, Catherine*, he thought. She had written: *Had coffee with Mrs. Evans. One of the boys is Phillip Johnson. It's the only name she'd give me.*

• • •

Pete stopped by his old high school, which was closed for the summer. The office was still open, however, and the secretary seemed eager to talk to Pete about Phillip Johnson. She didn't need much coxing before she brought the student's school records to Pete.

The photo showed a slender, light-haired youth with high cheekbones, widely set eyes and a masculine square jaw. His grades made Pete's appear scholarly in comparison. Johnson had been held back in seventh grade and barely achieved the 2.0 that was required for graduation. Also enclosed in the student file were reports signed by a Sergeant Hammerstone with the school police. During his four-year high school career, Johnson had been suspended several times for truancy, insubordination, and once for "habitual profanity, vulgarity, and obscenity."

Pete asked the secretary for names of other youths he might have palled around with, but that was when the secretary grew taciturn. She firmly closed the file and pulled it away from Pete. Shaking her head, she said she knew that "other people" had been around asking the same question. Her boss refused to give out their names. She would be in deep muck if she were to spill while the principal was out of town. So McGraw was back to square one, but at least he was on the trail of one very interesting person in Phillip Johnson, taking particular note of the police report's reference to "vulgarity and obscenity."

At headquarters, Pete wasn't surprised to find that the nineteen-year-old already had an arrest report for vagrancy and disorderly conduct. Nothing came of it. Only a slap on the wrist and a suspended sentence. No wonder: Johnson had Attorney Shaley, to represent him.

The home address given was a modest apartment house on G Street in downtown San Diego. The report was signed by his mother. Pete found that she worked at Kress's Department store.

Pete wondered how the likes of the Johnsons could afford this society lawyer.

Especially when Phillip's mother reared him singlehandedly on the limited income of a clerk working at Kress's Department Store.

The detective went to the store to take a gander for himself. So, out of uniform, he wandered from department to department. On the second floor, she was easy to find. She shared a very close resemblance to her son. Both were lean and fine-featured, with honey-brown hair, and deep blue eyes. In Pete's mind, she didn't *look* like a divorcée: She was soft and fine. She had style, not working woman roughness. A certain, ingrained class.   Cop instinct told Pete there was something "off." Phillip Johnson's mother was out of place at her job at Kress's.

Pete began keeping a surveillance on the Johnsons. He noted that mother left the apartment building regularly each morning around 8:15 for work at 9:00. Phillip, unemployed, was seen leaving later. Using his stoolie to follow Johnson, Pete was told that on two days the youth took the street car to Broadway and then walked to the San Diego Rowing Club. There, he rented a rowboat and took it out onto the water by himself.

Thinking that things would break at night, Pete began to ride the youth like a flea on a dog. The two cops, secreted in Pete's car, parked on the street outside the Johnson's apartment for five nights before things began to pop.

On the sixth night at 0130, they saw Johnson emerge from his apartment. He walked a half a block to the corner and waited until a black Nash came by to pick him up. Pete noted the license number. The two cops followed the Nash to Fourth and Broadway at a discreet distance. They observed the driver park the Nash and Johnson get out from the backseat. Johnson lit a cigarette and waited on the corner for about twenty minutes. Then he was joined by a group of males. The five men engaged in a conversation for approximately ten minutes. Johnson returned to the Nash and it drove him back to Johnson's apartment. Again, Pete parked a distance away and the two cops kept awake by smoking cigarettes and telling rasty stories. Then at about 0430, they saw Johnson once again leave his apartment. Again, he went to the corner and waited. The black Nash picked him up as before.

This time the Nash bypassed downtown, heading south towards the Mexican border, to an area on the *frontiera*. There, the Nash turned off the main road into the seeming open space of San Diego hinterlands. Pete parked and waited for nearly an hour before the Nash returned. It headed back to toward the city. Pete followed the car as it dropped off Johnson and watched as the youth closed the door to the apartment behind them. By the time they took up their chase once again, the Nash had disappeared.

The next day, Pete and Joe returned to the *frontiera*. They found the spot that the Nash had turned off the road. On foot, they followed tire tracks to their end and then combed the area for anything looking suspicious. They spent almost the entire afternoon walking the desolated dry wasteland, but came up with *nada*.

Later when Pete returned to headquarters, he ran the license plate of the Nash. The vehicle, as he suspected, had been reported as stolen. Pete drove to the apartment to pick up Phillip Johnson. Only an echo responded to his harsh raps on the apartment door.

Johnson had given them the slip.

Pete and Sera

Fifth Interview, November 1, 1990

ST. JAMES'S WHINING voice rang in his head after Pete hung up the telephone. He'd called the newspaper asking for Sera and ended up trapped in a long-winded conversation with the elderly editor. St. James vented to Pete some of his worries about retirement. He grumbled that old age, retirement, and mortality were unavoidable, but as far as retirement went he'd always planned to make it his own decision. Now an ambitious upstart was pushing him out the door. That had to be Richard Mosier, Pete assumed. St. James mentioned him frequently in their telephone conversations, which had become more regular since the article was published, and they had become reacquainted.

When Pete had been finally able to get around to the reason for his call, that Sera hadn't made their morning appointment the day before, nor had she called to cancel, St. James agreed with Pete's concern. He said it would surprise him that she forgot, because he knew how very interested she had become in the Abkhazian case and how she had been enjoying their interviews. St. James promised Pete that when he saw her, he'd have her get back to him with an explanation.

After disconnecting, McGraw collapsed heavily onto the sofa in the living room where he and Sera had conducted prior interviews. Her empty chair made him sadder. Pete had been looking forward all morning long to their appointment. When Sera wasn't at his home at precisely ten o'clock, he experienced first-date anxieties. When she made no appearance at all, Pete went into an adolescent pout. He shook his head, responding to his unfounded concern about Sera's welfare. But, it was uncharacteristic for her to simply forget; there had to be some major reason and he hoped she was all right.

Pete reached over and picked up his spiral notebook, which he'd placed on the coffee table that morning. He glanced through the agenda he had prepared for Sera. He had marked the word *Cover-up* with a bullet. McGraw had always been convinced that someone with money and prominence wanted the case closed in 1933, and that the reason behind the reinvestigation and ultimate closure of the case in 1990 was the same.

Another bullet on his agenda was placed next to the name *Phillip Johnson*. To this day, Pete believed without doubt that Johnson was involved in the kidnapping of Christopher Abkhazian. He planned to tell Sera about Johnson's apprehension and arrest.

Suddenly Pete remembered that he had placed a box of old goodies from his police years in the back of his clothes closet. He pushed himself out of the sofa and rambled back to his bedroom closet. He slid aside hangers and dove through boxes to get to the old box on the bottom of the pile, which was broken, bent, and yellowed from age. He pulled out the police journal he'd bought especially for his notes on the Abkhazian case and put it to his nose. It smelled musty and mildewed, but familiarity was priceless. He thumbed through the pages, smiling. It was like running into an old acquaintance.

Pete heard the telephone ring and Kate answer.

"It's Miss Schilling," the optimism of Mrs. Kersel's voice rang out through the house.

He took the telephone from his nurse, who was beaming, pleased with this turnaround of events that she hoped would ease his earlier disappointment.

"Hello, Sera," he answered. His voice sounded stiffer than he wanted. Trying to lighten his tone, he added, "I'm glad to hear from you. I missed you this morning."

"I didn't forget. I've been, um, incapacitated."

"I'm sorry to hear that. I know my social calendar isn't as busy as I'd like, but you might have called to let me know that you weren't coming—"

Ignoring his sarcasm, Sera said flatly, "We need to reschedule." There was an edge to her voice that Pete had never heard before. She continued: "I'm caught in a web of lies and cover-ups. I need to get substance—the truth—no more anecdotes just information—fact is, someone's trying to get me off the Abkhazian matter."

"What happened, Sera?"

"I've been—"Her voice faded.

"What happened, Sera?" He asked, more quietly this time.

There was a long silence on the other end of the line. He heard Sera sigh. Pete realized he was clenching the phone so hard his knuckles were turning white. Finally she spoke. "I was attacked last night by someone who made it as clear as he could that he wanted me to stop working on this case."

"Attacked?"

"I went to a party at the neighborhood bar, and someone must have slipped a date drug into my beer."

"Aw, shit, no. Are you all right?"

"Well, I *think* I'm all right."

She told him everything, opening the floodgates, releasing shame, terror, fear, embarrassment, and grief. "I was stupid. I should have been on my guard. During the past week, I've been threatened twice. I should have been more alert."

"Jesus, Sera. You didn't tell me that you had been threatened."

"First a telephone message was left by an unidentified caller at the paper warning me about working on this case, Pete. I don't remember how I got home last night. I remember little about the evening except that I spent it talking to a man I met whom I now believe drugged me."

"You hadn't seen him before last night?"

"He wore a costume. We all were wearing costumes. It being Halloween . . ." Her voice faltered into a sob. "I should have recognized his aftershave lotion, but I had too much to drink."

The cop in Pete started to emerge. "He wore a mask?"

"Yes, the Tick."

"The Tick? What's that?"

"It's a popular cartoon character. Well, not really popular. Perhaps somewhat of a cult thing. A television cartoon, Pete. Not everyone watches it."

"Was any part of his face left uncovered?

"Yes! His mouth. He had beautiful teeth."

"Good. What about his skin color?

"Dark-skinned. Latino? Perhaps light-colored African-American."

"How was he built?"

"I'm ashamed to say it, but he was very well built, and that's what attracted me to him."

"Don't be ashamed. We're getting someplace, Sera. Can you think of anything else about him? An accent?"

"No. Maybe–"

"Maybe what?"

"Oh, nothing. That's about all I remember."

"Maybe other customers who were there might remember him."

"I don't know."

"Did you ask any of them?"

"I gave a list of names of the people I knew who were at the bar to the policewoman who's running the investigation. I think by the time I ran into him, most of my friends had left. The bartender, Jake, might remember him. I gave his name to the police. Shit, Pete, that monster stood less than two feet from me. I was so stupid."

Pete swallowed a lump in his throat. "I don't know what to say. I feel like hell. I got you into this."

"I'm all right. I mean, apparently all he wanted to do was to scare me. He accomplished that. Today, I didn't go to work." Pete heard her stifle another sob. "I was supposed to get my review. Oh, hell. Obviously, I couldn't come to your house. But I'm not injured."

"Did you see a doctor?"

"Yes. I was examined at a clinic near my home." She paused. "So, Pete, you must understand my urgency. You have to tell me everything you know, no bars held. We're on a time thing here."

Pete chuckled, then he kindly corrected her: "It's *no holds barred*, Sera. It's an old wrestling term." He paused, then told her what he had put on his agenda for that morning's interview.

Finishing the conversation, she added: "By the way, I called Rose Abkhazian before I called you. I wondered if it might have been someone from the Abkhazian family who wanted me off the case, and thought of Rose. We spoke at length, and in the end I was convinced she didn't know anything, and that she was truly concerned about my safety."

"You were convinced?"

"Yes. I felt she was telling the truth."

"Sera, didn't you tell me that she didn't know very much about her brother's death?"

"That's right. Rose said her mother wouldn't talk about it when she was growing up."

Pete's voice dropped to a whisper. "Is she still alive?"

"Who? Oh, her mother. She told me that her mother died about a year ago."

Pete's voice was almost inaudible. "How did she die?"

Struck by something she heard in his voice, Sera responded kindly, "I think it was cancer." She waited a moment to continue. "Pete, did you meet Rose?"

"No. I never met her. I spoke to her. She said she'd call me back but never did."

"You saw her picture with the article in the paper?"

"Yes. She resembles her mother. But, not–I wish she had called me back. I would have liked to have heard about Catherine."

That being said, Pete fell into another extended silence. This time, his quietness signaled the conversation's end. Whenever the subject of Christopher Abkhazian's mother was brought up, Sera felt she had reopened scar tissue from a very painful wound.

Pete McGraw

"RISE 'N SHINE, Mr. McGraw!"

Kate Kersel pulled the drapes open and Pete blinked in irritation at the bright morning light. "Time for meds and breakfast."

"Not hungry," Pete grumbled, and turned over onto his side to face the wall, exposing his backside for her injection. So far this morning the pain hadn't begun. Before sleeping, he'd drunk his lytic cocktail and throughout the night, self-administered morphine via the pain pump. His nurse was conservative about giving him oral pain meds during the day (although he routinely popped a few without her knowing), but she was adamant about the morning injection. He kidded that she just liked to see his manly accoutrements. If she thought Pete's joke funny, she never let on.

"Well, you've got to eat. At least give it a try," she yammered as she jabbed him with the needle.

"Damn it, Kate!" Pete complained as he covered up. "Your injections are *gol*-dang lethal!"

Ignoring him, she asked, "Feel steady enough to get out of bed for the bathroom?"

"Yeah, yeah," he said, as he struggled to pull his legs over the side of the bed.

"You want to eat here or in the kitchen?"

"Here, I think." His feet hunted for his slippers. "Maybe I'll try a little breakfast in here, thank you. Maybe I'll go out into the other room later."

"I'll just straighten up your bed and get you some cereal while you're in the bathroom."

He shuffled back from the bathroom to a turned-down bed, pillows fluffed, and a breakfast of a small bowl of instant Quaker Oats with honey and brown sugar, the kind he liked, and cream and orange juice. His nurse was fiddling with the radio, jabbering nonstop as she scanned stations searching for news and talk shows. Pete especially liked to listen to Rush Limbaugh on AM 760 in the morning.

Now, there was a genius of a man who cut through the spin to get to the truth of it all, Pete thought. No pussyfooting around with pacifists. Time to get tough. The Persian Gulf was exploding, with Iraq invading little Kuwait. It was our national duty as guardian of the world to lead the United Nations' coalition of forces against the invading Iraqi forces. And Saudi Arabia looked to the U.S. and Russia for the protection it could count on. And didn't we need the oil from Kuwait for our protection?

Oh, settle on a station? The conflux of voices and music ...

The nurse continued her one sided chatter while she diddled with the knob on the radio. "I need to leave you alone for about forty minutes. I have a couple of errands I have to run."

"Sure. Okay. Dammit, Kate! I sure wish you'd land on something. Anything! That dad-blamed noise is driving me nuts!"

He heard her sigh while she continued to fool with the relic. A leftover from the seventies. A Philco. Did they even make Philco radios anymore? Still a good radio, just not as functionally precise as some of these newer devices, he supposed. True, stations sometimes faded in and out, or double broadcasted. Or even disappeared into a haze of static. But then again, it had lasted all these years. It wasn't like things today that were built to break down just as soon as you learned how to use them. Hadn't he heard something on that other radio talk show just yesterday about an entertainer back in the sixties whose real job was a radio repairman? It made Pete wonder if radio repairmen still existed.

"I've set the phone on autodial for paramedics, just in case of an emergency and you need someone here while I'm out. But if you stay in bed and listen to the—darn it! Where is that station you liked?" Fragments of music, static, and voices kept the room jittery with noise.

"Hold it right there," he said holding up his hand, "I like that song."

She stepped back, listened a minute, and gave a sideways smirk at Pete. "That's the religious station."

As he slipped his feet under the covers, arranged the tray table over his lap, and nestled back into the fluffed-up pillows, he repeated, "Keep that station."

She shrugged. "Guess a little religion might be better than seeing you get all worked up with that talk station host, what's-his-name, Limba."

"Limbaugh," Pete corrected.

Her green eyes crinkled up with her smile, and then she left him alone. He heard the front door open and close, and then the sound of her car driving down the street.

Pete jabbed the mound of oatmeal with his spoon a few times before tasting it. Like paste, it stuck to the roof of his mouth and the back of his teeth. He put the spoon down and sipped from the juice glass. The orange juice tasted sour and harsh. Grunting, he put the glass back and pushed the tray table out of the way. He lay back onto his pillows, suddenly aware of his solitude. In spite of the sunshine, the room was chilly. And it was quiet, aside from the music from the little radio next to his bed. He leaned over and turned the volume up a bit, then turned it a little louder.

The power of the soprano's voice shattered the silence in his bedroom.

When my heart is bowed in sorrow,
And it seems all help is gone,

Pete recognized the singer but couldn't quite recall her name. It was an old recording. Who was she? Her voice was clear, haunting, and captured the ache of the blues and spiritual longing. Bessie Smith, by damn, that's who it was! Only she could sing a hymn and make a believer out of anyone who was listening.

Jesus whispers: "Do not falter,
I will leave you not alone . . ."
Yes, there is sunshine
In the shadows
There is sunshine
In the rain
When our hearts are
Filled with pain

Pete shut his eyes tight against the morning sun's harsh glare and let the old song take him back in time, to a waning summer day, a long, long time ago.

It was just before dusk. The setting sun had flung a blanket of lavender and rose onto the California hills. The western horizon was painted in pale melon. Stars began to poke through the deep indigo evening sky. The earth had given up its heat, and now the air had a dusty and dry smell to it. And the desert breezes wrapped around a fellow in a friendly way.

For the two men who seemed disproportionately large in Pete's Ford, conversation was intermittent. They had rolled their windows down and sat with arms crooked on the doors. Hatless, the wind swept through their hair. They were a million miles from nowhere, and for the moment it felt good to speak only when necessary. Joe was with Pete that night, in Dehesa or what was facetiously called

East Jesus by city folk who never ventured out to this forbidding and rugged high desert, east of El Cajon.

Earlier that week the two partners had been strolling down Second Avenue when they noticed the poster, and more particularly the name "Abkhazian" appearing on it. They agreed it might be wise to go to Dehesa and attend the revival, to scout it out for people "of interest."

Pete had never driven to Dehesa. There was nothing out there for him, just rattlesnakes, sagebrush, and coyotes. As they left Highway 8 to drive east into the hilly terrain, they found that they joined a parade of cars slowly snaking down the macadam road into Dehesa Valley.

A sign advertised:

Fourth Annual Summer Christian Revival in Dehesa
August 9 through August 23rd
The Ecumenical Way
All folks welcome!
The Reverend Adam F. Abkhazian, Pastor
South Bay Baptist Church
The Reverend Michael Matthews, Central Presbyterian Church
Father Peter Delaney, Trinity Catholic Church
Message: Lambs among Lions – Christians among Sinners

Each car turned right off the main road onto a dirt road gouged deep by automobile wheels. Rusty barbed-wire fencing next to the road defined the boundary of the Sycuan Indian Reservation. "No Trespassing" signs were tacked to fence posts weathered by hot sun and whipping dust.

The road followed a landscape of sun-bleached boulder-laden hills. Looking ahead, they saw the winding trail of black automobiles, a string of army ants climbing the barren anthills. Pete and Joe were tossed hard against the back of the seat and doors as the car tires rolled in and out of ruts. Joe pointed out a coyote slinking into the brush, its tail caught between hind legs, terrified of the noisy, belching automobiles, the dreaded human interlopers.

Conversation was sparse. The two policemen were exhausted from their near record-setting ten-hour drive to and from Los Angeles the day before, when they picked up Phillip Johnson. Three refills of water poured into the overheating radiator and one flat tire lengthened the four-hour trip back to San Diego by an hour and a half.

The long drive from Los Angeles, however, allowed for continued questioning of their prisoner. After many miles, Pete had become completely convinced of the youth's involvement in the crime singularly and with a "ring of bad boys." Plus other stuff.

The Los Angeles Police Department had responded to the San Diego Police Department's all-points bulletin by wiring San Diego that they had a young man in their custody whom they had picked up for vagrancy and indecent exposure. The bulletin they'd received from San Diego pushed them to exert more pressure on Johnson. The exasperated youth finally confessed to killing the Abkhazian child. They were holding him for pickup by San Diego police.

"That's our man!" Pete had told Joe, and they went to pick him up.

On their drive back, they stopped a couple of times along the way to push their point in questioning their suspect. They arrived in San Diego after midnight and booked him. Only when they looked at him in the jail cell did they realize how bloodied up and bruised the fellow's face was from them pushing their point. Pete kept pressing though, knowing time was precious and he would lose Johnson to his big-shot attorney, Staley, and to the loss of the case. As he continued to beat him down, any sympathy he might have had for the youth was squelched when a certain arrogant look flashed in Johnson's eyes. Pete took on a fierce hatred for his prisoner.

And kept him nearly six hours in a small room with no water, food, or attorney in attendance. Finally the youth broke down and admitted that he'd "done it."

"Tell us your story."

The youth gazed from Joe's to Pete's faces, and exhaled long and deep, the air taken out of him. "Okay. Here's what went down. I was with my pals a few weeks back on a Saturday night. We were trolling the Stingaree."

"When was this?"

"I dunno. Guess the weekend before all hell started to break loose in San Diego."

"You're talking about Saturday, July fifteenth."

He shrugged. "Anyhow, as I was telling you, I was with my pals, and . . ."

"Who are your pals?" Pete asked, interrupting the youth.

Johnson held his index finger up, shook his head, scrunched up his mouth, and then winced at the pain from the bruises on his face.

"Nope. Not squealing on my pals. Anyhow, like I told ya, we was looking for some honeys to juke with and stuff when we run into this fellow. We had a few suds with him and got to talking, you know. We think he's looking for pussy, you know. We let him know we got connections, and then he takes this stash from his billfold. Shows it to us and tells us it's not pussy he's looking for. He likes boys. And he was going to pay us pay good money. He fans through the bills like a deck of cards. He's pretty darned selective about what he wants. No older than ten. A pretty face. Right off we think of the Abkhazian boy."

"Why him?" Pete asked, his stomach suddenly cramping.

"I dunno. He came to mind. He's a pretty."

"How'd you know him?"

"Know him? Nah. Saw him around. I dunno. We saw him walking to school during the school year. We messed around with him. The kid sort'ov irked us, if you know what I mean. A soft touch."

"You and your friends? C'mon, Johnson, fess up. If this wasn't your idea and it was somebody else's, don't take the rap for him. Come on now, come clean, who were they? Who was the leader of your gang? You're not going to carry this alone, are you? Was it David? David Cohn who thought of the Abkhazian boy?"

Johnson jumped. "Who's that?" he responded shrilly and unconvincingly. "Uh-uh. I told ya, I ain't spilling about anything except my own business in this affair, Officer. Those are my rules. I don't know anyone by that name, anyhow."

"Right," Pete responded, and then he changed his tone. "Go on with your story."

"We told the fellow we'd talk it over. Seemed like easy money. The plan was that I take the kid we bamboozled during the school year. Hooking him would be a piece of cake. He's scared shitless of us. Me and my buddy, anyhow. He'd be an easy fish to fry. We work out a plan, and at first it went like clockwork.

"On Tuesday we hung out on Fifth and B streets, until we see the kids headed towards the Bay. We talk at them a bit. Then me and my buddy, we split up then. I go it alone. Our plan is for me to hide him someplace and to meet up later, to do the business deal. So I get the kid on the street car. At first it was a game. Told him I was sorry we picked on him during the school year and I wanted to make it up to him. I'd buy him some candy at the end of the line where they have that ostrich farm. They sell candy, root beer, and stuff like that, plus he likes animals and he'd get to see the ostriches. It was funny the way at first he hesitated and then after a while he just went along with it. Easy as taking candy from a baby. So we ride to the end of the line and walk the rest of the way out to the ostrich farm, I buy him some candy like I promised, and we feed some seeds to the birds. All the time I'm wondering what I should do with him until we can make the exchange. That was when I see this dirt path leading down into Mission Valley. I tell him that I live in the valley, on a farm with horses and cows and a few chickens. It wasn't a long walk, I say; we'd just take a shortcut down. My mom would love to meet him, I say. I promise she'd have an apple pie waiting. His eyes got just as big as pies with that promise. Made me feel a little bit rotten, to tell you the truth. Shoot, I haven't had an apple pie myself in God knows how long. I had to find a place to hide him. And he was getting to be a pain in the neck with all that whining and complaining about how it was getting late and he should be getting back. But that pie did the trick, I'll tell you.

"We followed that trail next to the Cliffs Gardens and took it down into the valley. It goes across the valley to Camp Kearny. I know it's quiet and isolated there so we head in that direction. The kid, he's getting cranky. Pissing me off. It was hot. I kept him going. Sometimes pushing him, sometimes dragging him along with me by his hand. By the time we crossed the river, I almost had to carry him. He smartens up that there ain't no houses where we was. I get crazy. I just want him to shut the fuck up. When we finally get up onto the mesa I'm sick of the whole thing. I say, 'Hey kid, I have to take a piss. Look the other way.' That's the thing about that kid—he always does what he's told. What a fish! So, while he's looking the other way, I come up behind him quiet like, and I hit him in the head with this rock I found, just enough to knock him out while I tie him up. Remember, the plan was that I was going to go back later and pick him up after we fixed a drop-off place with that fellow, and had money in hand. When I left him there, he was alive."

"So, let me understand this. Was that the last time you saw him?"

"No, like I said, the plan was for me to go back later, and I did go back, but by then everything had gotten all botched up. We did our part. We were supposed to meet up with the guy for our payment. We waited, but the creep never showed up. That's when my buddy says he'd go with me to get the kid and then he'd take care of him.

"Say! I've got a brainstorm. Why don't we take a walk out there and I'll show you where I hid him. I could make a killing on this story, couldn't I? Like Northcott. Get famous. Get my mug plastered all over *Time* and *Life*. There's got to be some payola in that. Maybe, Officer McGraw, if you treat me good I might spread a little of the cheer your way later on. What do you think about that? We could do it, just you and I. It would make you famous. I could call it *The Death Walk*. That's a good one. *The Death Walk*."

Pete was able to take Johnson from the jail under his custody early the next morning, long before the milk trucks began making deliveries, before the sun came up, and before any action had been taken on his case. The two officers followed the youth down the trail at the end of the Number Seven line, into the valley. They forded a shallow part of the San Diego River. By the time they reached the top of Kearny Mesa, it was all a hollabello with the morning warming up, meadowlarks were flitting around mesquite bushes, and the world a conglomeration of their morning songs.

Johnson showed them where he'd dug a rock out of a hole in the ground to knock the boy unconscious. A short distance from the hole Pete could see how grass had been crushed down where Johnson said the boy had been left tied and unconscious. The youth circled around the area apparently looking for something. He smiled and picked up a rock. Looked it over and handed it to Pete. Pete studied it and felt sickened.

"Well I'll be damned!" Johnson chucked suddenly and bent over to pick out something from the grass. He held out his hand to show Pete what he'd found. Pete recognized the small beads as similar to ones taken from Johnson by the Los Angeles Police Department earlier. Before they left the mesa, Pete walked the rock over to the hole that Johnson claimed it came from. It fit perfectly.

Try as he might, Pete was unable to get Johnson to fill in a time gap between returning to the mesa with his buddy and the time the boy was unloaded, dead. Pete calculated that time gap could be as many as forty-eight hours that were unaccounted for. And each time Pete tried to get Johnson to admit that his buddy was in fact David Cohn, the youth's jaw would lock up like a good case of tetanus.

Joe broke the silence, responding to the question Pete had asked earlier. Pete's thoughts were brought back to the present as they bumped along on the dirt road towards the revival in the desert. "I think Johnson and the ring of bad boys are somebody's patsys."

"Yeah, I get that sense, too." Pete nodded in agreement; then began to talk his thoughts out. "There's a bigger fish in the pond, a criminal of the worst sort, that's for sure. Johnson's a link in the chain of desperados. Like you called him—a patsy. Those porno cards and all—. My gut tells me that there's an adult lurking somewhere behind this ring of bad boys. This is more than a wild bunch of youths. My take on it is—like yours—there's this butter and egg man, then the leader of the ring—David Cohn?—and then Johnson and some others we haven't identified yet. You bet: There's some big wig calling the shots. Can't you see the pieces coming together? First we get that fellow, Purdy, with those porno cards. He's definitely someone we want to put on the stand if we can put Johnson on trial—."

As they churned over the bumpy road, some other things ran through Pete's mind: the brouhaha the day before when they picked up the kid in L.A., their lack of sleep last night, and their compulsion to drive to Dehesa for the revival. Suddenly he winced when he remembered his wife's angry words.

He'd left the house, sandwich in hand, a bitch of a headache, and her caterwauling after him. There is nothing attractive about a woman whose mouth is spewing angry words with her face contorted and all pinched up.

Pete acknowledged that Connie had a right to be angry. This case was pulling him more and more away from home, bringing him home later in the night when she was asleep. He was drinking more and spending more time down in the Stingaree. No doubt about it, their marriage was drifting apart.

"Sure, you're going to a Baptist revival meeting!" she shouted after him. "Almost three in the morning when you came to bed last night. And you're gone all day today. What'd 'ya think? Think I fell off the turnip truck? I don't need a lie to punch me in the nose in order to tell the difference. I know you didn't drive to and from Los Angeles in a single day. You say you brought in a suspect for the Abkhazian boy's murder. Sure you did, Peter. And tell me, where does it say anything about it in the morning paper? And—when did you suddenly become religious?"

Pete didn't have the slightest idea of what to expect at a revival. His own modest experiences in church made him stereotype all churchgoing Christians as middle-class, staid, orderly, and reserved. He was blown away when he saw the tent.

"Holy cow!" he blurted. "It's as huge as the Barnum and Bailey Big Top!"

The two policemen stationed themselves at each of the entrances. Pete's eyes scanned the audience that kept flowing into the tent like rivers. He looked over at Joe, who was doing the same. Was the murderer in the crowd?

Pete recognized the diversity of the people the revival attracted. Though the majority of the audience appeared to be Caucasian, there were a few Negroes, a few Mexican families, sailors fresh from their ships wearing crisp, white uniforms, and families with children spanning all ages. There was a murmur of indiscernible voices, with an occasional *HALLELUJAH!* Or *PRAISE THE LORD!* Being shouted above the din. Friends hollered greetings to friends.

San Diego's own Negro gospel quartet, the Hallelujah Jubilee Singers, was to be featured at the revival that night. Pete heard this group on Christian radio station (not that he usually tuned in to that radio station). He found that he liked them and was looking forward to hearing them.

Reserved eagerness took the place of earlier fervor as worshippers began to take their seats. A few of the circles were breaking up with hugs and well wishes. As Pete scanned the sea of faces, his eyes came to a halt when they rested on the diminutive woman sitting quietly in the first row.

She wore a brown dress with white polka dots and a straw hat. She was looking down, drawing Pete's attention to her long and sculpted neck, which was bordered by a collar of lace. Other than the lace, the dress was simple and unadorned. As though she felt his eyes on her, she suddenly shifted in her chair, looked up, and gazed around. He could barely make out her profile under the hat, but he remembered her chiseled features, her soft brown eyes, aquiline nose, and Garbo cheekbones. He wished for her to turn; he willed her to turn. He wanted her to look at him. But although she didn't turn around, she stirred slightly as he held his gaze, and he knew she felt it.

Sitting next to her were her small children. She held the infant, Albert, in her arms. The child was still, probably asleep. The other two children were settled, not squirming like most kids.

The air in the tent was becoming close and heavy. Hand-held fans were beginning to wave in front of female faces through-out the congregation, creating a turbulent motion. Hats were being taken off briefly for handkerchiefs to modestly wipe away perspiration from feminine foreheads, cheeks, and necks. Men were removing their fedoras and jackets to sit informally in their suspenders, unbuttoned collars, loosened ties, and rolled-up sleeves.

But she sat regally, coolly detached.

The Reverend Abkhazian joined the other ministers on the wooden stage. He took his place at the altar. Together, he and the other leaders began to clap out a rhythm. The congregation joined. Then the quartet came onstage. They joined the clapping, and then broke into a rousing spiritual. A choir of well over one hundred sing-ers provided accompaniment, and soon members of the congrega-tion joined in singing:

"Preachers and teachers would make their appeal,
Fighting as soldiers on great battlefields;
When to their pleadings my poor heart did yield.
All I could say, there is something within."

In a single voice, the congregation echoed the chorus:

"Something within me, that holdeth the reins,
Something within me that banishes pain;
Something within me, I cannot explain
All that I know, there is something within."

After a while, it appeared that all who were coming had come, and were seated and participating. The flaps to the tent had been shut. Joe and Pete still stood sentry at each of the tent entrances. Pete's eyes found Joe's. Joe shook his head, indicating that nothing unusual had caught his attention. Pete nodded a reply that he hadn't seen anyone who looked out of place, either. For an instant, Pete felt very discouraged. Was this another futile attempt simply based on his hunches? Was it another waste of their time?

At the child's funeral, they had staked out the cemetery hoping the murderer might make an appearance, as some murderers were known to do to fill some prurient desire. At that time, they'd closely surveyed the nearly three hundred attendees for someone standing alone, someone wearing an inappropriate expression, someone who looked out of place. The only thing out of place was the cross put there by the parents of the Brooks girl.

Tonight, they'd driven all the way out here. Would there again be nothing?

He listened to the reverend's ramblings about sin-filled San Diego, about how Satan had joined forces with the Las Vegas League, about how the city fathers were transforming our city to a mini Las Vegas as they pressed to legalize prostitution, gambling, and heaven knew what else with the forthcoming end of Prohibition in December. Pete felt he had heard enough and left the tent to smoke a cigarette.

Once outside, he took a deep breath of the high desert air. He walked a way off from the tent, where the riotous noise from inside was muted. He struck the wooden match on the sole of his shoe. The match sputtered and blazed as he lit his cigarette.

Pete took a long drag on the Lucky Strike and looked at the night sky studded with stars. The air was warm. Bats flew crazily in the sky. The yellow moon lit a path on the hardpan as though the earth were water. Here he could hear the cicadas and the other songs of the night. Off in the distance, the yelp of a coyote was followed by the howling discord of its peers.

He'd almost found himself lost in the sounds, scents, and sweetness of the desert air when the tent flap was thrown open, momentarily startling him. He saw a sparse female figure step outside the tent and move quickly to the side, into the dark.

Seconds later, the tent flap opened once again. A young couple stepped out, arms around each other. They laughed softly and whispered conspiratorially. As the flap to the tent was held open, the light from inside illuminated the woman who had come outside earlier. He noted that the woman's face was buried in her white-gloved hands. She was crying. And in that instant, Pete also saw that she wore a dress with polka dots.

When the lovers were safely out of earshot, Pete called softly, "Catherine?"

"Yes. Who . . .?"

"It's Pete McGraw," he replied.

"Officer McGraw?"

He dropped his cigarette and ground it into the earth. "Yes. It's me," he answered, and walked slowly toward her.

She came toward Pete, one step at a time, apprehensively and cautiously.

As they drew together, she collapsed into him.

"It's all right, Catherine," Pete whispered into the top of her head. "Cry it out."

"I can't," she said, putting distance between them. But the tears came. Again she let him pull her to him. She sobbed against his chest.

This caught Pete off guard. He tucked his arms under hers and pulled her to him tightly. The two stood like that for a long time: she cried and he soothed. He longed for the desert music that just earlier had sounded so pleasant, not the boisterous vivacity coming from the tent, which denigrated the intimacy of the moment. Here, she sought solace. Here, he offered compassion. Pete buried his face in her thick, curly hair and breathed in the fragile rose scent of her body. He pulled his arms even more tightly around her so that the two stood in the desert darkness as one. Pete let her cry. And cry she did, as though her tears were limitless.

After a while, her shaking stopped. She stayed in his arms, not moving. Then, she looked up at Pete. Holding her so close, Pete studied her face in the faint light of the tent. Her features were perfect. She had an ethereal expression that he wanted to remember always. Unspent tears in her eyes caught the light enchantingly. Her lips were slightly parted, sensuously. Impulsively, he kissed her. In her soft, melting responsiveness, the sweetness of that first kiss exploded into fiery passion. With his mouth, he tasted her, consumed her femaleness, felt the core of her desire. He took her head between his strong hands, looked into her liquid eyes, and then ran his mouth over her eyelids, her moist cheeks, and her pulsing throat, the smoothness of her porcelain neck, her ears, and her lips. For several moments, they remained embraced. Then, Pete began to guide her toward an area of absolute darkness, to seek the solitude two lovers needed.

"No. I can't," Catherine said, and put her hand on his chest in soft protest. Pete released her and let her step back, slightly away from him. "I'll be all right. Just give me a moment."

Pete turned away and gave her the additional space she needed to compose herself.

She began to hiccup. They both laughed. "I'm embarrassed, Mr. McGraw."

"Why?" Pete said, running his hand through her hair. "You needed to cry."

"I did." She hiccupped again. "Why do I always seem to hiccup after I cry?" Pete leaned down and kissed her forehead gently.

"Should I thank you for giving me what I needed and couldn't ask for? I've craved to be held. Held, like you held me just now. My soul cries for human passion. In the loss of our son, in my grieving, I'm afraid my physical needs have become manic."

"We all react to grief in different ways, I think."

"My husband doesn't respond to my urgency."

"Oh God! How much I've wanted to hold you in my arms since the first time I saw you, Catherine."

She hiccupped. "Don't say that. It's wrong for you to want me." She hesitated, and quietly added, "That's not completely true. I've wanted you to hold me, Pete. I've longed for your strength to buoy me. Your compassion. Your friendship. I've sought affection that I've been missing in Adam. With Chris's death he closed up. That's how he has handled his grief. And here I am, a sponge. Ready to absorb all your affection, compassion, and loving. I know my husband wants to give me it, but can't."

Pete once again covered her wet face with kisses.

She put her hands against his chest and again gently pushed herself away. She looked up at him. "Do you understand that I love my husband? At least, I like to think I do. Everything is so jumbled up inside of me." She hesitated, and then she asked, "May I ask you a favor?"

"Anything. Anything at all." Pete smiled at the new inflection in her voice.

"May I have one of your cigarettes?"

Pete chuckled as he lit two. He steered her over to a flat rock, where they sat and smoked.

"Catherine, I have something to tell you. But you have to keep what I tell you to yourself."

"What is it?"

"You have to promise. It's too important that this doesn't get out."

"I promise."

"I think we have our man."

"Is it Johnson?"

"I believe he's involved and a very important key."

"Then . . . who?"

"I can't say right now."

Pete told her about Johnson's capture and his confession, side-stepping anything having to do with their "Death Walk."

When he finished, she shivered violently and crushed out her cigarette. "I will keep this information to myself. Thank you, Officer McGraw. As long as I live, I will never forget your promise to me and your resolve to make it come true. And your friendship." She kissed him on his cheek and left him alone on the rock, where he sat for a few more minutes, his gut churning with emotion.

Once inside, Pete looked toward Joe and was surprised to see him motion with his thumb to meet outside the tent.

Once again, Pete left the commotion inside the tent to the quiet of the night. The transition gave him an overwhelming sense of relief. He lit another cigarette and inhaled deeply, listening to the conflux of noises. Above the dull roar of the audience inside and nature outside, the reverend's guttural voice rose and fell in cadence as he strove to bring his points to the hearts of the listening audience. Soon the sound of scuffing feet joined the babble as Joe skirted the tent to meet him.

"Over here!" Pete called. He took out another cigarette and lit it from the end of the one he smoked, handing it to Joe as he joined him. "What'cha got, pal?" he asked.

"Take a gander over by the south side of the stage, Pete. There are two fellows that stand out like sore thumbs."

When, a few moments later, Pete stepped inside the tent, he immediately recognized the two men Joe was talking about.

He wondered why he hadn't noticed them before. As Joe said, they did stick out from the rest like sore thumbs. The service had ended and the audience was shifting from their seats into small, amicable groups. Generally a pleasant ambience filled the tent. The two sour-faced men standing partly hidden in the shadow of the stage were the exceptions to the congeniality. Most of the men in the congregation had dressed down for the heat, with rolled-up shirtsleeves and trousers; these two were suited up with collared shirts and neckties. Most of the men in the audience were now bare-headed; these two kept fedoras on their heads. While the men in the congregation were mingling, they stood alone and apart. One of the outcasts was picking wax from his ear with his nail clippers and the other's face was stretched into a bored yawn.

"Yeah. I saw them," Pete acknowledged when he joined his partner outside.

"That shorter one—I've seen him around City Hall," Joe said.

"Yup, me too. What's your thinking?"

"My gut sense is that they were sent here to keep an eye on the good reverend."

"You might be right at that. I'll tell you what. I'll get my stoolie on this. He'll find out what's behind them. Good job, partner!" Pete said, as he swatted Joe on his back.

• • •

The sound of car doors opening and shutting pulled Pete out of the darkness of old memories into the bright present. Again he found himself in his bedroom that was awash with light, no longer outside in the desert on a summer's night. From where he lay, he watched his nurse lean into the car through the open passenger door. She removed three brown bags of groceries, shut the door with her heel, and headed up the sidewalk to the front door.

There was more static than music coming from the old Philco as it had lost the sound waves. Irritating noise, it was. A cacophony of voices and jarring notes from songs. Pete reached over and shut off the radio.

He heard the front door open and close, and the nurse's footsteps on the wooden floor as she went to the kitchen. Then he heard a rustle of paper, the refrigerator door opening, water being run, and cabinet doors slamming shut, as she put the groceries away. Comfortable sounds. Comfortable, pleasant sounds. Soon, he knew, she would be headed back to check on him. Her delightful round face, broad with a smile, and tenderness in her blue eyes. Oh, he'd had so many women in his life: a wife; lovers too numerous to count; Mrs. Kersel—

—and Catherine.

Pete pulled open the drawer of the nightstand. Under all the things stuffed in the small drawer, he finally found what he was looking for.

One of these days, he thought, he'd have to go through that drawer and destroy everything he didn't want others to see. After—

But right now that one small age-old, mangled black-and-white snapshot gave him more comfort than all the sweet smoke in a Chinese opium den.

My God, but wasn't Catherine beautiful? Didn't her hair smell like the out-of-doors? Didn't her dark eyes flash and pierce his soul? She could be tough or she could be soft. Her skin was like the inside of a rose petal.

Pete held the picture to his nose and inhaled deeply of the imagined roses and fresh air. Fragments of thoughts flooded his brain, as though it were but yesterday. *Damned rascal time. Man's delusion. Just a mortal's invention, a feeble attempt to understand the Master's chronology. God knows no time. To God it was but yesterday.*

It was a summer's night down on the sand in Ocean Beach, within earshot of the hurly-burly of Wonderland Amusement Park. Beyond the San Diego River channel, where it flowed into the Pacific, waves peaked, and green iridescence flashed from a red tide lit by the full moon.

On the stiller water, the many-colored lights of Mission Beach homes bounced cheerfully as they were reflected on the ripples.

He recalled standing knee-deep in the surf, casting his line aimlessly into the waves.

He imagined the smell of the salty sea air, catching the flash of the crest of a breaking wave in the moonlight, and the feel of sand between his toes.

Now even after the near eternity of another world, the memory still sizzled.

In his room, he imagined the heat of the flames from the bonfire he'd built for her comfort as she watched him fish. She waited, sitting on a towel on the sand. He had turned around to say something, but then he fell silent. Almost reverently. He remembered not being able to call out to her. The classic features of her beautiful face were painted rosy and warm orange in the light of the fire. Instead of speaking, he left the fishing line to its own work, knelt behind her, and put his arms around her.

His eyes had misted. Did they water from the pungent wood smoke of the fire or from noticing the goose bumps that had sprouted on Catherine's thin white arms in the coolness of the evening? Or was it from the sudden awareness that this was but a moment in time, never to happen again?

It was but a fleeting happiness that they shared: the young Irish-American cop and the older, dark beauty who had been matured by childbirth and mellowed by sorrow. It—whatever *it* was that they shared—passed too quickly to be tangible. It was simply a beginning without an end.

Thinking about the lies they'd had to tell others in order to get there that night made Pete smile ruefully.

Those few stolen moments with sand between the sheets and their bodies as they made love. Her smooth, clammy skin, her soft voice in his ear, the tears, and then their combined shrieks of passion. All had seemed boundless and free and eternal; but they knew all was actually fragile and perishable, to be trapped in the web of separate lives constrained by commitments, conventions, and contingencies.

They awoke in the thrashed sheets of the bed in the morning and made love once again. He remembered their foggy walk next to the crashing ocean breakers, below squawking seagulls circling in the sky above them, a reverse tornado, and two pairs of footprints in the sand on the beach.

But that was—his thoughts dissipated like bubbles in air.

Pete's fingers squeezed the corner of the picture of Catherine as though by squeezing it, his heartache would be lessened.

She'd been so young when this picture was taken. He had demanded that she give it to him. He wanted to keep it. And she gave it to him. He'd kept it for all these years.

The picture had been taken before they had met, before the other children had come, when she was the mother of only one child: a very young son by the name of Christopher.

It was probably taken when Catherine was newly married, the young wife of an earnest and stalwart minister.

She couldn't have known what life held in store for her when this picture was taken.

Does anyone ever?

If she had known, she wouldn't have been smiling with so much abandon.

Who took the photograph? Who was Catherine smiling at? What had been said to make her smile like that? It was, after all, a very foolish smile, but it always made him glad. She looked strong, vigorous, and alive in that picture, a Catherine he had never known—or, may have known for only those few fleeting moments in time.

Pete heard the tinkling of glass striking glass as his breakfast made its way down the hall on the tray in Mrs. Kersel's hands. Pete took one last look at the picture and then put it back into the drawer. He carefully covered it with other stuff in order to hide it.

Sera

SEVERAL DAYS AFTER my second meeting with Richard, when he had made a commitment to help me find something else to work on that would be publishable more readily than the "old time-pisser of the Abkhazian case, St. James's pet, Richard proved that he was as good as his word. And as it happened, I was caught completely off guard when he called at one thirty in the morning, awakening me from a serious sleep.

"Be speedy," he urged.

I splashed water on my face, tied my sleep-matted hair into a ponytail, slipped on my sandals, slammed the door shut behind me, and hustled to my car, which I'd parked on Mission Boulevard.

The dull yellow streetlight made my little '83 Volkswagen Beetle look miserably forlorn. It sat humbly between two splashier, shinier, and newer cars. The night mist had settled on it. The front windshield was dark, wet, and gaping, looking tragically human.

I slid into the vinyl seat, damp from the night air, and shivered. As I fumbled the key into the ignition, I caught my reflection in the rearview mirror, which made me smile. For all the discomfort I felt and in spite of my grumbling, I was totally elated. And this eagerness glowed back at me in my reflection, even in that dim light. Up until now, nobody at the paper had told me that my presence was "urgently required," as Richard had just said. There was little traffic at that hour, and I made it to the *Observer* offices in record time.

I knocked on the conference room door.

He got right to the point. A tunnel had been discovered at the Mexican border earlier that morning.

It was connected to a storage warehouse facility in Otay Mesa, in the American *frontera,* and an automobile salvage lot near the other side of the fence in Mexico. The D.E.A. was on site doing the initial crime scene investigation there. Television news with its broad-cam had just arrived on the scene.

I was to cover the tunnel's discovery for the morning edition. There was a good chance that this article would make the front page of the local section, or even the national front page—with my own byline. The Associated Press was already interested in buying the story. This would be a great opportunity.

A deadline for the draft was given. I had just over two hours to interview, investigate, and get it written.

What had been learned from the D.E.A. was that several tons of marijuana and cocaine had been seized during its delivery to the tunnel entrance in Mexico. There was evidence that human smuggling recently occurred in the tunnel as well. My responsibility was to gather information for an article that would expand on television's morning edition's "Breaking News."

Richard walked with me to the elevator. "I told you I would shoot something to you," he said. "Now, go forth and make me proud!"

I met the staff photographer outside the newspaper building. While he drove, I read off driving directions and filled him in on the information I'd learned about the tunnel's use.

Beyond the forbidding twelve-foot-high chain-link fence enclosing the property, the television news truck was parked with its lighting scaffold extended. Massive bright lights focused on the entrance of a building there, and people scurried around like flies on a jelly sandwich. The news anchor was giving her report to the cameraman.

I walked close by her, eavesdropping on what she had to say, and caught the words "longest tunnel discovered in over a decade" and "smuggling drugs."

There was a crude cement-block building on the lot. In the front of the building, yellow police tape had been hung across the entrance where D.E.A. officers guarded the unit, standing at regular intervals, fully armed. Aside from the woman's voice, there was a deadly silence in the air. Faces were grim.

I showed my press identification and one of the officers lifted the tape to let me through. He directed me to the officer in charge, Captain Hamilton, who was engaged in a conversation with another officer just inside the unit. The officer told me that Captain Hamilton had been expecting someone from the paper and was ready for the interview. I thanked him and walked over to the building, to the two uniformed officers, who looked very officious—and impressive in size and brawn.

They were just finishing up their conversation as I approached them. Again, I held out my identification. The captain introduced himself as Doug Hamilton. An agent for the D.E.A., he would be the media spokesman working with the San Diego unit of the International Border Tunnel Task Force. He said this was his second tunnel of this sort.

Hamilton explained that the tunnel started here in Otay Mesa and ended on the other side of the border, just outside the city of Tijuana. He confirmed what I overhead the anchorwoman telling the camera just now: that it was one of the longest smuggling tunnels uncovered in this vicinity in recent years. He added that it spanned 2,400 feet, the length of approximately eight football fields, and that roughly two and a half tons of marijuana and raw cocaine had been excavated from the tunnel.

"How was the discovery made?" I asked.

I was told that the surveillance operation began about five months before, when members of the San Diego Tunnel Task Force received information concerning a cross-border tunnel.

"Nothing was said to any of the press at that time because, of course, we waited until the tunnel was put to its intended use. The success of the surveillance and final crackdown was an international feat, with this agency working in liaison with Mexican and American border-enforcement officers. It's been a long time coming; it was all a matter of timing. We knew from our sources that there was a major shipment of marijuana and cocaine on its way. We kept watch for this shipment. When the plane brought it to a landing field in the hills, about fifty miles south of here in rural Mexico, the *Federales* were ready for it and let us know it had arrived. They tracked it using clandestine observation, aerial photography, and radar. We were ready at this end of the tunnel.

"Of course we only got the peons—just the delivery boys. They're in custody now. We're not overly optimistic. We won't get much out of them, if anything. It's what we find in the samples that will be interesting to us. When we get them, we'll get the lab to run tests."

"What kinds of tests?"

"Chemical analysis. The tests should tell us if this cocaine shipment can be tied to the Cali Cartel down in Colombia. We'll do a comparison study between what we find here and what we have already acquired from Cali in another bust down south. Recently, Cali has shifted to trafficking more cocaine because of its higher street value and its relative ease in trafficking. Why this bust is important to the D.E.A. is because up until this seizure, the Cali Cartel operated mainly out of Miami, with its air connections by way of the Caribbean. This would mark the beginning of a major Colombian connection through the California-Mexico border, at least the first that we know of. Once we identified it, we would attempt to trace it to trafficking cells in Mexico and cells in our own country."

I asked about the Cali Cartel, and specifically about the business empire it created and how it rose to international power. I learned that it destroyed its archrival, the Medellín Cartel, by ruthlessly collaborating with the Colombian police in supplying information about Medellin members. This practice ultimately resulted in a violent and deadly standoff between the Medellin Cartel and the Colombian military. Rather than the power play of violence that its predecessor had used, the Cali employed more subtle business practices, such as utilizing legitimate enterprises throughout the EU and Spain for money laundering. Borrowing a successful technique of the Medellin Cartel of using lightweight airplanes to transport drugs into the U.S. interior, Cali purchased and controlled an island in the Caribbean that they used mainly for the purpose of refueling these airplanes. I learned how the Cali Cartel separated its groups into cells so that each group knew little about the others; how its technology was state-of-the-art, encrypting communication so that it couldn't be hacked into, bugged, or traced; and its practice of hiring internationally renowned legal experts to protect themselves from prosecution by D.E.A. and U.S. prosecutors. The Cali Cartel kept its reputation for high-quality cocaine by importing expert chemists into Colombia from such distant places as Japan.

"You've got to admire this tunnel, though. It took a tremendous amount of effort to construct it and not be caught doing it. Not to mention manpower. Time. And a whole lot of money." He shook his head in disbelief. "Just excavating and removing the dirt without being seen is astonishing."

"That this was done right under our noses, with patrol helicopters systematically patrolling this area of the border from the air, is huge," the other D.E.A. officer added.

Captain Hamilton nodded grimly.

"When was it constructed?" I asked.

"At least from what we're seeing here, it was finished fairly recently. But tunnels have been used for smuggling for a long time. I've got my hunches that a tunnel, perhaps not of this sophistication or length, might have been situated here for decades."

"But you don't know for sure."

The captain shook his head. "The Drug Enforcement Forensics Team will have to answer that question. They'll look behind the cement on the walls for water marks in the compacted earth, I suspect. If they can find the dumping site of the excavated dirt, they might be able to make a judgment call. Like I said, I think it has been here for a while. It might have been updated with lighting, ventilation, and reinforcement of the walls, but a tunnel could have been here a long time."

"This tunnel isn't unique, you say? There are others?"

"There are other tunnels, but none so far of this sophistication."

"You keep using the word *sophisticated*. Could you elaborate on what you mean?"

"Lighting. Ventilation, as I mentioned. Cement reinforcement. Communication system, a radar system—which probably addresses your observation about surveillance. It has been very well maintained, clearly expecting high financial returns. A *lot* of money went into improving the tunnel. And drugs are only part of the picture. There's human smuggling and human trafficking as well. Its maintenance and concealment illustrate the scope of the drug war, the vast amount of financial reserves that are involved in getting illegal drugs and people into America, and unfortunately the weakness in our current border system in stopping these things from coming in.

"Follow me closely, Miss Schilling. We're done with the initial part of the process—removing the contraband. But it's dark in there. I think you'll find this experience of walking the tunnel interesting and want to describe it in your paper."

We entered the building that housed the tunnel entrance. In it was a square room with cement block walls, a metal roof, and a single door and front window. It was sparsely furnished with a metal military-style desk and three four-drawer file cabinets, a wall clock, and an outdated calendar brandishing nudes. Two Naugahyde chairs and a table covered with old magazines took up one corner. Curious, I picked up a couple of the magazines and noted that the name and address labels had been torn off the covers. It looked like a typical office one would expect to find in a business of this sort. A thread-bare carpet covered most of the Saltillo-tiled floor. The corner of the carpet had been pulled back, revealing a trapdoor in the floor, now exposed and yawning. The metal cover that had originally sealed it had been moved aside. Several tiles that had been removed were piled nearby.

The entrance to the tunnel was a square a little over three feet wide. A retractable ladder was extended into the void below. Captain Hamilton was already halfway down the ladder before I managed to shuffle my gear around and began to climb down behind him. It was about a fifteen-foot drop to the tunnel floor. As I descended, the air became cooler and damper.

"See there?" He pointed to a rope and pulley. "The stairs can be lifted out of the way for handing down merchandise. That's one of the possible indicators that this site was used for more than one type of smuggling. We've seen some pretty crude elevators installed in other tunnels. But this tunnel is shallow enough for hand-to-hand distribu-tion of cartons or bundles from up above down to another person in the tunnel. Smuggling of the other type would use this ladder."

The tunnel was about seven feet high, judging from the distance above Hamilton's head, and about five feet wide—narrow enough to touch both sides with fully extended arms. Light bulbs were strung along the center of the ceiling, throwing faint puddles of light onto the rough hard-packed floor. Whitewashed cement thinly coated the hard-packed earthen tunnel walls.

I followed closely behind the captain as we plodded deeper into the tunnel. Our footsteps were muted by the earthen floor and the air was damp and musty. Between the puddles of luminosity created by the ceiling fixtures, it was almost pitch.

For what seemed a very long time, we walked in silence. The more distant we were from both ends of the tunnel, the darker and damper it grew. The feeble light overhead was nearly completely absorbed by the gloom. The captain's form frequently lost its human shape and tangibility as distance increased between us. He would become merely a deeper, darker silhouette. Occasionally, he stopped to let us catch up to him realizing our tentativeness in that dark and creepy place.

When the photographer, who followed me, took occasional pictures during the walk, the shock of the bright light would leave me temporarily blinded. Then my vision would return to normal, and it would become so dark, even with the overhead lighting, that I needed to use my hands against the hard earthen walls to feel my way. Ironically, even with male escorts, I needed to keep reminding myself that I was safe. I consciously fought growing claustrophobia.

I began to compare my experience with the experiences of others who had possibly walked through this terrifying, stifling tunnel before me. I realized how insignificant my own trepidations were when compared to the risks, dangers, and exploitation others had faced. The thought of their apprehension, as they walked this same black walk that I now took, was chilling. Some may have made this walk filled with hope, with dreams of the future that America promised. Others came with guns held to their backs. These faced lives of abuse, slavery, and cruelty.

The sigh of relief I breathed when we ascended from the tunnel was audible. Fresh air replaced the musty, damp air we'd been breathing and the flood-lights from the television van were a welcome sight. We thanked the officers for their assistance with the story. Then, loaded with thoughts, feelings, and information we drove back to the newspaper to put together the article.

I was amazed at how easily ideas jelled into written observations and how words flowed. When at last we'd finished, I knew that my photographer and I had done a good job of putting the article together. The pictures that he took captured the insidious atmosphere inside the tunnel, while my article included frightening statistics showing the immense increase in the use of international tunnels, as well as a numbing description of human smuggling. I confidently submitted our product.

Instead of being exhausted from lack of sleep, I was jolted with exhilaration and decided to work on a few ideas that hit me about the Abkhazian case. I spent the rest of the early morning hours squinting at old microfilm. Later, when the morning edition rolled off the press, I was right there to take in hand one of the first issues. I trembled as I scanned the front page. As I read *Largest Tunnel Discovered: Over Two Tons of Marijuana and Cocaine Seized at Mexican Border*—my headline—my excitement was palpable. There, under the title, my name appeared: *By Sera Schilling, Reporter.*

Pete McGraw

WHILE PETE WAS sleeping, Mrs. Kersel put the morning newspaper on his bedside table with a smile on her lips. It was all she could do to resist awakening him. The nurse had folded the paper with the article topside so that Pete would see it the moment he awoke. Before bringing the paper back to his room, she'd taken a yellow highlight pen to the byline: *Sera Schilling, Reporter.* Now she wanted to be there when he picked it up and read it, to share his happiness with him.

It was Pete's morning ritual to reach for the paper first thing in the morning before getting out of bed. He'd occasionally take a pill to offset any pain, read the paper front to back, and let the medication take effect before Mrs. Kersel brought him his breakfast.

This morning he reached for the newspaper and was surprised to see that one of the articles had been highlighted in yellow. He blinked rheum from his eyes to see more clearly, read the headline again, and read aloud: "Largest Tunnel Discovered: Over Two Tons of Marijuana and Cocaine Seized at Mexican Border. By Sera Schilling, Reporter.

"Hot damn! She got her contract!"

His nurse must have heard his exclamation, because within seconds she was standing at the door. She came in, and together they read the entire article aloud.

"We ought to do something to celebrate with her," Pete decided. But what? Flowers were too *girlie* for Sera. Champagne? No, she drank beer. What could they do to show their support of the upwardly mobile young newspaper reporter? After a few minutes' discussion, they decided that a desk plate would do. One with her name imprinted: *Sera Schilling, Investigative Reporter.* Hadn't she shared her dream with Pete of becoming an investigative reporter? Well, she was on her way, and they wanted her to know that they were behind her on her professional journey, starting with this first step.

Pete continued reading the paper against the background of Mrs. Kersel whistling in the kitchen, as she prepared his breakfast. He wanted to whistle, too, or to sing. He couldn't be much prouder if he had been her father. Sadly, she'd told him that she hadn't known her father. That was one hell of a burden for a young gal to carry.

He lay the paper down on his lap and thought about his own career—its gigantic leaps and its thudding crashes. For one particular memory, even pain pills wouldn't alleviate its physical pain.

He took a minute to watch a scrub jay on the eucalyptus branch just outside his window. Something startled the jay. It squawked and pumped its wings to fly out of sight, the bold blueness of its feathers filling him with pleasure. Didn't Connie feed the scrub jays? Didn't she leave peanuts just inside the kitchen door? And didn't one fearless female come into the kitchen to receive her meal and peck it from Connie's hand?

Connie.

Hadn't Connie put up with a lot from him? Pete recalled when everything turned upside down in his life.

• • •

The last of summer days in 1933 languished along with the season's pending end. The expectancy of school reopening in September offered welcome relief for parents of antsy children. It meant that they could finally relinquish to others their tight hold on their children. Conversely, most children began to resent the repression of overbearing parents who had been traumatized by the Abkhazian boy's death. They recalled summer holidays before this one that had seemed unlimited in freedom, sunshine, and space: The city was their playground. Now, they wanted to go back *to* school. There, unspent energy finally could be expended on playgrounds, playing with chums they'd missed over the summer holiday; school: where kids could be kids!

As August days eased by, the mood of the entire city seemed to temper into simpler routines. The agitation of early summer was beginning to dissipate into the more mundane concerns of home and hearth. Children's laughter began to once again punctuate the over-fence chatter of mothers.

Since the sheriff's department had taken over the investigation of the Abkhazian boy's death, articles were to be found on the back pages of Section A, instead of the front page. They leaned towards accidental death. Ever-increasing evidence pointed that way, according to Carver's nightly radio appearances.

The editorial section continued to take stabs at Chief Doyle. He was on his way out; he hadn't been all he was cracked up to be.

And San Diego's hero, Pete McGraw? He fell from grace with a picture that was caught by a newspaper photographer and published on the front section of the local section. It was of Pete escorting a woman "known to be of questionable repute" in the Stingaree.

Reporters began hounding Pete. Then they hounded Connie.

At first Connie greeted the reporters warmly, trying to keep emotional control by presenting a cheerful countenance. Then the doorbell nagged. Over-eager reporters with revolting questions unnerved her so much that she avoided answering the door altogether.

In the beginning, she made an effort to keep up her normal activities, trying to ignore the gossip and the slights of friends. After a while, she began to distance herself, closeting herself away in her little home, and suffering.

While she suffered, her husband struggled. Connie didn't know what double binds Pete had made for himself. These involved his boss's demands, his buddies' trust, and his affections. And like predacious crows taking chunks out of his self-esteem, these were devouring his confidence, his self-worth, his identity—and even his resolve to stop his growing addiction to alcohol.

One of the dilemmas Pete faced had to do with respecting authority. Pete had been raised by strongly moral parents to respect authority. When, six years before, he joined the force, he served under the last of the strong leaders who had resigned his position because of a heavy-handed city council. After that chief left the department, Pete served under a series of lackluster leaders. None earned his respect. He had hoped Doyle was different, but he was proven wrong.

For one thing, Doyle was a poor cop. He threw Pete into command of the Abkhazian boy's death, which was a good thing at the time, but soon Pete realized he'd been given the command impulsively. As it was, he began investigating the boy's death too late. Like the rest of the fellows in the department, Pete felt that if they had gotten on the case immediately after the boy went missing, they might have even found him alive.

And now that the sheriff's department had taken control of the investigation, Pete was stripped of the title of chief detective, to street patrol.

Another thing that was gnawing at Pete was his relationship with other officers in the department. Most of them were his friends, for heaven's sake. And teamwork and unquestioning comradeship were paramount in such a potentially dangerous profession.

As a boy, Pete proudly observed the respect the department showered on his father. Senior McGraw earned an almost epic reputation for integrity and honor that lasted even after his death. Pete had to wonder what his father would have thought about his son allowing himself to be placed in such an abhorrently compromising situation as ratting on his cronies. No, Pete thought, Doyle had completely misjudged his father. He would have flat-out refused to do it and would have walked out if the degrading command had been given to him.

But, hell, this was the Depression, and a paycheck was a paycheck.

Pete met with Doyle weekly to report what he'd found on kick-backs. Unfortunately, one of the officers saw him go into Doyle's office and close the door behind him. Word got around that McGraw had succumbed to the detestable position of the chief's stool pigeon, and then everyone started to shun him.

Another double bind was in his marriage. Pete wanted more than anything in the world to stay loyal to Connie. But those promises faded. One night when Pete got home especially late, he saw the note on the kitchen counter. He didn't need to open it to know its contents. Connie was spending a few nights at her parents' home. This began a swinging-door relationship: she would be there, then here, then there. And then she wanted to make it permanent. He didn't blame her for leaving. To be fair, Connie had all the reason in the world to leave him.

Then, one morning, after an entire night of philandering, imbib-ing, and still half drunk, on impulse Pete called the Abkhazian home and asked for Catherine. He was told that she was practicing down at the church. He drove to Chula Vista, parked his car on the street behind the South Bay Baptist Church, and quietly took a seat in the last row and listened to her practice on the church organ. For nearly three hours, he sat alone and unobserved in the darkened sanctuary.

He found that he discovered a kind of peace there that he craved, and going to the church to listen, to watch her, became a habit. No one knew he was there. *She* didn't know he was there.

Dwarfed by the cherry wood console of the huge pipe organ, the tiny woman worked both hands and feet. Her hands slid across the keyboard while her feet busily worked the pedalboard. She took on a bit of a comical look, like a wind-up doll. Her curly head bounced, her elbows flew, her knees rose and sank, and her back muscles rippled under her cotton dress.

Sometimes he would enter the sanctuary noiselessly and see her sitting silently, staring at the stained-glass window, with reflections of red, blue, and gold coloring her face.

Using any excuse whatsoever, Pete also frequently dropped by the little bungalow on 47th Street. Sometimes he would find Catherine at work, practicing the piano for an upcoming concert, for church, or for self-improvement. She'd welcome him with a nod, briefly explain the music she was working on, and ask him to take a seat until she finished. Then she'd lose herself in her music.

In those electrifying moments of listening, while chords and trills and runs reverberated and set the air to humming, his own heart raced.

On other visits to the Abkhazian house, the dreaded mother-in-law would answer the door and silently and grimly motion him to the backyard, her probing eyes cutting into his soul. In the backyard he'd find Catherine bent over, working alone in her garden, clipping and pruning her beloved roses. He would stand silently in the shadow of the magnolia tree, watching her completely absorbed in her work. She would be wearing her gardening apron, her gloves, and a straw hat under which her dark curls coiled onto her porcelain neck. When he interrupted her, their eyes would lock. The intensity of this connection would catch him off guard. But her eyes lit up. She'd smile at him. And the spell would be broken.

One time he found her working on a particular rosebush that seemed the smallest and yet most fruitful in her garden, thriving with deep red blossoms and lush green leaves. He complimented her on it. She seemed pleased that he'd mentioned its beauty. It was her creation, she explained. She had grafted this rose before her son died. It had been accepted into the American Rose Society. She named it Blood Red Rose for its color. She placed a hand on his arm and led him over to the rosebush. She took her clippers, found a perfect bud, cut it, and handed it to Pete. She told him that on their way to church every Sunday, she would choose the most perfect rose to take out to Glen Abbey Cemetery. She would then place it at Christopher's grave.

She took Pete to where she had cultivated other rosebushes of the same variety and gave him a small pot with one of them in it, suggesting he add it to his own rose garden.

He had.

• • •

The memories seemed to drain Pete of all his earlier happiness and excitement. But he forced himself out of his bed and into the bathroom, where a change of clothing would be waiting for him. The one thing he was adamant about was keeping neat as long as he could during this soul-destroying, body-decaying disease. Kate understood his compulsion and kept his shirts and handkerchiefs ironed, his pants pressed, and his suit jackets hung tidily on hangers.

After he dressed, Pete considered the two important things he'd just now put on his agenda for the day: He would call and order a desk plate for the future investigative reporter. That was number one. The second thing he'd do was try to get out to the garden to that rosebush and see how it was faring. Better than he was, he hoped.

Pete and Sera

MRS. KERSEL'S FACE lit up when she opened the door and saw Sera standing on the porch.

"Did you get Pete's gift?"

"Yes! The desk plate!" Sera flushed with pleasure. "You were so very thoughtful."

"Mr. McGraw thought you probably didn't already have one."

"That's absolutely right." She lowered her voice. "I'm not yet an investigative reporter, though, Mrs. Kersel."

"He knows that, Sera. But he holds high hopes for you!" She ushered Sera through the door she held open. Still smiling, she said, "Pete felt well enough to enjoy the outdoors today. He's out in the backyard." She beckoned for Sera to follow her through the house to the dining room, where the French doors had been opened and fragrant breezes blew through.

As Sera stepped out into the backyard, her face registered her astonishment at the dazzling garden, still strikingly prolific with late roses bursting in a kaleidoscope of brilliancy.

"Mr. McGraw," the nurse yelled out in a chipper voice, "Miss Schilling is here!"

"I'll be there in just a moment." The old man answered from somewhere within the vibrancy.

Sera's eyes followed the sound of the snapping of pruners to see Pete's gloved hand tossing dead leaves and spent flowers into a pile by the side of the garden.

"Make yourself comfortable," Mrs. Kersel said to Sera. "There's lemonade, so please help yourself. He'll be out soon. It's surprising that he felt well enough to do what he's doing."

"I'm in shock," Sera whispered to the nurse. "The last time I was here, Pete was so weak. How could he now be so full of energy when he has cancer?"

The nurse shrugged and smiled. "Nature of the disease, I guess. Mr. McGraw is a fighter. And that garden means the world to him. He's been determinedly getting out there for as long as I've taken care of him."

"Is there a chance—" Sera let her question drift off.

"You mean, can he beat the cancer? No. He still is on borrowed time. We must make the most of these days when they happen. Now, you settle in and enjoy this beautiful weather."

Sera listened to the clipping, watched the cuttings being tossed, and thought that Pete McGraw was the most unusual character she'd ever met. When he first telephoned the newspaper about this case, she envisioned an old, infirm curmudgeon. Then, when St. James described McGraw as a cross between a real-life superman and one of those old-time hard-boiled private eyes of the Bulldog Drummond, Boston Blackie, or Dick Tracy variety, her curiosity peaked. When she finally met the man, she found him courteous, candid, and sharp.

Sometimes flashes of that tough-but-troubled, brutish, and alluring younger man shined through his age and illness. When he was younger he was a giant of a man—virile, with rugged Irish features. His eyes, now in old age, were rheumy and faded, but they were still very blue. When Pete smiled, one forgot the poor teeth, the stubble of whiskers, the nose that was somewhat bulbous, and the sallow complexion, because his smile made his whole face crinkle up merrily. It was impossible to see Pete smile without smiling back.

She set up her equipment and began to thumb through a steno pad left on the table. The pad, with *Abkhazian – 1933* written on its cover, had only one page used. It was in Pete's handwriting and of bulleted notes. This, she suspected, outlined his agenda for today's interview. There was also a leather-bound, clasped journal on the table. Despite her curiosity, she was reluctant to open up the seemingly personal and very old journal.

After a short while he emerged from the garden, opened the shed door, tossed his pruning shears and gloves into a container. He stood watching her pensively as he wiped his hands and forehead with a bandana he'd taken from his pants pocket. "Glad to see you've made yourself at home. Do me a favor and pour me a glass of that lemonade. I'll be right over." Finally the bandana was tossed among his tools and the shed door closed. He ambled over to the table, pulled out the chair opposite her, and sat down on it heavily.

"Mrs. Kersel picked that up at the K-Mart for me to jot down notes in our interviews," he said about the steno pad. "Didn't you think last time when I outlined what I was going to talk about, it helped to keep me on track?"

Not giving Sera the chance to respond, he picked up the other, beaten-up leather notebook. "See here? I also had a chance to sit down with my old police journal since I saw you last." He picked it up and handed it to her.

The musty smell and time-blurred pencil, with notes scrawled across pages dating from July 1933 through the end of August 1933, attested to its age and authenticity. Pages had become yellowed and brittle, and were pockmarked with deterioration. The farther into the notebook, the sparser his notes became—perhaps a date here, a number there, an initial, arrows, or notes in the margin;

crudely drawn maps and sketches were the only notes by the last page.

Sera looked up when she'd finished glancing through the pages of the frail, old book.

He laughed at her puzzled expression. "I'm afraid it's Egyptian hieroglyphics to others. I call it McGraw shorthand. I'll tell you what, Sera: I'm going to give this notebook to you today. You might be able to interpret it and fill in the gaps from our interviews. You can keep it as a souvenir, or throw it away."

The old man reached across the small patio table and took her hands into his old ones. "I can't tell you how terrible I feel about getting someone as sweet as you involved with something as loathsome as this old case. I now realize it was my ego that I wanted to polish that compelled me to dig it up again. I didn't want to die with this case unsolved. You have done an admirable job of researching. Up until now, nobody supported me, or even listened to me. Now Sera, if you want to stop working on this case, I can't blame you. You're on the road to a successful journalism career, and getting to the bottom of this old case *ain't* going to stop the world from spinning. Now, more important than putting closure on this case, I can't go to my grave with any sense of peace knowing that I put you in danger."

McGraw's uncommonly sentimental outburst took Sera by surprise. Her eyes welled up. She gave his gnarled old hands a sound squeeze. "I won't give it up and I'll never throw this away," she said about the notebook. "We're a team. I won't let down my end."

He grinned. "Okay then, are you ready? Let's begin our work for today!"

"Ready!"

Pete picked up the pencil, opened the pad to the first page, and with a definitive stroke, checked off the first bulleted note. "I'm afraid we've some ugly stuff to cover today."

She nodded thoughtfully. The whole thing was pretty darn ugly.

"Last Thursday we left off talking about Sunday, July twenty-third, after the boy's body was found. The next day, Joe and I went down to the waterfront once again. That time, we were going to interview the port pilot, a man by the name of," he consulted his police journal, "Captain Dalton Jones. This guy knew all about high and low tides, tidal drift, water temperature, unlogged or unusual ships in the harbor—things I thought might help determine where and when the body went into the water. It turned out to be time well spent: not only did he have good maritime information to share with us, he had a very definite opinion regarding the length of time the boy's body had been in the water, based on over a quarter century's experience and observation."

Pete shuffled through the pages in his notebook. "In Jones's opinion, the body hadn't been in the water for more than twenty-four to forty-eight hours. He based that estimate on the temperature of the water."

"Dr. Caswell's opinion was the same as your port pilot's."

Pete nodded somberly. "A day—or two at the most—."

"So, since the body was found floating on Sunday morning, it was probably placed in the water no earlier than Friday or Saturday."

He nodded grimly.

"So, if he went missing on July eighteenth and was put into the bay on July twenty-second or twenty-third, where was he for the three to four days that aren't accounted for?"

"I can account for one of those missing days, but the rest of the time remains a mystery. I've considered this over and over. I came up with a theory, but wasn't able to check it out."

"You said you can account for one of the days the boy was missing?"

"I interviewed a suspect—

"—who would have been Phillip Johnson," Sera suggested, consulting her notes.

"I always thought Johnson was a member of David Cohn's ring of bad boys. Johnson said the boy was alive when he handed him over. I believe that's true and he handed him over to David Cohn."

"Where was he kept?"

"Remember the Cohns had a tannery—"

"—that would fit. It was in Mission Valley."

"Yes."

"Was it checked for evidence?"

"No, unfortunately the building was destroyed in a fire before I could check it out. And remember, I only had a short time to work on the case before it was sent over to the sheriff's department."

"That is unfortunate. Back to the port pilot. Did he have an opinion of how or where the body was put into the water?"

"Yes."

"Boat or pier?"

"Pier."

"Why not from a boat?"

"We checked out boats logged for that night. There were no suspect boats recorded by the guards who were on duty during a twenty-four hour block of time."

"So the next questions would be: Where?"

Pete turned the steno pad around towards Sera and doodled a rough map of the San Diego shoreline. "This is how it was in 1933. There were quite a few loading piers in the San Diego harbor back then. This pier on the right was the one at the end of Broadway, the Broadway Pier. Next to it, this shorter one, was Pier One. This third pier on the left is Navy Pier. You can see that Broadway and Navy Piers are longer than the one in the middle, Pier One. The longer piers catch the tidal pull. Navy Pier would have been the least obstructed if there were a southerly current, which would have taken it out to the vicinity of the turning basin.

"During high tide, the current sets a southerly course; during ebb, it sets a northerly course. In order for the body to end up floating around the turning basin, the currents would have to have been in a southwesterly direction."

"If it had been thrown from the end of Pier One, it probably would have remained close by, as that pier is much shorter than the other two and doesn't get much of a tidal stream. Also, it probably would've gotten stuck in the mud and weeds at that point."

"Okay. So I get it. It would have been Navy Pier which was the most open to the southerly currents and deeper water. Next question: When?"

"See here, I've got it in my notes. On Monday, July twenty-fourth, high tide on Friday through Saturday nights occurred between 0832 and 0934. Sunset was at 0909. The culprit would have put the boy's body in the water after it got dark, after nine o'clock Friday night."

Sera held her hand to interrupt him. "But although it seems logical and fits with currents and the time of sunset, how could a person dispose of a body in such a busy place and not be seen?"

"That's a good question. For one thing, the waterfront typically was empty down there at night during the thirties. It wasn't busy like it is now with downtown residents walking their dogs along the boardwalk in the evening, or tourists riding in those fancy Cinderella coaches with the fine horses pulling them, or bicycle rickshaws, or lines of folks waiting to board one of the scenic bay cruises, or street musicians. All of that wonderful activity that we enjoy now in our beautiful Embarcadero did not happen then.

"You have to visualize the waterfront in the thirties. It was dark. There were only a few streetlights, if there were any at all. There weren't any Carnival Cruise ships all lit up; there were fewer houses across the bay in Point Loma. There were few reflections in the water to light it up. There was mucky sand, wooden piers, small sailing vessels and the like that were anchored close in by the shore. At night, when the fishermen and longshoremen left, all you'd see were sea rats of the human variety: transients, bums, and other unsavory characters."

He continued: "At both Broadway Pier and Navy Pier, there was a night watchman on duty at all times. He alternated his watch duty between those piers, which were maybe a hundred and fifty yards apart from each other. We checked the watchman's log with Captain Jones. There were lapses in time. A car could drive out to the end of the Navy Pier, do the deed, and then turn around and leave without being seen. There was a gate at the entrance on Pacific Highway. The gate was always kept open. This pier was wide enough to allow a car to drive out to the end, turn around, and return through the gate it had entered. Broadway Pier is narrower. A car could fit, but just barely. It could drive out to the end, but it would have been obliged to back up the length of the pier in order to get off since the pier wasn't wide enough for a car to turn around. Backing up without much space on either side would have been nearly impossible to do without going overboard into the water. Even on a moonlit night.

"Our conclusion? The boy's dead body was tossed into the water at the end of Navy Pier, between twenty-four and forty-eight hours before its discovery; and after nine o'clock in the evening." He paused to offer, "Would you want a refill of lemonade?"

Sera held her hand over the empty glass and shook her head. He poured the yellow liquid from the pitcher into his own glass. The ice cubes chinked against the glass.

"I'd like to hear more about Phillip Johnson." she said.

"Yes. That's bullet number two on today's agenda. When I first got Johnson's name as a person of interest, I followed him and then had my stoolie follow him. After a few days, he reported back to me. He mentioned following Johnson to the rowing club and movies. These were innocuous enough. Then he followed him to a couple of the clubs in the Stingaree and bought a deck of pornographic play-ing cards from him. He caught him selling marijuana. Joe and I were able to follow him down to the border, but our surveillance ended at the turn off where his car drove into the desert down there. We went back to check it out the next day. We didn't find anything, but had enough of the other stuff to bring him on pornography and dope charges.

"Then the bastard flat-out disappeared. I made calls to my connections in municipalities as far away as Los Angeles that we were pursuing Johnson as a person of interest in a murder case. Before long, I received a telegram from L.A. It said that Johnson had been picked up for loitering and indecent exposure in Westwood. Joe and I drove up there and brought him back to San Diego. Johnson spilled everything. He sounded pretty proud of having committed this crime. He thought he was up there with criminals like Northcott."

"Northcott?" Sera interrupted.

"The Wineville Chicken Coop Murders up in L.A. around that time, perhaps a year or so before. Northcott became somewhat of a sensation as a serial murderer of over twenty young boys." Pete added, "And apparently a role model for the likes of Johnson."

She held up a finger for Pete to pause and flipped through the pages of notes. "You mentioned chicken. The chicken feather in Christopher's shoe that you found—"

"Yes, you see the connection." Pete described the "Death Walk," the rock and it's matching hole, the matted grasses, and the red beads. "Remember the missing marble?"

"Yes! The orange cat's-eye marble Mrs. Abkhazian said was missing from Christopher's collection."

"It was in Phillip Johnson's pants pocket."

Sera shook her head. "So, what happened to Johnson?"

"Oh, Johnson did stand trial. But not for homicide."

"Hmmm. Even with all this evidence?"

"No. He was tried for a misdemeanor—"

"A *misdemeanor*?"

"Yes. The charge was obstruction of justice. He got six months at a juvenile center that Sheriff Carver ran. I don't think he even served those six months before he got out. After that we lost track of him. Heard he moved somewhere up north. As far as I know, he never returned to San Diego." Pete pushed the journal towards Sera. "It's yours now."

The old man picked up his lemonade, drained it, put the glass down thoughtfully, and said: "Losing control of that case hit me like nothing else in my life." Falling silent, he studied his aged hands on the table. "You said that it was important for me to be completely honest with you— alcoholism. It got bad. I want," he paused, looked up at Sera. His blue eyes crinkled up humorously, *"no bars held."* Sera smiled at his reference to her earlier colloquial blunder and let him continue. "Before Doyle left, he demoted me to patrol along with decreased pay, and gave me the most God-awful job of spying on my buddies. The newspaper looped me with the chief, and published shameful things about me. Connie left me. Doyle moved on. I was fired because of my drinking by the incoming chief. Hell, Sera, I would have drowned in alcohol if I hadn't had two strong lifelines to grab onto."

Sera put her notepad on the table and laid down her pencil. She leaned toward Pete and quietly asked, "Who were your lifelines, Mr. McGraw?"

He was pensive for a moment, then said, "One was Catherine, the boy's mother."

He paused as he became choked up, dabbing his eyes with his handkerchief and then honking into it.

"Catherine became my lifeline to sanity. The things she did for me!" He turned away. The ensuing silence, the unspoken words found meaning in her young heart, and she looked down at the table and waited for him to continue.

"The strength and the determination of that woman lifted me out of the gutter. Because of Catherine, I was able begin my sobriety, grant Connie the divorce she sought, and eventually get my job back at the police department."

He stopped and gazed into Sera's eyes, examining them for judgment. McGraw saw only sympathy written on the features of her face.

"And who was your second lifeline?" she asked.

"My dog Gus. You smile, but if I hadn't had Gus, and Catherine of course, my life would have been over. Some say God sends angels to help us in life. Not that I'm religious. But Irish as I am, I believe in angels. They can be of the canine variety as well.

"Many nights I'd stumble home, and God only knows how I did that. This was after Connie left and I lived alone. One of those nights, I tripped over something in front of my front door. It was a mangy, lame shepherd. He was a sight. But he cleaned up well and stayed with me for another three or four years, until he died. He was my best friend in the world."

Before Sera left, Pete asked Mrs. Kersel to bring him the little gift he had for his star reporter. When the nurse returned, she held a glass vase with a small bouquet of robust, deep red roses.

"Yes, they are very beautiful," Pete agreed as she admired them, "and they are very special roses. Remember that I told you that Catherine was a gifted woman? She was many things: a wonderful mother, a concert pianist, and she propagated roses. These came from a bush she gave me before they moved to Missouri."

"They are not only beautiful but very fragrant," Sera said, her face nearly buried in the bouquet.

"Yes, they are. You know what she named them?"

"What?" Sera smiled, then shivered with his response.

"Blood Red Rose."

Sera

IT WAS LATE Saturday morning and I would have preferred to sleep in, but the sun's rays flooded my cave with searing light. I grumbled, stretched, and scuffed over to the window to look out onto a day that was already vigorously pulsating. The ocean sparkled under the blue sky. Out in the water, surfers waited patiently in the too-calm sea for the perfect wave. Walkers, skaters, and bicyclers kept up a steady stream on the boardwalk. Bikini-clad sunbathers headed to the beach to take in a little of the rare November Santa Ana sunshine.

After a cup of coffee, I felt eager to begin the agenda that had formed in my head. I picked up my attaché and drove to Presidio Park via Starbucks for a second cup of "high test" coffee. My agenda included going through all the information that I had so far accumulated on the Abkhazian case since Pete McGraw's initial telephone call.

The Serra Museum sits atop Presidio Hill. It was here in the old Spanish presidio that California began. Its location is one of the most beautiful in San Diego.

By climbing the stairs to the tower inside the museum, one views the city spreading out below like a colorful carpet. To the north is Kearny Mesa and the lovely, pristine campus of the University of San Diego. Beneath the hill, one looks down onto cliffs that fall sharply into Mission Valley, where two major interstate arteries converge. To the west is the blue water of the Pacific Ocean; to the east are the rounded coastal Cuyamaca Mountains.

I found a table under the leafy branches of a California oak tree where it was comparatively quiet, a short distance from the playground and athletic field hosting little boys' soccer games. Presidio Hill was always windy, and now there was a little bite to the air. It wasn't uncomfortable, but it made the warmth of the coffee I'd picked up welcome and the onion bagel taste better. Finally I was ready to begin my work.

First I removed the yellow legal pad from the attaché. It was nearly filled with notes I'd taken since I'd begun working on the case. Then I took out all the loose papers and sheets of photocopied microfilm. I removed the mini cassette tapes of Pete McGraw's interviews and paired each with its typed transcript, flattened crumpled pages of information that had been jammed into the bottom of the attaché, and found a rock to use as a paperweight. Pausing to read through each page as I placed it in the pile, all the places I'd been and the people I had met struck me. The last things to come out of my attaché case were the first items I'd used in my research: the sheriff's department's forensic team's newspaper article, the perpetual calendar, and my timeline, which had grown more detailed since I'd begun it on the first day of my assignment and with the last day of Christopher Abkhazian's life.

I reviewed the photographs I'd copied in the historical society's archives. Among them were various street scenes of old San Diego. One picture showed the busy corner of Broadway and Fifth streets. Included in the photograph was Kress's Department Store, where the boys had played in the toy department just before Christopher Abkhazian disappeared. Horse-drawn wagons shared the street with cars. A streetcar, loaded with passengers, took up the center of Broadway under a ceiling of wires. The photo was dated June 1930. This was what Jackie Cohn and Christopher Abkhazian might have viewed in downtown San Diego.

Another photograph showed the San Diego waterfront, circa 1930. Tuna boats were moored to posts on a wooden pier with off-duty fishermen standing in small groups, relaxing and talking. Hemp fishing nets were strung out to dry. In the background, a steamer with black smoke trailing from its smokestack crossed the bay.

There were photographs of Balboa Park, including the Pepper Grove. One of the San Diego Zoo showed a line of customers awaiting entry. I studied the faces wondering if any of the people Pete mentioned were in the line. There was also an old black-and-white aerial photo taken around this same time. The picture showed the agricultural valley that Mission Valley used to be, with farms, livestock, and a swollen San Diego River. Camino Del Rio was the only road through the Valley then. It ran parallel to the San Diego River. Unlike busy Interstate 8, there was absolutely no traffic on that narrow, two-lane road when the photograph was taken.

In the same aerial shot, I noticed that the Valley appeared much narrower at the point where I imagined Christopher and Phillip Johnson crossed it, between Presidio Park and Kearny Mesa. Interestingly, the vertical cliffs on both elevations were gentler slopes at the time, before Caltrans and commercial development altered the topography for the interstates. The ostrich farm and the trail behind it leading into Mission Valley were caught in the photograph.

I compared this aerial picture to a 1930 street map, and could trace what I believed was the route Johnson had taken with Christopher to get from the ostrich farm to Kearny Mesa. It occurred to me how easy it would have been then to walk it, with no interstates and the San Diego River only a trickle in the dry month of July.

I had newspaper photos of the Abkhazian family, Pete McGraw, and other key players in the long-ago drama. One was a picture just after the boy's body had been taken from the bay. The sheriff's dinghy was in the background. I could barely make out McGraw among a group of officers and doctors who were huddled around the boy's body on Broadway Pier.

I sorted through copies of Christopher's birth certificate, his erroneously dated death certificate, and the duplicate autopsy report done under the authority of the San Diego Police Department. I read over my notes from my interview with the San Diego medical examiner, Dr. Caswell.

I'd yet to open McGraw's police journal to study it since he gave it to me. Now, as I held it in my hands, I felt the verve of excitement that always happened when I found a unique, personal, and precious primary source.

On the cover was *Pete McGraw, Chief Detective, San Diego Police Department*, and underneath that, *Official Police Journal of Crime Investigation, July 1933, Abkhazian* was written in his bold, scrawling script.

I carefully fanned through its pages, looking for things he might have tucked inside, and found only two items: a rust-colored feather and a rosebud. I took the fragile bud and tenderly held it in the palm of my hand. Though it was shrunken and desiccated, its color tarnished, I knew instinctively that it was Catherine's rose, *Blood Red Rose*. I put it back in its place carefully, to keep it from falling apart.

Page by page, I reviewed Pete's notes on his investigation of the case. The first pages followed the movements of Chris Abkhazian on the day he disappeared. Pete had written the names and addresses of merchants and others he'd questioned, beginning with the hobby shop owner, the jewelry shop proprietor, and the store clerk and security guard at Kress's Department Store. There were notes he'd taken of his conversations with Stoogies, Dudley, and the Cohns. I compared his timeline to the one I'd made and found them closely parallel. Pete's route could be traced on the city street map. I had to smile when I recalled his warning that I wouldn't be able to read his handwriting. True, the pencil had faded and become blurred, yet it was easy to make out street names, people's names, stores, times, and dates.

He'd listed important details from both of the autopsies. I found these notes located in two separate places in his notebook, as they should have been, given the first autopsy took place on July 23 and the second was on August 5, under the authority of the sheriff's department.

Throughout the notebook, I noted that Pete used initials for people's names. Most of the names were easily recognizable. *C.A.* was, of course, Christopher Abkhazian; *Cat.A.* was the boy's mother, Catherine Abkhazian; *A.A.* was the father, Adam Abkhazian, and so on.

Pete's shorthand seemed incomprehensible at first glance. He'd made notations like *Saw A.A./M.E. – P.J. Others (?)*. After some thinking, I understood this concerned the time that Catherine gave Pete Phillip Johnson's name in the note at her concert. *M.E.* was Mildred Evans, the schoolteacher. The question mark after "Others" indicated the ring of bad boys, but their names were still unknown. I tried to put together the members of that ring: Phillip Johnson, David Cohn, and the *"Ss"*. So far I hadn't been introduced to anyone with a name beginning with "S" at least in Pete's police journal. And noting how Pete had referred to them as "*the* Ss," I wondered if they were related. Perhaps brothers? Father and Son? Husband and wife?

On another page Pete wrote: *P.M. / J.C. at O.B. (Scared! Brother? Ring?)* I thought this note related to the time Pete had taken Jackie to his fishing shack in Ocean Beach for interrogation. After that Pete'd written: *J.C. lying/BP/C.A./drowned*. I recalled the sheriff's investigator's deposition of Jackie Cohn. In the deposition, Jackie stated that he witnessed Christopher Abkhazian fall off Broadway Pier to accidently drown. I knew that Pete didn't believe this story and was convinced that only tremendous fear could compel Jackie to tell such a self-condemning lie. My hunch was validated when I read a note that Pete'd made: *Jackie lied to protect his brother, or to protect himself from him.*

It occurred to me, thinking about Jackie's statement, that there was another inconsistency in Jackie Cohn's deposition. This was when he said Christopher had fallen into the bay from Broadway Pier. According to all the experts' opinions, including the port pilot and Dr.

Caswell, this would have been improbable given the tidal currents and the location where the body was found floating in the turning basin by the sailors. I was convinced that Christopher went into the water at Navy Pier.

On another page, Pete noted picking up *P.J.* (Phillip Johnson) at the *L.A.P.D., Central Precinct.* This page contained details: time of pickup and names of Los Angeles police officers to contact for further questioning if necessary, time of arrival in San Diego, and time of booking.

"DEATH WALK" was the heading, written in capital letters, on another page. The date was the day after Pete had brought Johnson back to San Diego from Los Angeles before his arraignment. Pete had drawn a crude map. On it, he'd painstakingly noted various points of interest along the so-called death walk.

Pete stuck the chicken feather in the pages regarding the trail through Mission Valley. He'd noted that it was from a Rhode Island Red. I found it very intriguing that Pete had kept what was possibly material evidence.

The death walk began at Fifth and B streets, sometime after noon, at the end of the Number Seven line, where Pete's notes suggested that Phillip Johnson had connected with Christopher Abkhazian.

On his map, Pete marked the trolley's route and placed an *X* at the end point, on Park Avenue several block south of the ostrich farm. A large circle was drawn around an area near the end of the line and labeled *Ellis Sundry Store, 4103 Park Ave/confirmed red licorice.* Another *X* marked the ostrich farm, and a line indicated a sand rock grade leading down into the valley. The San Diego River was marked and labeled *dry bed.*

On the north side of the Valley, he'd marked *K. Mesa,* which was Kearny Mesa, where *BROOKS* was underlined and written in capital letters.

Her name compelled me to dig out the newspaper article about Virginia Brooks. Brooks, a young girl, was murdered a few years prior to Chris's death. Her body was discovered on Kearny Mesa. In a case chillingly similar to Christopher's, this little girl was sexually molested and savagely mutilated.

The parallels were astounding. My mind ran wild. It occurred to me that the Brooks girl's murderer was never found. Whoever it was still had been free to roam the streets of 1930s San Diego at the time, three years later, when Christopher was killed.

McGraw painstakingly described the long trail Phillip had taken the men on, ending with the chilling description of his attack: *Struck C.A./back of head with rock.* Pete noted that Johnson had *produced rock as evidence. Rock showed possible bloodstain. Viewed hole where rock was removed/matches rock shape/crushed undergrowth shows evidence of violent act/5 red glass beads found in grass/similar red beads taken from P.J. front right pants pocket @ L.A.P.D. P.J. cool, collected, talks fast and brags.*

Pete noted that Johnson's bail was paid by his mother and that he had been released into her custody two days after capture. Johnson's mother was a Marston's Department Store sales clerk. McGraw made notes regarding Johnson's arraignment: *August trial set. Muni.Ct., D.A./misdemeanor. Judge Hudson.* It was easy to comprehend that notation and the frustration the lower court caused McGraw by the heavy underlining under "misdemeanor" and "Muni Ct." Johnson escaped the stronger sentence requiring a felony trial.

On another page: *Exhumation/All evidence to L.A. Wagner – Toomey, Shea attended autopsy: vic. acc. drowning – all mutilations marine animals or ship engines.* A bold slash had been drawn across the page. Across the line, Pete had written *Slides fr. orig. aut. to Wagner, All evidence lost.*

I went to put Pete's notebook back into the attaché case, but as I picked it up, a folded piece of thin, blue lady's stationery fluttered to the table. The paper was so fine, I opened it carefully. The precise and legible calligraphy had faded. Letters and whole words had disappeared. It took a while to put together its composition.

Dear Pete:

I happened to run into Catherine Abkhazian the other day and asked her about your health. She told me you had returned from Paradise Valley and were back at your home. The ladies of the Committee of Six Hundred join me in wishing you a full and speedy recovery. We are hopeful that soon you will be fit enough to continue our combined efforts of investigating the Abkhazian boy's murder. We have appreciated and miss your professional guidance. I, for one, have missed your sense of humor. Your sobriquet, "Irish," wasn't a misnomer.

I would like to discuss some recent developments with you at your earliest convenience. I will, however, let you rest for a few more days before I telephone you to set up a meeting. In the meantime this letter will bring you current on what our committee has done on the investigation of the Abkhazian case while you were hospitalized.

Our own investigator, Monte Clark, is now firmly convinced that there is more to the Cohn boy's story than he is telling. Mr. Clark believes Jackie is terrified of his older brother, David, and his gang. Jackie is lying to protect himself, Mr. Clark told me. On one or more occasions Mr. Clark came close to breaking the boy, but Jackie would button up and then Mr. Clark couldn't get anything else out of him.

Clark, in questioning Jackie's school mates, happened to question a girl by the name of Hannah Smith. She told Clark that she overheard her father talking to Jackie's older brother in Smith's office at her home. The fact that Jackie's brother was meeting with Hannah's father at his house surprised her. Hannah mentioned that she heard Christopher Abkhazian's name brought up in this conversation.

Hannah is the daughter of William Chester Smith (I know him by name only). Smith is of an old San Diego family. He is a wealthy and prominent real estate developer. He has a ranch in

Chula Vista, where his wife, Charlotte Delancy (of the Scottsdale Delancys), and he entertain many notable personages frequently. In addition, my informants tell me that he carries a heavy dose of clout at City Hall.

This may or not be significant, but I thought it interesting enough to mention it to you. When you get back into ship shape, you may want to check out Smith and why Christopher was a subject of this meeting.

I do not believe in coincidences.

You always held the frame of mind that there's some bigwig who is the kingpin in all of this. We aren't overlooking Phillip Johnson's culpability, nor David Cohn's for that matter, but like you, our committee is leaning toward someone else as the heavy hand in Chris's death.

I am working on trying to get the grand jury to look at an appeal of Johnson's sentence for that misdemeanor case— BEFORE WE LOSE HIM! I also petitioned them to reconsider Jackie Cohn's testimony. We'll see where that gets us. If we can get the judge to vouch for us, we might have a good chance at it.

In the meantime, please take good care of yourself. The ladies need your guidance in our ongoing commitment to bring justice to the Abkhazian family. We need you; and, we need you in good health.

Yours for Integrity,

Mable A. Sterling, Chairwoman, Committee of 600

I added Smith to my list of names to look up, still wondering who the *Ss* that Pete talked about in his journal were. My list of names was growing: Phillip Johnson, David Cohn, Jackie Cohn, Hannah Smith, W.C. Smith. And the *Ss.*

I looked around Presidio Park. The mothers and their sons had left the soccer field. Now the park was quiet. The sun had slipped into the west. Shadows from tall eucalyptus trees fell long on the grass. The wind had died down. I was alone, except for two people. A sweater-clad woman walked her white Pomeranian around the perimeter of the grassy area, stopping intermediately to let it sniff and raise its small hind leg. A man sat at a nearby picnic table. His head was down. He seemed to be immersed in what appeared to be the newspaper's crossword puzzle.

It was time to leave and postpone my research until another day. I had a ticket for a Lenny Kravitz concert at the Sports Arena that night. Now that was something to look forward to!

• • •

On Monday morning I went to San Diego High School to view old year-books. 1933's class of graduating seniors included a picture of Phillip Johnson. He was a good looking in a rough, rakish way, the kind of ruffian some girls would find alluring. Most graduating students had a short list of activities, their college aspirations, and a brief depiction written under their pictures. Johnson didn't have anything but a curt caption: *Reckless and Wild.* I didn't get the impression that he won any popularity contests at San Diego High. The omitted caption said it all: What is left unsaid, sometimes says a whole lot about a person.

In the senior section, I also found David Cohn's picture. No college, no caption, no sports or other after-school activities were published under his picture. I glanced through the Ss in the same class, making a mental note of their names.

Jackie Cohn and Hannah Smith were members of the freshman class, as I knew. On Smith's page, along with other names beginning with "S," a student by the name of Harold Sanders was pictured. Recalling the name "Sanders" from the graduating class, I flipped back to seniors. True to my hunch, I found a student by the name of Marvin Sanders. The fact that the two boys, although different ages, resembled each other made me suspect they were brothers. And, like David Cohn and Phillip Johnson, there were no activities listed under Marvin Sanders' picture. Three boys-plus-three-non-involved students-equaled-three high school outcasts. Had I found the names of some of the members of Pete's so-called ring of bad boys: Cohn, Johnson, and the Sanders' brothers?

Since Harold would have graduated in 1936, if he were a freshman when his brother graduated from San Diego High School in 1933, I pulled the 1936 *Gray Castle*'s yearbook from the shelves and found Harold Sanders' graduating photo. The caption under his picture read: *Bound for the Military.* Considering that World War II was revving up in Europe, it would fit that a student in 1936 might go into the military.

Unlike his brother and his friends, Harold was on the high school football team, involved in several other after-school activities, including Boy Scouts. And with the reference to military service, it was obvious that he, unlike his brother, had ambitions.

Hannah Smith was in the same graduating class as Harold at San Diego High School. Her graduation photo stood out from those of other girls because of her beauty. She was active in after-school clubs. Her caption read: *Our Homecoming Queen is headed for Wellesley's ivy towers in the fall.*

Leaving the high school, I drove back to the *Observer* for information furthering my yearbook finds. I also planned to connect to police and military records.

Marvin Sanders, Jr. died in 1947, at the age of thirty-two. He left a wife, Eleanor, and a brother, Harold. There were no children. Marvin, the obituary went on to mention, was the son of "prominent photographer Marvin Sanders, Sr."

On hunch, I called the police department. Their records listed a 1934 arrest of Marvin Jr. for racketeering. He had been sentenced to jail, where he served from July 1934 through January 1935. In March of 1936, he was arrested for driving under the influence of alcohol and public intoxication. He was sentenced to ninety days' confinement. In 1941, Sanders was convicted of assault and sent to the state prison at Tehachapi to serve a three-year sentence.

Since Eleanor Sanders, his wife, wasn't listed in San Diego obituaries, I looked her name up in the telephone directory. Finding no listing, I suspected Eleanor would be in one of several places. Given her age, she might be in a nursing home, or she might have moved away from San Diego.

There was fascinating material in the archives about the boys' father, Marvin Sanders Sr.   Fascinating, if it were relevant to my research on this case. Sanders was a "prominent photographer" in San Diego. He died in 1949, at Paco Vista Sanitarium. The short biography summarized his life: one that began in obscurity, mounted into local and national repute, and catapulted into alcoholic ruin at the end.

Sanders's parents had both died from influenza, leaving their only child, Marvin, an orphan at nine years old. He was raised in a Catholic children's home in Kansas City, Kansas. At sixteen, Marvin left the institution to "paddle his own canoe." He rode the rails as a hobo, and was said to be "glad for it." It was during this time of hoboing that Marvin became interested in photography. A few of his photographs were published in the periodical, *Americana.* In a biography of the same issue, Sanders was quoted as saying: "I photographed what I saw along the rails, not sensitive to what my pictures took in: only what they gave out." He settled in San Diego, married, and continued to develop his skills in photography. In time he became the Marston's Department Store photographer, gained membership in the prestigious Daguerre Society, and earned many photographic awards, including the highest honor: the Diamond Medal in the Aledus Boe Photographic Competition. His subtle use of lighting and the dramatic posing of subjects were professionally recognized as "the best in his profession." I noted, with interest, the article's remark: *Sanders's areas of specialty were children and young adults.*

Harold Sanders, Marvin Jr.'s younger brother, didn't appear to have an obituary. Assuming he was still alive, I again consulted the current San Diego telephone directory and found a listing for a Harold Sanders at 3702 Van Dyke Street.

Further research of Harold Sanders's life indicated that there was absolutely nothing unfavorable reported about him. His name never made the newspaper—aside from sports articles featuring high school football games. He didn't have a police record, nor was he involved in any court proceedings. It seemed that, especially when compared to his older brother, Harold lived a clean but rather non-descript life. Military records indicated that he had enlisted in the United States Army in 1940. He was honorably discharged in 1945, after serving active duty during the Second World War. After his stint with the military, he graduated from San Diego State University with a 2.6 grade point average, earning a B.S. in engineering.

David Cohn's biography was as miserable as his buddy Marvin's. Cohn had multiple arrests for drunk and disorderly conduct in San Diego: September 1932, October 1932, December 1932, and May, 1933. Cohn was arrested for "indecent exposure in May of 1933, as well. After the last arrest, his San Diego trail abruptly stopped. A national search engine led me to Newark, New Jersey. I called and spoke with a reporter from the *Newark Star-Ledger,* who gave me the following information:

Cohn's police records in Newark consisted mostly of misdemeanors during the mid-thirties. He spent jail time for drunk and disorderly conduct, being a public nuisance, driving while intoxicated, and loitering around an elementary school play yard. Cohn served time in prison following pornography charges in 1948. He died at the age of forty-nine, in 1963.

David Cohn's death notice mentioned a younger brother, Joshua, who was a resident of New York City at the time. Jackie might have changed his name to Joshua in an attempt to put the past behind him, so I ran a search on a Joshua Cohn. I was stunned by my discovery.

Joshua Cohn, a.k.a. Jackie, had indeed turned his life around by pursuing his talent on the violin. I was able to put together a picture of an astonishing man, a man who had overcome inconceivable child-hood trauma.

I found three obituaries: in the *Newark Star-Ledger*, the *New York Times*, and the *Washington Post*. As a child prodigy, Joshua had been accepted at the prestigious Juilliard School in New York City, and studied under the tutelage of esteemed violinist Bernard Giltheim. Though his classical techniques were said to be "eloquent," Joshua's true enjoyment came from traditional and beloved Israeli folk tunes, when "sparks flew when his bow touched the strings." Joshua per-formed at many concert halls in major cities in the United States. These included New York City, Chicago, and St. Louis, Missouri. Cohn's overseas performances were popular in London, Rome, Paris, and other major European cities after the war. He was philanthropic, supporting multiple charitable organizations. Jackie/Joshua was also generous in making personal appearances at family and community functions. Cohn died in 1988, from natural causes, at sixty-four years old.

Phillip Johnson's tawdry biography was diametric to Jackie's. Johnson lived his life in an obscure, immoral, and criminal way. His squalid life was traceable by police records, just as his friend Marvin Sanders's had been. Johnson was incarcerated in a California youth facility in August of 1933, for a misdemeanor of obstruction of jus-tice, as I knew. I followed Johnson's trail to the Bakersfield area. Police records there indicated that in 1936, and again in 1937, he was arrested for "lewd and indecent exposure." In 1938, Johnson was arrested for pornography, and in 1939, for child molestation. For this offense, he served a two-year sentence. In 1946, Johnson was tried and convicted in the Bakersfield Superior Court for first-degree murder. I researched this murder and found only a short note in the Bakersfield newspaper of his arrest for the sexual assault and murder of a vagrant, LeRoy Hiddinsbrook, who was fifteen years old. Johnson was sent to San Quentin, where he died in 1953, of an undisclosed cause.

Much like a jigsaw puzzle, the pieces were fitting together. The picture was becoming clear. Although it appeared that Pete's version of the crime was most probably true, I needed something concrete on which to hang his theory before even attempting to write a rejoinder to the sheriff's article. I looked over my notes and recalled that two witnesses might still be alive and living in San Diego: the widow of Marvin Sanders, Jr., and Harold Sanders. Harold Sanders's statement might be what I needed to tie up the loose ends of my investigation into the cold case of Christopher Abkhazian.

I called the number listed in the telephone directory for Harold Sanders. A woman answered with a strong Mexican accent and identified herself as Mr. Sanders's housekeeper. I introduced myself and explained the purpose of my telephone call. The housekeeper politely and pointedly told me that Mr. Sanders was *"confinar"* and unable to get to the telephone just at that time, but she would give him my phone number. Before I let her hang up, I requested that she ask Sanders a couple of questions just to verify that he was who I wanted. She reluctantly agreed, and after a few minutes returned to the phone with affirmative answers. But he still didn't want to talk to me. I begged her to try to convince Mr. Sanders of the importance of a short interview. Once again, I held the phone waiting for a response. Sanders said that he wasn't interested in talking about the old crime. She then hung up, leaving me with a dead line and the irritating bark of the dial tone.

Later, when I heard the telephone message from Harold Sanders, I was shocked. He could see me the next afternoon.

The concept of meeting him flooded me with conflicting emotions: excitement and apprehension. On one hand he might be able to supply me with some of the missing information I needed. But what was I walking into? Although everything I'd read about Harold Sanders said he lived a respectable adult life, he was a witness to an atrocity, or worse—perhaps a participant in the crime. Another thing to consider was my personal vulnerability: Someone was desperate to have this case forgotten and I was in the way. Was Sanders involved somehow in my recent attacks? Would I be safe gong to his house alone?

• • •

Sanders's housekeeper ushered me into the living room, where the elderly man was crumpled in a wheelchair like a discarded marionette. The table next to him had an ashtray brimming with spent cigarettes. There was also a half-empty glass of milk and a plate with an uneaten ham-and-cheese sandwich. The room was dim so that the table light was on. The air was dense with cigarette smoke.

He didn't say anything as I walked into the room, but continued to suck on an unfiltered cigarette, spewing gray smoke from his nostrils and sour-looking mouth. His gaze followed me as I crossed the room to stand in front of his wheelchair. I extended my hand to shake his, in introduction. I held it out stupidly, because he ignored my gesture.

Sanders was elderly, skeletal, and worn. His neck, arms, fingers, and legs were wasted branches of an emaciated trunk. And he was completely blind.

When I spoke, he glanced up at me with hollow, unfocusing eyes. His hair was yellow-gray and his complexion ashy. Tightly drawn facial skin drew cavernous shadows under his protruding cheekbones.

I watched a curious assortment of expressions flash across his features as I spoke about the importance of this interview. His brows drew together into a frown: displeasure. His mouth curved down into a grimace: shame. He shivered violently and jerked his face away from me: guilt. Then he turned toward me once again, but kept his eyes

lowered: conflict. Finally he raised his head, nodded in self-affirma-
tion and swallowed resolutely.

"It's time," he said finally, his voice cracking with emotion as his
face drew tight.

I knew I'd get my answers.

"Oh, shit!" he suddenly bellowed out. "Shit and damnation!"

His fingers fumbled for the ashtray to extinguish his cigarette.
Finding it, he thrashed the butt into the mound of ashes until it collapsed into shreds of tobacco. "Shit!" he roared once again.

Unexpectedly and suddenly, he picked up the ashtray and flung it
so fiercely across the room so that it shattered against the wall, scattering shards of glass, ashes, and cigarette butts on the hardwood
floor. The housekeeper let out a shriek from somewhere in the back
of the little house. She rushed into the room, and when she saw the
mess on the floor, groaned: "¡Ah mi Dios! ¿Qué pasa? ¡Mi Dios!"

The scene might have been laughable had it not been so tragic.
I considered the frail man—the blind, crippled, forgotten old man—
and felt sickened by my role in reopening the wound that had been
hidden for so long under scar tissue.

The housekeeper left to get a broom. The old man fell silent as
she swept up the mess. Muttering in Spanish, she returned to the
kitchen, broom and dustpan in her hands.

After a while, Sanders sighed deeply and waved toward the sofa,
indicating for me to take a seat.

"You understand," he said as I arranged my things, "I don't like to
talk about this."

"Yes," I giggled nervously. "I think you have made that perfectly
clear." I glanced up to see how he took my sarcasm. His face remained
taut.

"You know, I could simply tell you to get lost." He lit another cigarette and fumbled on the table for the ashtray, forgetting that it was
no longer on the table. "Damn it, Sylvia," he yelled. "I need another
goddamn ashtray!"

After the ashtray was replaced, the maid left the room, and he was once again situated and smoking in his compulsive fashion, I heard him grumble, "I don't get it. After all these years—hell, why doesn't the damn thing"—he waved his hand in front of him—"just go away?"

I reassured him that I would keep his name anonymous. I was out for information only.

He knew about the newspaper article closing the case as accidental. "For me, it was a relief. But sounds like Irish never got over it," he said. "It's like a fucking parasite sucking the blood out of the guy."

"So you remember Pete McGraw?"

"Yes, of course. He was a good cop, in spite getting kicked off the force. The booze got to him. I knew about his drinking before I went overseas. When I got back I heard he'd been reinstated. Old Irish was a pretty slick investigator." He gave an indignant chuckle. "Hell, even after he'd been fired from the police, he had this Sherlock Holmes kind of obsession about solving this case. Shoot, even as time passed, even though I was only a kid and only marginally involved with the whole mess, he was a fucking monkey on my back. I got to hoping that he had kicked the bucket or just moved on. Everyone else had—my father, brother. Johnson, I heard, was in prison and died there, too. Don't know what happened to the Abkhazians, or for that matter, the Cohn family. I got to feeling pretty safe because they all moved on in life. Except Irish."

I filled him in on what I'd found about the Cohns. He was quiet and interested. He said, "That Jackie was a good fiddler even back then when he was a kid." He took a drag on his cigarette, deep in thought. Then he spat out: "It was them others. Those lowlifes. I wasn't there when the boy died. But the circumstances that led up to his death were not accidental. Those cold case investigators got it all wrong."

I wrote as fast as I could, trying to keep up with his narrative. As a younger sibling, he'd been proud to be "invited" to be a member of his older brother's secret gang. It started out with him going along with the others just raising hell. Various pranks and even some petty thefts. Razzing the Abkhazian boy was kind of a joke at first. Then it got ugly. First they beat up the boy. Then—

"The things they did!" Sanders spat out. "I never saw it, but I heard… It was them two—Johnson and David Cohn. They were sick. It makes *me* sick."

Doctor Caswell's voice rang in my head: *"Ante mortem sexual attacks were brutal and multiple,"* he had said.

"Who was in your brother's gang?" I asked.

"Johnson, David Cohn, my brother, and me, I guess."

"What do you know about the boy's abduction," I said.

"Most of it was what I heard from the others…" Harold Sanders began and then talked nonstop for nearly two hours, sweating and crying, spitting out names like they were poison, at times shivering, sighing, and cursing. By the time he finished, I felt as if I personally knew each of the sordid characters in this obscene story. His story fit the final pieces into the puzzle and validated McGraw's story.

I noticed that during his story, Harold hadn't smoked. Now he sighed and reached over to the table next to his chair and took his pack, shook out a cigarette, and lit it. I waited for him to take a few drags before I said, "Thank you. Now, perhaps ghosts can rest." I paused, then added: "One more thing: I wonder if you remember anything about a family by the name of Smith?"

"Smith?" he asked, scratching his chin. His face was relaxed. He smoked in a more leisurely and gratifying manner.

"Do you remember having a classmate by the name of Hannah Smith?"

The old man smiled. "Oh, yeah, I remember Hannah. She was a little dolly. All the fellows liked her. But, she was too good for the likes of us. Her father was a big-shot in real estate. The Smiths were rich. What do they have to do with this thing?"

"Perhaps nothing. Their name just came up."

"Hold on a moment! I seem to recall that there was some scuttle-butt about dishonest dealings with city hall and Smith. Something about water. Jeez, I can't remember now"

We let that hang. I quietly packed up my paperwork. As I left the room, I stopped by his wheelchair and once again offered him my hand. This time he sensed my gesture and reached over to shake it.

Sera

DURING THE TIME that I was involved in the Abkhazian case, there were significant management changes taking place in my department of the *Observer*. Not that these changes came as a surprise. Richard Mosier had taken over St. James's position as senior editor. Now he called me into what was now his office for a meeting. It seemed strange to see Richard sitting in what had been St. James's office.

Richard had replaced the old man's oak furnishings with sleek modern furniture. Soft popular music gave off a calm yet upbeat ambience to the boss's office. It somewhat relaxed me, as I'd been a little jittery all morning wondering what Richard wanted to see me about.

"Sit!" he cheerfully demanded, reminding me of the way St. James once welcomed me. I sat in one of the black leather and metal chairs arranged in front of Richard's desk.

Richard had positioned silver framed photographs of his wife and children on the corner of his desk. *Definitely setting boundaries*, I thought, considering my handsome boss. He now wore a self-satisfied grin as he watched me take in the new surroundings. He reclined in his ergonomically correct executive chair. I caught his eye and playfully cracked a smile. Pointing at the coffee carafe that was choking out a brew, I asked, "Did you really mean to put the coffeepot in the same, exact spot that Albion used to put his?"

This set off a round of waggish memories about the elderly St. James. We recalled the tepid, bitter coffee that he poured from the harvest-yellow Melmac coffee carafe left over from the seventies and the cups he served it in, with brown coffee stains permanently etched into the plastic.

"After those memories of St. James's famous coffee, would you *like* a cup of coffee?" Richard offered. "I promise that it's Starbucks and the cups are new. See here?" He picked up an empty porcelain cup and tipped it so that I could check out the inside for stains or chips. "The enamel is still quite spotless." Still chuckling, he poured two cups of coffee and handed one to me.

"You might be interested in hearing that you were the subject of a conversation I had with our publisher a few days ago. He was interested in knowing what you were working on.

He was favorably impressed by your article on the Tijuana tunnel and the responses the paper got from our advertisers. He wondered why you were still spinning your wheels on the Abkhazian case. When he said that, it caught me off guard. I didn't know he knew or cared about what you were involved in. He was emphatic—said he wants you to drop that case, Sera. He even suggested that we set you up with something else 'more tailored to your talents,' is the way he put it."

"Uh-uh," I said, shaking my head. "I'm nearly done. I have enough sound information to write that rejoinder to the forensic team's article. Richard, I'm going to finish it and then get it published—whether it's here at the *Observer* or someplace else."

"Sera," Richard replied, "When David pressed me to have you give it up, I couldn't tell him, 'No,' because he and I come from two different points in this business. But, finish your work and hand it in. I'll make the judgment call. Advertisers are his concern; readership is mine."

"Thank you," I said, my gut churning. I took a sip of my coffee. As I set the cup down, I noticed my hand was shaking. What had inspired me to say what I'd just said? I wondered.

Richard continued. "We discussed the other reporters' high regard for the quality of the research you did for them. We agreed that you have excellent writing skills based on this recent tunnel article and other assignments that you've been given. I told him what you said in your interview, that your ambition is to become an investigative reporter. I have no doubts that you will achieve this goal, Sera."

His confidence in me made me smile. I said: "Then you under-stand how much I want to get to the bottom of the Abkhazian case."

"Yes," Richard chuckled lightly, "Your tenacity is impressive. But to get back to our discussion, we came up with an idea for you."

I felt a flutter of excitement in my stomach. "And that would be?"

"That you have a column of your own."

"What kind of a column?" I asked, cautiously interested.

"A whistle-blowing, watchdog type of column, wherein your inter-ests, skills, and talents would be integrated."

"How often would this column appear? Daily? Weekly? Monthly? Would I still be a full-time employee?"

"We discussed the options and agreed that bimonthly might be a good start. And yes, you wouldn't change your employment status."

"How would I choose my subjects?"

"They'd come from me; or, you would find your own subjects. You'd have to pass them by me for approval, of course."

I exhaled, and relaxed back into the chair, thoughtfully drained the coffee in my cup. After a short time, I plopped the cup on Richard's desk and smiled broadly at him. "I might use the Abkhazian case for my first column."

"I'd have to approve it. But possibly—yes."

After I left Richard's office and before I continued to work on the draft that was now potentially my new column, I stopped by my desk to look through my mail and telephone messages. I was surprised to see that Rose Abkhazian had called. I returned her telephone call immediately.

Rose said she had been thinking about my recent call, in which I told her about my attack and the threats I had gotten because of my investigation of her brother's murder. She said it terrified her that someone wanted to hurt me. She admitted that although she didn't agree with the purpose of my efforts to reopen the case to new investigation when I called her at the start of my investigation, she respected my determination to see it through. She offered to help in any way she could.

The name, Hannah Smith, was seared into my brain ever since reading the letter from Mabel Sterling. Now, I wanted to check her and her family out. I needed more information on Phillip Johnson as well. So once again, I joined the extensive line of customers waiting in the county's records department.

The birth certificate read that Hannah Smith had been born to Charlotte Delancy and William Chester Smith in 1920. William Chester Smith was born in 1893; his parents were Beulah Morgan and Harold C. Smith. There was no certificate on file for Harold C. Smith. Phillip Johnson was born to Helen and Willis D. Johnson in 1914.

I took this information back to Ichabod's Den. First I consulted the circular file for Hannah Smith's obituary notice. Hannah Smith (Owens) died in 1985, leaving a daughter by the name of Miriam Delancy Owens.

Hannah's father, W. C. Smith, "The Professor," died in 1950, at the age of fifty-seven, from natural causes. He had a lengthy obituary recounting his philanthropic work, his elected position on the school board, his successful and vast lemon orchards in Chula Vista, and his real estate development. Smith's survivors included his widow, Charlotte Delancy, and daughter, Hannah Smith Owens.

The obituary for Harold C. Smith read that he was a lifelong resident of Chula Vista and died in 1958, at the age of eighty-five. He had been a cattle rancher in the Sweetwater–Otay Mesa area. He passed away "peacefully" at the Fieldside Nursing Home in Chula Vista.

I stared at the circular file for a while, wondering how I could tie these names—these lives—to the Abkhazian case. Mrs. Sterling's letter had said that Hannah Smith overhead her father talking to David, about Christopher Abkhazian. Smith and Cohn did seem to me a peculiar duo. The families might have known each other socially. But David? Why would David be at Smith's house and discussing Christopher Abkhazian?

I took several boxes of microfilm to the viewing table. Before feeding the first film into the machine, I mentally prepared myself for a long afternoon of intense reading, focused concentration, prolonged sitting in that God-awful metal chair, and trying to fit together snatches of information so that they would make some iota of sense.

Hannah Smith Owens was the subject of my first search. After a long, excruciating effort, I felt I had enough information to piece together a picture of the girl Mabel Sterling wrote about in her letter to Pete McGraw in 1933.

Hannah Smith grew up experiencing both the rural climate of agricultural Chula Vista and the urban sophistication of San Diego's elite society. She enjoyed holidays on the family ranch in Chula Vista. During the school year, Hannah attended San Diego High School. I knew she graduated from there in 1936.

Articles about Hannah Smith appeared in society pages of the newspaper and local magazines at various times of her life. She was a natural beauty that photographers adored, a fresh-faced blonde with a prominent dimple in her cheek that she showed off with a wide, photogenic smile.

The first photograph I found had been taken of Hannah was when she was a teenager. It made the front page of the local section. She was pictured, along with her horse, at a jumping competition that had been held at Agua Caliente. The article mentioned that she walked away with three blue ribbons and a jackpot amassing nearly five hundred dollars, a goodly amount that would equal over five thousand dollars in 1990.

In 1938, Hannah's coming-out picture appeared in the newspaper's society page. She was photographed along with a group of other debutantes at the Cotillion Ball. All the young women appeared groomed, poised, and happy. They were similarly dressed in long, flowing white gowns. Hannah was positioned in the center of the first row. It struck me that the photographer might have placed her center-front to highlight her beauty by framing her with the other, less dazzling women.

Since I had begun reading old San Diego newspapers, I discovered my enjoyment in some of the more period pieces, articles that appeared in the Women's Section regarding fashions, interior décor, advice, and gossip, including Helga Smiley's gossip column, "San Diego Undercurrents." Purely for entertainment in the course of my more rigorous research, I'd occasionally scroll through the pages to read Smiley's column. Often I would find myself chuckling out loud at the witty way Helga would sling the nastiest slander onto San Diego's fairest. This slander she called, "Whispers."

I wasn't completely surprised to find Hannah Smith's name appearing in one of Helga Smiley's columns, being that she was from one of San Diego's most prominent families. It mentioned that Hannah had recently graduated from Wellesley College in Massachusetts, with a B.A. degree in Liberal Studies. Smiley's column hinted that Smith had been seen at various social functions on the East Coast, "On the arm of a certain gentleman of Main Line blue blood, who is rumored to be more than simply an escort."

Sure enough, on June 13, 1942, Hannah Smith and DeWitt Clancy Owens exchanged marriage vows at the First Presbyterian Church in San Diego.

DeWitt Owens had been a graduate student in business at Yale while Hannah Smith was a Wellesley College undergraduate. According to Smiley, Mr. Owens came from a Philadelphia family, and

Hannah's father had convinced him to move to San Diego to join the Smith family's land development business.

The wedding photograph depicted an elegant bride and groom with their entourage of twelve attendants for each. Both sets of parents were in the photograph. Hannah's father, W. C. Smith, was a striking gentleman, with white hair and a dramatic handlebar mustache. He wore tails, a top hat, and a gold pocket fob. He towered over his wife, Charlotte, whose lowered gaze gave her a demure look. Even though some of her face was in shadow, it was apparent that Hannah inherited her mother's beauty. Seated in the center of the wedding portrait was old Harold C. Smith, the granddaddy of them all.

After I finished following Hannah Smith's thread, I looked for further articles about William Chester Smith, Hannah's father. I discovered that Smith was a financier for major improvements of the Lower Otay Damn near the Mexican border in South Bay. As I spun the microfilm ahead to read other articles regarding Smith's part in that project, I found one of particular interest and with a possible connection to my focus in searching for a power monger who might have somehow figured into the Abkhazian case by the name of "Smith." Over the course of three days, several articles appeared in the newspaper's local section regarding allegations that had been made of W. C. Smith's attempts to bribe a city official for the diversionary use of water from Lower Otay Damn for his lemon orchards. Not surprisingly, these allegations were later proven "unfounded" and not pursued any further. I checked the notes I'd taken from my interview with Harold Sanders and now understood his implication about Smith's possible crooked City Hall dealings.

This led me to a news search of city councilmen and other municipal employees. I found that at the time of Christopher's death, there were some pretty dirty individuals in City Hall. It took a pretty piece of time and many spools of microfilm to follow the threads into the future to see how the men holding office in July 1933 had lived out their lives. Much to my astonishment, taking bribes was not the only issue for which two of these individuals were ultimately found culpable. Pornography was. These two men eventually sank from City Hall politics to incarceration in San Quentin Prison as sex offenders and for selling child pornography.

I couldn't tie pornography in the city council to the Abkhazian case, but the coincidences of a pornographic ring involving city leaders, the theory of a boy who was initially procured for sexual purposes, and the possibility of a powerful individual at the helm with resources to cover up any dirty dealings seemed too coincidental to overlook.

Pete McGraw always had the sense that there was a "biggie" at the center of it all. He had suggested that it was this individual who pulled the strings that manipulated the "ring of bad boys" that included Phillip Johnson and David Cohn. Pete knew that Phillip Johnson was involved in bootlegging and smuggling alcohol. He knew that Johnson was a social misfit with sociopathic and monomaniac traits. Johnson was also young and malleable. He would have been a perfect pawn for a powerful person, working through the manipulating skills of David Cohn—might that powerful person have been Smith?

I scrawled *Is William Chester Smith the biggie?* Across one page on my legal pad.

Paco

PACO WALKED INTO Tony's New York Pizza knowing he would find *la güera*, Sera Schilling. She was easy to find. All caught up in talk with some *chica*, sitting in a booth, sharing a pizza. She didn't see him as he stood in the doorway watching them. It hit him, she might recognize him from Halloween night. Best to keep his back to her. So he slid into a table near their booth, ordered a slice of pizza and a draft. Then settled back in the chair to get an earful.

Sal had given him the go ahead to step things up. "She" was tired of playing games, whoever the *fresa* who was paying him was. Paco had to admit that at first the little games were amusing. Halloween night was *brillante*. But game playing wasn't his talent. When he was hired to do a job, he wanted to get it done and over with. The *fresa* was dragging her fuck-ass feet. Now time was dragging on—hell, *she* was dragging on. She just didn't get *it*. He'd seen her go to the old cop's house, talking to other people, sitting in the basement of the newspaper pouring over microfilm, going in county buildings—she like fucking Fido—sinking her teeth into bloody meat and holding on. This assignment should have only taken a few days. Hell, he had other things to do. Sal thought she would be an easy mark. Scare her off, that's what they wanted. Halloween should have ended it. Couldn't make things much clearer than that. Now Paco was beginning to feel the fool. And there was nothing he hated more than feeling like he was being made to look foolish. No *bruja* does that! Last night, when Sal called and said "she" was getting nervous and said to do the deed, Paco was relieved. Make it fast and clean, Sal said. Get rid of her, and then get his ass back to L.A.

At Tony's, he listened. Finally he heard something to pay attention to. The *chica* was saying Sera was being stupid when she swam in the cove at La Jolla, alone, especially when lifeguards weren't on duty. This idea brought a smile to Paco's lips. Hot damn, he thought. That's it! It *could* get pretty rough out there in the ocean. Paco rotated his shoulder and neck as he thought of once again putting his own swimming talents to good use. When the waitress brought him his order, he said he had a change of plans, to box it up for him. Some pressing business. He downed his beer while she went to get a box. Where could he find a wet suit to rent for himself at this time of the year? Did stores still rent swim gear in the winter?

Pete and Sera

Seventh Interview, November 7, 1990

I IMMEDIATELY FOLDED up a draft of the article that would begin my new column at the *Observer*, the rejoinder to the sheriff's forensic team's article. It was to be published in the paper the next day under my new column, but I wanted Pete to know about it before it made ink.

Instead of finding the street quiet as usual, there was a moving van parked in front of McGraw's bungalow, with guys loading it up. My heart fell. I wasn't prepared for that. I parked my car, and went up to the front door of 421 Lomas Street realizing that this visit might be one of my last. Stood in the doorway. Announced myself.

The heavy drapes had been pulled open, and sunshine blazed through the glass, highlighting the drama with ghastly insensitivity. Boxes, crates, loading gear, and husky masculine movers changed the ambience of the normally quiet living room into total bedlam. Mrs. Kersel sat rigidly, pasty-faced, in "my" chair. She didn't hear me come in. She didn't see me standing there. Her eyes were glued on her patient. Pete sat huddled in the corner of the sofa. It was all wrong.

I crossed the room, sat down on the sofa next to Pete, and kept quiet.

Pete's voice was husky and ragged. "I'm going to Valley View Nursing Facility, Sera. You know what that means."

"Don't—"

He interrupted me with a wave of his arm. "All this stuff. Nothing but shit." Following the direction of his pointed finger to his "ego" wall, I saw how the photographs had left behind square reminders with darker paint. "Well, it's going into storage. What the hell else does one do with it all, anyhow? Who wants it?"

The old man's anguish was contagious. I simply nodded, sympathetically.

With effort, Pete made a conscious attempt to lighten up. Smiling weakly, he pointed at the manila folder I was holding in my hands. "What'cha got there, Sera?"

"Something you might find interesting, Mr. McGraw."

"Now, what have you got?" he repeated, smiling—that wonderful smile.

I pulled the article from the folder and handed it to him. Pete read the caption. His mouth spread wide and tears glistened in his eyes. "Read it out loud to me. To us."

Pete and Mrs. Kersel listened as I read my article. Pete nodded his head from time to time. When I finished, I glanced at their faces. The nurse looked pleased—Pete didn't say anything. He didn't need to. The tears in his eyes and the gentle uplift of his lips said more than words.

I handed him the folder with the article, telling him to keep it. "It was all your work, you know." As I began to stand, to leave, Pete McGraw put his hand on my knee to stop me. "After all these years—" His voice caught. He cleared his throat and began again. "After all these years that I've tried to get someone to listen to me. What you've done has meant so much. I made a promise, you know. Catherine left town trusting my promise. I had almost given up. And then you came through. I don't know how I can thank you."

"Pete, it's what I do. It's my job."

"It—the case and the boy's death—has become more than that to you, I think."

I nodded. "It has. And *you* have."

"Sera, I hate to ask, but there's something I'd like to ask you to do."

"Of course. Anything, Pete," I said.

"You remember that rose I brought you from my backyard? That was the day that I gave you my old police journal. It was the one called Blood Red Rose."

"I remember it."

"It was Catherine's rose. I told you how she gave me my rose bush." In Pete's idiosyncratic way, his dour expression melted suddenly into a smile, sunshine breaking through heavy clouds. "Holy smoke! That rosebush is three times your age, Sera."

"Yes. It's an old bush."

"It's in the far west corner of my rose garden. You'll see it near a yellow hybrid and in front an orange climber. You'll know the one I'm talking about."

"What can I do for you, Pete?"

"I know I'm asking a lot. But it would mean the world to me. Before you leave today, get the clippers from Mrs. Kersel." He looked around at the disarray and added, "That is, *if* you can find them in this mess, Kate."

"I can find them. I know just where they were packed."

"Sera, would you clip a few of the prettiest roses? I'm pretty sure there are a few still in bloom. When you came by that day, I saw a few buds that looked like they'd be opening up. Last of the season, you know. First and last of the season always are the most beautiful, aren't they?

"What I want to ask you to do is to put a few of them by little Chris's grave. That's something I planned on doing myself. Before . . ." His voice slid off. "Well, anyway, I'd be happy to pay for gas."

"You don't need to do that. I'll be very pleased to do it for you, Pete," I said, meaning every word.

"He's buried out at Glen Abbey—that's off the I-805 in Chula Vista. It's a lot, I know. It's just that I don't know anyone else who . . ."

"I'll go right after I leave here, Pete."

And I did. I drove to the cemetery where the little boy had been buried on a sunny afternoon, long ago. The secretary in the office had no difficulty finding the lot number, and furnished me with a map of the grounds.

The winding drive was beautifully verdant, manicured, and lovely. Using the map, I found the vicinity of Christopher's gravesite, parked the car, and headed up a small hill in the direction of a pond with a fountain at its center. When I reached Christopher's grave, I was surprised to find a half dozen roses already there. They were the same variety as the ones I'd clipped from Pete's garden and still fresh. The thought that Chris's younger sister, Rose, had her mother's rose, as did McGraw, sent a shiver up my spine and tears to my eyes.

I added Rose's bouquet to Pete's. Combined, they made a full and very pretty bouquet. I found an empty cemetery-issued metal container on another gravesite. "Borrowing" it, I filled it with water, stuck it in the ground at the head of the small grave, next to the gray granite marker, and placed the red roses in it. I read the inscription on the marker: *Christopher M. Abkhazian, "Darling Son," June 2, 1926– July 23, 1933. Rest Now, Beloved.*

• • •

After I exited Glenn Abbey, I drove to downtown Chula Vista and found a small coffee shop. From a corner table, I watched customers come in and out, greeting each other in cheerful camaraderie. I noticed that eyes would dart in my direction and just as quickly look away from me, the outsider in this small enclave of regulars. I stood out like a sore thumb, being tall and light haired amongst a group of Spanish speaking *amigos.*

Over my steaming latte, I got to thinking about my recent assignment to the tunnel not too far from there. I grabbed a pen and doodled a rough map of the tunnel vicinity on a paper napkin.

Johnson and the rest of his gang, or anything about the Abkhazian case, hadn't been on my mind at that moment, but the sketch reminded me of Pete's story about driving out to the Mexican border to case an area where he had followed Johnson in 1933. I remembered the officer telling me that tunnels were common in the thirties and that this tunnel probably had been there for a long time. Smugglers used tunnels for bootlegged booze then; now they were used for humans and drugs. Could it be that Johnson and his buddies might have been in the same area when Pete followed them that night? Pete thought they were smuggling, but couldn't prove it. Could they possibly have used a tunnel if they were smuggling? Was it a similar tunnel? Or could it have been the same tunnel?

The idea electrified me.

I had to check out this remote possibility. It would become a gnawing curiosity if I didn't put it to rest in my mind.

• • •

I left the coffee shop and drove downtown to the newspaper. My mind ran wild considering the links in the case. Pete followed Phillip Johnson to Otay Mesa. The Smith family was linked to Otay Mesa and a lemon ranch there. Sterling's letter put David Cohn in Smith's company. Hannah and the Sanders' boys were schoolmates. The Cohns, the Sanders, and Phillip Johnson were members of Pete's so-called "Ring of Bad Boys." These were all linked to Christopher Abkhazian.

Finally settled in Icobad's Den, back on the microfilm machine, I began re-reading the articles accompanying Johnson's trial for "obstructing justice," but with new interest. In a photograph accompanying one of the articles, Johnson stood next to his mother, Helen, and their attorney, Staley. Helen Johnson was "Hollywood beautiful," as McGraw had said.

I raced through the microfilm for that period, looking more closely for anything further about the Sanders's boys, the Cohns, and Phillip Johnson. I found nothing.

Half on a whim, I pulled up Helga Smiley's "San Diego Undercurrents," and focused on articles within a month's span of Johnson's trial, thinking Helga might have found some dirt to dig up on ol' Phil or his beautiful momma.

One of Smiley's columns "whispered" that Johnson's mother, Helen Johnson, was the daughter of prominent landowner, entrepreneur, and cattle tycoon Harold C. Smith. Smiley even went further to "whisper," that Helen had been legally disowned when she eloped with a "flimflam drifter by the name of Willy Johnson," (in Smiley's words). She and Johnson apparently had a son together.

I recalled from my notes that Harold C. Smith had two children: a son, William Chester Smith *and* a daughter by the name of Helen.

William Chester Smith's daughter was Hannah.

Helen Johnson's son was Phillip.

Hannah Smith and Phillip Johnson were cousins!

I shot back into my chair, blasting out a loud expletive with the shock of my discovery: *They were fucking related!*

From my earlier research, I knew that Phillip Johnson died in prison. He left no offspring of record, so I focused on the Delancys: Charlotte Delancy, W. C. Smith's wife and Hannah Smith's mother.

I checked W. C. Smith's obituary for the date of his death and confirmed that he had died in 1950. Through his will, Charlotte—his wife—would have been deeded the property, possibly including the area of Otay Mesa where the tunnel I'd toured was situated.

Through Charlotte, who died in 1963, ownership would have passed to her only surviving daughter, Hannah. Images of Hannah as a bride on the arm of DeWitt Clancy Owens came to mind.

Using the circular obituary file, I found that Hannah Smith Owens died in 1985, leaving only one child: a daughter, Miriam. Was Miriam Owens still alive?

I didn't find any death notices for a Miriam Owens. So far, so good. It occurred to me that now I needed to get more information on this individual from records at the county offices. While I was there, I also would go to the land department and trace ownership of the land deed for the parcel where the Tijuana tunnel I'd recently visited was located, to confirm my hunch that it was in the same area.

Before I left the building, I went up to the second floor to my desk and looked through my notes on the Tijuana tunnel. I had jotted down the coordinates of the specific land parcel on which the warehouse at the end of the tunnel was located in Otay Mesa. These coordinates were N94°40'39°.

Now I felt as though I couldn't move fast enough. I left the building and raced to my car in the parking lot, slammed the car door shut, fumbled with getting the damn key into the lock, and drove to the County Administration offices, beating every red light on Broadway.

After a few inquiries, I found the location of the property on the San Diego County Assessor's map. It directed me to the Book of Parcels, Number 667. The parcel number of the Tijuana tunnel was 667-050-40. Its coordinates were N94°40'39°.

I looked up the land deeds for this property and discovered that in 1925 (and still in 1933), this portion of the property was owned by W. C. Smith. It had been deeded to him in the Last Will and Testament of H. C. Smith, his father. I followed ownership records until I got to 1990, and found that this parcel of land was currently owned by an M. Delancy. Miriam had been deeded the land under her mother's maiden name and hadn't changed it for some seemingly unfathomable reason—unfathomable until now.

My hunch was right. The tunnel I'd toured and described in the newspaper was still being used for smuggling drugs and people.

And it was owned by Miriam Delancy—probably married. What was her married name?

At county offices I found a marriage certificate for Miriam Owens and Robert B. Priestley. It was issued on January 21st, 1971.

Back at Icobad's Den I ran searches for Robert B. Priestley and was astounded by my oversight: Robert B. Priestley was a candidate currently running for a congressional seat in the upcoming election.

I looked for any other articles on the Priestleys and found several, one of which appeared on San Diego's society page. This had a picture of the couple with a group of other social notables at a recent charity ball. Miriam was pictured on the arm of her husband. She was dressed in a flowing white gown and wore her blond hair in an updo. She had that blazing smile of her aunt's—a Helen Smith smile—and like her aunt, Miriam was (in Pete's words) "Hollywood beautiful."

I found an empty table, opened my attaché case, and dumped all my papers on the surface, anxiously looking for any information I could to sketch a family tree of the Smith family. I copied the marriage certificate of Miriam (Delancy) Owens and Robert (Breckenridge) Priestley.

The pieces fit together and the picture, a terrifyingly clear picture, had taken shape.

As I put my papers back into my attaché case, I gazed around the busy room, looking for someone—who? Sensing something—what? I looked down at my hands and saw they were shaking. A river of perspiration was flowing down the middle of my back.

I had stepped on a land mine.

By linking a family-owned piece of land that was currently used for smuggling to 1933, when Phillip Johnson may have accepted bootleg liquor, I unlocked the family secret of none other than a congressional candidate's wife. And to reveal this secret would be fatal to her husband's political aspirations.

I wondered if Robert Priestley had any idea about the connection of land ownership to this tunnel. If not, it had to be his wife, Miriam, who was so very threatened by my investigation into the Abkhazian case. She would rightfully think that any information about the tunnel could be easily linked to the dark horse of her ancestry, Phillip Johnson, then to the ring of bad boys, and ultimately to Christopher's death.

I realized my danger: Miriam was so desperate to keep this closeted away that she'd stop at nothing to keep it that way. The attack at the Surf Rider bar? It was a warning. Miriam Priestley had given me a warning.

Sera

SEVERAL WEEKS HAD passed since my first article in my new column made ink. I published the article about the 1933 case, as I'd told Richard I would. In it, I used the sheriff's forensic team's article to frame the more intriguing aspects of old San Diego, the Abkhazian case, and the findings of Chief Detective Pete McGraw. Critical of the forensic team's conclusion of accidental death, I described the research I did and my ultimate opinion. I was careful to avoid any hint of a connection to the Priestleys; that would come in time.

The article received mixed reviews. It was well read: Richard received a surprising number of telephone calls. Some were positive and flattering; others weren't so complimentary, including one from ex-deputy Sheriff Robert Tindall, who blasted the *Observer*, defending the work his team had done.

Both Miriam Priestley and Pete McGraw had moved on in their personal lives. The congressional elections voted Robert Priestley in as San Diego's congressman and pictures of him with his wife, Miriam, appeared regularly in the paper—both of their handsome faces wearing confident smiles. They would be moving to Washington, D.C.

Even McGraw moved on from obsessing over the Abkhazian case to sharing my enthusiasm about my new column, which I talked over with him during my visits to Valley View.

While Pete's health deteriorated rapidly, our relationship deep-ened. When I visited Pete at the facility, it was like visiting a family member. I felt he thought the same of me.

With the passing of time and the changes taking place in all of our lives, it seemed clear that Miriam Priestley considered my article the end of my involvement in the Abkhazian case. In it, she hadn't been implicated. After it, I received no further "warnings." I thought I was safe, until—

—One late afternoon day, I decided to go to the Cove for a quick swim. I'd left the newspaper, telling Betty on my way out that I was off for a swim at the Cove.

Not surprisingly, the beach at La Jolla Cove was deserted. Only a few tourists milled about the park. The sun was weakening and the stiff, afternoon coastal winds blew. The small, wooden life-guard stand above the Cove beach had been boarded up for winter. The blackboard tacked there had scrawled across it: *See you next summer!*

Short of time and bursting with anticipation, I charged down the cement steps toward the beach, set my swimming bag with my towel and terry-cloth sweats on a rock, tugged on my wet suit, zipped up its front, grabbed my goggles and cap, dashed into the water. As I tucked my hair into my cap, I scanned the water for other swimmers. I didn't expect to see any, but there was one other swimmer, around a quarter-mile out.

When I am swimming alone, I sense my vulnerability. I know I am constantly exposed to elements beyond my control. I realize my human limitations. And usually I listen to my instincts. But deter-mined to swim, I ignored them that day. I should have, because some-thing was definitely *off.* The ocean was murky and ominous, seaweed drab. There was a peculiar denseness to the water, it moved like mol-ten lead. The usually cheerful little white buoys marking distance now pitched and fell recklessly in gigantic swells. A strong undertow tugged treacherously at the sandy beach. The sky was dark, and clouds hung on the ocean's horizon.

Instead of giving in to wise apprehension, I dove into the water, to power through the breaking waves at the narrow mouth of the Cove; then beyond these waves, to cross riptides. And finally, once past these, to swim freely in the open water, keeping my eyes on my goal, the buoy.

In the open water my strokes become regular, my breathing even. I lift my head to scan the water in front of me and around me for the other swimmer, for sea life, for seaweed floating enmasse on the water's surface that could catch stinging jellyfish or tangle kicking feet.

On my left was the western horizon, where the white ball of the sun floated behind gray clouds. Every so often the sun's errant rays broke through the cloud bank and shot into the water like arrows, puddles of light.

The sun, so low in the sky, reminded me that my time was limited. The fog was moving in toward land. Already, puffs of low, thick clouds had formed and were moving through the sky above me. I didn't want to be in the water after sunset. Given the heavy clouds, it would be uncommonly dark then.

Sea lions lay on rocks on the cliffs, barking hoarsely. Seagulls circled in the sky, their cries raucous. Pelicans swept overhead in a perfect "V" formation, uniformly flapping their wings and following the front-runner synchronously. Not breaking formation, they dove down to skirt the ocean's surface and then rose up into the sky to paddle on through the low clouds above.

I looked back toward land. The park above the Cove beach was empty with the exception of one person, sitting alone on a cement bench, gazing out at the water.

I had almost forgotten about the swimmer I'd seen just before I began my swim, when I saw two arms rising and falling on the surface of the water heading back toward the beach from the buoy. Comfort in a stranger. Two in the water.

We grew closer. Details sharpened. He was male, wore a black cap, and goggles. A wetsuit covered his arms, but they were strong. He cut through the water like a knife through butter.

We swam the same path of the narrow channel: I out, and he in towards shore.

Seagulls dove and brawled. Waves shattered on rocks by the deepening caves as lights began to sparkle in homes braced on the cliffs above. The sun touched the ocean's far edge, turning the water a dull gray.

At a point it seemed to me that we might collide if one of us didn't change direction, so I altered mine. After a few strokes, I realized that he changed his to adjust to my redirection. Once again we headed toward each other. I veered to the right and continued. He changed his direction, too— to the left. I did the opposite and he counteracted it. Thoughts—fears—awareness crept into my thoughts.

When only a few yards separated us, I stopped swimming, treaded water, momentarily frozen. The terror of it! Like a tsunami, strength and power grow silently. Its absoluteness captivates and locks in its victims. He churned towards me, powerful arms pulling him, head lifted in focus, and the taut line of aggression of his mouth.

Adrenaline kicked in.

I turned toward shore, digging my arms into the water. My muscles teaming together, thrusting me, my arms pulling, my legs pushing. Before long, I felt myself cutting through the ocean swells, a torpedo.

But my staying power didn't last. The shore grew closer, but I began to tire. Waves, swells, and tidal currents thwarted my speed and endurance. My heart pounded against my chest. My breathing became rapid and shallow and ineffective. My arms cramped up. I began to take in water. My lenses fogged. I shoved them up on my forehead, but the salt in the water stung my eyes and clouded my vision.

I looked toward shore, waving and calling out to the lone person. He stood. He reached his hand to his brow. Scanned the ocean and looked in my direction. I waved my arms frantically. I tried to call out, but my feeble voice was drowned out by the waves, the cawing of birds, and the yelping of sea life.

Helplessly I watched him leave.

It was me against the swimmer.

Without daring to check, I sensed that the gap between me and him grow tighter.

Suddenly, his hand grabbed my ankle, pulled me back. I tried to kick my leg free, but his fingers were iron. I screamed at him, and sensed a smile. It was a cruel smile. Behind goggles, his eyes were distorted, hard, and predatory.

He put his arms on my shoulders and dug his fingers in. Down, I went. His body's weight towering over me.

Then he let go.

I kicked wildly to escape, to swim away.

I made little distance when grabbed my leg and pulled me back to him. He wrapped his arms around me, holding me so close that my face was smashed against the rubber of his wetsuit.

"Let me go!" I begged. "Please!"

He laughed.

Then he pushed me under the water again. I hadn't had time to take a breath. He held on, his talon-like grasp holding my shoulders. I couldn't escape. My lungs were burning. I thrashed my legs and arms in panic. I tried to claw at him, but my hand slipped on the rubber of his wet suit. He let go of my shoulders. I surfaced. We were so close. He laughed again. Still struggling for air, I tried to breathe. I spat salt water from my mouth.

He lunged at me and pushed me under. I began to sink.

Deeper into the kelp forest.

In my half-conscious state, I was aware of a confluence of noises in my head: muddled voices, snatches of conversation, and chanting phrases: "No water in the lungs," and "Blood red Rose, Sera."

Then a deep baritone voice, commanding me: "No!"

I felt a surge of adrenaline. I began to kick: up, up, up, until I pushed through the surface. I sputtered, coughed out water, and suck in all the air my lungs could hold.

Through tears and still coughing, I saw my attacker treading water a few yards away from where I surfaced. He dove and disappeared. I waited and looked around. There were no telling bubbles surfacing near me. There was no movement. This was the time to get away, but my legs had become rubber.

A wave crested and broke in my face. I swallowed salt water. It burned my throat. I choked.

Like a whale breaching, he shot up next to me. He put his hands on my head and using all his body weight pushed me under.

I hadn't any strength left.

I felt him let go and kick away from me. I felt his legs sweep by me as he swam away.

Still I sank.

Deeper into the darkness.

I had all but given up when I felt fingers lock under my jaw and the brushing of legs pull me up. I vaguely recall hearing the *clop, clop* of a helicopter, a siren, and a confluence of other shore noises, before I lost consciousness.

•   •   •

Later that night, recovering after being given a tranquilizer, a shot of adrenaline, and a bowl of beef broth, I lay under crisp sheets and a heated, woolen blanket at the hospital. A nurse was fiddling with something and saying something about a visitor. "No visitors!" I protested. She agreed and told me to sleep for a while. I burrowed into the warmth of the bed.

I don't know how long I slept, but morning sunlight awakened me. I sat up sleepily in the hospital bed and looked around the room. How unaware I'd been of the activity surrounding me! While I slept, several bouquets of flowers had been put in vases on the bedside table. Now a breakfast tray was set out for me, and I was ravenous.

It was a morning of interrogations by police. It somewhat calmed me knowing that a twenty-four hour guard sat outside my door, especially when I learned that even with all the police activity at the Cove the night of my attack, the man who attacked me had managed to get away. When I asked to speak to an agent of the F.B.I., because of the more extending aspects of the attack, it wasn't long before I had two young men listening with gravity to what I had to tell them about the tunnel, the old case, and the connection to the Priestleys. The release of the responsibility and feeling that I would be protected by the strong arm of federal law reassured me. I also knew I would have full rights to the story in time as well.

Just when I thought I couldn't face another visitor, my door opened a crack. I heard a voice call out, "Are you accepting company?"

I responded affirmatively, and Rose Abkhazian stepped into the hospital room. Her face was half hidden by the long-stemmed flowers in her hands. She put them with the others, chuckling about her lack of originality. Then the older woman reached over and placed her hand gently on my forehead.

"You want to know how I knew you were here?" she asked kindly, still smiling. Not waiting for my answer, she said, "Yesterday afternoon, I called your newspaper. You weren't there. I left a message. When you didn't call back, I called again. That time, when you didn't answer, I spoke with the operator and asked her if she knew when you would be coming back. She said you had left work early and were swimming at the La Jolla Cove. I really wanted to speak to you, Sera, to thank you for seeing this case through and for your wonderful article. Your article provoked more questions, especially after your attack on Halloween night, which made it obvious to me that there is much more to this case as you have felt all along."

"I got to thinking about you swimming in the Cove, especially after that other attack, so I drove there to check on you." She smiled and said with emphasis, "And, I am so glad that I did."

The tears slipped down my cheeks when I pictured the person on the bench. It was she, not a man. I took her hand and squeezed it.

"Just get better," Christopher Abkhazian's younger sister said.

Pete and Sera

Last Interview, November 23, 1990

ABOUT TWO WEEKS had passed since my attack when I received a call from a caregiver at the hospice facility where Pete had been moved, advising me to come in and say my last goodbye to Pete McGraw. When I saw his wasted body in the hospital bed, tied to tubes and catheters, I was overcome by sadness. I sat down heavily in one of the chairs and wept. I realized how deeply I had come to feel about the old man and how much my being with him meant to me.

The door to his room opened and Rose Abkhazian came in. I stood up and we hugged each other for a long moment. She sat down next to me, and I found that we both averted our eyes, away from Pete.

After a long while, I felt Rose's elbow nudge me, and I looked to see that Pete had opened his eyes. We moved closer to his bedside. His face held no expression; gone was the wonderful smile that I used to see. But when he recognized me, his eyes crinkled into fondness. He whispered, "Sera."

Only that.

Rose stood quietly next to me. Pete's eyes moved from me to her. The old man nodded faintly and held his hand out. She took it in her own and smiled, looking deeply into his eyes. I saw an uncanny bond between them that was odd for two people who had had spoken on the telephone but had never before met. I found my eyes glancing at each of them, seeking understanding. It was when I saw that their eyes were the same shade of blue that I understood that Rose was Pete's daughter. I watched a tear roll down his cheek. The intimate drama caught my breath.

"I never knew," Pete murmured with combined astonishment and acceptance.

"She never told you about me. She only told me at the end of her life so you and I might have the possibility of meeting," Rose responded quietly.

"Did she . . . did she suffer?"

"She suffered. Yes. But she suffered quietly throughout her entire life. You know that. She took her suffering in death just as she took everything else in life, graciously. Mother was a strong woman."

"She pursued her music," Pete said. It wasn't a question.

"Yes."

"I used to love to hear her play."

"She became quite famous."

Pete nodded that he knew. "She was also very beautiful woman. I didn't want to let her go. But I had to. She made me promise that I would never contact her again when your family moved east. Then she was pregnant when she left San Diego."

"Yes."

Pete gave a deep sigh and said quietly, "I loved her."

I shook from emotion.

"And she loved you," Rose responded softly.

"Mrs. Kersel—my caregiver?"

"Yes. Mother provided for your care, if it should become needed, in her trust."

As Rose and I left the hospital room a little while later, we heard Pete McGraw once again thank us. We turned to respond, but he had closed his eyes. His face was relaxed. The old man had fallen into a peaceful and contented rest

Epilogue

AS HE WELL deserved, Peter William McGraw, esteemed Medal of Valor recipient, was put to rest with full military-style honors by the San Diego Police Department. In keeping with his request, he was buried at a preselected and prepaid plot located at Glen Abbey Cemetery.

I drove three cars behind the hearse, which trailed a parade of motorcycle policemen up the winding road in the cemetery. I had driven the same route only a few weeks earlier to place roses at Christopher Abkhazian's grave—the roses Catherine had named Blood Red Rose.

An open wound in the ground marked the spot of Pete's final resting place. I was escorted to the small grouping of folding chairs usually marked for "family of deceased." I realized, as I sat next to Rose, that she was his only family and thought it honorary that I was to be seated there.

During the several minutes before the somber procession began carrying his casket from the hearse in the parking lot down below, I took in the surroundings. It didn't surprise me at all when I noticed that Pete McGraw had selected a gravesite just above Christopher's grave, a little higher on the hillside. It occurred to me that Pete chose this site deliberately, so he could continue to keep watch over the child. This was a child he'd never known alive, yet a child he loved so greatly that he had been haunted by his death throughout his life. I whispered this observation to Rose who nodded and smiled with a distant look in her eyes.

The burial was a final phase of a three-day observance celebrating Pete's life. It began with a two-day casket watch in the mortuary at Glen Abbey. A team of two honorary guards stood vigil, each for a period of thirty minutes, rotating to fresh teams ceremoniously and punctually. One formally uniformed guard stood at the head of the casket and the other stood at the base. Their presence gave a solemn respectfulness that hushed any light conversations. But visitors were sparse, according to the signatures on the guest book. I read the names of Mrs. Kersel and Rose Abkhazian, and I recognized some of Pete's neighbors by their addresses.

Now on the hill, the sorrowful notes of bagpipes captured our attention. Six honor guards carried the casket up the steep grade. Behind them was a steady stream of blue uniforms. Following the police were dignitaries and a handful of select acquaintances.

Albion St. James moved with the group. He looked older than when I'd last seen him and walked up the steep hill with apparent difficulty. Retirement had aged and weakened him. He used his cane to steady himself as he made the climb. No longer was Albion St. James the great and terrible Oz of the *San Diego Observer*.

There were prayers, invocations, and speeches made by city dignitaries, including the mayor, city councilmen, and the chief of police. St. James read a respectfully light and informed biography he'd written about Pete. The irony of Pete's life of obscurity and his death suddenly brought to life with hyperbolic words and lit with passionate zeal amused me. "Irish" was probably somewhere up there and chuckling as he watched the pomp his death was being given. I imagined how he'd chuckle, how his eyes would crinkle, and how he'd call it all "blarney."

Somberly, six policemen folded the flag that had been draped on Pete's casket and handed it to Rose. After the flag ceremony, a firing party of seven policemen gave the ultimate honor of a twenty-one-gun salute. When the last shot rang into the hills, Pete's rosewood casket was lowered into the grave. The bagpiper, costumed in his native plaid wool, tasseled knee socks, boots, and a kilt, piped the sober notes of the hymn "Amazing Grace." The chief took the podium for the last time and uttered dismissal instructions. The contingency dispersed.

I remained alone in my chair for a few minutes, choosing to make my exit from the cemetery solitarily. Before I left his gravesite, I placed one of the two roses I'd brought with me on Pete's grave. Then, I walked down to Chris's and placed the other on it.

• • •

An F.B.I. agent and I met frequently in the days that followed Pete's burial. The agent was adamant about the urgency of getting this case into the hands of the bureau and out of mine. He emphasized that the expediency was for my safety. I agreed to give him all the details of my investigation of the boy's death leading up to the land deed in Otay Mesa owned by the Smith-Priestley family where the tunnel was located. In return for my information, the F.B.I. committed to giving me the story first. Always cautious about my safety and privacy, the agent selected meeting places where we wouldn't be observed. He instructed me to make telephone calls using only public pay telephones. Although I continued to be terribly paranoid, no further warnings, threats, or attacks occurred.

A few weeks after Pete's burial, I was surprised by a telephone call from Pete's lawyer inviting me to a reading of the Last Will and Testament of Peter W. McGraw.

I took a seat in the reception area and began to nervously peruse magazines when the door opened and Rose stepped in. We were equally surprised to see each other. After an awkward conversation, we took seats in front of the attorney's massive cherrywood desk, which was cleared of papers except for the bound will and two small boxes. One of them I recognized as the velvet box that held the Medal of Valor. The other box was a mystery to me.

Before reading the will, the attorney explained the terms of the trust that had been set up by Catherine Abkhazian in 1938, when she first began a savings account from money earned from her concerts and recordings. She requested that the trust be kept a secret from Pete until just before his death. It had remained a secret from her husband for his entire life. She employed a private investigator hired by the law firm to report back to her in Missouri about Pete's well-being while she was alive. Since she died in 1970, the trust was put in the hands of a trustee of the law firm. When Pete McGraw was dying of pancreatic cancer, Kate Kersel was hired as a full-time caregiver. Pete never knew where the money came from for his medical care and hospitalization. This was in keeping with Catherine Abkhazian's wishes.

Then the lawyer read the will. It was pretty straightforward. As he neared the end, he smiled at us and lifted the two small boxes. He handed the box that held the Medal of Valor to Pete's daughter. The other, he gave to me with a pair of scissors to cut through layers of Scotch tape that had sealed it shut.

Inside the small box, there were two keys. One was a larger, well-used steel key and the other a shiny, brass key with the number B35. Baffled, I asked what they were for. The attorney smiled and placed a business envelope in my hand. I had a lump the size of a boulder in my throat and my hands shook after I'd read the document. Inside the envelope was a grant deed to ownership of the residence at 421 Lomas Street, Pete McGraw's house.

The other key, the attorney explained as he handed me the contract, was to the facility where Pete's furniture had been put into storage. Then he read the words that Pete had obviously instructed to be written into his will. What he wrote caused bittersweet chuck-les from us. Seeing my tears, the attorney pushed a box of tissues across the desk to me.

Pete had instructed: "This crap is for Sera to use as she sees fit. It is being given with no obligation and/or guilt for tossing what she doesn't want."

• • •

Since then, my life has moved in other directions at breakneck speed. Before this event became clouded and its value diminished, it was my intention to record it factually and straightforwardly.

I am still employed by the *San Diego Observer*, which has changed ownership and name twice since the days I received the telephone call from Pete McGraw.

Over the years I received several offers for much more lucrative and impressive career opportunities by national magazines and other big-city newspapers. These might have seemed tempting to any other ambitious journalist, but not to me. Richard took the bait and moved to Atlanta to work for *Turner News*. He took his office furniture with him, leaving behind an empty office.

As St. James, I preferred the more traditional style of furniture. I used McGraw's old roll top desk in my office, and nailed his serenity prayer on the wall over it.

I have continued to live a single life and reside very comfort-ably at my home at 421 Lomas Street. I keep up the rose garden in the backyard and replanted the garden by the front door, so my front yard is in keeping with the well-maintained font yards of my neighbors. A golden bougainvillea is trellised over the front-door entrance, and the brass number over it, "421," has been cleaned and shined.

I am most content when I wind up Pete McGraw's antique Victrola and place the needle on one of the several 78 records he kept. I sit

down on the old sofa near the fireplace and relax to the old recordings that were housed in the old cabinet. My favorite is "Moonlight
Sonata" by Beethoven. There is something very haunting about the
way Catherine played it.

Made in the USA
San Bernardino, CA
07 January 2016